NOW'S THE TIME

The Ladies Who Brunch Book Three

HARLOW JAMES

*To any woman who has felt like a broken heart would never
mend...this one's for you.
And now's the time to open yourself up to the possibility of love
again.*

"Grief is the price we pay for love."

Queen Elizabeth II

Contents

Prologue

Penelope

Age Eighteen

"And what did the coach say?"

"He said I need to report the first week of July so I can start training with the team." Jacob reaches over, grabs my hand, and lifts it to his lips as he continues to drive. And every time he does that—kisses the back of my hand—I fall a little bit more in love with him.

Riding in his truck, one of my favorite places to be, I look over at my boyfriend. He's driving me home where my parents are waiting on us for dinner. It's just a few weeks before graduation, and the anticipation of our future together is making my heart race every time we talk about it. "It's all happening, babe," he says. "Everything that we want and have worked for is coming together."

Shifting my body in the seat so I can tuck my legs under me and turn in his direction, I study his profile the same way I've done for the past two years. "This was the plan, Jacob. This is your dream. You know just as much as I do that hard work pays off, baby—you and I are living proof of that. And the support of our town has only pushed you to make your dream come true. Soon, everyone will know who Jacob Peterson is."

"It's *our* dream, *our* future, Pen. Ohio State is one of the top seeds in the nation for college football. It's my gateway to the NFL. And the fact that you got in and we won't be apart for four years is just the cherry on top."

I clear my throat. "And don't you forget that I'm giving up UCLA for that," I tease, even though I don't feel salty about that at all.

He smirks, glancing over at me before shifting his eyes back to the road. "I won't. But I also don't want you to hold it over my head, either." Brushing a hand through his light brown hair, he exhales heavily. "Are you sure you're still okay with giving up that school, Pen? Because if you really want to go there, we can make this work." The cool spring air blows right through the open windows of the truck, making my hair go wild while I try to catch his gaze again. "I don't care if we have to do long distance. I don't want you to give up on your dreams for me and then resent me down the line. But—"

"Jacob, stop." He leans back in his seat while clenching his jaw, silence descending on us for a moment. "It's just a school, and I know that if I were that far away from you, I'd regret it. I'd be miserable. Wherever you are is where I want to be, too."

That blinding smile of his is back as he exhales, his whole

body relaxing. "You are the only thing that matters to me, Penelope. Well, you and football."

"I was gonna say . . ." I laugh out loud, my eyes drifting out my open window and over the residential roads of our small Ohio town, soaking up the distant sunset that's painting the sky in hues of oranges and pinks. Watching the sun rise and set is one of my favorite things in the world, and it only reminds me to soak up this precious moment even more.

"Sure is a beautiful one tonight, huh?" Jacob asks when he catches me staring at the colorful sky.

"It's funny how it happens each day, and yet, no two skies are the same. I can't get enough of them."

"And each time I watch you stare at one, it makes me even more grateful for all the sunrises and sunsets I get to experience with you—and every one that is yet to come."

Love spreads like a warmth through my body as I look out the windshield, taking in the only place I've called home since I was born. Sure, there's an entire world out there to discover, but once Jacob entered my life two years ago—the new student in school who caught the attention of every girl—some kind of cosmic shift took place, and I knew my life would never be the same. Girls from every grade threw themselves at him, but his eyes landed only on me. And after I made him work for it, of course, I realized that home wasn't just a place—it could also be a person.

And so Jacob became my home and the biggest part of my life moving forward.

"What's your mom making for dinner tonight?" he asks, pulling me back to the present as we get closer to my house.

"Chicken enchiladas."

"My favorite."

I smirk. "I know. That's probably why she's making them. I swear she likes you better than me sometimes."

"Wouldn't you rather your parents like me than not?" he asks on a chuckle.

"I don't know. Sometimes I think the fact that they actually *love* the boy I'm dating has prevented me from being able to tap into my rebellious side. I always envisioned myself singing "*Papa Don't Preach*" at some point while I'd get to argue with them about how much I loved some boy they didn't approve of. And because you're basically the best guy on the planet and treat me with the utmost respect and adoration, I don't get to fight with them." I shoot him a teasing glare. "In all honesty, you're cramping my teenage-girl style, Jacob Peterson, and now it's making me question things."

Jacob throws his head back as he laughs. "God, you're something else, Penelope Klein." He pulls my hand to his lips again and reverently presses a kiss to my skin.

Two years of dating has made us closer than ever, especially as we talked about our futures beyond high school and what they would look like. We ultimately realized we wanted one with the other person in it. Jacob made it very clear that I was the girl he wanted to marry, even after I challenged him on that declaration for several months. But when I finally gave in to what I felt for him and offered him all of me in return, I knew he was the man I was supposed to be with.

Even though the idea of being someone's wife was never an aspiration of mine growing up, visions of a life with Jacob became all I could think about—following him to Ohio State, being behind the scenes when he gets drafted to the NFL, becoming a football wife to the top quarterback in the League, having little miniature

Jacobs and Penelopes that every married couple in America would envy because our kids would be the cutest fucking kids on the planet, and creating a life and empire with the boy that made me rethink everything I thought I'd wanted for my life.

We aren't naïve. We know the odds are stacked against us. We know people think we won't last six months as a couple once we get to Ohio State even though we'll be on the same campus, that the allure of dating someone new or the stress of classes and him playing on the football team will tear us apart.

But what we have is the real deal, young love that is strong enough to stand the test of time.

Unfortunately, though, time wouldn't be on our side . . .

Chapter 1

Penelope

Present Day

"The party is here, bitches!" Holding up two bottles of champagne, I stand in the doorway of Amelia's house, eager for the alcohol to take my mind off of several emotions this day brings up as well as the fact that my job is insane at the moment and I'm seriously considering running off to Bora Bora without telling a soul just so I can have a moment of peace and quiet without my phone going off.

"Aunt Penelope, you said a bad word." Oliver, the cutest six-year-old boy to grace this earth, runs right up to me, craning his neck so he can meet my eyes.

I drop my arms and look down at him. "You're right. I'm sorry, Ollie. But one day, when you're an adult, you'll understand why we say bad words all the time."

"Why?"

"Because life fucking sucks." I wink at him and then head toward my best girlfriends in the kitchen. "I brought the champagne, ladies."

If anything keeps me going in life, it's these women. Honestly, they'll never know how much meeting them changed my world after the summer my life fell apart. Charlotte, Amelia, and Noelle are the sisters I never had, the three people that made me want to live when I thought my life was over. Meeting them my freshman year at UCLA was the best thing that ever happened to me.

And now we're all entering the phase of our lives where my girls are catching feelings for men and starting to build futures with them—or they are just catching sperm, like Noelle.

But that's a whole other story I can fill you in on later.

Charlotte claps her hands. "Good thinking. We didn't get to have brunch this morning because *someone* was too busy preparing for a Super Bowl party," she says with a side glance in Amelia's direction.

Every Sunday, my girls and I go to Frankie's Diner for a champagne brunch. It's our ritual, but life sometimes gets in the way of it, which I get. Hence why I brought the champagne here so the tradition can at least live on in that respect.

Ethan, Amelia's boyfriend and Oliver's father, releases her as she moves toward the cupboard to fetch champagne glasses. "Hey, this was Ethan's idea, so if you want to blame anyone, blame him."

"I'll take the blame," he says, kissing Amelia on the cheek. "Besides, that just means I got to enjoy her this morning instead of her running out the door to meet you girls."

"That'd better mean you got laid, Amelia," I interject. "Otherwise, that's just a waste of a Sunday morning without brunch."

If there's one thing I'll always advocate for, it's sex. But not just any sex, *good* sex—the kind that all women deserve. Because lord knows there's a difference between sex just for fun and the kind that makes you feel like you can let that sexual kitten out of the closet long enough to appreciate the fact that you have a vagina and there are men that know how to make it purr, if you catch my drift.

Seriously, more women should be grateful that we have the capacity for multiple orgasms and demand to find a partner who can make that happen. But if not, at least there are battery-operated toys that can fill that hole, no pun intended.

"Don't worry. Ethan made sure staying home was worth it." Amelia smirks in his direction as he grabs a beer and proudly struts to where the rest of the boys are sitting on the couch.

"So how are things going? Are he and Oliver officially moved in yet?" Charlotte asks once Ethan is gone just as Noelle comes into the kitchen from the bathroom.

Amelia met Ethan last summer when he opened his practice in the same complex as Amelia's office. She's a marriage and sex therapist, and he's a divorce lawyer. You can imagine the disdain for each other that developed almost instantly when they met, but all I saw were fireworks. Sure enough, after a delivery of three-hundred dildos to his office to show him not to mess with my friend, he finally admitted that he wanted her.

Like any fresh relationship, there were a few learning curves, but with a little tough love from me, Charlotte, and Noelle, Amelia and Ethan were able to sort out their issues and move forward, culminating with him and his son moving into her house.

"It's almost official. Next weekend should be the last move with a bunch of little stuff. Oliver's room is already set up, Ethan donated a bunch of their furniture since most of my stuff was newer and was already here anyway, and they've pretty much been sleeping here for the past week, so I'd say everything is basically finished."

"We're so happy for you, Amelia." Noelle gestures to Charlotte and me, and we both nod.

"Thank you. I'm insanely happy."

"Good. And if he ever messes up again, just let me know. I can deliver three-hundred tubes of hemorrhoid cream to his office with the click of a button." A second later, my cell phone rings. I stare down at the screen once I pull it from my pocket. "Jesus, why on earth is my boss calling me on a Sunday like this?"

"Does he not usually call on Sundays?" Amelia asks.

"Every once in a while because PR never stops, you know? But this is like the fifth time he's called." Sure enough, there are five missed calls from him.

"Should you call him back then?"

"Ugh, I really don't want to think about work right now. I just wanted to get champagne drunk with my girls and watch hot men run around in tight pants." I groan. "But I'd better see what he wants before I get too drunk to have a normal conversation with him."

Noelle chimes in. "Do you even know *how* to have a normal conversation?"

"Hardy har har." I know I'm the queen of giving my friends shit, so even though I act like it bugs me, I love it when the girls give it right back.

I grab a potato skin and then saunter off toward the stairs to go somewhere quieter. Once I reach Amelia's room at the top of the landing, I take a seat on the bed and hit my boss's name to call him back.

"Penelope." Charles answers after one ring. "I'm sorry to bother you on a Sunday."

"No, you're not, but I appreciate you acting like you care."

He laughs. "You know me too well. Anyway, I'm sorry but not really sorry to interrupt your weekend, but an event popped up that I need you to assist with. It's in two weeks."

"Who dropped the ball this time?" I ask, knowing that the only reason he would give me such short notice is because someone isn't doing their job.

"It doesn't matter. All I need is for you to be there to manage a few things and make sure our company doesn't look like we can't handle our shit."

I've worked for Edelman PR Company out of their Los Angeles office for the past five years, and in that time, I've made a name for myself as a rep that my boss can count on because I truly am a badass bitch. I manage clients such as fast food companies, department stores, and even celebrities, though I'm very selective about which celebrities I choose to take on. There's just a certain line I can't cross there for personal reasons, which I won't get into at this time.

Sighing out loud and pinching the bridge of my nose while I mentally recall every event on my calendar for the next two weeks to ensure there's no conflict, I accept defeat. "Fine. Who's the client?"

"It's Zio's Vodka. They're revealing a new line of flavored vodka and seltzers and sponsoring a night at *Loft 24*. You've worked with Hayes Weston and his employees many times before, so I know they can trust you to make sure the night goes off without complications. Just delegate what you need done to your team, and don't let me down. Zio's is making a name for themselves, and I want them to know they can count on Edelman's to make sure everyone knows who they are."

"I understand. I'll make sure the night is flawless."

"I know you will," he says, and I swear I can hear the smile in his voice.

"Now, if you don't mind, I have a Super Bowl party to get back to."

"I didn't know you were a football fan. I thought you always avoided sports."

"I do on a professional level, but let's be honest, Charles . . . I'm really just here for the booze and food."

He laughs. "That sounds more like you. Enjoy the rest of your day, Penelope. I'll see you in the office tomorrow."

"See ya then."

Hanging up the call, I stare down at my phone before pushing off the bed and walking to the window to take in Amelia's neighborhood. I berate myself for not saying no to Charles, even though I know how to say no when it counts. This was just a battle I didn't feel was worth fighting, and honestly, alcohol companies are clients I know how to please with my eyes closed.

A family walks down the sidewalk in front of Amelia's house, pushing a double stroller as the mom and dad laugh at each other before the man bends down to kiss his wife's temple.

And just that sight has a flash of memories lunging forward, a mixture of reality and visions of a future that I don't let myself think about very often. But they slam into me, reminding me of a life I was supposed to have but never got to and the decision I made to never let that be a possibility again.

Shaking off the rush of emotions that just bombarded me, I turn and head back downstairs, knowing that a few glasses of champagne and more snacks that I refuse to feel guilty about today will help distract me from thinking about how different a day like today would have been if my life had turned out the way I planned.

And maybe that's why I don't bother planning much anymore except when it comes to my job.

When I enter the kitchen again, the sound of Ethan, Damien, and Nick screaming at the television helps drown out my thoughts, especially as I see a glass of champagne waiting for me on the kitchen counter. I grab the bubbly liquid and another potato skin and then head into the living room to join my friends who are more like my family since I haven't really seen mine in twelve years.

"What did your boss want?" Noelle asks me as I sit down next to her.

"He needs me to run point on a vodka launch party in two weeks. It's for a new client, and he's afraid the agent he assigned doesn't know their head from their ass, so I have to step in and show them how it's done."

"Which you will," she says.

"You know it, girl." We clink glasses just as the whistle rings out from the television.

"Damn! Come on, Kansas City!" Ethan shouts. "This game better not be like this the entire time."

"Like it would be any different if Dallas were playing," Nick mutters under his breath. Ethan is a diehard Dallas Cowboys fan, and Nick, Amelia's brother, loves giving him shit about it. And I'm not gonna lie, I usually get in on that action, too.

"You're just pissed that New Orleans didn't make it so you could drool over Maddox Taylor on the screen the entire time," Ethan counters.

Nick puts a finger in the air. "As a heterosexual man who is in a very loving relationship, I have no problem admitting that Maddox Taylor is a fine male specimen. But didn't you hear? Maddox's contract is up this year, and rumor is that New Orleans is gonna let him go."

"What?" Damien, Charlotte's fiancé, Ethan, and Jeffrey, Damien's colleague and good friend, all turn their heads in Nick's direction.

"Yeah. Don't you guys keep up with this shit?" Nick asks, his mouth and eyes wide.

They give Nick a collective blank stare.

"No, man. Sorry I'm not reading the gossip magazines. I've been kinda busy," Ethan mutters as Nick shakes his head.

"And you call yourself a football fan."

Snickering, I chime in on the shit talking. "I even know that, Ethan, and I only watch the game for the men in tight pants."

This is what I let them believe, anyway. The truth is, I know the game better than most of them since I grew up around it. Besides, being the star quarterback's girlfriend in high school almost required me to understand the game just as well as he did.

Commotion explodes from the television, pulling everyone's attention back to the game.

"Touchdown!" Oliver shouts before breaking into his victory dance, and everyone laughs as the boys take turns showing off their best touchdown celebrations.

And then a twinge in my chest takes life again as I remember the boy who used to celebrate each one of the touchdowns he helped make happen, too.

God, it seems like a lifetime ago and yet like it was just yesterday in the same breath.

"It's good to be back at Frankie's, ladies," I declare as we clink our glasses of champagne together and settle into our seats. We just placed our orders for breakfast, and now it's time to catch up with my girls. I made sure to give my main man, Frankie, the attention he deserves: a little harmless flirting that he enjoys just as much as I do.

Noelle starts brunch off with a bang. "So this week, I get the results back on my fertility testing." No topic is off-limits when the four of us talk, and honestly, that's how it should be with your girlfriends. Our brunches are the time when we catch up on each other's lives, process what we're feeling, and bitch about everything in between.

It's also when I enjoy endless mimosas and giving my friends shit while simultaneously having their backs—it's a delicate balance.

"Are you nervous?" Charlotte asks, leaning forward slightly in her seat.

Noelle nods. "Definitely. I know that I obviously *feel* fine and healthy, but I'm afraid these tests might show something that will make this process more difficult or stressful. Ideally, if everything looks good, I move forward with the required counseling, choose a donor, and then hopefully do my first intrauterine insemination next month." She takes a deep breath. "I just hope it works. I have to keep reminding myself that just because I'm subtracting the man from this equation doesn't mean that pregnancy is guaranteed. All of the stars still have to align to make this happen, and even then, there's no telling if this will all work out the way I want it to."

"Counseling? They're making you do counseling beforehand?" I ask, my brows pushing together.

Amelia, our resident therapist, chimes in. "Oh, absolutely. I'm glad the clinic you chose is requiring it, too." She reaches across the table and places her hand on Noelle's. "Obviously, I support your decision, as do we all, but there are plenty of emotions to process related to having a child, especially in this manner. The acceptance that you'll be a single mother, the judgment you'll receive from family and friends who may not support your decision, and the consideration of how and when you'll tell your child how they were conceived. It's a lot to think about and not a decision that should be rushed."

Charlotte interjects before Noelle can speak. "*Are* you having second thoughts, Noelle?"

Noelle clears her throat. "No, but the longer it takes, the more it seems like there are hoops to jump through at every turn, and I'm afraid all the waiting might be for nothing. Ultimately, though, I've made my peace with this decision. I know that I don't need a man or to be in love to become a mother, and this avenue gives me some control over the choice. Even though I know there are many aspects of this process where I have no control over what might happen."

"Did you bring the catalog of sperm donors? You know I'm going to be pissed if you didn't include me in that part," I say, trying to lighten up the conversation. Judging by the eye rolls and chuckles, it did the trick. Not that I didn't want to continue talking about the realities of the situation, but comedic relief is my specialty. It's helped me cope with many issues in my life, and I'd like to think it's what my girls have come to expect and appreciate about me, too.

Noelle's eyes light up as she reaches down to grab a few papers from her purse. "Oh, yeah. Now, these are the ones I've narrowed it down to. Naturally, I wanted input from my girls, but I thought it best to go through the list first before I enlisted your help so we all weren't being pulled in different directions and I wouldn't feel even more confused."

Shaking my head, I grab the papers from her and begin fingering through them. "I still think it's a shame you don't get to see their dicks before making your final decision."

Charlotte huffs out a laugh. "Eliminating the whole dick thing is mostly the point of doing things this way, Pen. Why should it matter?"

"I know, but what if she has a boy?" I toss my thumb toward Noelle, who's sitting right next to me. "Wouldn't you want to know if your child's dad was on the teeny-weenie committee? Or if he's packing a bazooka in his pants?"

Amelia shakes her head while laughing. "What if she has a girl?"

I hum in thought. "Well, then I guess that argument is invalid. And Noelle has a nice rack, so hopefully her daughter inherits that, too."

Noelle rips the papers from my hands. "Glad to know where your priorities lie."

"Hey, you know I'm just joking. But seriously, what is it that you're looking for? Then maybe we can use that to help you decide."

Noelle's face instantly softens. She knows this is just how I am, and I appreciate that. "I think coloring is important, because I want my child to look like me. So brown hair, light or dark . . . but I've always envisioned a baby with bright blue eyes." She shakes her head at herself. "But obviously, none of that matters, just that the baby is healthy, so family health history is my biggest concern. Breast cancer is already on my side from my mom's mom, so I'd like to avoid potentially passing down those kinds of risks to my kid through their father as well. But honestly, I just feel like I'll know when I come across the profile. Does that sound crazy?"

Charlotte shakes her head. "Not at all. That's your female intuition at work, and we all need to listen to her when she wants to be heard."

"Absolutely," Amelia adds as Noelle gives us each a few papers to sort through as we speak. "So, Penelope, how are things with you? When is that vodka launch party?"

"This weekend. And I'm still mad that you bitches aren't going. You used to go to all of my events. Now it's like you're too cool to be seen with me," I whine playfully.

But it is true. Whenever I gave them a date and time, they used to be there. However, in the last year or so, and especially once Charlotte started dating Damien and Amelia found Ethan, their attendance has dwindled.

The sad effects of falling in love, I suppose.

Charlotte speaks up first. "I know, but Damien and I have so many appointments this weekend with wedding vendors. Now that we've found our venue, it's time to make a bunch of decisions. I just know by the end of the day, I'm going to be exhausted."

Charlotte and Damien are getting married this June at a beautiful hotel in Dana Point, the Waldorf Astoria Monarch Beach Resort & Club. Her parents are footing the entire bill, too, which is the least they could do after the shit Charlotte went through with her mother. They're slowly healing their relationship, but I don't blame her for keeping her distance given everything that happened.

And I may have a little bit of experience in distancing from the parents as well.

"I get it. It's just more fun for me if I know you girls will be there to talk me down when I'm on the verge of punching someone."

Amelia chimes in now. "You've got this, Pen. But I have to say, it sounds like you're a little resentful of your job right now. Is everything okay at work?"

I narrow my eyes at her across the table. "Are you going into therapist mode with me right now?"

She smiles knowingly. "A little. I just can't remember the last time, if at all, that you sounded like you genuinely didn't want to head up an event. You normally are chomping at the bit for that kind of stuff."

Sighing, I reach for my mimosa and take a large drink, setting my glass down before speaking again. "I don't know. I'm just not feeling very challenged at the moment. Everything just kind of feels monotonous, you know?" My friends all nod. "You guys all have things changing and happening in your lives, and I'm just kind of standing still."

"Maybe it's time for Penelope to get a boyfriend?" Noelle nudges me with her shoulder from her seat beside me. "When's the last time you went on a date?"

A snort leaves my lips. "Yeah, I think this is the time to remind you that I don't date. Not my style, girls." Then I turn in my seat to face Noelle head on. "Besides, aren't you the one who decided to forgo dating altogether and move straight toward having a kid on your own because you were so fed up with men?" She sighs and then nods. "Exactly. So why are you trying to feed me to the sharks? No, thank you, ma'am. All I need is a good dicking. Haven't had one of those in a while, surprisingly, so I am definitely overdue."

"That *is* surprising for you. You're in such a rut that it's extending to your sex life. I'm in shock." Charlotte reaches for the champagne to refill her glass just as Frankie comes by with our food.

"Beautiful ladies, your breakfast is served." In his thick Greek accent, he begins unloading plates of comforting breakfast food in front of each of us. Since my sweet tooth was awake with a vengeance this morning, I ordered the waffles with strawberries and whipped cream, my favorite thing on the menu.

"Frankie, you're a doll. I hope your wife knows how lucky she is to have you."

He beams down at me with pride. "Oh yes, Miss Penelope. She knows. But it never hurts to be reminded that I can take care of all of you ladies as well. It's appreciated."

Amelia smiles over at him. "We always appreciate you, Frankie."

"And we would love another bottle of champagne when you get a chance, please," Charlotte adds, holding up the empty bottle.

"Your wish is my command, ladies. I will return shortly."

Once we all get our food the way we like it with sprinkles of salt and pepper or slathered in syrup or ketchup, Amelia turns the questions back to me. "Whatever happened to that bouncer at that club who you were hooking up with?"

"Tony?" I ask around a mouthful of waffle.

"Yeah, him. I thought you liked him. He checked all of your boxes, no?"

"Yes, he did. But let's remember what the boxes are, shall we?" I wipe the corner of my mouth with my napkin and then begin listing items out loud, ticking them off on my fingers as I do. "One, he has to be taller than me. Sorry to the short guys, but I'm nearly six foot, taller than that with heels. I don't want a man cowering just because I'm looking down at him." Charlotte snickers but tilts her head in agreement. "Two, he has to be able to hold a decent conversation. Not that I ever plan on doing much talking with the guy once I decide I'm going to let him into my lady garden, but I prefer to talk to a man that doesn't have the IQ of a napkin."

Noelle snorts. "Oh God, please don't call your vagina that. Do you say that to them?"

I purse my lips at her and narrow my eyes. "Of course not. That little metaphor was just for you girls."

Amelia giggles, and then I continue. "And three, he has to have an ass. I mean, even if he's not the largest guy on the planet in other areas, a nice, plump, hard ass makes up for that. Especially if he likes to be spanked."

Charlotte spits mimosa across the table. "Dear lord. You spank men?"

I shrug nonchalantly. "Why not? If women like it so much, who's to say men don't enjoy a little love tap, too?"

"You are seriously deranged, Pen. I feel like I just learned about this entirely different side to you, which is scary considering

I feel like I already know way too much about your sex life as it is."

"You're welcome," I state matter-of-factly as I spear a piece of my waffle and plop it into my mouth. "But my point is, there are plenty of men that fit that bill. Why limit myself to just one? And Tony . . . well, Tony wanted more, and you know that's not my style."

Noelle chimes in. "So that's it? That's your criteria to allow a man into your bed?"

"Well, first, we never go to my place . . ."

"Now you really sound like a guy," Charlotte mutters, but I can tell she's just being sarcastic.

"Come on. Would you want some potential stage-five clinger to know where you live? It's shit like that that makes me grateful I never took Tony back to my place. Because once he started to catch feelings, I know he would have shown up to my house and started begging me to reconsider."

"But have you thought about reconsidering?" Noelle asks.

"Reconsidering what?"

"Trying for more with him? Or any man, for that matter? You never let things go beyond the physical, Pen. I'm not shaming you for it. Please know that's not what I'm saying." I nod, urging her to continue because I know my girlfriends would never look down on me for enjoying sex and actively seeking it out. No woman should ever feel ashamed for that. "It's just that, now that I think about it, in all the years that we've known you, I don't believe you've ever had a boyfriend," she says, tapping her chin. Then she peers across the table at my other two friends, who are studying me as they question the validity of her assessment.

"I'll save you some time, ladies. Noelle's right. I haven't. I don't date. I told you this way back when the four of us became friends freshman year of college."

"But why, Penelope?" Charlotte asks softly, emotion clouding her voice now. "You have so much to offer someone. I guess I'm just trying to understand—"

"I don't need a man to be happy, okay?"

"We know that," Amelia interjects. "That's not what we're saying. But don't you ever wonder if you can have more by just letting someone in?"

Sucking my lips in, I stare down at my plate, my appetite gone.

My friends are concerned, and their questions are only coming from a good place right now, I know this. But the truth of the matter is, I've never told them exactly why I don't date.

I just always played it off, stating there were too many men out there to enjoy to commit to only one. I just want to live my life with no regrets before potentially settling down with someone.

Penelope Klein is just down for a good time, not a long time.

They don't know that falling in love is the thing that almost destroyed me when I was younger, and I don't know if I could live through that again.

After a few moments of silent contemplation, I decide to throw them a bone. "My one brush with love didn't end well, so I vowed never to go there again."

"You've been in love?" Charlotte asks, her eyes practically popping out of her head.

"High school love, girls. And it was the real deal. But—"

"What happened?" Noelle cuts me off. "And why on earth haven't you ever told us this?"

"It . . . it didn't work out, okay? And I don't like talking about it." I sit up taller in my chair, straightening my shoulders and shaking my hair back into place. "So now you know, but please don't go any further with your questions because there is nothing more to say."

Amelia licks her lips and then takes a bite of her oatmeal, chewing slowly as she locks her eyes onto me. I hate when she does that, because I know that therapist mind of hers is at work, dissecting all of my issues from my childhood that I've yet to deal with.

Well, news flash, I don't need a therapist or one of my best friends to tell me that. I already know my mind is full of some fucked-up issues that would probably benefit from some emotional unpacking. But I also know that there's no reason to bother when I'm living my life just fine and have been for years.

"Just say it, Amelia. I know you're psychoanalyzing me over there right now."

She swallows, wipes her mouth, and then reaches for her drink. "I'm not going to say anything, Penelope."

I glare right back at her. "Really?"

"Yup."

Charlotte and Noelle watch us, their eyes bouncing back and forth as we continue our stare-off.

"And why not?"

"Because you'll talk when you're ready. And when you are, you know where to find me so I can recommend you to someone who can help you process everything you're keeping inside." She taps her chin. "Now that I think about it, I don't know why I didn't see it before."

"See what?"

Noelle mutters out of the corner of her mouth. "She is reading you so hard right now, Penelope, that it's starting to freak me out."

"Join the club," I mutter back. But then I decide that if Amelia is going to continue to be cryptic about what she's thinking, then I'm going to take this opportunity to change the subject. "You know what? It's fine. You can go on thinking you have me all figured out. But the only thing that matters is that I know what I want, and a monogamous relationship is not it." Wiping my hands off in front of me dramatically, I continue, "Well, now that we've gotten that conversation out of the way, let's turn the tables on someone else, shall we?"

Noelle pushes her plate to the side and grabs her stack of potential sperm donors again. "Anyone in the mood to go shopping for sperm?"

"Always down for shopping, but this is definitely a purchase I want no part in," I reply, grabbing the papers she handed me before out from under my plate. "I am merely here to help you spend your money and find your baby daddy."

Charlotte and Amelia share a look before we all settle in and get to work trying to find Noelle's diamond in the rough.

Chapter 2

Penelope

"**K**risten, did you forget how to speak English tonight? I said check in with the bartenders to make sure they had enough bottles of each flavor, not flirt with the one behind the bar. News flash, he's gay anyway, so you're wasting your time."

Her eyes narrow as she stares up at me. "I did check in with them. They said they were fine."

"Really? Because I just had to deliver a case of the apple-flavored vodka because they ran out. So try again."

"But I—"

I hold up my hand to cut her off. "No, I don't want to hear your excuses. Next time, don't even bother going over there empty-handed. Bring something with you even if you don't think they need it, because the last thing we need is for them to have to work twice as hard to do their jobs. The last thing we want is our client worried that we can't make sure their product is stocked so customers are getting their fix within seconds. That's how you keep clients happy, Kristen. You make sure they never have to worry about their product being accessible."

She sighs but reluctantly nods. "Okay. Fine."

"There's a reason why I'm the shit, Kristen. Listen to what I tell you, and you'll go far in this business. You have the potential, but your head isn't focused on the job. Tonight isn't about *you* having a good time. It's about everyone else having a good time. Save your flirting and pick-up attempts for when you're off the clock. Now go. Make your rounds. Make sure each station is stocked, including the ice luge. I want to see a fresh stack of vanilla vodka over there, stat."

She nods again and then scurries away, giving me a moment to catch my breath and exhale the frustration building up inside of me.

It's the night of Zio's launch party, and now I see why Charles wanted me here. These interns are young and clueless, but I have no reservations about setting them straight. Even though this wasn't an event I wanted to be at, knowing my boss wanted me here does make my chest swell with pride.

"Damn. Bossy and beautiful."

Spinning on my heels, prepared to lay into the man for his blatant eavesdropping, I'm caught off guard when the face staring back at me is one I didn't expect to see tonight, particularly because I didn't see his name on the list. But I definitely recognize him, as I'm sure the rest of the crowd in the club does, too.

"I'm sorry?" I find my footing again, but I'm stunned speechless by the view of this man in real life. Because let me tell you, the television cameras and stadium lights don't do him justice.

Maddox Taylor, quarterback for the New Orleans Saints, is

standing right in front of me, one hand casually placed in the pocket of his black slacks, the other holding his drink as he smirks down at me, a gleam of pleasure in his hazel eyes.

Standing at least a few inches taller than me, he commands the attention of those around us with his confident stance and the curve of his lips, even though I can tell he's not trying to. Though he's dressed like every other guy in the club tonight—a button-down shirt with the top two buttons undone and his sleeves rolled up to his elbows plus slacks to adhere to the dress code—he has a presence that makes him stand out against every other male in the room. He's the definition of tall, dark, and handsome, but there's a hint of mischief in that grin, and I can't deny that I'm intrigued, especially when I shouldn't be.

"You put that girl in her place. Stern but not overbearing. It was impressive." He continues to compliment me in a voice laced with a small southern twang as my brain tries to process how I feel about this conversation in the first place.

"Well, I am a pretty impressive woman."

The corner of his mouth lifts, his eyes practically dancing as he watches me, assessing my reaction. "That you are."

Hey, I'm no stranger to harmless flirting. Hell, usually I'm the one who initiates it. But I don't know if I'm completely off my game tonight or if the shock of seeing him here is what's really throwing me off.

I'm pretty much immune to meeting and conversing with celebrities now, given how often it happens in my line of work. But Maddox Taylor is football's notorious playboy, at least that's what the media portrays, the guy everyone is watching to see if and when he'll be in the public eye next—and the last person I anticipated being here tonight all the way out in California when his team and home are halfway across the country.

Lifting his hand from his pocket, he reaches out to shake mine. "Maddox Taylor, by the way."

"I know who you are," I reply as I intercept his hand and reciprocate the movement. Warm skin and his very large hand envelope mine, and suddenly a rather massive spark of lust ignites between my legs. You know what they say about a man with big hands . . .

Looks like my lady garden is waking up.

"You may know my name, but you don't know *me*."

His rebuttal catches me by surprise. "True."

"This would be the time when you tell me your name," he says, the two of us still shaking hands slowly as we stare at one another. I'm waiting for his eyes to drop down to my cleavage or my body incased in a lavender hip-hugging dress that makes me look like Sandra Bullock in *Miss Congeniality*. Which is exactly why I bought the thing—such an iconic movie and scene. And I look fucking amazing in it.

"What if I don't want to?" Dropping his hand, I smile up at him teasingly.

"Well, how am I supposed to hold a conversation with the most beautiful woman in the room if I don't know her name?"

Rolling my eyes, I gently release his hand from mine. "That was cheesy, but I'll let it slide. I'm Penelope."

His smile grows. "Nice to meet you, Penelope."

Not quite sure how to take his earlier compliment, I flash him a tight-lipped smile and then reach for my clipboard again and pretend to get back to work. I can feel him staring at me while I fake reading through the list on my paper, and the heart palpitations rocking my body have me remembering the last time a man made me feel this way. I feel like I'm crawling out of my skin.

"Why did Barbie get kicked out of the toy box?" he asks, and my head twists to find him still staring down at me with a grin on his beautiful full lips. *Damn, I bet that mouth possesses just as much skill as the man has on the football field.*

"What?"

"It's a joke. You look like you could use a good laugh, so I'm gonna tell you a joke." He shrugs and then takes another sip of his drink. "But I have to warn you, I only know dirty ones, so that's what you're going to get."

Fighting my smile, I pull my clipboard to my chest and then turn to face him head-on again, tilting my head to the side as I narrow my eyes at him. "Well, I happen to love dirty jokes, so I'll bite. Why did Barbie get kicked out of the toy box, Maddox?"

He leans in, giving me a full view of every fleck of gold in his eyes, every speck of dark hair in the stubble on his jaw, and a fresh wave of his masculine scent, clean and spicy. "Because she kept sitting on Pinocchio's face saying, 'Lie to me, lie to me!'"

A roar of laughter leaves my lips as I toss my head back. "Oh God. That's a good one. I might have to put that one in my arsenal from now on. My girlfriends will love that."

Shaking from his own laughter, he stands taller, clearly proud of my reaction. "Glad you appreciated it. It's one of my favorites."

Studying him, I peer up into his eyes. "Who would have thought that Maddox Taylor had talent on and off the football field?"

He leans into me again. "Oh, believe me, Penelope. I have plenty of talents that nobody knows about."

"I'm sure you do, and that's exactly why this conversation is going to end right now." Taking a step back so I can gain a little more control of my body given this visceral reaction that I'm having to him, I scour the room, remembering that I'm here to work, something I just spent ten minutes berating Kristen for forgetting. "Well, it was nice to meet you, Maddox, but if you'll excuse me, I have a job to do."

"Oh, of course. But I'll be here all night if you need another joke to help you relax."

Oh, I'm sure there are many ways you could help me relax.

No, Penelope. He may be hot and check all of your boxes, but he's off-limits. You know this. Remember the rules. No athletes.

Wait, does he check all of your boxes? What about his ass?

With a curt nod, he walks off, giving me a perfect view of his backside, and *good lord*. I think God spent extra time sculpting those round globes. Well, that, and all the time he must spend in the weight room has definitely paid off.

Biting my lip, I continue staring for an unknown length of time, completely mesmerized by Maddox's ass and practically salivating from just our short interaction. It's been a long time since a man has intrigued me to this degree, and it's been an even longer time since I've seen an ass on a man like that.

The problem is that the man getting that reaction from me is *him*.

Just to set the record straight, I sincerely think that an ass on a man is one of the most underrated body parts to appreciate. I mean, I know forearms are sexy, and I love a nice pair of bulging biceps and massive shoulders just as much as the next girl. But a nice round ass? One that is completely bitable and so hard you could bounce a quarter off it? It's like being teased with a juicy piece of medium-rare steak and fighting every urge to sink your teeth into it, even though you know it would be delicious and satisfy a very savage craving.

Unfortunately, biting a man's ass is frowned upon in public.

But in private? You'd better believe I'll be appreciating that man's bedunkadunk in full if he'll let me.

"I guess I can wait until you're done." Garret, my amazing assistant, comes up on my right, startling me from my blatant appraisal of Maddox's ass.

"Shit, Garret. You scared me." Placing my hand over my chest, I feel my heart beat wilder than it was when Maddox was standing right next to me.

"I didn't mean to, Pen, but I don't think I've seen you stare that hard at a man before, ever. And I don't blame you, honey. Maddox Taylor is grade A prime choice beef." He bites his own lip as he tips his head to the side while watching Maddox walk away. "He is definitely droolworthy. Which reminds me, you have some drool dripping out of the side of your mouth right now."

"No, I don't." I frantically swipe at the corner of my mouth then glare at Garret when I realize he was lying.

"Not yet, but it was coming."

I clear my throat and then change the subject, slightly irritated that Garret is calling me on my shit. "Tell me again why you're over here? Is everything okay?"

"Oh, yeah. The president of Zio's is getting a little tipsy, so I thought I would come let you know in case you wanted to check in on him or switch his orders to water. Everything else is good— Kristen helped restock the bar, the second round of hors d'oeuvres and tasting pairings are being served as we speak, and the ice luge is a huge hit. Good idea with that one."

"Everyone loves an ice luge, especially after a few shots of vodka." I wink at him and then glance out over the crowded dance floor. "Four years in a sorority proved that to be true."

"Well, your experience and expertise are easy to admire. And I'm not the only one—apparently you have a not-so-secret admirer for the evening that you can't seem to shake." Garret tips his head to the side of the room where Maddox is standing, his eyes locked on me. "You have to go talk to him again."

Humming with nervous energy, which is very unlike me, I shake my head and stare down at my clipboard again. "I'm working, Garret. And besides, I'm not interested."

He steps up right in front of my face so we are staring into each other's eyes. "Really? Could have fooled me with the way you were gawking at his ass earlier."

"The man plays football for a living. Of course he has a nice ass. I was merely appreciating it. There's nothing wrong with that. An ass like that covered in spandex is why most women watch the sport to begin with."

He shakes his head. "And gay men, sweetheart. But I saw you two talking. He had you laughing and smiling like a smitten girl."

"Me and the word 'smitten' do not belong together. I don't get smitten with men. It's more like the other way around."

And that's the truth. I'm gonna toot my own horn for a minute and brag about my ability to mesmerize the male population. I've got a curvy body, long legs, and a sassy mouth. Most men can't resist that.

"Well, Maddox is clearly interested in you, so what do you have to lose? Plus, he's a football god. Any heterosexual woman would be a fool to turn him down. Believe me, if he played for my team, I wouldn't think twice about cashing in on his interest."

"Well, you can be very persuasive. Maybe you should take a

chance and see if you can bring him over to your side of life?"

Garret laughs. "If I thought I had a chance, I would. But he is clearly vying for only one woman's attention tonight, and that woman is you, my friend." With a pat on my shoulder, he walks off, leaving me vibrating with uneasiness as I glance in Maddox's direction, watching him converse with the man standing next to him, someone he is clearly familiar with. He's laughing, drinking, and partying, solidifying the image that so many football fans know him for maintaining: the life of the party, the man who's down to have fun and not worry about how that paints his occupation and team in a negative light.

And then a parade of twenty-something blondes skip up to where he's standing, each one fighting for his attention, and all of the men around him gleefully absorb the interest.

But when he sees me staring, his gaze locks on mine again. He lifts his drink in acknowledgment and then takes a sip, his eyes never leaving mine.

Temptation builds in my body, a reminder that it has been awhile since I've enjoyed some male company. But then my subconscious wins as I remember my rules.

But what is the saying? Some rules are made to be broken, right?

I t's well past one in the morning and the club is packed, bodies gyrating as the bass of the music pumps through the walls and everyone's bloodstream. Now that the busiest part of the night has passed, Charles comes over to me and congratulates me on a job well done.

"Thank you again, Penelope, for stepping up. I knew I could count on you." He hands me a glass of a mixed drink that hopefully contains the green apple flavored vodka that I've been dying to taste. "You've earned this."

"Yes, I have, as well as a bonus for putting up with interns all night." Taking a drink of the alcohol, I welcome the warmth it covers my body in and the sour taste on my tongue.

"I'll see what I can do." He winks. "But just know the reason I wanted you here is because you're who I want them learning from. You're helping mold the future of this company, and I want them to learn from the best."

"Well, when you put it that way . . ."

"Excuse me." A familiar voice pulls our attention to my left where Maddox stands, eager to encroach on our conversation. Extending his hand out for a shake, he announces, "Maddox Taylor. You're Charles Edelman, correct?" he asks as my boss stretches his hand out to greet him.

"Yes, sir. And Mr. Taylor, it's an honor to meet you. I'm a big fan."

"Thank you."

"Are you enjoying the party tonight?"

He casts his eyes over to me quickly and then shifts back to Charles. "I am. Attending tonight sort of happened on a whim. I wasn't supposed to be in town, but a last-minute meeting pulled me to LA and some friends of mine insisted I come along, so I did. Even though my agent won't be happy if my face ends up in a picture online," he jokes.

"You do have a bit of a reputation, don't you, Maddox?" I interject.

He arches a brow at me. "Keeping tabs on me, Penelope?"

"Being in PR means it's my job to keep tabs on everyone. Knowledge is power in this industry; you must know that."

Charles grins. "She's right. And believe me, Maddox, Penelope is always right. I may not be married, but I've been around long enough to know that women have that magical intuition that can't be ignored." He places his hand on my shoulder, beaming with pride. "This is why Penelope is the best rep in our company. I know now more than ever not to argue with her."

Maddox chuckles as someone calls for Charles across the room. He holds a finger up to them before turning back to us.

"If you'll excuse me, duty calls. Enjoy the rest of your night, Maddox. And Penelope, nice work tonight. You're officially off the clock. Now go have some fun." With one more proud smile, he saunters off, leaving me alone with the man who has my body humming with energy for the second time tonight.

"Now that you're done working, care to have a drink with me?" Maddox asks, stepping right in front of me so I have no choice but to look at him.

My mind is telling me to say no, but my vagina? That bitch is clearly not listening to any of my other body parts. "I suppose one drink won't be the end of the world."

His triumphant smile makes my stomach flip. "I'm sure there are worse things you could endure, like dealing with interns for the rest of the night, right?" With his hand on the small of my back, he leads me to a VIP booth tucked into a corner that's really made for two people, although I've seen far more than that squeezed into the small space. The spot where he's touching me is on fire, even with the barrier of fabric between our skin.

I wonder what his hands would feel like elsewhere.

As we settle in, he spreads his legs, and just the sheer size of him has me fighting to take a deep breath. I like a large man, like I told the girls, and Maddox definitely fits the bill.

He's likely six feet and three inches of solid muscle and brawn with a face very similar to Jimmy Garoppolo. And the way he's wearing that simple white shirt and black slacks only notches up his sex appeal.

"Don't take this the wrong way, Penelope, but I've been waiting to talk to you again all night."

"Really? And why is that?"

"Because it's not every day that the moment I see a woman, I'm captivated by her."

I roll my eyes, even though the compliment sits in the center of my chest. "I'm sure you say that to all the girls. I've seen the pictures of you with women, Maddox. I know you're not hurting for any female attention."

He leans forward in the seat, so close that I can count his eyelashes. "You should know better than anyone not to believe everything the media says, right? I mean, if you're the best at your job, I imagine you would at least know that. Not everything is as it seems."

"And what do you mean by that?"

He shifts back and lifts his drink to his lips. "Exactly what I said."

Silence descends on us, and I'm not sure if it's awkward or intentional as I process his words. So instead, I decide to change the subject. "You said you came out to California unexpectedly? What are you here for?"

He nods. "A meeting with my agent and a few endorsement deals. Boring stuff that I don't particularly care about. I just want to play football. Although, if I had run into Steve

Harvey while I was out here, I probably would have shit myself."

"Steve Harvey? Really? That's very specific."

His face instantly lights up like a little boy who's just been asked who his favorite superhero is. "Hell, yeah. The man is one of my idols. I was just scrolling through Reels on Facebook one day and came across a bunch of Family Feud videos, which is, like, the best fucking show ever. Seriously, if I ever had a chance to be on there, I might pass out from nerves."

"What?" I laugh. "You play football on live television in front of millions of people, but meeting Steve Harvey would make you pass out?"

He shrugs. "What can I say? I idolize the guy. He has so much wisdom, shoots straight from the hip, practices what he preaches, and he's hilarious. Plus, he pulls off a bald head and mustache with so much confidence, any man should look up to him for that alone."

"And you decided all of this after watching Family Feud videos and clips of him on his talk show?"

"Hell, yeah. I was entranced. Suddenly hours had passed as I watched hundreds of clips and just listened to everything the man had to say. Some stuff gave me fucking goosebumps. What's not to love?"

"So are you saying that when you grow up, you want to be like Steve Harvey?"

"Fuck, yeah! Where do I sign up?"

Laughter escapes from my lips. "You do realize you're the number two quarterback in the NFL, right? Most men would make something like that their aspiration in life."

His smirk is instant. "So you *have* been keeping tabs on me. I knew it, Penelope. I could see that hint of stalker in your eyes." His playful demeanor is in the same league as my own, and I can't say that I hate it.

Instead, I roll my eyes. "Don't flatter yourself. I was raised to watch and know the game. I know many stats about many players, not just you."

"Let me guess, you were 'just a small-town girl, living in a lonely world . . .'"

A snort leaves my lips. "Quoting Journey now?" I shake my head. "You are quite the enigma, Maddox."

"How so?"

"First, the dirty jokes, which was unique, I must say. Next, an infatuation with Steve Harvey. And now, you're using carefully placed lines of popular eighties ballads in conversation?" I lean back and glare at him. "Who *are* you, Maddox Taylor?"

"I'm just a regular guy, Penelope. What you see is what you get. The last thing I want is for you to think I'm sitting here because I'm not genuinely interested in you or I'm trying to be someone that I'm not."

"Interested?"

He leans forward again, leaving only a few inches of space between us. "Very interested," he rasps, and the gravel in his voice has goosebumps breaking out over my arms.

We sit there in a stare-off as I feel my pulse pick up speed. But in the next breath, my mind is reminding me that I'm teetering on the edge of dangerous territory.

I feel like I'm not in control of what's happening here, which is definitely not what I'm used to.

I'm usually the one that makes *my* interest known. It's how I know I'm safe, that feelings won't be involved, that a man knows exactly what an interaction between us will be with no misconceptions: a transaction.

But there are just too many flags here that are telling me Maddox Taylor is a man that could pull me back to a place that I mentally keep buried in the past.

The physical similarities, the personality, the profession—it all has me fighting a trip down memory lane.

But then again, I've become an expert on separating feelings and sex, so I should be able to do that with him, right? I mean, it has been awhile for me, which is definitely out of the ordinary. He's obviously shown his interest, and the man has an ass that won't quit. I'd be stupid not to take him out for a test drive if that's what he's offering.

Any other time, you wouldn't think twice about taking a man up on his offer, especially the blatant one he's putting out on the table. Hell, half the time, you're *the one putting the offer down.*

So what if he's a football player? It's not like he lives here. It's not like you'll ever see him again. This isn't about fairytales, rings, and babies. This is about lust and orgasms, and hopefully multiple ones.

Before I can make my decision officially in my head, Maddox speaks and breaks our stare-off. "Who's the most popular guy at the nudist colony?"

Choking back laughter, I bite. "I don't know, Maddox. Who?"

"The guy who can carry two cups of coffee and a dozen donuts."

It takes me a minute, but once the punchline hits, I cackle out loud. "Oh my God!"

Laughing, he leans back in the booth again. "I told ya. Dirty jokes break the tension every time."

Sitting up taller on my side of the booth, my decision made about seeing where the night takes us, I decide to give him a little taste of his own medicine. "What do a penis and a Rubik's Cube have in common?"

Delightful glee spreads across Maddox's face. "Are you trying to tell me a dirty joke, Penelope?"

"Yes, I am. And I hope it's not one you know."

"I actually haven't heard this one, so I'm definitely intrigued." He adjusts himself in his seat. "I don't know. What do a penis and a Rubik's Cube have in common?"

"The more you play with them, the harder they get."

The laughter he grants me is like a reward I didn't know I wanted. And right then and there, I should have known that Maddox Taylor was trouble, in more ways than one.

"So tell me I was right about the small-town girl part . . ."

After another round of drinks, I'm feeling a little tipsy, and Maddox—clearly tipsy himself—decides we need to take a few shots, so the waitress scurries off like her ass is on fire to fulfill his request. In the time that we've been sitting here, I've learned the man likes to indulge a bit in the off-season, and it looks like we are both well on our way to making that happen.

"You are."

He eyes me as he contemplates his next words. "And let me guess: You were the rebel child in high school. Always sneaking out and seeing how far you could push your limits or what you could get away with."

"Why do you say that?"

"You just don't seem like the type of woman who likes to be told no, that you're a woman who knows what she wants and goes after it." He licks his lips slowly, and I'm not sure if it's supposed to be seductive, but it definitely catches my attention. "Am I right?"

"Oh, you're definitely right about that. But sadly, my rebellious side didn't quite blossom until college."

"And where did you go to school?"

"UCLA."

"Damn. Bossy, beautiful, and brainy. Triple b's. You're a catch, Penelope."

I reach up and cup my breasts. "Add in these modest B-cups up here, and you can make it four b's. I *am* a catch, Maddox, but I'm not looking to be caught."

His eyes never leave mine, not even to glance at my chest that I just fondled in front of him. "And why is that?"

"Because I prefer to be alone. Less drama that way. I don't need a man for a long time, just for a good time." Staring down into my glass, I lift it and take a sip, biting my straw between my teeth before I glance back at him.

He raises his eyebrows and then nods. "I see your point. Although, why can't the good time last for a long time?"

"Because something bad always happens sooner or later. And I'd rather not stick around and find out what it is."

A second later, the waitress returns with the shots Maddox ordered earlier, effectively ending that conversation. Though I can see the wheels turning in his mind from my answer.

"Thank you," he says, smiling up at her before directing his attention back to me, handing me my own shot. "Here."

I take the small glass from him and hold it out in front of me.

"So how many of these do we plan on taking before we address the inevitable end to this night?"

"Which is?"

"Me in your bed. That's why you're investing all of this time talking to me, right?"

One of his brows rises. "Is that what you think?"

"Am I wrong?"

"Partly." He clinks his shot glass against mine, and I take that as a sign to sling my shot back, soaking up the burn as the vodka slides down my throat. We both drop our shot glasses on the table, and then I lean back again in the booth, wincing just slightly and feeling warm all over.

"So which part am I wrong about?"

"The part where I planned to go home with anyone tonight."

"You're telling me that you had no intention of showing up here and finding someone to warm your bed? In a second, you'll tell me the story about how, when you were young, you went backpacking across western Europe . . ."

He chuckles before he slides closer to me in the booth, the heat coming off his body warming mine up even more. "I appreciate the *Friends* reference, but the truth is my bed has been pretty cold for a while, Penelope."

"So has mine."

"But that doesn't mean I expect anything to happen with you tonight." He reaches over and grips my chin slightly as his eyes bounce back and forth between mine. "Why don't you believe me?"

Because believing you would crack open this little ball of hope that I've buried deep in my chest, the ball of hope that allows me to crave more from a man than just one night.

Maddox is funny, playful, and obviously attractive. Any other time, I wouldn't question what I'm feeling. But with him, there's a subconscious conversation happening in my brain that I can't quite hear—or maybe I'm just choosing not to.

But before I can answer, he continues. "Look, despite what you may think, I want you to know I saw you across the club when I walked in tonight and just knew I *had* to talk to you. But I also know that I can't be the only one of us that feels this kinetic energy bouncing between us." He leans in further, dragging his nose up my jawline before his lips land at my ear. And I swear, I can feel my pulse pounding as I wait to hear what he has to say. "My body is vibrating with adrenaline right now just being near you. I don't even think I feel this way on the football field, Penelope, and that's saying something. Tell me I'm not the only one who's feeling this."

"You're not," I reply on a whisper and way too quickly, practically panting. *Dear lord, this man is making me weak.* And right then and there, I know I'm powerless over what happens next.

When he presses his lips to the skin right under my ear, my breath hitches, and he pulls back. "Then let's just enjoy each other and see where the night takes us." *Please say it's back to your bed, because now that I've given myself permission, it's all I can think about.* "Do you want to take another shot? Will that help you relax?"

"Maybe." I watch him stand, grab the shot glass from the table, and then walk around to my side of the booth so he's standing behind where I'm sitting. "What are you doing?"

"Helping you take a shot."

"From behind me?"

He moves his mouth to my ear again. "From behind is one of

the best positions, don't you think?"

I have to bite my lip from moaning out loud as visions of Maddox behind me in other circumstances flash through my mind. "Definitely. Although for someone who said their intentions aren't what they seem, that was a pretty suggestive comment."

"Not suggestive, just honest. Now just trust me." He tips my head back so I can see him above me but upside down. "Open your mouth."

"Bossy much?"

"You've already established *you* can be bossy, so now it's my turn." Smirking down at me, I watch him lick his lips as he waits for me to comply with his request.

So I do. Very slowly, I part my lips and wait for what he's going to do next.

"Try to keep your throat open. I'm going to pour the alcohol in slowly, and if you can swallow it as it's going down, it will make this easier on you."

"Sounds like you've said those words a time or two before," I counter. "Lucky for you, I'm good at swallowing."

My ears may be deceiving me, but I swear, I hear a small growl come from him. "You're not making it easy for me to be a gentleman, Penelope. I'm trying really hard to be on my best behavior . . ."

"Well, where's the fun in that?"

Shaking his head, he brings the shot glass over my mouth, and I wait for him to direct me again. "Open up."

Leaving my mouth parted once more, I stare up at him and watch the concentration on his face as he tips the glass over slowly and the vodka hits my tongue. The sensation is foreign, particularly because I'm taking a shot in an entirely different way, but as soon as I open up my throat and feel it slide down, another spark of adrenaline rushes through me as pride spreads across Maddox's face.

"Attagirl." At a painstakingly slow pace, he finishes emptying the shot into my mouth while slowly sliding his hand down the column of my throat with a soft graze of his fingertips on my flesh. My heart threatens to jump out of my chest from the caress, and once he's done, he drags his fingers across my collarbone as he releases me. I swallow the last little bit, still with my head tipped back. "How was that?" he asks as our eyes stay locked on one another. Mine trail him as he starts back toward his seat, forcing me to finally drop my head down.

Borderline orgasm-inducing just watching your face and feeling your hand on my throat. "Interesting. Different. Who taught you how to do a shot like that?"

He rounds the booth, and instead of going back to his seat, he motions for me to scoot over as he slides in next to me. "I picked up a few useful things in college besides how to play football."

"Is that right?"

"Like I said earlier, I'm a man of many talents, Penelope."

"I think I'll be the judge of that."

My libido is primed, and now I'm fully invested in discovering all of his skills. Here's hoping that in a matter of minutes we'll be moving this evening forward to the part where all of the orgasms will be delivered.

But a voice behind us bursts the bubble we're residing in very quickly. "Maddox?"

He twists in his seat, and I look past him to see a beautiful petite blonde in a skintight red dress, giggling as we both stare at her. "Hayley?"

"I'm ready to leave, Maddox." Twirling a piece of her hair around her finger, she wobbles on her heels, clearly drunk and clearly anticipating leaving the club with the man I just spent the past hour with.

"Yeah. Okay." He turns back to me, his brow furrowed but his intentions clear. "I'll be right back, all right?"

"Um, yeah. Okay . . ."

Hayley peers around Maddox's shoulders. "Maddox is gonna help me get home tonight." She giggles again. "He promised me earlier."

My brows pinch together this time. "Sure."

Maddox stands from the booth but stares down at me, cupping my jaw. "Don't go anywhere, Penelope. I'm not done with you."

I don't say anything as he walks away, but mostly because now I feel like a fool.

Of course this woman thinks she's going home with him tonight. I recognize her as one of the blondes who were swarming him while he stood around with his friends earlier. I'm guessing that while I was busy working, he was giving her his attention and reeling her in with his suave demeanor and smooth words.

It would only make sense for a man like Maddox to have a backup in case the time he invested in me didn't pan out. And a move like that definitely fits with his rumored playboy persona.

An unfamiliar twinge of jealousy builds in my chest, and that sign right there tells me to get out of this situation before I get in too deep, become just another one of his conquests, and wake up with regrets in the morning. So not my style.

I am all for a one-night stand, but not when the vulnerability that's enveloping me right now tells me it's better to avoid potential feelings altogether, especially now that I have a way out.

Without wasting another second, I stand up and move toward the back of the club, arriving at the office where I locked up my purse. I grab my bag, say a quick goodbye to Garret, and then make a beeline for the back door so I can walk out to my car, reaching for the Mace in my purse before I go outside.

Safety first, ladies—always.

Disappointment flows through me, but I shove it back down as I try to regain power over my feelings about the night. I'm taking control back, leaving before I can be left, and accepting that not all things pan out the way we think they will.

I have some firsthand experience with that.

But before I can reach for the handle on the door at the end of a long hallway, a strong hand grips my upper arm and stops me in my tracks.

"Where are you going?"

Spinning around, I meet the angry eyes of the man I was just running away from.

He came back?

"I'm leaving. Just like you were doing with Hayley."

The groove in his forehead gets deeper. "No, I wasn't. I told you to wait for me, that I would be right back. But when I got to the booth, you were gone." Our eyes bounce back and forth between each other's. "Why?"

I motion for Maddox to let go of my arm, and he does so willingly. "I wasn't going to wait around when I wasn't sure that you were actually coming back."

"But I told you I would return." He crowds my space, forcing me up against the wall so his chest is pressed into mine, our lips mere centimeters apart. "I meant what I said."

"Forgive me for not wanting to look like a fool, but it seems

Hayley was under the impression that you would be going home with *her* tonight."

His face softens as realization dawns in his eyes, and then a grin graces his lips. "You're jealous."

"Ha. No, I'm not. I don't get jealous." *Liar, liar, pants on fire, Penelope.*

"It may not be normal for you, but that's exactly what you're feeling."

"Keep flattering yourself, Maddox. Now, if you'll excuse me, I need to go." I move to push against his chest, but he reaches up and encircles my wrists with his hands, holding them tightly between us, brushing his thumbs over my skin.

"So that's it? You're ready for this night to be over?"

"You even said yourself that you didn't expect anything, so . . ."

"I don't. But you and I both know where this was headed."

"Maybe I changed my mind."

His face scrunches up. "I don't think you did, because your body is telling me something completely different than what your mouth is."

My heart rate picks up. "And what is that?"

His eyes dart to my neck as he presses the length of his body against mine. I can feel just how hard he is, which is making this entire situation even more difficult to navigate.

"Well, given I can see your pulse thumping in your veins, I'd say you're turned on and scared. Also, your pupils are dilated, which could mean a multitude of things, but I'm going to chalk it up to the obvious fact that you want me just as badly as I want you. But mostly, all I can focus on is how your eyes are glittering from the light above us right now, and watching you debate what to do with yourself is turning me on even more. And your nipples are hard, but not as hard as my dick is right now, Penelope . . . because being pressed up against you is a thousand times better than I thought it would be when I first saw you tonight."

"Maddox . . ."

"Give me tonight. Trust me to give us what we both need. Who wants to live life with regrets, right? Who wants to wonder 'what if'?"

God, do I have experience in that area.

I take in shallow breaths as I slowly let myself melt back into the decision I had made earlier in our booth. But before I can say anything, he leans down and softly brushes his lips against mine. It's so subtle, I would barely classify it as a kiss.

But the fireworks that explode in my nerve endings is enough to make me give in.

Maddox releases my wrists right before I reach up and grip the back of his neck to pull him down to me, pressing my lips harder against his mouth this time so he knows that I'm in. I'm *all* in, and I'm not backing out now.

My body wants this. My mind is made up. And my gut? Well, she's not exactly on board, but that's for a variety of other reasons I'd rather not process at this moment.

A deep groan travels up his throat, the vibrations hitting my tongue as he swipes his across mine and a whole new rush of desire runs through me.

"Fuck, Penelope . . ."

"Shut up, Maddox, and keep kissing me."

He chuckles and then grabs on to my hips, pulling my pelvis toward him as our tongues tangle and my internal body temperature rises a few hundred degrees.

Then this kiss morphs into one that I feel all the way down to the tips of my toes.

My skin is on fire, my vagina is throbbing, and my lungs are fighting for air as we make out like two horny teenagers in the hallway of the club.

One of his hands finds my hair, burrowing deep in my thick tresses. He pulls just slightly as he maneuvers my head the way he wants, nipping and licking at every corner of my mouth until I can barely recall where I'm even at.

That is until he breaks me from the time warp we'd fallen into.

"Come back to my hotel with me," he growls deeply as we part, heavy breaths mingling between us.

"I thought that was implied by that kiss. You'd better make this worth my while, Maddox Taylor."

"If there's one thing I know how to do well, it's use my time and skills to the best of my ability, particularly under pressure."

"I guess you might have some experience in that area."

Pressing one more chaste kiss to my lips, he backs away, grabs my hand, and then leads me outside to a waiting car.

I don't question why it is there or where we are going. I just let Maddox Taylor, the NFL star quarterback, take me back to his hotel so he can fuck me—and hopefully, I can survive it.

As soon as the light on the lock of his hotel room's door turns green, Maddox opens and closes the door behind us. We are a tangled mess of limbs as we stumble down the hallway, gripping onto any clothing we can grasp while sucking each other's faces off.

"I can't wait to lick every inch of you."

"Less talk, more action, buddy," I tease him as he pins me up against the wall and holds my wrists in his hands above my head.

"I want you to let go a little, Penelope. Trust me."

"Trust is a strong word, Maddox, and don't take this personally, but we just met. Trust has to be earned. I prefer just hoping that based on the rod I felt in your pants earlier and the big game you talked before that your intention is to fuck the shit out of me—and that you can deliver on those promises."

He chuckles and then bites my neck lightly, making me gasp. "Oh, that's exactly what I intend to do, but I need to know that you're not going to fight me the entire way like you've been doing all night." When he leans back and stares down into my eyes, my throat squeezes, making it hard to breathe.

"A woman who doesn't fight back is boring, don't you think?"

He grins delightedly. "In certain instances, yes. But you also seem like the type of woman who doesn't want to give up control but really needs to. And I'm asking you to give it to me tonight."

Gulping down the lump in my throat, I debate his request for a few moments before I finally give in. With a nod, I grant him permission to take control, but only because I know that this will be a one-time thing for both of us. Why not try something new?

You only live once, right?

"Attagirl." He releases my wrists and then finds the hem of my dress, peeling the stretchy purple fabric up my body slowly until it bunches at my hips, exposing my lower half to him. And except for the small triangle of gray lace covering that sweet spot between my legs, I'm entirely bare as the cool air in the hotel room hits my skin.

He slowly lowers his body to the floor so he's on his knees—

and I have to say, the sight of a man like Maddox Taylor on his knees before me is one I won't soon forget.

With smooth and clear intention, he runs his hands up my legs from my calves to my thighs then back around to my ass, grabbing a handful of my flesh in both of his large hands and giving it a good squeeze. "Damn, these curves."

"Thanks, I grew them myself."

Startling me, he smacks my ass cheek lightly. "You and that sass."

"It's part of the entire package. Take it or leave it, Maddox."

He lowers his head to my slit and drags his tongue up it through the lace. "Oh, I plan to take it and then some." Hooking both of his thumbs under the strings at my hips, he lowers the fabric to my ankles, waiting for me to slowly step out of it, taking in the small triangle of hair I keep trimmed above my slit while the rest of me is bare. "This is sexy."

"Glad you approve."

His eyes lift to mine. "Where did you come from, Penelope?"

"Well, legend has it that women are from Venus and men are from Mars, so . . ."

He bites the inside of my thigh and then licks over the spot. I groan from the sensation, his teeth and tongue teasing me and making me even wetter.

"Honestly, I wouldn't really have cared what you have going on down here. I just know that now that I've seen it, I want to lick every inch of you until you're screaming my name."

I grip the short strands of his hair as he descends on my pussy, and with one long stroke through my slit again, this time with no barrier, I can feel my eyes roll into the back of my head. Maddox licks me from bottom to top and then fixates on my clit, circling and flicking the nub with his tongue. Just that right amount of pressure has me holding my breath, waiting to see what he does next.

His hands grip my ass again, pulling me closer to him to give him better access, and I widen my legs to grant it to him. He laps at me, sucks and nibbles, and I groan louder as I pull his hair, flexing my hips forward when I begin to lose control of my body.

"That's right, Penelope. Ride my face, sweetheart."

"More, Maddox. Please . . ."

He sticks his fingers in his mouth to wet them, and then he sits back on his heels and runs them through me, coating them in my arousal. When he slowly slips them inside me, stretching me around him, a violent shiver runs down my spine to my toes.

"Fuck. I want to devour you." He leans in again and flicks his tongue on my clit as he slowly moves his fingers in and out of me. "I want you to come on my face, Penelope, and then I'm going to fuck you with my cock until you can't stand."

My legs start to wobble from his words.

Pressure builds in my core, and I find myself gasping for air and reaching behind me with my free hand to grab the wall for balance, riding the tidal wave building in my body and heading to crash on the shore. I mumble incoherent words while pulling on his hair with my other hand so hard I'm surprised it hasn't fazed him.

Or maybe he's just too busy and drunk on my pussy to care.

"You're close, aren't you, Penelope?"

"Yes. Keep going, Maddox." I pull him closer to me.

"Tell me what you need," he mumbles against my slit.

"Keep doing what you're doing." He strikes my clit again and then sucks it between his lips. "Yes, just like that."

He takes his time building me up, reading my body for the signals I'm giving him. I find myself transported to another place, one where the pleasure I'm feeling from his hands and tongue is different than other men that I've been with.

It's powerful. Consuming. Overwhelming and chaotic.

It's making my heart and mind frenzied as I battle between staying planted in reality and letting this all-consuming pleasure overwhelm me and pull me under.

I grind myself on his mouth and feel him hook his finger up inside of me, detonating a whole new cluster of sparks as he coaxes my G-spot and licks my clit simultaneously, bringing me over the edge.

"Fuck, Maddox . . . yes . . . yes!" And then I explode, riding his mouth, letting pressure and pleasure consume my limbs and nerves. I buck against him, thrash against the wall, practically wild with pleasure as Maddox keeps licking and sucking while I ride out my climax.

I feel like I'm floating, taking forever to come back down to earth, until I hear and feel him start to stand.

As I fight to regain control of my breathing, we stand there in a stare-off, waiting for someone to make the next move. So I sink down to the floor, eager to return the favor.

He watches me as I lock eyes with him and reach for his belt, loosening the buckle and sliding the leather free. I unbutton his slacks, slide down the zipper, and stroke the hard length of him behind black boxer briefs.

"You want my cock now, Penelope?"

"Fuck, yes, I do."

When I pull down the band of his underwear, his cock springs free, and my eyes widen on instinct. He is thick, long, proud, and . . . *pierced.*

"Damn, even more surprises," I announce, peering up at him as I begin to stroke his shaft.

"It's a reverse Prince Albert," he informs me.

"I know. I've seen pictures but never the real thing."

"Wait until you feel it."

I'm practically salivating at the thought. "Can't wait."

"Take off your dress so I can see all of you while you suck me off," he commands, and the switch in his voice from compassionate to dominating is one I wasn't prepared for, but I'm not complaining about it one bit.

He was right. I want to fight him. I want to tell him to fuck off.

But there's a part of me that knows right now kneeling before him and following his orders is one of the hottest moments of my life.

Resting fully on my knees, I grab my dress and peel it over my head, tossing it aside before reaching behind me and pinching the clasp on my bra, freeing it from my body as well.

"God, I want to bite your tits."

"Let me suck your cock first."

His dick literally jumps in front of me at the idea. "With pleasure. Bring that beautiful mouth to me."

Holding his dick in front of my mouth, he waits for me to open my lips and welcome him inside, but instead, I stick out my tongue and lick him from base to tip.

He lets out a groan of pleasure and then watches me while I do it again, feeling him grow harder against my tongue. I circle the tip first before taking him back into my mouth as far as he'll go. It's not easy; Maddox is larger than most in both girth and length. But his reactions—the way his eyes become hooded, the groans leaving his parted lips, and the flex of his abs as he lets me work him over with my mouth while restraining from shoving his dick as far back in my throat as it can go—are what's really making me drip between my legs.

It's the way he's unraveling before me that makes me feel more powerful than I can ever remember feeling.

And I never question my power as a woman.

"You have to stop," he finally grates out, pulling his cock from my mouth and reaching down to help me up. When I'm on my feet again, he pulls me into his chest, buries his hand in my hair, and kisses me again as we walk further into the hotel room toward a dining room table, a table I didn't realize was in this suite when we entered because I was preoccupied.

As he spins me around, I catch the view of the skyline around us. We're up high enough to see the freeways full of speeding cars below, office windows still illuminated in other buildings, and city lights twinkling on the hills in the distance.

"Quite the view, isn't it?" he whispers in my ear as he stands behind me, guiding me to the edge of the table and lying me down on it so my stomach is flat with the glass surface, my ass perched in front of him.

"It's all right."

He chuckles. "Yeah, I agree. It's definitely nothing like the view in front of me right now."

I peer over my shoulder to see him staring down at my ass as he unbuttons his shirt, peeling it open to reveal his tan and sculpted chest with muscles that have been carved and defined through years of hard work and dedication. Tattoos cover both arms—one all the way down to his wrist, the other covered just to his elbow—and his nipples are pierced as well, adding even more body jewelry to the mix.

My vagina definitely appreciates the bad boy vibes, such a contrast to the man that gave me his undivided attention tonight.

"And what view is that?" I ask, shaking my naked ass at him as he tosses his shirt to the floor and pushes down his briefs and slacks, discarding them and his shoes off to the side—but not before he grabs a condom from his wallet.

As he tears open the wrapper and covers himself, he says, "The one of the sexiest woman I've ever met bent over the table right now, ready for me to fuck her."

Goosebumps erupt over my skin. "Damn right. Now get to it, Mr. Taylor. Put your money where your mouth is."

He closes the distance between us, eating up the handful of steps with his muscular legs and all-around solid physique. The man is large for a quarterback, that's for sure, but he obviously knows how to put those muscles to good use.

He rubs his cock through my wetness, humming in approval as I grow antsy and try to force him to slip in before he's ready.

He smacks my ass in warning. "Patience, Penelope. I'll give you what you want, babe—what we both want."

"What the fuck are you waiting for?" I ask as he shoves two fingers inside of me, stroking me deep and thoroughly, eliciting a moan from deep in my throat. "Shit. Oh, yes . . ." I close my eyes and allow him to play my body like a fiddle for a moment while I wait for his answer.

"Someone needs to be fucked, doesn't she?"

"That's why we're here, isn't it?"

"Yes, ma'am. But remember, that's not the only thing I want from you, Penelope."

"What do you want?" I groan as I close my eyes, melt into the table, and move my body in time with Maddox's fingers sliding in and out. "Because I can tell you what *I* want, and it starts with d, ends with k, and *I see* it between us, staring back at me."

Maddox laughs before growing serious again, pausing his fingers. "Are you going to let go?"

I freeze, remembering what he asked me for earlier.

Leaning over me now, he rests his solid chest on my back, leaving his fingers buried inside of me. "Let me experience all of you tonight, Penelope . . . since this is all that we get."

His words feel so final, but he's right. Why hold back when we only have tonight?

"Give me your cock then, Maddox, and I'll give you what you want."

With a nip of his lips on my neck followed by the drag of his tongue, he removes his fingers from me and then lines up his cock with my entrance, pushing in slowly as we both moan aloud our relief.

I'm fucking breathless as he rears back and pushes in more, stretching me around him, filling me up, and cupping my breasts now as he thrusts forward and hits me as deep as he can go.

"Oh, fuck, yes."

"Goddamn, woman. I knew you'd feel incredible."

He thrusts again and again, forcing my body to slide across the glass as he hovers over me and our skin slaps together. Just that sound has pressure building between my legs, that and the feeling of his piercing inside me.

His movements are intense, strong, and precise, and my nerves come alive in every limb as our bodies touch and grind. It's been so long since sex has been this good, since I've had this kind of chemistry and comfort with someone so soon.

Not since . . .

Not allowing myself to go there right now, I focus back on the physical feelings because that's what I normally do. I focus on his cock, my pussy, my breasts, the tingles and sparks—all of the components of sex that don't require feelings so I can shut off my brain and keep those pesky emotions out of it.

Maddox releases my breasts, and I feel his weight shift off of me as he grips my hips for leverage and pounds my pussy even harder than before, standing up so I can see his reflection in the glass in front of us. And damn is he all man.

If football didn't work out for him, the man could have a very successful future in porn. He's got that clean-cut yet dirty look to him, like the way Thor Bradley can transform from lumberjack to a man you'd take home to meet your mom. I'm sure women would be searching for and watching the hell out of that.

Maddox pounds into me hard, taking me by surprise and bringing me back to the moment. "Oh, God. Fuck."

He reaches forward and grabs a fistful of my hair, pulling me gently until I'm upright so my back is pressed to his chest. "This is what you needed, isn't it, Penelope?"

"All women need a good fuck from time to time."

"Just good?" he growls in my ear.

"Care to make it great?" I challenge him as I feel my walls clench tighter. He's so deep like this, using his powerful legs to thrust harder inside of me as I stand in front of him and look out the windows at the view.

The thing is, this *is* great, phenomenal even—but I want to see what else he has to offer.

He slips out of me and spins me around, lifting me up by my waist and wrapping my legs around his. "Don't worry. I'm just getting started."

He takes my lips captive, owning my mouth with his as he walks us further into the room. Then he surprises me when he spins around and falls to the giant bed, him lying beneath me and me straddling him, our mouths still locked.

He kisses me like he's starving for my lips and tongue. He devours me as if each taste isn't enough. He holds my head in his hands like I'm both precious and his—and that has me breaking us apart before those stupid emotions can come into play again.

"I want to watch you ride me, Penelope. Fuck me hard, and make yourself come."

Licking my lips, I obey his order without hesitation—which I can tell he loves by the gleam in his eyes—and situate myself over him, lining him up with my core again before sinking down hard and fast.

And if I thought he was deep before, that doesn't even compare to the fullness and pressure I'm feeling from his cock in this position.

I begin circling my hips, lifting and lowering myself while using his entire length to hit every spot inside that I can, grinding on his pelvis on the way down for maximum benefit.

He just watches me with his hands resting gently on my hips, his gaze locked on mine as I move my hands to my hair and bend my head back, really giving him a show, pushing my breasts out as I work for my orgasm.

"Jesus Christ. I will never forget this sight."

"I'll never forget this cock," I announce breathlessly as I feel myself grow closer to my release.

Maddox sits up and finds my nipple with his mouth, engulfing my modest breasts in his big palms, squeezing and licking and sucking on them as I pick up my pace.

The added sensation has me inching closer and closer to the finish line, but Maddox is a gentleman—even though I doubted it for a second—so he reaches down to where we're joined, lightly brushing my clit to help me get there.

"Come for me, Penelope."

It only takes a few moments before my orgasm slams into me. "I'm coming! Oh God, Maddox!" The orgasm that rips through me is more powerful and intense than the first, and I ride it out just as wildly as Maddox holds me to him, continuously applying pressure to my clit.

I can feel his eyes on me even though mine are closed. I figure he's studying my reaction and the unashamed pleasure I'm feeling and outwardly showing. I'm letting go like he wanted, and I'm terrified at how easy it feels to do so.

Before I realize what's happening, he rolls us over, brings my legs over his shoulders, and begins to pound into me, taking me by surprise in the best way.

"I hope you're up for round two later, because I can't hold back any longer. Watching you come again was pure fucking torture."

"Maddox," I gasp on his next thrust, weaving my hands into his hair as he fucks me—legitimately, powerfully, and intensely. He fucks me so hard I can barely breathe.

Yes, please.

So I egg him on. "Yes. Fucking come. Please. Keep fucking me, and come inside me . . ."

Sweat drips from his brow as his pace becomes relentless, his eyes staring down into my own like it's only the two of us in the world right now. And just when I hear his groan of release, he rears back and thrusts forward so hard I scream while he's pinning me to the bed.

Then I watch him come undone.

Every muscle in his body strains as he lets go and finds his pleasure. And damn, it is a sight *I* will never forget.

But then something else happens—he collapses on top of me when he's through, and instead of fighting to break free from the cage of his body, I welcome his weight. I run my hands over his back and lie there for a minute, wondering why my brain is suddenly confronting the fact that for the past twelve years I've accepted nothing but loneliness, detached hookups that have done nothing but provide the physical release I needed to survive.

But this hookup was not like that.

And at this moment, I already know—something has shifted inside of me. Something has changed.

So later that night, after round two, I leave as soon as Maddox falls asleep, knowing that I wouldn't survive a round three.

I wouldn't survive another moment of being vulnerable with him.

The next day, I lock the cages back up in my brain and chest, burying the night I had with Maddox Taylor, the quarterback who reminded me too much of my past.

But you know what they say: The past will always come back to haunt us at some point.

And sometimes, it happens when you least expect it.

Chapter 3

Penelope

Six Weeks Later

"Garret! I need coffee!" Shouting out of my open office door, I hope to God Garret is at his desk so he can hear me.

His head pops in two seconds later. "Starbucks or the coffee cart downstairs?"

"I don't care. I just need caffeine. And then I need you to get the DoubleTree rep back on the phone so we can go through the details of their new campaign one more time before our meeting next week."

Garret groans as his eyes roll into the back of his head. "God, those chocolate chip cookies are the best. I seriously don't mind *not* staying in a five-star hotel when I know there are cookies involved."

"Grab us a few cookies from the cart, then, when you get the coffee, and then get back here. My inbox is bursting with unread messages, and my phone is ringing off the hook." I lean back in my chair, steepling my hands. "What the hell have you been doing all morning, Garret? My inbox never looks like this."

He stands fully in the open doorframe now, biting his lip and fiddling his fingers with a hint of excitement in his eyes. "There's a rumor going around the office."

"Oh God. How many times do I have to tell you there's always a rumor going around here?"

He shakes his head and takes a few steps closer. "No, this is huge. Representation for a big affiliate just came by and requested Edelman in repairing an image." He claps his hands and bounces. "It's like a home makeover, but for an entire team."

"News flash, that happens a lot in this line of work." And then his words register. "Wait, did you say 'team'?"

"Yes, and Nancy was telling me it's for—" Garret gets cut off by Charles, my boss, appearing right behind him, his brow pinched tight.

"Penelope? You busy?"

"I'm always busy, Charles," I fire back with a shrug and a smile because he should know better than to ask that question.

"Silly me. Of course, but I need to speak with you. In my office. Now."

Nerves build in my chest at his tone. "Okay . . ."

Garret's eyes grow to the size of saucers as he watches me stand from my chair and round my desk.

"Will this take long? I have some phone calls to return and a meeting right after lunch."

"No, not too long. You should be fine." Charles glances at Garret as I walk past both of them.

"Please get my coffee, and I'll see you in a few." I nod confidently at my assistant before I follow my boss down the long corridor of offices and enter his right behind him.

"Take a seat."

Hesitantly, I follow his directions. "Is everything okay? Am I in trouble for something?"

His face instantly softens. "Oh no, Penelope. Not at all. Actually, I need to ask you for a favor, and I'm afraid you'll tell me no."

Now my curiosity is piqued. "Well, if you already know my answer, then why are we having this conversation?" I tease.

He huffs out a laugh. "Because I respect you enough as a professional to give you the opportunity to tell me no before I disregard your opinion anyway."

I squint across his desk at him. "What's this about, Charles?"

"Well, I remember when we hired you that there were professional boundaries you told me you didn't want to cross, and I've respected them so far. But that's been years now, and today a new client came by and . . . now I need you to take on this project because there isn't anyone else I would trust more. Plus, you've met a player related to this team before, so there's familiarity that I think will make the professional relationship work out well."

"I already know I'm your favorite, Charles, so there's no need to kiss my ass." He laughs and nods in agreement. "But what makes this client so special?"

"I'm surprised you don't already know. You're usually so aware of any type of news . . ."

"I've been busy, in case you haven't noticed. And the Double-Tree account is proving to be quite involved."

"Well, if you take on this client, I will gladly lighten your workload, particularly because this team will need undivided attention. For what they're paying, we're going to give them the best. And that's you," he says, pointing a finger across the desk at me.

Now I'm irritated that he keeps dancing around the pertinent information. "Who is the client, Charles?"

"It's the Los Angeles Bolts. They are looking to build buzz around the upcoming season given their less than stellar record in recent years. And they just signed Maddox Taylor as their new quarterback, so they have a lot riding on this season."

My stomach drops, and I swear my face goes white. *Do I look like I'm going to be sick? Because that's exactly how I feel . . .*

"No." It's my first natural response, but it comes from a defensive place deep in my gut.

It's been six weeks since my night with Maddox, and flashes of that rendezvous still haunt me at all hours of the day.

I broke my one cardinal rule—*no athletes*—thinking I had things under control. We met, there was attraction, and so it should have just been casual sex like it always has been before. But my stupid mind played tricks on me, and then my stupid emotions got involved. What's even worse is that I haven't felt inclined to fuck anyone else since our night together, even though I think it would help me move past the monumental experience.

I think Charles is talking to me still, but all I can hear is a ringing in my ears.

"Look, Penelope. I know you said no athletes, but—"

"Charles, there has to be someone else. I am sorry, truly, but I have my reasons for not taking on cases like this."

"What if I told you that I already told their representation you'd do it?"

Clenching my teeth together, I glare at him, contemplating how to murder him. Wanting to murder your boss for making an executive decision isn't a healthy daydream, I'm sure. And a therapist might have a field day unpacking that one. I'll have to ask Amelia when we have brunch on Sunday.

"Why would you do that?"

"Because you're the only one I trust. I even told Maddox you were the best of the best the night of the Zio's party. So how would that look if they came here by recommendation, and I gave Maddox and the team to someone else?"

"It would look like I wasn't available. That I had other clients I'm committed to. Like—"

"Knock, knock." Julie, Charles's assistant, knocks on his office door as she opens it. *Seems pretty pointless in knocking if you're not going to wait to be invited in, Jules.*

"Yes, Julie?" Charles asks.

"Mr. Taylor and representation for the Bolts are here."

"Great, send them back, please."

I twist around to face Charles again once Julie leaves. "We're meeting with them right now? You're not going to let us finish this conversation?" I ask, panic resonating in my body, mainly due to the fact that in a matter of seconds I have to come face-to-face with the man I ran out on six weeks ago.

"There isn't one to be had." He runs a hand through his hair. "Look, I will gladly give you a bonus, I'll reassign a few of your clients, and if this goes off well, there's a promotion with your name on it, Pen. Senior Brand Strategist for whatever client you want on our roster. You name it, it's yours. But I need you to agree."

"Why is this so important to you? Why does it matter so much that you're willing to go back on the *one* stipulation I asked for when I started working here?"

He stands from his desk. "Because Maddox Taylor is an NFL player that everyone knows and everyone is watching. And now he's playing for the Los Angeles Bolts, and the team made an investment in signing him that needs to pay off. Plus, this could be huge for this firm, Penelope. You and I both know that. Most sports teams do their own PR in-house, but the team had some recent restructuring and decided to hire outside. So I want my best employee to help my most high-profile client. You can't blame me for that."

"Oh, I can blame you all I want," I counter, "but I see your point, too."

Another knock rings out, and this time when I turn around, I'm met with hazel eyes that have haunted my mind for the past month and a half.

"Penelope," Maddox says in a deep lilt that makes my heart skip a beat. "It sure is nice to see you again."

And right then and there, I know I am fucked. And not in the good way like when Maddox fucked me that fateful night.

Chapter 4

Maddox

Do you believe in fate?

When asked that question, a lot of people tend to have a very strong opinion on the matter. I, for one, don't usually. I tend to feel that life happens as a direct consequence of our choices, some we like and some we wish we could take back because of the outcome that follows.

But right now, standing in the same room as the woman who cast her spell on me almost two months ago—well, it's hard not to believe in fate in a moment like this.

God, she's even more beautiful than I remember, but by the look in her eyes, she's not happy to see me at all.

Well, this meeting wasn't necessarily planned, but it's gonna happen, and I'm damn sure not going to let her run away this time.

"Mr. Taylor. Mr. Nelson. So nice of you to hang around for a moment so I can introduce you to Penelope Klein, our representative that will be working on the Bolts' account." Charles Edelman practically runs around his desk, right past Penelope, to kiss both of our asses again. "Penelope, you remember Maddox, right?"

She clears her throat, and a veil of professionalism slips right over her face, covering up the shock that was there before. "Yes. How are you, Mr. Taylor?"

I intercept her outstretched hand and grin back at her, enjoying this second encounter almost as much as our first—*almost*. "Great. Happy to be here in California. Eager for a new season with a new team," I reply, using the rehearsed response I agreed to, when in reality, I'm still accepting the change that uprooted my life in a matter of weeks. "But the best part is seeing a familiar face again." I wink at her, and I swear I see her plotting my death as she smiles tightly.

"And this is Liam Nelson, the representative for the team," Charles continues as Penelope drops my hand and shifts to shake Liam's.

"Nice to meet you, Mr. Nelson."

Liam arches one brow at her, his doubt obvious on his face. I can almost hear his internal dialogue as he takes in Penelope, and I know we're going to have a lengthy conversation about how blatantly gorgeous she is and how I have to keep my dick in my pants in order for this little arrangement to work.

Well, news flash to Liam, but a football team consists of fifty-three men who are all going to look at Penelope the same way that I am once they meet her.

But I'll make sure everyone knows not to even think about crossing that line.

Oh, you mean the one you've already crossed, Maddox?

If only Liam knew that my dick has already been well

acquainted with the woman standing before us, then we'd have a much bigger problem on our hands.

Flashes of our night come back to me like wildfire—especially the end, when I woke up in the morning and realized she left without saying goodbye.

In all honesty, I'm not sure I was expecting much more than that, given that we agreed to just one night. But I know I can't be the only one who felt something more between us, and now I have a way to find out just exactly what that *more* might be.

The trade wasn't unexpected, but being picked up by a team in California was. Based on what my agent said, it sounded like Baltimore was more interested in me. No player's happy about being traded, and lord knows I threw my own hissy fit with the news, especially because the move took me away from my family and the organization I've worked hard to build for the past six years.

But seeing Penelope's face again chisels away the chip on my shoulder I've been walking around with since I had to accept the fact that I would be moving across the country. Lo and behold, the universe made a few decisions that landed me right back in front of this woman, and I can't say that I'm mad about it—although it appears that she is.

Contrary to what the media portrays, I'm not the one-night-stand type. In fact, since I've been in the NFL, I haven't taken a random girl home at all. Not even once. I had a friend from college who would scratch the physical itch I needed to appease from time to time. But like any casual relationship, most things like that must come to an end eventually, and it did about four months ago.

The pictures of me leaving clubs and events with a woman on

my arm are not what they seem, but I'll be damned if I try to explain that right now. I have my reasons for keeping that information close to the vest, too.

"Yes, well, Charles says you're the best, and I'm sure you're aware that you have your work cut out for you," Liam says as he drops Penelope's hand and crosses his arms over his chest. "The Bolts are a newer franchise to the NFL with a lackluster fanbase, so there is a lot of pressure to make this season the best yet. And now with the addition of Mr. Taylor, it seems we have a carrot to dangle to get the fans excited. We just want to make sure they bite."

"Penelope is aware and knows the stakes are high. But I assure you, she's perfectly capable of accomplishing the task at hand."

I turn to him. "I appreciate your help, Charles. After speaking with you during the Zio's launch party, I knew your firm could help us out."

That's right. It was *my* suggestion to use Edelman PR when I met with the team representatives and coaching staff. Public perception is key to generating excitement and buzz for sports. Just as a teacher fosters relationships in a classroom that makes learning more meaningful, football players can do the same in their communities to connect with fans.

It's not just about throwing and catching pigskin. It's about building relationships through a game that people love to watch. Since that's part of what made my time in New Orleans so successful, I want to continue that here, but I know that won't be easy given the pressure to bring a team that only won three games last season out of that losing streak.

"We will do everything we can to ensure your future is bright and long with the Los Angeles Bolts." Charles smiles.

Penelope clears her throat, commanding our attention. "Well, I'm sorry to run off, but I have a meeting I need to prepare for." Then she turns to me, and I can see her pulse hammering in her neck. "I will be in touch soon, Mr. Taylor and Mr. Nelson, so we can sit down and assess how to move forward with what you have envisioned." With a curt nod and granting me no opportunity to respond, she takes off out of Charles's office, leaving dust behind her as she disappears.

Liam blows out a breath. "I'm not sure Miss Klein is what we had in mind in a representative, Charles," he says, his voice full of irritation.

Charles, to his credit, picks up on his insinuation instantly. "I assure you, Mr. Nelson, Penelope is the best. I hope your reservations aren't of the sexist variety, otherwise, we might have a different problem on our hands."

I decide to step in before this gets out of control. "I trust you, Charles, and know just from my brief interaction with Miss Klein before that she is the right person for the job." The need to see her again slams into me abruptly, so I find a way for me to leave. "If you don't mind, I need to use the restroom, so I'll leave you two to discuss any last-minute details. Just let me know what I need to do from here."

Without any hesitation, I walk out of Charles's office and begin searching for the brunette who's been appearing in my mind for weeks, practically running down the halls and gazing into any open door. I'm hoping that once we have a moment alone, I can ask her a few questions that may clear up some of the awkwardness between us.

Of course, I can't help but be amused by this turn of events, either, and perhaps fate is dealing me a hand I would be stupid to ignore.

It only takes me asking one person where Penelope's office is before I head in that direction, passing by her assistant on the way in.

"Oh my God, it's true!" The man sitting at the desk just outside her office squeals as he leaps from his chair and clasps his hands over his mouth. "Maddox Taylor is here!"

"Yeah. Hey." I reach out to shake his hand. "Nice to meet you."

His hand trembles as he meets me halfway. "Holy shit, your hands are huge."

"Well, they come in handy for throwing a football," I joke.

"Oh, I'm sure they come in handy for other things, too," he says, eyeing me up and down now, blatantly checking me out.

Eager to not make this more awkward, I change the subject. "Say, is Penelope free? I need to speak with her really quick."

"I think it's sweet that you're asking for permission because you definitely don't need it. But even if she weren't free, I would let you do whatever you want. Go right on in." He waves his hand to the side as if he's laying out a red carpet for me to walk on, and I give him a nod as I go straight to her door and open it, not bothering with knocking.

As soon as she comes into view, I grin at the sight in front of me. Pacing with her hands in her hair, the woman looks like she's on the verge of a mental breakdown as she talks to herself.

"Fuckity fuck!" she shouts just before turning around and realizing I'm there. "Oh my God! Maddox, what the hell?"

Closing the door behind me, I stand across the room from her, taking her in but trying not to poke her even more. "Sorry. I didn't mean to scare you."

"Oh, sure. Just like you didn't mean to show up at my place of employment and fuck up my day?"

"Not exactly the welcome I was expecting, but sure, we can go with that."

"What are you doing here, Maddox? Is this some sick joke?"

"Why would me being here be a joke?"

She throws her hands up. "I don't know! Forgive me, but I'm in a little bit of shock right now. You're supposed to be in New Orleans, clear on the other side of the country!"

"I got let go and then picked up during free agency. It all happened in the last few weeks, but it comes with the job. Not every team is forever."

She shakes her head. "I'm aware of how the NFL works."

"I didn't say you weren't." We continue to stare at each other, her chest rising and falling rapidly, my heart hammering uncontrollably from just being in her presence.

And then a light bulb comes on overhead. "What does a perverted frog say?"

She drops her hands as her mouth falls open. "Are you kidding me right now?"

"The tension is too high in this room, so I need to defuse it."

Rolling her eyes, she sighs while pinching the bridge of her nose. "I don't know, Maddox. What?"

"Rubbit."

The corner of her mouth twitches, but she covers it up quickly. "Cute."

"No, *beautiful*." Her head lifts, and she watches as I cross the room toward her. "Fuck, you're more beautiful than I remember, Penelope."

Shaking her head, she begins to retreat. "No, Maddox. You can't say things like that." I get within inches of her before she yells, "Stop!"

I freeze. "Why?"

She lowers her voice suddenly. "Because this can't happen again. You're a client of mine now. Anything that happened before is in the past, and that's where it has to stay." She pushes back her shoulders, finding her resolve, but I can still see the confliction in her eyes.

Grinding my teeth together, I nod. "Right." I acknowledge her point, but it doesn't mean I have to like it. Hell, I feel like every time I'm near her I have no control over my reaction to her. But then, suddenly, the reality of our situation pummels into me. "You're right."

She exhales. "Yes, I am," she says while nodding, as if she's convincing herself of the same fact. "So while I know that we're surprised we've found ourselves in this predicament, we need to remain professional."

My dick twitches at her sternness, but my mind knows she's speaking the truth. Even though it was my idea to use Edelman PR once the Bolts sent over my contract and we discussed the promise for this upcoming season, I never imagined Penelope would be the one they assigned to the account. "I can do that."

She nods again. "Good."

But then I decide to push this boundary and see if what I felt between us before is still there. Because I know my body is humming with need for her again, remembering every sound she made while I fucked her, how soft her fucking skin is, and the fact that no other woman has intrigued me the way she has since or even before her.

Penelope Klein has fucking hypnotized me.

I take a few steps toward her again as her eyes go wide. Her feet start moving until her back hits the glass wall of windows behind her. "Maddox, what are you doing?"

"I just need to ask you a question before I leave."

She swallows hard. "What?"

Leaning down, I run my nose along the column of her throat, and I'm rewarded with a small hitch in her breath. "Why did you leave without saying something?"

"Huh?" Her hands reach out and grip my biceps to hold her steady. And just that subtle touch has my dick growing hard in seconds.

"That night. You left. I woke up, and you were gone."

"Okay . . ."

"Why didn't you say something?"

She finally snaps out of the breathless haze she was in. "What was I supposed to say? It was a one-night stand. We fucked. We had fun." I press my lips to her skin, and she shudders. "It didn't mean anything."

And that has my head popping back up. Staring down into her eyes, I watch her struggle with her composure right in front of me.

"You sure about that?"

"Yes . . ." she says, but I hear no confidence behind it.

"Hmm . . . okay." I take a step back and watch her sigh with her whole body, but then she squints at me. "If you say so." Spinning around, I head for her door, but her voice stops me before I get to the exit.

"Maddox?"

I twist my head to face her. "Yeah?"

"This has to stay between us. You haven't told anyone, have you?"

"No." *Except for my cousin, Leslie, but Penelope doesn't need to know that right now.* "But I understand. Don't worry, our secret is safe."

"I'm serious," she continues, walking toward me now on unsteady legs. But damn, the woman can fake confidence.

If I wasn't so hyperaware of how her body moves and I didn't possess an uncanny ability to read her, I'd think she's found her certainty again. But I can tell she's still rattled.

"This is my job. If word got out that we—"

I hold my hand up to stop her. "I get it, Penelope. We're good."

Her shoulders drop, and she half smiles. "Okay. Thank you."

"Yup. See you soon. Have a good rest of your day."

I reach for the handle and exit her office, heading back to Liam and Charles, hoping the two of them have ironed out the details of our contract without punching each other so I can get home and rest before I report to the practice facilities tomorrow for my workout.

I also need to do some thinking, because this thing between Penelope and me isn't over. It just got a lot more complicated, but it's definitely *not* over.

And I need to figure out a way to make sure she knows it, too, without either of us losing our jobs.

Chapter 5

Penelope

"Is Noelle coming?" Charlotte asks Amelia and me as we sit at our table at Frankie's.

"When I was texting with her last night, she said she was," Amelia answers. "But I also told her to see how she felt this morning and that if she didn't want to come, we would understand."

Just as I go to say something, a figure to my left has me looking up. And there she is—our friend who'd realized her first implantation failed when she got her period a few days ago.

"Hey, gorgeous."

She rolls her eyes at me and then plops down in the chair to my left. "Hey."

Amelia and Charlotte share a look before Charlotte slides a fresh mimosa across the table to her. "The good news is you can still drink champagne with us for another month."

"Ha. Yeah. Thanks."

Slinging my arm around her shoulder, I pull her into me. "I'm sorry, babe. Truly. I know you wanted this."

She sighs and then takes a sip of her drink as her eyes well. "I did, but I also knew that there was a possibility it wouldn't work on the first try." Wiping under her eyes, she stares at the table in front of her. "My doctor told me not to get my hopes up, but I did, and now I'm just reminding myself that there's always next month."

"Yes, there is. And the month after that. It's gonna happen, Noelle. I can feel it."

"Yeah?" she asks hopefully, turning so we're face-to-face.

"Absolutely. My nipples are getting all tingly just thinking about it."

A snort leaves her lips as she laughs, and I congratulate myself internally for making her smile. *Mission accomplished.*

"You have problems, Penelope," Charlotte teases.

"I know, but I'm not lying. Sometimes my nipples will tingle when I have a good feeling about something."

Funny thing is, though, they were *not* tingling when I saw Maddox a few days ago at my office. My vagina was throbbing, but there were *no* tingling nipples. No indication that having him as a client was a good thing at all. Just my needy pussy remembering how his pierced dick rocked my world and wondering when it is gonna happen again.

It's not. It can't.

But you know how you tell someone they can't have something, and it just makes them want it even more? Well, now *I'm* in that fucking situation, and it's not one I'm used to being in.

I always get what I want. And what I want is Maddox's dick again.

"Is there anything we can do to make you feel better?" Amelia asks Noelle, pulling me back to the conversation.

"No, I'm okay. I've made my peace with it. It will happen when it's supposed to."

"How about a little retail therapy?" Charlotte suggests. "Every girl needs a little retail therapy now and then."

"That and vibrator therapy," I add.

"You go shopping for vibrators when you're sad?" Noelle shifts to me again, her eyebrows lifting to her hairline.

"No. I lay all of mine out on my bed and go to town for a few hours on and off until I can't stand up straight or I pass out, whichever happens first."

"*Hours*? How does your clit not burn off?" Charlotte practically shrieks.

"Lots of training, ladies. Lots of training."

Charlotte leans back in her chair and shakes her head at me while smiling. "I just can't with you today."

Batting my eyelashes, I say, "You love me."

"How's work going, Penelope?" Amelia asks as we all take drinks from our glasses.

"Oh . . . it's . . . going."

"That doesn't sound very convincing."

I've been struggling with what to tell my friends for the past two days about my little work situation, but I know that if I express how detrimental it is to have Maddox as a client, then I have to explain what happened between us.

And I don't feel ready to admit it, which should be a red flag all on its own.

In any other instance, I would have no problem telling my girls about my phenomenal sexual experience. But this one is laced with emotional baggage and unethical work relationships that together form one big clusterfuck of problems I'm choosing to ignore right now.

I can't tell them what happened, not yet—well, at least not in great detail. Vague details should be okay to give, though, right?

"Uh, well? This week, I kind of got thrown off by a surprise client my boss assigned to me who I wasn't exactly thrilled about."

Charlotte leans forward, always the one down for some gossip. "Who is it?"

I sigh. "The Los Angeles Bolts."

Her eyes go wide. "The football team?" And then it dawns on her. "Oh, God! You can't tell Damien, Ethan, Jeffrey, or Nick. The four of them won't leave you alone."

"Ha! Yeah, they definitely can't know, at least for the time being. Maybe soon I can introduce them to the team at an event or something and watch them all cry like teenage girls seeing *NSYNC or the Backstreet Boys in concert for the first time." The girls giggle. "But I'm not happy about this new role of mine because my boss basically told me that I was taking on the client without considering all of the other accounts I'm managing right now. So now I have to dedicate my life to the team for the next few months as I try to make them look like one big happy family when they're not tackling each other on a field, fighting over a football."

"An entire football team? Of hot, muscular men in tight pants?" Noelle asks, now fully invested and looking like she's feeling lighter than she was when she arrived. "That sounds like heaven to you, Pen. You're sure you're not going to enjoy this even a little bit?"

"Um, no. I don't like dealing with athletes. Most of them are entitled assholes or have huge egos that truly need to be knocked down a peg or two."

"Didn't Maddox Taylor just get traded to the Bolts?" Amelia asks, pulling our attention to her. I arch my brow at her, and she continues. "What? I heard Ethan talking to Nick about it at dinner the other night."

"Yes, he did. He actually came by the office with the team representative to meet me. And he's probably going to be the biggest pain in the ass. And not the type of pain that actually feels good, like a decent spanking."

"Well, if there's anyone who can handle him, it's you, Pen," Charlotte declares. "You'll put him in his place, I'm sure."

Licking my lips, I tilt my head to the side. "I'm gonna try. It's just . . . complicated."

"How so?"

Frankie comes by and saves the day as he drops off our food. I peer up at him and smile. "God bless you, Frankie."

"Miss Penelope, God blesses me every Sunday when I get to see you beautiful women." He sets down ketchup, hot sauce, and extra napkins. "Is there anything else I can get for you ladies?"

"Everything is perfect, Frankie, including you." I blow him a kiss before he walks away and then dig into my waffle with strawberries. I've been thinking about this for the past twenty-four hours, and it's just as delicious as always.

"So if you only have one client, which I'm sure is a lot since it's really an entire team, your work schedule should slow down a bit, right?" Amelia asks around a bite of her omelet.

"Yes and no. I have a few things to iron out this afternoon after I leave here so I can pass off a few accounts, but then I need to come up with a game plan to make these men uber-lovable and get the people of LA to care about their football team."

"Let us know if there's anything we can do to help you, Pen," Amelia says. "Lord knows, I owe you a favor or two after how you helped me with Ethan."

"I don't think three-hundred vibrating dildos will help this situation, but I'll keep your offer in mind. Thank you."

Charlotte starts giggling. "I still can't believe you did that." Then she stops and stares at me. "Who am I kidding? Yes, I can. And what's scary is that I know you're capable of so much more."

I point my fork across the table at her. "Damn right. And these men don't know the half of it yet, but they're about to find out what will happen if they mouth off to Penelope Klein."

With renewed confidence in my ability to handle Maddox and keep things professional thanks to my girlfriends, I march into my office Monday morning with a list of ideas to put into motion before my first meeting with Liam to discuss strategy.

But in the back of my mind, I know the stakes are high here. Not only did I get the vibe from Liam that he doesn't believe in my abilities, but if this whole process doesn't go well, it's my reputation on the line.

Being a woman in a field like PR still comes with stigma, particularly when it pertains to sports. I remember getting looks from men in college when I would show them up in football knowledge or disagree with a play called by a coach. And I hate when my integrity and skills are questioned, especially for no other reason than because of what I have between my legs.

But ultimately, my loyalty has to remain with Maddox and the team. No matter how awkward or unfortunate this situation is, I have a little bit of experience with people holding you to unrealistic expectations or believing the worst in you, and I'll be damned if I let that happen to him, too. From what I've read in the past two days, a lot of outlets think he's pissed about leaving New Orleans, and if so, then I need to show them he's here for the long haul with confidence in his new team.

He definitely has the skills to take his team all the way, skills that had me riding his cock all the way to orgasm land.

Oh, Jesus. Here I am thinking about him again in a very unprofessional way. Perhaps the man has already burrowed himself into my subconscious and now I have a soft spot reserved for him and his dick.

If that's the case, though, then it doesn't look like things may pan out for me in the end.

Let's just hope I can keep my legs closed in the process.

Chapter 6

Maddox

"You ready to get on the field today?" Hayden, our rookie running back, comes up to me as I close my locker door, and I jump.

This is only the third day I've been at the practice facilities, and of all my new teammates, Hayden has been the most welcoming. He's also young and doesn't think before he speaks.

But I get where the other players are coming from. The new guy comes in with high expectations, and suddenly they have to learn how to work with a different leader at the helm. Not to mention that everyone's in a sour mood after a shitty season. Brock Miller, the former QB, was a stand-up guy, too, so it definitely makes things a little awkward. It's not like I'm replacing someone that nobody liked.

I've only been with New Orleans since I was drafted to the NFL, so this experience is new to me, too. I've never had to acclimate to a brand-new set of players and command respect while simultaneously earning it. New Orleans made it to the playoffs every year I've been on the field as well, so it's different knowing this team has been disappointed in that respect. Add in this whole Penelope conundrum, and my head isn't exactly screwed on correctly at the moment.

At least it's the off-season—I have time to get mentally prepared for the entire season later.

I pull an earbud from my right ear so I can hear Hayden better. "Definitely. It'll be nice to see how everyone gels."

"We've got a solid offense, Taylor. I think you'll be impressed. We just need someone to run it confidently on the field."

"I'm gonna try my best." Hayden's brow furrows as he leans toward me, searching for something. "What?"

His eyes move around the room. "What is that noise?"

"What noise?"

He looks down at my earbud and then rips it from my hands, placing it in his own ear and grinning like a fool once he hears my song.

Oh boy, here we go.

"What the fuck are you listening to?"

"Only the best music from the best decade," I reply confidently.

He starts to slide his feet back and forth, side to side, while holding his hands out to me like he's performing a serenade. "Goddamn, I forgot how good this song is!"

Vince, our center, comes by at this very moment. "I'm afraid to even ask what the fuck is happening right now . . ."

"Taylor gets down to Cindy Lauper songs while he's lifting weights." Hayden beams as he dances.

"Shut the fuck up," Vince replies. "Are you serious?"

"Yup! 'Time After Time,' to be exact." Hayden continues to belt out the lyrics as Vince eyes me with a raised eyebrow.

"Mostly just eighties tunes in general." I shrug.

Vince nods in understanding. "I can respect that. And hey, we all have our quirks, right?" He tosses his thumb over at Hayden. "This moron listens to a romance reader podcast on flights to away games."

Hayden immediately stops dancing and points at him. "Don't knock it, alright? I've learned a lot about women by listening to that podcast."

"Apparently not enough since you're still single," Vince teases.

I stand back with my arms folded, watching the dynamic between these two. Shit-talking of any degree between men, especially in professional sports, is a pastime that should be revered. Men giving each other a hard time is a way we bond, one that will ultimately help me win over my new teammates if I learn to get in on the action sooner rather than later.

"Not ready to settle down just yet, my man," Hayden preens. "Too many women willing and ready, am I right, Maddox?"

"Sure, Hayden," I say, turning back to my locker to make sure I locked it.

"Well, I heard the PR rep the team just hired is a Cindy Crawford look-alike, so maybe I'll test out my female expertise on her."

I clench my fists at the mention of Penelope. I know the team's been talking about what's going to happen over the next few months, how we all need to buy in to build the image they want to portray to the fans. But it just hit me that soon Penelope will be exposed to all of them, and lord only knows the vulgar insinuations that will come out of their mouths once they see her. Because Hayden's right—Penelope *does* look like she could be Cindy Crawford's doppelgänger.

Though honestly, I think she just stands out all on her own.

"I personally can't wait to see you crash and burn in your pickup attempts," Vince chimes in, "but you need to remember how much you're being paid to throw around a football and dedicate your energy to that, Palomar." Hayden's only been active for a year, so he's still green in terms of knowing the shit, both good and bad, that can come with this job. "Fucking remember how many men would kill to be in your shoes, and don't make an ass of yourself because you're too preoccupied with getting your dick wet."

He hands me my earbud as he looks at Vince. "Message heard loud and clear, Sargent. Thanks for making me feel like an ass."

Vince gets in one final dig. "Well, you look and smell like one, too."

I huff out a laugh and then face Hayden. "I know I'm new, but trust me, I want a shot at the playoffs just as bad as the rest of you. I came close before, but we never could pull off the big win. We all need to focus on the team right now, okay? We have a lot of work cut out for us over the next several weeks, and I have a lot to prove, too, so perhaps my motives are partially selfish. However, if I find out you're making Penelope's life difficult in any way, I'll make sure you pay for it. Are we clear?"

Hayden smirks. "Loud and clear." And then he licks his lips. "Penelope, huh? You already on a first-name basis with the rep?"

I'm on a far more intimate basis with Penelope than just knowing her first name. Like knowing how she fucking tastes —everywhere.

My heart starts to hammer, but I hold my composure. "Yeah, I am. I went with Liam to meet her. And she's damn good at her job, so don't give her shit. Now let's get back to training, shall we?"

Vince slaps my shoulder. "Sounds like a plan, QB."

Right now, because it's the off-season, players have the option to train on their own or come in to keep in shape, which is what the three of us are here for today. But after the draft in a few weeks, the team will be doing OTAs, or organized team activities, which consist of no-contact drills and mostly weight lifting in preparation for training camp. The players aren't required to attend all of them, just those ten days when every player must be there, but it's a great way for the team to bond in the off-season —and definitely something I'm taking advantage of given the trade.

So my plan for the next few months is to show up four hours a day, four days a week, and prove that I'm committed both to this team and to win while also making time to meet with Penelope.

She might think this thing between us is done, but my gut tells me it's not. And I'm hell-bent on figuring out why.

"Alright, let's get out on the field so Coach doesn't get his panties in a wad," Vince suggests as the three of us walk through the locker room, bypassing other players who are also preparing to head to the field.

"You've seen Coach's panties, Vince?" Hayden shoves his shoulder. "Didn't know you swing that way . . ."

"What if I did?" He glares over at him.

"Hey, I'm all about love is love. Just didn't know you had the hots for the coach."

I roll my eyes and then shove Hayden to the side. "Shut the fuck up, man, before Vince and I both knock you out."

"Aw, my life has been threatened. Now I really feel like you're a part of the team, Taylor."

After a great introduction to some of the players and coaching staff I hadn't met yet and a few chances to run some plays I'd been studying, I shower in the locker room and change, headed toward my meeting with Penelope.

Liam is running behind, so I'll have a little bit of time to feel her out without his presence. We spoke on the phone last night, and he made sure I understood how important it is that we follow the guidelines set forth by the team.

Negative press is the last thing they want surrounding my trade, but it's already blowing up all over the internet, insinuating I'm mad about the move when I'm not. I mean, no player likes when they have to switch teams, especially when their team's winning streak is strong and they've been there for years, but it's part of the job. Although being farther away from my cousin and her family is the biggest sore spot for me.

Paparazzi were camped outside the practice facilities today as the players were leaving, snapping pictures and calling out questions as they did. I kept my head down and headed to my truck like I've done many times before, knowing that even one wrong look can be misconstrued. The last thing I want to do is feed the gossip, especially when I have my own personal issues with the media.

The biggest obstacle I face is the pictures of me leaving parties and events with women. I'm not going to apologize because I like to socialize and relax when my job is physically and mentally grueling, but the context of those pictures definitely doesn't paint me in a good light.

During the season, I limit my alcohol intake tremendously, so it's not like I'm out to get drunk. But on New Year's Eve, as I was leaving a party, paparazzi snapped a shot of me as I helped three girls out to their ride to leave.

To any outsider, it looked like I was about to get down with three women at the same time. But that wasn't it at all. I was making sure they got home safely because I know how quickly a night can turn when alcohol is involved.

But that's a story for another time.

Hopefully, I won't be put in a position where I have to explain this to Penelope, especially given our history. I don't want her to think she's one of a dozen girls I've taken home, because she's not. She's the *only* one, and I know that detail is only going to create more of a problem the more time we spend together.

My phone rings through my truck's Bluetooth as I drive to Penelope's office, my cousin's name flashing across the screen.

"Hey, Leslie," I answer and instantly hear chatter in the background.

"Hold on. Sorry." She exhales roughly before I hear a door shut. "There. Now I can hear you better. The office is chaotic today."

"That's good, though, right?"

"Yes. We're doing a registration fair, so Tabitha and Brett are running around like crazy, and the place is packed. The program is only growing, Maddox. You should be proud."

After I was signed to the NFL, one of my goals was to give back to the town where I grew up, so I started a football camp for kids and make sure I appear each summer before my own NFL training camp starts. My cousin, Leslie, handles all of the logistics for me, and now the foundation we've established also gives out thousands of dollars in scholarships each year to high school seniors as well.

She also helped create the hotline we established after tragedy struck our family, and it sucks that I can't be close by to help her as much as I did before.

"Glad to hear it."

"You sound like you're driving. Where are you going?"

I come up to a stoplight, and as soon as the truck comes to a complete stop, I run a hand through my hair. "Well, I just left my workout at the practice field, and now I'm on my way to meet with the PR rep the Bolts hired."

She clicks her tongue. "And how do we feel about them?"

I momentarily contemplate just how honest I should be with Leslie. She's my cousin and one of my best friends, really. We're only four months apart, so we grew up together like siblings. She was the person I told when I lost my virginity, she was there when I thought I'd hit my low point in my career and couldn't trust anyone . . . and I also told her about Penelope after I returned from my trip to California almost two months ago.

Plus, I really need someone to remind me about everything at stake here if I can't control myself around her.

"It's Penelope," I finally answer, waiting for her response.

"Wait? *The* Penelope? The one from California?"

"Well, since I'm now out in California, that would make sense, don't you think?"

"No need to be a wiseass, Maddox. She's the PR rep the team hired?"

"Yup. One and the same."

"Jesus," she huffs. "How the hell did this happen?"

I run my hand through my hair. "Well, it's partly my doing."

"Maddox!"

"Listen, I didn't do anything on purpose. I just suggested the team use Edelman PR because I remember them being responsible for the Zio's Vodka party I attended when I was out here last."

"The one where you met Penelope . . ."

"Yup. I didn't know they'd assign *her* to the team, obviously. And believe me, she was just as shocked as I was about this development."

"So what does this mean?"

I sigh. "Fuck, Leslie. She's so fucking beautiful, my dick jumped when I saw her again."

"We've discussed the penis talk, Maddox. I love you, but I don't need to know anything about your dick."

Chuckling, I signal to turn into the parking garage down the street from Penelope's office, ducking as I drive through the different levels looking for a spot. For the record, I know the top of my truck is low enough not to hit the ceiling, but I still duck every single time.

I can't be the only one, right?

"Sorry. But damn, Leslie. All I keep thinking about is our night together. Hell, for the past two months, I've thought about it a lot, more than I should probably admit. The one time I give in to temptation ends up being with a woman who made an impression on me, and now I'm going to see her day after day. We're going to be working together, essentially."

"And that's the problem, Maddox." She cuts me off. "I'm sure it's not ethical for her to indulge in relations with a client, and you just got traded. I'm also fairly confident that the Bolts don't want a scandal of you hooking up with their PR rep. You've been able to keep lots of things out of the public eye for a long time, and that's exactly how it needs to stay. Wouldn't you hooking up with Penelope behind the scenes kind of undermine what they're trying to do?"

I pinch the bridge of my nose. "Fuck, I know. You're right."

"Glad you can admit that. Most men can't admit when a woman is right."

"You know I'm not most men."

She hums. "No, you're not, which is why I know this must be hard for you . . . no pun intended."

"Just for the record, you're the one who made a penis joke that time."

"I did. Shit."

We both share a laugh before I let out a frustrated sigh. "I just don't know what to do, Leslie."

"There's not much you *can* do, Maddox. Just focus on football. Maybe when the contract with her firm is up, you can revisit your connection if you feel it's still there."

"Oh, it's still there," I interject, remembering how Penelope reacted when I cornered her in her office on Friday, a move that was risky but confirmed what I already know—that the chemistry between us is just as strong as it was two months ago.

"I'm not going to lie, though, your reaction to this woman is a little concerning."

"She's not Brittney, Leslie."

"I know. But you didn't know who Brittney really was even after you'd been with her for a long time."

Biting my lip, I battle with her reminder of how I've been

fooled before. But Penelope is different. She's *not* Brittney, and something deep in my gut tells me that.

"Just behave yourself, Maddox. This is your career and your livelihood, the goal you've worked toward since you were seven and played your first season of peewee football. It's all you've ever talked about. No woman is worth jeopardizing that for. Remember how close you were to losing everything once."

I swing my truck into a parking spot and shift into park. "Yeah, I know. You're right . . . again."

"Good luck with your meeting, and we'll talk soon. I know you haven't been gone long, but I already miss your face."

After New Orleans decided to let me go, I spent some time at home in Newberry Springs, Texas, before I was officially picked up by the Los Angeles Bolts. My parents were thrilled to have me around for a while, naturally, and of course I spent as much time as I could with my cousin helping out with the foundation. It was humbling being home and living a normal life for a while, but nothing is ever concrete when playing for the NFL, and my glimpse of normalcy with my family was too short-lived.

"Miss you, too, Les."

"But I'll see you in a few months for camp, right?"

"Yes, you will."

"Now, go meet with Penelope, and be the professional I know you are."

I love that she has faith in me, but at the same time, I'm still a man—a man who is insanely attracted to the woman I'm about to have a conversation with for God knows how long. "I'll try."

I hang up and rest my head on the seat behind me, closing my eyes while trying to convince myself that I have everything under control.

But my chest is tight, my palms are sweating, and my head is filled with thoughts of Penelope and everything I already know about her that has me wanting to know more.

My cousin may have faith in me, but I'm not sure I have enough in myself.

So much has changed in my life recently, including wanting a woman I know I can't have, and I'm not sure if that's a boundary I want to honor or not.

"Mr. Taylor. It's so good to see you again." The man I met last time outside of Penelope's office leaps from his seat as soon as I round the corner.

"Hey. Same to you . . ."

"Garret," he finishes for me. "I'm Garret, Miss Klein's assistant."

"Nice to see you again, Garret." He smiles and then starts twisting as he stands there. "Is Penelope in her office?"

"Oh, yes! She's ready for you whenever you're ready to go in." Waving his hands toward the door, he slides out of my way, allowing me to reach for the handle.

"Thanks."

"My pleasure. I hope you have a great meeting!"

Amused by his excitement, I knock on Penelope's door and wait for her acknowledgment to enter this time.

"Come in!"

Walking inside, I brace myself for the professional demeanor I anticipate receiving from her. And sure enough, she sits poised behind her desk with her hands clasped in front of her, smiling as we make eye contact.

"Good morning, Mr. Taylor."

I arch a brow at her as I close the door. Apparently, she's in a better mood today—a pretending-like-nothing-happened-between-us mood, it appears. "Good morning, Miss Klein."

Her face falls for a moment when she realizes I'm alone. "Um, where is Mr. Nelson?"

"He'll be here late. He didn't tell you?"

She flashes me a tight-lipped smile, her expression full of irritation. It's the type of look that warns me to sleep with one eye open if I'm around her for any length of time. "No, he did not."

"Well, he mentioned it to me when we spoke last night. It's fine. I'm sure you and I can find something to talk about in the meantime." I cross her office and take a seat in one of the gray chairs across from her desk, reminding myself to behave while fighting the instinct to take in every detail about her. "So how are you this morning?"

"Great. Fantastic. Busy," she answers while shifting papers around her desk, avoiding my eyes.

"You forgot beautiful."

That makes her head pop up. "Maddox . . ."

"So tell me what you have in mind for the team for the next few months." I cut her off, not wanting to hear a lecture from her this early into our meeting. But I just couldn't help being reeled in by how stunning she looks today.

The long locks I remember having wrapped around my fingers are shining in the light coming through the windows, the slight tint of red more apparent now in the sun. Her hazel eyes are wide and framed by dark lashes that stand out against her tan skin. Her lips are full and a perfect pink with a freckle just above her top lip at the corner—a freckle my eyes instantly gravitate toward. Just staring at her mouth is reminding me of what those lips felt like pressed up against mine and wrapped around my cock.

Fuck, Maddox. Focus.

"I'd like to hear your ideas and see if they're in line with what Liam wants. That was one thing he asked me to do before he arrives, so I'm just following instructions," I continue, shrugging while smiling at her. "If anything sounds like it might be a bad idea, I can at least warn you before he arrives."

She licks her lips, sits up straighter in her chair, and clasps her hands again. "Okay, then. We can discuss that." Suddenly, she reaches for a pen and begins to tap it against the papers in front of her, glancing down at her list before lifting her eyes back to me. "First, I plan on being at the practice fields this week to get some pictures and clips of the players working out together and training. I know not every player will be there, but showing the team in the off-season will be a good place to start proving to the public that you are getting along well with your new teammates. It will also help build excitement for the upcoming season."

"I like it, and I think Liam will, too."

"Great. Next, I've spoken with the Los Angeles Children's Hospital to do a visit with their patients. We can bring in some kind of activity for the players to do with the kids, take pictures— and make donations, of course."

"I did something similar in New Orleans, and it was always a great time."

"Perfect. I have another event at the end of May I'm still waiting on confirmation for. It's for one of the no-kill animal shelters in the area. They hold a fundraising event that's quite popular with the community and would be great for positive exposure. One of my best friends works for a magazine that is a sponsor every year, so I think it will be easy to get into. I'm just waiting to hear back from their rep."

"You've been a busy woman since last Friday," I tease, but I'm impressed. Charles was right to give this job to Penelope, and I think Liam will be pleased with the direction she's suggesting. Charities and community businesses are the types of entities we need to reach out to in hopes of gaining support back. We need to meet the citizens of Los Angeles, the men and women that keep the town moving and prospering, and show them they have our support and that we're proud to be a part of this area.

"Yes, I have. But so far, that's all I've got, aside from normal game-related press and a few articles lined up with interviews of several key players, such as yourself. I will also be attending the draft in Vegas and managing press while I'm there. And there are quite a few organizations I'm still waiting to hear back from, but by Wednesday, I should have a few more events lined up."

"I think Liam will be happy with your ideas so far. And I'm sure the team will be, too."

"I've already been in contact with Kathy at the training facility at Cal Lutheran University, and we will be using one of the conference rooms big enough to fit everyone so I can present our game plan."

Suddenly, the reality of over fifty men plus the coaching staff meeting Penelope has my pulse racing again—because I know exactly what they're going to be thinking when they see her. It's probably going to be along the lines of what I thought when I saw her for the first time.

That night at Loft 24 was so fucking unexpected. It was one of the only moments in my professional career that I allowed myself to act impulsively, especially after I vowed a few years into my collegiate career to be extremely selective about any woman I enjoyed physical activities with. Normally, I've got my head on straight, keep my personal life close to the vest, and never let a woman derail me. One time was enough—who needs to deal with that shit twice in their life?

But the second I saw Penelope walk through the club, I was captivated. Not only was she gorgeous, but after eavesdropping on her conversation with that intern and talking to her myself, I knew she was different. She is smart and sarcastic. Beautiful and bossy. Bold and unapologetically herself. And the fact that she basically didn't bat an eye in my direction made me want to know her even more.

For me in particular, looks only carry a woman so far. I want a woman who can challenge me, who doesn't just want to talk to me because of who I am and what I do for a living. Someone who can hold my attention.

And that's exactly what Penelope did that night, what she is still doing now.

"Have you ever been in a room with that many football players at one time?" I ask, watching for her reaction.

"Do you think I can't handle myself around all of those men, Maddox?" she retorts, crossing her arms over her chest.

"Not at all. I think I'm more scared for them."

She chuckles. "As you and they should be. But this won't be my first time handling a bunch of boys with overgrown egos and an abundance of testosterone."

"And just when have you done this before?"

Her eyes fall to her desk as she uncrosses her arms. "Um, just a long time ago."

That's all I get, and something tells me she doesn't want to elaborate on the subject. More than anything, a part of me wants to know why.

"So is there anything you think I should be aware of pertaining to the team or the players?" Her head pops back up as she slips right back into her job.

"Not that I know of. You've got to remember, I've only been here for a few weeks now. I've met some of the guys but not all. And of those I've met, I know there are some good men on this team. Family men. Guys with good hearts who just want to play football for a living. But I also know that they want to win, and so do I."

"Well, teamwork is built outside of the field as much as it is on it."

"You sound like you have some appreciation and under-standing of the game, Penelope. Do you have some experience with a football team?"

"Secondhand experience. Sorry to disappoint you, but I've never played football before. This is my first time doing PR for a team, though."

I narrow my eyes at her. "Damn. Why am I now envisioning you in football pads and a helmet regulating grown men on the offensive line?"

She snorts and rolls her eyes. "Because you're a guy. And I find it disturbing if that vision is one of your fantasies, Maddox. That's the type of thing you may want to see a therapist about."

Perhaps, but the vision of her in my jersey with my name splayed across the back is coming in quickly to replace that one.

"I didn't know it was a fantasy of mine until it was your face I was picturing, although the sight of you wearing my jersey and nothing else might just top it." She blushes but then covers her cheek with her hand to try to cover it up. "But based on what you're saying, you know the game. I can hear it in your voice. You're one of those women who probably understands the mechanics of it better than some men."

The smile she gives me is one of pure pride. "You bet your ass, I do."

Throwing my head back, I let out the laugh she inspires in me. "I fucking love it."

"Glad you approve." She relaxes into her chair as we stare at one another.

"You know, I wouldn't mind picking your brain about a few things sometime," I suggest. "I mean about football, of course."

Her shoulders fall along with the smile she just gave me. "Maddox . . ."

"Or about Los Angeles. You know I just moved here. I don't know much about the city, and with the exception of four hours a day, four days a week, I have plenty of downtime to explore a bit."

Wearily, she takes the bait. "Well, what are you into?"

"Food, culture, and seeing the little spots that most people miss."

"There's no shortage of food everywhere you turn. Any small hole-in-the-wall spot is going to give you some of the best Mexican food of your life. There's a place called Chevos near UCLA that my girlfriends and I used to go to late at night during college. They have some of the best tacos, burritos, and salsa you'll ever taste. Although, most of the time we ate there, we were drunk, so take that with a grain of salt."

I laugh. "Everything tastes better when you're drunk."

"Absolutely. You also must go to Frankie's Diner. My girl-friends and I go to brunch there almost every Sunday, and you won't be disappointed by anything on the menu, including bottom-less mimosas."

"You like a champagne brunch, huh?"

"Only with my girlfriends," she clarifies. "If you get really bored or want some adventure, you could visit the popular tourist spots—Warner Bros. Studios, the Getty, Griffith Observatory, Disneyland, Six Flags, Universal Studios, Staples Center—the list goes on and on. Do a Google search, and you can plan out your entire summer with things to do, Maddox."

"Yeah, I could. It would be better with a guide, though, or someone to tag along and keep me company, someone who knows me and who I can trust. I don't suppose you know someone who might be available, do you?"

She shakes her head at me. "Look, I know what you're doing—"

"And what is that?" I ask, trying to keep a straight face because I know I'm pushing her limits right now. But when she's frustrated with me, it only makes me want her even more.

I wonder why that is?

Because she's not throwing herself at your feet like every other female you cross paths with, Maddox. Duh.

Because she's intelligent, sarcastic, kindhearted, and beautiful. That's why.

"Look. As I said on Friday, we have to pretend like what happened between us never happened, Maddox."

"Remind me again why that is, Penelope," I reply, even though I know why already. But I want to hear it from her mouth. Maybe if I hear her say it, something will stick—because right now, all I want is to move around her desk, lift her up on top of it, kiss her until we both can't breathe, and devour that sweet spot between her legs.

The skin on her neck turns red, and I swear her thoughts are mimicking my own.

She clears her throat while trying to appear composed. "Because you are my client now. In fact, the entire team is, and if this goes wrong, it's both of our jobs on the line. The last thing either of us needs is bad press. I have enough work cut out for me with this job just because I'm a woman, and on top of that, my boss is counting on me to do it well for the firm. Plus, a football team is not a client I would normally take on, so I have to make sure I'm focused so I don't make a misstep." She points a finger at me now. "And *you*—you have a lot to prove to a new team. Don't you care what people think of you? Don't you want the fans to know you're dedicated to the Bolts and not letting some woman you had a one-night stand with derail your focus?"

"My focus is fine. In fact, I don't feel like I've been this focused in years . . ."

Focused on one woman, that is.

A knock on the door halts our conversation.

Both of us turn in that direction as the door opens and Liam appears. "Sorry I'm late, you two." He shuts the door behind him and then takes a seat in the empty chair right next to me. Bouncing his eyes between us, he furrows his brow. "Is everything okay?"

Penelope clears her throat again while shooting me a glare. I smirk back at her before she directs her attention to Liam. "Everything is fine, Mr. Nelson. Maddox and I were just discussing the events I have lined up, and he agreed everything sounds promising."

"Well, I'm ready to be filled in as well, and then I have a few thoughts of my own to add, naturally. We want to make sure that our vision is in line with what Edelman PR suggests. Ultimately, the Bolts franchise needs to approve every appearance, event, and press release to make sure the best interest of our players is being met." He drops his eyes up and down while glaring at Penelope—and if I wasn't a better gentleman, I'd punch the man for his lack of respect and belief in her.

"Of course."

I sit back in the chair and watch Penelope deliver the same information to Liam just as she did with me, and by the end of the meeting, I've made up my mind.

Penelope may think that what happened between us can't happen again. And she's right. It shouldn't. But she doesn't realize that I can be one determined motherfucker when I want to be. And right now, I'm determined to get Penelope to admit that she still wants me.

Let the games begin.

Chapter 7

Penelope

"Damn. Bringing out the red dress today, huh?" Garret walks into my office just after he arrives. I've been here for the past hour preparing for my meeting this morning with the entire Bolts franchise, vibrating with nerves.

"Red is a power color, Garret. It says don't fuck with me because I know what I'm doing."

"Do you know what you're doing?"

I glance back at him over my shoulder as I stuff another file folder into my bag. "For the most part. About ninety percent, I'd say."

"Your missing ten percent wouldn't have to do with that Adonis Maddox Taylor being involved, would it?"

Just the mention of his name has my pulse spiking. "No, it's just . . . uncharted territory for me."

"Being attracted to a man?" he prods with a smirk.

"No. Dealing with athletes. It isn't my normal clientele."

Garret walks further into the room. "Well, I, for one, am jealous as fuck. You get to boss around over fifty grown men, men who I would have no problem letting crack my spine." He visibly shivers. "I wonder if any of them are secretly gay and you could hook me up?"

"I'll keep my eyes and ears open just in case."

He dramatically bows in front of me with his hands clasped together. "Thank you." And then he's standing, moving for the door. "Is there anything you need from me before you leave?"

I scour my office, thinking back to my meeting with Liam and Maddox just a few days ago. Being in the same room with Maddox again and trying to pretend like his presence didn't rattle me was one of the most challenging things I've had to endure in a while. I mean, if there's anything that's come out of being assigned to the Bolts, it's that my job has officially become exciting again—just not in the way I was anticipating or needing.

Visions of our night together flashed through my mind while words of the professional variety were leaving my lips. It's like I was living outside of my body, watching myself putting on a skit, acting like another woman, not the one I've been fighting with ever since Maddox showed up in my office last week.

During our meeting, I was looking into his eyes, but all I could remember was how he looked at me when he hovered over me. He was engaging in our conversation, speaking in that deep, raspy voice of his, but all I could hear was the sounds he made when he found his release, pinning me to the bed beneath him.

Once Liam entered the room, he sat there smugly while I filled Mr. Nelson in on everything we had already discussed. Meanwhile, all I could think about while Maddox was sitting there was his dick and how phenomenal it felt inside of me.

And that piercing.

Jesus Christ, I have issues. The girls are right.

What the hell did I do in a past life to deserve the shitshow I'm currently dealing with?

I think this is more about what you've done in this life, Penelope.

"Nope. I think I have everything. The PowerPoint is on the drive. My laptop is in the bag with all of the research and stats I pulled over the past week. And I made sure to put on an extra layer of deodorant this morning. I think I've got it handled."

"You do. You've got this. Now, go make those grown men scared of you, and let me know if there is a physical examination component to this job that may require my assistance."

Little does he know, I've already been up close and physical with Maddox Taylor—and he's as fit as an ox.

"You'll be the first one I call."

After a little butt tap of encouragement from Garret, I leave the office and head across town toward Cal Lutheran University, where the private practice fields are located for the team. I crank up some Eminem, Snoop Dogg, and Lil' Wayne to help ease my nerves. There's something about listening to gangster rap that makes me feel like a badass bitch, especially going into a meeting of this magnitude.

When I arrive at the practice fields on campus, I park in the designated area, head toward the athletic facilities, and go through a security checkpoint before I head for the conference room where I know an abundance of testosterone awaits me.

"Miss Klein." A voice to my left has me twisting in that direction, and I catch Liam walking toward me.

"Mr. Nelson. Good morning."

"You ready?"

"Born ready. Just lead the way, please."

"Hmm," he hums and then turns back the way he came from, beckoning me to follow him. If I had a free hand, I'd flip him off behind his back. Sadly, my hands are full, so I make sure I do it in my mind only. Probably safer that way, anyway.

When we arrive at the room, Liam holds the door open for me so I can walk in and survey the space ahead of him. At least he's gentlemanly enough to hold open a door for a lady.

Rows of seats are lined in stadium-style seating, cascading up the wall like the inside of a lecture hall. A whiteboard and projection screen is situated in the front of the room, ready for my presentation. The walls are beige and empty except for a few banners with the Los Angeles Bolts logo splayed above the door we just walked through.

"IT just came in and made sure power was hooked up for you. You should be able to plug in any technology you brought with very little trouble."

I set my bag on the table in front of the whiteboard. "Thank you. I'll let you know if there are any issues."

His phone dings, and he buries his head in the screen. "Great. I'll be back with the team at the top of the hour." He lifts his phone to his ear and turns to exit the room, leaving me alone.

I take a deep breath and then get to work, oblivious to how fast time is passing. I plug in my laptop and go through my presentation, practicing walking across the space. This isn't my first rodeo, not with a presentation of this magnitude, but my nerves are still running high.

"Where is Peter Pan's favorite place to eat?"

Gasping, I spin around and come face-to-face with Maddox, who's grinning like a fool.

"Holy fuck, Maddox!" I place my hand over my racing heart. "You scared the shit out of me."

"Eloquent choice of words there."

"Don't judge me for the language that just came out of my mouth," I fire back, standing tall as I finally take him in. He's wearing netted black shorts and a light gray tank top, his hair slicked back with moisture. His tan skin is glistening with sweat, and he smells divine, like a man who overexerts his body for a living—a body I remember being impeccably shredded and hard.

"Why don't you try warning a person politely before sneaking up on them next time, and maybe you won't have so many vulgar words spat in your direction?"

He licks his lips as he fights a grin. "My apologies, but you didn't answer my question."

"What was your question?" I honestly don't remember what he asked because I was too busy trying not to pee and shit myself.

He steps closer, leaning in toward my ear and leaving very little space between our bodies. I catch a whiff of him again, but this time I smell soap. I guess what I thought was sweat is actually residue from his shower. The clean spice of his soap and his natural scent fills my nostrils, and suddenly I remember inhaling him during our night together and thinking how I could sniff him all day like a crackhead and it probably still wouldn't be enough.

"I asked, where is Peter Pan's favorite place to eat?" he whispers in my ear, his breath tickling my skin and erupting a flurry of goosebumps down my arms and up my neck.

I rear back and stare into his eyes, knowing I'm about to either laugh or shake my head at him. Probably both, if I'm being honest. "I don't know, Maddox. Where?"

The corner of his lips lift as he gazes into my eyes and says, "Wendy's."

"Well, I'm just embarrassed with myself for not getting that one," I say as I smile and step back from him.

"You should be. That one was easy. But hey, it helped you relax, didn't it?"

Suddenly, it dawns on me that we're no longer alone as dozens of men begin to enter the room, forcing me back to the reality of why I'm here.

Creating even more distance between us, I say, "For a moment, until I realized there were probably many witnesses to our little interaction just now."

"What's the matter, Penelope? You don't want to be seen talking to me?" he asks as he circles around me, but I continue to stare forward, smiling in greeting as players and coaching staff walk past, their eyes dancing as they size me up.

"If you want to keep your dick and balls intact, I suggest you find a seat, Maddox, and pretend as if the only way we know each other is on a professional level."

"And if I don't?" I turn to find him glaring down at me in challenge.

"Don't say I didn't warn you . . ."

"Gentleman, please, take your seats. Miss Klein will begin her presentation in just a few minutes," Liam speaks into a microphone as he walks over to us with it in hand, pulling it away from his mouth to offer it to me. "Forgot to give this to you earlier, Penelope. Half of these guys have taken one too many hits to the head, so they may be hard of hearing."

I smile and then intercept the microphone. "Thank you."

"Maddox, why don't you go find a seat?" he suggests before he gets pulled in another direction.

Maddox leans in to whisper in my ear. "Just remember, Penelope. If you get too nervous, just picture everyone in the audience naked." Then he marches off, shaking hands with a few of the men I recognize on the offensive line: Vince Dayton, the center, and Hayden Palomar, who is one of the best rookie running backs in the League.

Maddox takes a seat in the front row next to the other men I just recognized, and then I stand there, counting man after man traipsing into the room, feeling sweat drip down my spine as pressure mounts in my chest.

There are so many men. Professional athlete men. Men who could probably crack a watermelon in half with their legs.

It's a thing. I've seen it. Look it up. You won't be disappointed.

At that moment, on the verge of throwing up, I decide to try Maddox's trick. I scour the crowd, trying to picture all of these men naked, even the coaching staff who I can tell don't partake in the same physical workouts as the players.

But then it hits me . . .

I'm in a room full of some of the most spectacular male bodies in the world. There are so many dicks in front of me, and normally, I would be more than intrigued by the smorgasbord of options. I'd be trying to catch the outline of them through their shorts or pants, attempting to determine who's a grower and who's a shower. And I'd be more than intrigued by who was rocking the turtleneck underneath or who was cut and ready for action without a wardrobe change, if you catch my drift.

But my dick radar must be broken—because there's only one dick and one man I care to see naked, and it's one I already have.

As if he knows I'm thinking of him, Maddox smirks in my direction. I catch his reaction just long enough to remind myself that I need to keep it together.

My vagina and brain may be malfunctioning right now, but I'm still Penelope Klein—and it's time to make sure the Los Angeles Bolts know who they'll be working with for the next four months.

It's showtime.

"**M**iss Klein, it's a pleasure to meet you." Coach Williams comes up after my presentation to shake my hand. "Likewise."

"I really like your ideas and know that my players will be active participants as long as it doesn't jeopardize their time on the field or potentially injure them."

"That's the last thing we want now, isn't it, Coach?" I ask, and he nods. "With Palomar and Taylor at the helm this year, you need your offense in top shape if you're going to win games, and I can respect that. But I also know that we need to highlight the bond between the offense, too. Look at Dak Prescott and Ezekiel Elliott of the Cowboys. Everyone loves the two of them together. Their bromance translates to chemistry on the field, and fans pick up on that. Hopefully, the next few months will strengthen the team in that manner as well, and you'll be happy with the results you see on and off the grass, sir."

His brow lifts as he nods again. "You're right. Well, here's hoping you can work your magic and that it will translate to some winning games."

"I can do my best, sir. But you and I both know that winning games is your job." I wink at him just as I feel large bodies come up behind me.

"Would it be inappropriate to tell you that listening to a woman talk about football like that was one of the hottest things I've ever experienced?"

I twist to find Hayden Palomar smiling from ear to ear as he stares down at me. "Yes and no."

Maddox comes up behind him and smacks him on the back of the head. "Yes, it's fucking inappropriate. Now apologize."

Hayden rubs the spot Maddox just hit. "Jesus, dude. Penelope just said we're supposed to be building a bromance, and here you are, smacking me around."

"Don't act and talk like an idiot, and then you won't get hit."

Hayden tosses his thumb at Maddox. "My QB here seems to be in a mood."

Now that I look at him, his demeanor seems a bit more intense than it was when he surprised me before the meeting.

"Your head is gonna get a few more hits if you don't watch your mouth, Palomar."

Vince Dayton comes up beside Maddox now and slings an arm over his shoulder. "Relax, Taylor. We've already talked about how Hayden has verbal diarrhea. And now we know it seems to get worse around a beautiful woman." He extends his hand to me. "Vince Dayton. Nice to meet you, Miss Klein."

"Penelope, please."

"Penelope. Please, forgive my boys here. They don't seem to know how to behave around women."

"And you do?"

He grins. "My wife seems to think so."

"Well, lucky her."

"I'm the lucky one, Penelope. She puts up with my ass and this job. But I admire what you're trying to do for this team, and I'm excited to be a part of it. I just wanted you to know that."

"Well, I appreciate that, Vince. Thank you."

"You're welcome. Now, if you'll excuse me, I'm headed home to spend some time with the family. My girls are waiting for me in the pool, and I'd much rather be with them than referee these two idiots."

"It was nice to meet you."

"Likewise, Penelope. See you soon." With a tip of his chin, he saunters off, leaving me with Maddox and Hayden standing next to me.

The room is mostly cleared out now, coaching staff returning to offices and players headed home since the workouts were earlier this morning. Liam is nowhere to be found. I'm guessing that means I'm free to leave as well, so I turn to start packing up my things. But all I feel is a searing heat on my back.

"Hey, Penelope?" Hayden says, pulling my eyes to him over my shoulder.

"Yeah?"

"In all honesty, I'm pumped about this. I know that giving back is one of the best things about this job, and I haven't really had a chance to discover how to do that on my own. Last year was a blur just trying to survive my first season, so I'm eager to be everywhere you want me to be this summer, all right?" He leans in a little closer to me now. "And if you have any tips on my game, I wouldn't be opposed to hearing them, too . . ."

That has me smiling. "I'm not sure you could handle it, Hayden."

He covers his heart with his hand. "Are you gonna be brutal?"

"Honesty is the only option when it comes to football, don't you think?"

He casts a glance at Maddox, whose eyes haven't moved from me since Vince left. "I like her."

Maddox grunts. "Yeah."

Okay, then . . .

"See you soon, Hayden."

"See ya, Penelope. And Maddox, I'll see you tomorrow."

Maddox finally shifts his focus to him. "Stay outta trouble, Palomar."

Hayden shakes his head as he walks away and leaves me alone with Maddox again.

"You rocked the presentation. Every guy had their eyes on you," he finally says as I begin packing up my laptop.

"Thanks. I just hope they were actually listening and not staring at my tits."

"Highly unlikely," he fires back, a playfulness returning to his voice again. "What are you up to after this?"

"Headed back to the office. My inbox is full of emails, and I have some phone calls to return plus a meeting with Charles."

"Wanna have dinner? I promise, I'll take you somewhere nicer than Wendy's. Unless you want me to eat that . . ."

I spin to face him, my heart beating rapidly from his suggestion and my vagina clenching from the idea as well. But I'm more frustrated with his offer after our discussion earlier and the fact that he's not comprehending the seriousness of all of this. "No, Maddox." My eyes dart around the room that I realize is now empty except for us. And thank God, because if someone had overheard his question, we'd have another mess on our hands.

"Why not?" he smiles like he's allowing himself to relax again now that Hayden isn't here flirting with me and there aren't any witnesses to our interaction. "It will just be two friends having dinner and perhaps getting naked afterward. Nothing wrong with that."

I place my hands on my waist and watch his smile grow wider as my frustration with him builds. "Why on earth are you happy about this? I feel like I'm living in a fucking nightmare, like I'm being punished for having good sex with a man I wouldn't have entertained otherwise."

"Glad you can admit it was good. I was aiming for great, but I'll just need another night, then, so you can improve your assessment."

"How can you not see how bad this is, Maddox?"

He finally stops grinning and lowers his voice. "Because it's not for me. Like the great Steve Harvey says, 'Gratitude erases negativity.' Maybe you should try to see the positive in this situation instead of the negative, Penelope."

I tilt my head and arch a brow at him. "Quoting Steve Harvey right now? Really?"

"Damn straight, woman. Instead of continuing to remind me that anything between us can't happen, why not ask yourself what positive thing might happen if we *do* spend time together?"

Um, I'm going to lose my clothes again. That's *what might happen. And as much as I know it would be amazing, it's bad. SO bad.* "Like what?"

He takes a step closer, and my skin comes alive again. "Like us getting to know each other more. Wouldn't it make your job easier if you knew the star QB of the team you're representing inside and out?"

I know what you feel like inside of me, *and that's enough, as far as I'm concerned.* "Maddox . . ."

"Like how I hate anything cinnamon flavored, but my favorite pie is apple pie, which is full of cinnamon. Or how if my closet isn't organized by color, it freaks me out. Or how I despise watching baseball on television but love going to a live game. That I hate cheese unless it's melted, and I always call my mom after every game I play no matter how late it is." He leans in closer to me again and lowers his voice. "Or how after we slept together two months ago, I swore it was the alcohol that made me think it was the best night of my life. But now I know . . . it was you."

I swallow hard before taking a step back.

"Are you honestly going to stand here and pretend that you don't think about that night—about *me*—at all?"

I try not to hesitate, but I fail. "No. I don't."

"Liar," he fires back.

Irritation bubbles inside of me because it seems that Maddox is too stubborn to take a hint. So I decide to pull a little reverse psychology on him.

He grins again as I stand there and come up with something that will kick him down a notch or two. "Actually, I did have a dream about you last night."

"Oh?" Glee springs to his face. "See? You don't have to lie anymore, Penelope. It was a sex dream, wasn't it? Did I blow your mind just as hard as the last time?"

"No, you were the cab driver while I blew Robert Downey, Jr. in the back seat."

He freezes, narrows his eyes, and then asks, "RDJ is your dream guy?"

That reaction right there, his shock and disappointment? That's exactly what I wanted. "He's my *everything* guy—cocky but not too much, extremely good-looking in that older man kinda way, and he used to be a bad boy . . . he's *every* girl's kryptonite. Plus, he masquerades as a superhero."

"You know he just plays that part, right?"

"No. RDJ *is* Ironman, Maddox. He was born to play that role. In fact, I'd be surprised if he didn't come out of his mom in the famous red suit ready to fight bad guys and spit off sarcastic remarks. I would let that man do very bad things to me."

"So you had a dream about Robert Downey, Jr. . . . well, at least I was in it."

I place a palm on his chest and instantly regret it. His pecs are hard and warm, his body intoxicating as I stare up into his sparkling hazel eyes. But I need him to hear me. "You're missing the point, Maddox. It wasn't you. It *can't* be you. And I need you to hear me when I tell you: What happened between us was a mistake. We've already talked about why this can't happen again. That night was fluke, a case of bad judgment and even worse decisions on my part. Believe me, I'm not usually a woman who regrets her sexual conquests. In fact, I'm generally quite proud of mine. No woman should be made to feel bad about appeasing her sexual appetite. But with you? I had a momentary lapse in judgment. I don't normally hook up with athletes, football players in particular . . ."

"Why not?"

I sigh and close my eyes. "It's just one of my rules, okay?"

He takes my words with a grain of salt, clearly not truly

listening because it wasn't what he wanted to hear. "Well, you know what they say: Some rules are made to be broken."

"Breaking it once was a mistake. But doing it again? That would be a choice, one I can't risk the consequences of."

I turn around, ready to run out the door to get away from the man who's far too tempting and turning my world and determination upside down.

"You don't think finding out what's between us is worth the risk?"

"No." I face him again while hiking my bag on my shoulder. "I don't. Now if you'll excuse me, I have a job to get back to."

"I won't stop believing, Penelope. I'm gonna hang on to this feeling," he says, placing a hand over his chest, referencing Journey again.

"You sure are something, Maddox Taylor." And all I can do is shake my head and laugh while he watches me hurry away.

He calls out to me one more time before I exit the building. "This isn't over!"

But I don't respond again. I just keep running—out of the room, away from the man my body keeps forgetting I can't have, and out to my car, where I stare at my reflection in the rearview mirror and remember the last boy I fought my attraction to.

I lost that battle, but I can't lose this time. The stakes are too high.

And no dick is worth my job. Not even the anaconda on Maddox Taylor.

Chapter 8

Penelope

The next few days I spend with my media crew at the private practice fields getting video and pictures of the players on the team training and running a few drills together. The amount of players there is minuscule, but the draft happens this week, which will fill any empty spots on the roster before the season. And once rookie training camp is over, OTAs will start, and there will be far more players attending practices. But enough players were around while I was there to display sportsmanship and camaraderie that we can feed to the public in healthy doses.

I spoke with one of my contacts at *The Los Angeles Times* earlier this week, and an article is set to run this Sunday in the sports section highlighting Maddox's new position on the team and how early training is going during the off-season. I got a few statements from him yesterday before he left the locker room, but the vibe between us was different.

He wasn't flirtatious. He wasn't playful. He wasn't pressing me to go to dinner with him. And when I thanked him for the interview, he walked away after giving me a simple "You're welcome."

It seemed like he finally accepted what I said to him about the two of us, even though his last words to me earlier this week were "This isn't over."

So why was I filled with disappointment?

Because you didn't want him to stop pursuing you, Penelope. Duh. Even Amelia would point that out at the drop of a hat.

But my girlfriends don't know what happened between Maddox and me two months ago, and they certainly don't have any indication of the turmoil I'm in now.

They wouldn't understand why being near him makes my chest tight and my stomach churn because he was the first man to make me feel something in a long time—twelve years, to be exact.

And I know that I can't explain how Maddox is making me feel without telling them about Jacob, which is something else I've never done.

In fact, since I moved out to California for college, I've never told a soul about him—not even the girls I consider my sisters. Granted, our friendship blossomed over time since our freshman year at UCLA. But even after I knew those women would be in my life until I took my last breath, I still kept my past with Jacob to myself. I left him and our relationship back in Ohio and shut off a switch in my brain, the one where I let myself grow feelings for another man. Because how could I ever explain to a new one why I'm so messed up from the last?

How on earth could I possibly get someone to understand that I'm the reason Jacob died?

It's a guilt I carry with me every day. It's the reason I haven't been back home in twelve years. It's why the future I thought I had with him is buried deep inside: so I didn't have to deal with the pain of losing every dream I had of our life together.

He was my everything. My first and only love.

And he died.

So I ran.

I started a new life in a new state where nobody knew me, where people wouldn't make comments about how sad it was that he was gone too soon, how sorry they felt for his family, or how I must be feeling knowing I was there and played a part in his accident.

As I get older, I think some parts of it get harder. Because there's not a day that goes by when I don't wonder what our life would be like right now if he were still here.

Would Jacob have made it to the NFL? What team would he be playing on? Would we be married and have kids yet? Where would we be living, and would I ever get used to the fact that my husband was a professional football player?

These are all questions I ask myself randomly, and lately, they're even more prevalent because of the man who has intruded on my life. The man who reminds me way too much of Jacob.

Maddox.

Something about him keeps me second-guessing this entire situation. Obviously, the potential threat to our jobs is the biggest obstacle we face. But more importantly, it's the familiarity he gives me, the way he reminds me so much of Jacob and the connection we shared.

The laughter, the teasing, the chemistry.

I know—at seventeen, what the hell did I know about chemistry? But as a thirty-year-old woman, I know much more about sex now, believe me.

And all I know is there was *love* with Jacob—and that's something I haven't experienced since him because I've never allowed myself to.

I'm not saying I love Maddox. Hell, I barely know the man.

But I did love the way he made me *feel*—seen, interesting, desired, wanted, and *alive*.

It's been too long since I've felt those things, and that's the scariest part of it all: The feelings, both old and new, are all ones that I don't want to deal with right now.

By the time the week is over, I'm even more confused about what I want from him. He's backed off, which is what I asked him to do, but now I just feel used and irritated, and I'm not exactly sure why.

I'm sitting at my desk, reading through the article I approved to run in *The LA Times* on Sunday, when I jump at a knock on my door.

"You have a delivery," Garret announces as he strides into my office holding a bouquet of stunning lilac calla lilies.

I stand from my chair, walking over to him to intercept the arrangement. "What the hell? Who are they from?"

"I don't know, Penelope. Is there a man in your life I don't know about?" With one hand on his hip, he eyes me as I set the vase down on my desk and search for a card. But there's nothing.

"No, Garret. There's no man."

"You sure about that?"

"Last time I checked, it's been a long time since a dick has come in contact with this vagina, all right?"

He laughs. "A simple 'no' would have sufficed."

"And since when do I offer a simple reply?"

"Touché. Well, do you have any idea who they could be from?"

I feel a tiny sliver of hope when I consider who they *could* be from, but I don't dare voice that aloud. Especially because that hope is yet another reason why they *shouldn't* be from him. "No."

"Pity. They're beautiful. And I know they're your favorite."

"They are." Instinctually, I reach back and rub the skin on my shoulder where my calla lily tattoo rests, my unique floral tattoo that me and the girls got during the summer between our freshman and sophomore years of college.

When we realized the bond we shared was special, we wanted something to cement that. So we each got a tattoo of our favorite flower on our shoulder, a way to connect us together while still celebrating our individuality.

The truth is, I never really cared for flowers much, but I remember dozens of calla lilies at Jacob's funeral, so that's what I chose as a reminder of him as well—a detail only I know, of course.

And then it hits me—the last person who saw that tattoo.

Maddox.

Could these really be from him?

"There's a gift, too," Garret announces as he reveals a small white box from behind his back with a yellow ribbon tied on the top.

"Well, why didn't you say so?" I rip the box from his hands.

"I wanted to make you sweat a little."

Yanking the ribbon, I turn toward my desk chair and resume my seat. "Tell me why I don't fire you again?"

"You'd miss me too much," he tosses back without pause.

When I lift the lid and see what's inside, I instantly know my intuition was correct.

"What is it?" Garret asks, leaning over my desk.

Twisting to the side, I hide the box from view. "Nothing."

He narrows his eyes at me and places his hands on his hips. "Really? After all that, you're not going to let me know who they're from?"

"You don't need to know everything."

He gasps. "But I'm your assistant!"

"Well, then you'd better get back to work."

"Fine. Whatever." He throws his hands up in defeat. "I'll just have to ask around if anyone knows. You know how gossip flies around this office."

"Good luck with that."

He shuts the door behind him as I place the box on my desk and take one of the apple-flavored Jolly Ranchers out of the box along with the note inside.

Unfolding the paper, my heart picks up as I take in the masculine handwriting staring back at me, scanning the words at lightning speed for a message.

Penelope,

Calla lilies and anything sour-apple flavored—two things I will never be able to see again without thinking of you.

I don't know when I'll see you next since the Children's Hospital event is a few weeks away, but just know you'll be on my mind until then, like you have been since the night we met.

I told you this wasn't over, and I'm standing by that.

I tried my best this week to show you that I could be professional when I need to, but now I'm trying to tell you what I'm really feeling.

I'm not the type of guy who takes no for an answer, especially when it's something that I want.

And I want you.

I want your time and friendship. I just want to get to know you better—because the parts of you I know so far, I really like. But I know there's more to you, too.

So I'll ask again . . . why can't you give this a chance?

Until next time,

Maddox

Sighing, I toss the note on my desk and then unwrap the candy, twisting the plastic free and plopping it into my mouth. It tastes just like the sour-apple vodka we were drinking that night, and now I'm even more confused.

I've met stubborn men in my life. Hell, my own father is just about as stubborn as they come. But Maddox's stubbornness isn't menacing or a turnoff. On the contrary, it ignites a flurry of excitement in my gut. He may not have listened, but deep down, I don't think I wanted him to.

And now he's proving himself in more ways than one.

God help me.

"You look stressed," Charlotte announces as I take my seat at our table. It's Sunday, which means it's brunch day, and boy, do I need some champagne.

With the draft commencing this week, I was busy following the team representatives to Las Vegas for the festivities, releasing a statement to the press as soon as they secured their new wide receiver, Jake Young, in the first round. The new rookie will arrive tomorrow and then attend rookie camp this week with the rest of the draft picks and free agents all vying for a spot on the team.

But that means I haven't seen Maddox in over a week, and the fact that I'm acutely aware of that is a problem.

There was a bouquet of calla lilies waiting in my hotel room for me when I arrived in Vegas and a massage paid for by Steve Harvey—a gift that I gladly partook in the last night I was there after being on my feet all day.

I sent him a text thanking him for the gifts but never got a response—which makes me wonder if something happened between then and now that made him change his mind. And not knowing is making me even more eager to see or hear from him again and figure out what the hell is going through both of our heads because all I know is that mine is spinning.

"I guess you could say that." Reaching for my mimosa, I drain about half of it while my friends watch, waiting for me to elaborate. "What?"

"Care to talk about it?" Amelia asks.

"Um, well . . ."

Noelle pipes up. "How was Vegas? Was the draft everything you thought it would be?"

I've watched many NFL drafts in my life and came to the conclusion that there is a lot of waiting, and you just never know what might happen. This year was no exception. But being there in person was a reminder of how much energy exists in the football world, a world I hate to admit that I've missed.

"Seeing one live is definitely a much cooler experience than watching it on television. And there were so many men, ladies. A penis palooza!"

"Did you end your dry spell, then?" Charlotte asks. "I mean, you *did* say it's been awhile, right?"

"Honestly, after the days were done, I was so exhausted that I just went straight to bed. I did get a massage one day, though. That felt great."

"Nice."

I twiddle my fingers for a moment, wondering how to ask for advice without asking for advice. I know I could just come out and say what's going on with Maddox, but I'm just not ready to open up that can of worms.

"Say . . . can I ask you girls about something? It's for my . . . friend."

Sure. There you go. Let your friend be the one with the messed-up head, Pen. Good thinking!

Charlotte stares at me then blinks dramatically. "You have other friends besides us?"

"Funny. And yes, I do. Who knows if you bitches will up and forget about me before we ever make it to the nursing home?"

"Aw, Pen. We could never forget about you," Noelle assures me. "Mostly because you wouldn't let us." She winks.

"Damn straight. Anyway . . . this friend of mine is talking to this guy who they're interested in but really shouldn't be."

"And why not?" Amelia questions.

"Because they had a one-night stand and thought they'd never see each other again, but now they keep running into each other and the guy is insistent that they spend some more time together to get to know one another. The guy seems to think they have a connection worth exploring."

"And why doesn't your friend want to get to know him? Was the sex bad?"

"Uh, no. Not at all. It was mind-blowing, actually," I say and then look up to find them all studying me. "According to my friend, that is."

"All right. So the sex was good, but nothing else is?" Charlotte continues.

I shake my head. "No, there's definitely a connection. But the guy . . . he . . . has a job that kind of creates a problem for my friend."

Charlotte rolls her eyes. "Oh, Jesus. I'm getting confused. Names would be helpful, Pen. Who is this friend?"

I look around Frankie's while I come up with a name. Unfortunately, the first one that pops in my head is not a fictional person. "It's . . . uh . . . Garret!" I practically shout, very pleased with my answer.

"Garret? Your assistant?"

"Yes!" *There, Garret. Now you're part of the gossip. I hope you're happy and pleased that I'm using you as my scapegoat.* "But don't tell him I told you about this. He's still really unsure about everything with this guy, and I don't want him to feel like I'm betraying his trust. But you girls are much more experienced with this type of stuff, so I knew you could help me tell him what to do."

Amelia chimes in. "First, don't *tell* him what to do. Simply offer a suggestion, and let him make that decision, okay?"

There's my therapist friend coming through. "Yes. Of course."

"Second, what is the problem with this guy's job? Is that the biggest hang-up?"

"It's a big issue for him, yes." *Think, Penelope. What job could this guy have that seems like a dealbreaker, an occupation that would make most people cringe?* "Oh! He's a taxidermist!"

All of their faces scrunch up. "A taxidermist?" Noelle asks for clarification.

"Yes. You know, the people who stuff animals after they've been killed?"

"I'm familiar with what a taxidermist is. That's just not a job you hear about every day." *No, it's not, but it was the first thing that popped into my head.* "So this is a problem for Garret?"

I nod a little over-enthusiastically, but instantly my mind is dedicated to this story. "A big one. See, Garret grew up on a farm and loves animals. He hated when any of them died, but he knew it was part of life. However, when an animal did die, his family never kept the body around, you know?" My friends are all staring at me like I've grown two heads, but I'm in this now, so I have to see it through.

"So when he went to this guy's house, it just brought back all of these memories for him. And he's struggling with that because he really likes him. He's thoughtful, funny, and makes him feel wanted. But his job might be a dealbreaker."

Amelia chimes in again. "Well, coming from someone who's living with a man whose job was also once a dealbreaker, I feel equipped to offer some insight on the matter."

"Yes, please do."

We all shift our attention to Amelia. "A person is not their job. What's important here is how this man makes Garret feel because, ultimately, work is work. You can separate jobs from relationships. There are healthy boundaries you can put in place there. But if this man is making Garret feel anything that leads him to believe investing time in the relationship may be worth it, then he owes it to himself to explore that. Speaking from experience, of course."

"Are you sure? Even if it brings up bad memories for Garret?" My heart is pounding as I wait for her answer.

"What Garret needs to ask himself is if those memories are fear or something else—because if they are fear, it's something he can work past. But if it's more of a traumatic feeling, then that's something deeper that needs to be dealt with through counseling."

I drop my voice. "What if it's a little of both?"

Amelia stares at me, and I see the light click on in her head. Fuck, she knows this isn't about Garret at all. "Then he needs to be honest with the guy if he really wants to see what's there. And I bet if the man truly cares for Garret the way I think he does, he'd be willing to take things slow, make sure Garret feels comfortable, and even compromise about not flashing his job in front of his face."

I swallow down the emotion in my throat and turn to find Noelle and Charlotte staring at us.

"Um, wasn't Garret born in New York?" Charlotte asks, her eyebrows scrunched together.

"He was, but there are farms in New York. Google it." *Sounding a little too defensive there, Penelope.*

"I mean, I know. I just didn't think—"

Luckily, Frankie comes by at that moment with our food, halting the conversation.

I pick up my glass and drink the rest of my mimosa as Amelia's words sink in. And with a side glance in her direction, I realize she's studying me like a math problem she's trying to figure out.

I'd have to be honest with Maddox about why he scares me if I chose to explore this thing between us. It's the only way he would understand why I'm so afraid.

But can I do that? Could I really open up that part of my past for a chance at a future?

More importantly, do I even *want* that? I've been living my life for me for the past twelve years without ever considering dating another man. And now because of *one* guy, I'm willing to change all of that? That doesn't sound healthy.

"It only takes one, you know. The right one."

Noelle's words pull me back to the conversation. "Wait, what?"

"Sperm. I had my second implantation almost two weeks ago, remember?"

"Oh, yes. That's right." Thankful that we're moving on to a different topic, I immerse myself in the conversation. "So when can you take a test?"

"Technically, not until Wednesday, but I got a few of those that are supposed to detect early, so I might try one tonight or tomorrow." She's beaming with excitement, but I see reservation in her eyes, too.

Charlotte reaches for the champagne to fill us all up. "I would wait for the morning. They say your morning pee is the best one."

"I know, I'm just excited. And nervous. I'm trying not to get my hopes up because being disappointed last time was rough. But I don't know . . . I just feel good about it this time."

I pull her into my side. "Then keep that positivity, and let us know as soon as you find out the results. I mean, we could all drive over in the morning and be there with you for support if you need us to. I can chant through the bathroom door while you pee if it will help."

Noelle shoves me off. "I think I'll be okay."

"The offer still stands if you want it."

For the rest of the meal, we discuss Charlotte's upcoming wedding and the Puppy Palooza event next month that I was able to get the Bolts to be a part of.

By the time we're all full and the champagne has worn off, I'm more than ready to head home and take a nap, which is what I do most Sundays after brunch. But as I head toward my car, Amelia comes up behind me and pulls on my arm.

"Hey."

I spin to face her, grateful that she's alone. "What's up?"

"I wanted to talk to you about Garret."

"Oh." My pulse instantly spikes. "Okay . . ."

"Garret isn't the one who needs the advice, is he, Pen?"

Our eyes bounce back and forth as she waits for me to reply. And without thinking about it too hard, I finally cave. "I think you already know the answer to that question."

"I think I do, too, but I want to hear you say it."

"Yes," I manage to croak out as she smiles softly. "I wasn't talking about Garret."

"Wanna talk?" She gestures to my car, and I nod, unlocking the doors so we can both slide in. Once we're comfortable, she grabs my hand and holds it in hers over the center console.

"What's going on? I know you're hiding something, and the only reason I didn't call you out on it in front of the girls is because I feel like it's a big thing, Pen. And if you're not willing to tell us all, there has to be a reason. You never hold back talking about anything normally, so I'm not going to lie, I'm a little concerned." She stares at me, and my heart starts racing even faster. "I would never have gotten through all of the crap with Ethan if it wasn't for you. So now, if you'll let me, I'd like to return the favor."

I sigh and lean my head back against the headrest. "I met someone."

"I kind of figured. Is this the man you, or should I say Garret, had a one-night stand with?"

I scoff. "Yeah."

"Okay. So what happened?"

Twisting my head so I can see her again, I finally admit my conundrum out loud. "I slept with Maddox Taylor back in March." Her eyes widen, but she doesn't say anything. "We met at the Zio's Vodka party my boss asked me to run point on. Initially, I blew him off. But he was relentless and charming." I turn back to stare out the front windshield again. "I felt something with him, Amelia . . . something I haven't felt in twelve years."

"Does this have to do with your young love you mentioned a few weeks ago?"

All I can do is nod because I feel emotional and am afraid to speak.

"I see."

But then I decide to rip off the Band-Aid because I know Amelia won't judge me. And maybe it's time to let it out. "He was a football player, too. And he . . . died."

I hear her deep exhale. "I'm so sorry, Penelope. My God, you've been carrying this around for twelve years, haven't you?"

"Yeah."

Stroking the back of my hand with her thumb, she stays quiet for a moment, giving me some time to process the fact that I finally spoke about the confusion I'm feeling. And I'm grateful for that because I'm barely holding it together right now. My hands are shaking, and my heart is galloping in my chest. But knowing that she's here and now someone else knows has also given me a slice of relief.

Amelia rubs my hand again and clears her throat. "So back to Maddox for a second. Based on what you said in Frankie's when we thought you were talking about Garret, is Maddox trying to date you?"

"I guess? I mean, yes and no." I run a hand through my hair. "Obviously, I didn't think I'd ever see the guy again. He was in town for a few days, but he played for New Orleans. He wasn't supposed to be in California ever again, so I thought I was safe. That's why I gave in to what I felt for him. The choice to be with him is one I wouldn't have wavered on before because I have always stayed away from athletes ever since Jacob. But Maddox was . . . enticing, to say the least."

"I remember that. Even in college, you wouldn't even smile in an athlete's direction."

"Exactly. So when I decided to go for it, I convinced myself it was just a fluke. I gave in to my body's reaction to him, but there was something different about him. Obviously, I didn't anticipate him being traded, and I sure as hell did not anticipate being assigned to work for the Bolts, yet here I am." I tuck my leg underneath me as I turn to face her again. "This is my job, Amelia. And Maddox is my client now. I tried to get him to understand that nothing more can happen between us, but he keeps telling me that he's not taking no for an answer. That he won't stop believing that us crossing paths again happened for a reason."

"Wow. And how does that make you feel? Do you want to explore something with him?"

"I . . . I can't decide. On one hand, I can say without a shadow of a doubt that it's been twelve years since a man has made me feel anything close to what Maddox makes me feel."

"Which is?"

I stare out the front windshield as I put my thoughts into words. "Like I want to see him every chance I can, like I want to talk to him just to find out what's going to come out of his mouth, that I just want to be in his presence." A smile graces my lips as I recall our previous conversations so far. "He's cocky, but in a charming way. He tells me dirty jokes to lighten the mood or help me relax when he senses that I'm stressed. And he even sent me calla lilies twice now because he says they remind him of me."

"Your tattoo?"

"Yeah."

"But he makes me laugh." I chuckle, thinking about how he uses humor to defuse a situation just like I do. "He's unexpected, but he's also comforting—being around him makes me feel like this girl I left behind in Ohio . . ."

"He reminds you of home."

I close my eyes. "He reminds me of a lot of things—and of Jacob."

"Was that . . ."

"Yeah."

She takes a deep breath and waits for me to look at her again. "Look, I can speak to you as a therapist, or I can speak to you as your friend. But either way, I have one question to ask you."

"Okay . . ."

"If Maddox wasn't a football player, if he wasn't your client, and all of the other circumstances were the same, would you be hesitating as much about what to do?"

"Um . . ."

She holds her palm up. "Don't answer yet; just think about it. Because, like I told you when we thought you were talking about Garret, if it's just fear, you can work past that. But if it's something else, you need to find out what's holding you back and work through it. I've known you for a long time, Penelope, and I always knew there had to be something you were keeping locked inside all of these years, something you've used humor, sex, and vulgar language to cover up."

"You have to admit I am funny, though."

She chuckles. "You are. But I also know that you have one of the biggest hearts of anyone I know. You love fiercely, and you have a protective streak of us girls that is not to be messed with. There are so many parts of you that deserved to be loved, too, even the parts you keep hidden. I'm not saying Maddox is the man for you, but if he's making you feel like a piece of the old you is resurfacing, I think you owe it to yourself to find out why he makes you feel that way—and if letting her out is really as bad of a thing as you think it is."

Chapter 9

Maddox

"Nice job today." Hayden comes up behind me in the locker room, wiping the water from his hair with a towel. The team had our first OTA today with a full roster, and I have to say, we have some work to do, but things look promising.

"Thanks, QB. Young has some speed on him," he replies, referencing the rookie wide receiver the team drafted who proved his skills during rookie camp. "I think he's going to be a solid addition to the offense."

"I agree. We just need to get those plays down now. Most of the work will happen during training camp, but the more we can mesh together before then, the more productive camp will be with the entire team there."

"Time to get our bromance brewing, then. I don't want Penelope to think we're slacking." He winks as he drops his towel and reaches for a pair of briefs. "My plan tonight is to stuff my face, study a bit, and then get to bed early so I'm fresh for the kids tomorrow." He shoots finger guns at me as he snaps the band of his underwear around his waist. "I can't wait to see what Penelope has in store for us."

About half the team is going to the Los Angeles Children's Hospital tomorrow to visit children in the cancer ward and those who are recovering from illness and surgery. This is one of the first major events that Penelope signed us up for to build the team's image and to give back to the community, and I'd be lying if I said I haven't been counting down the days until I get to see her again.

Between the draft and the workouts, we haven't crossed paths too much. And I've been trying to back off so I wouldn't scare her away even more. I can tell she's skittish, that she's fighting herself and her attraction toward me, even though we both know the risks given our professional relationship now. I'm fairly certain that if our jobs weren't such an issue, she would be much more willing to oblige my request to get to know each other better.

My gut is telling me that taking it slow and steady with her is the right thing to do, but I also don't want her to think that I'm going to give up without a fight.

It's why I sent her the flowers I noticed etched into her skin and candy that reminds me of the way she tasted the night we met. It's why I hope to break down her walls a bit more tomorrow while we're at the hospital, show her who I am and that she doesn't have to be scared of me.

I want her to know that my interest in her is for more than just sex. Don't get me wrong—the woman made me lose my fucking mind the night we slept together. Details about her body and the things it can do have plagued me since then. But now I want to know and discover even more.

I won't deny flirting with her, telling her dirty jokes, or reminding her of how good we were together is becoming a favorite pastime of mine, especially because of the way her cheeks flame and fire burns from her eyes.

After the draft, rookie camp occupied most of my time as I watched the potential players fight for a spot on the team permanently, not to mention meeting with the coaching staff to talk strategy. But tomorrow, we'll come face-to-face for the first time in over a week, and my body is primed just thinking about it.

Playing a professional sport gives me so many opportunities and freedoms that quite often are taken for granted by other players. I recognized that when I signed my first contract, and I vowed not to be one of them. So during my six years on my former team, I volunteered and made appearances a lot during my off-season, giving back where I could. It's why I started the football camp in my hometown, and it's why when Penelope suggested visiting the Children's Hospital, I was on board. I know the entire team will benefit from the humbling experience it's sure to be.

Not only that, but it will give me a chance to show her another side of me, the one that isn't just a professional football player— the one who has his own fears, too.

"You're serious?" Colton Cross, one of the defensive linemen, asks as we stand in a semi-circle listening to Penelope explain the rules and activities for our visit today.

She holds up one of the wigs and smiles proudly. "Yes."

Hayden stands beside me and rubs his hands together. "I am so fucking in. This is gonna be great."

Colton huffs. "A tea party? You want us to dress up for a fucking tea party?"

Penelope stands her ground, placing a hand on her hip. "Yes, I do. These kids are stuck in this hospital for weeks at a time battling illness, cancer, and recovering from life-altering surgery while you get to run around a football field tackling grown men to the ground while getting paid millions of dollars to do it. So yeah, Colton Cross—I want you to dress up and make them smile, unless you're too scared that wearing a dress and wig will jeopardize your manhood?"

Holy fuck, I think I'm in love.

Colton rolls his eyes but relents, snatching the wig from her hands. "Fine."

"Thank you. And I'll make sure to get plenty of pictures of you to use as blackmail if you feel the need to fight me again."

Hayden steps in front of Penelope, wielding a fairy wand like a sword. "Don't worry, Penelope, I'll defend you."

She laughs and then starts handing out costume accessories to the guys. "Thanks, Hayden."

Even though Penelope eloquently proved her own point, I feel like now's the appropriate time to step up as the unofficial leader of this team and hammer home the expectations of my fellow players.

"I don't want to hear anyone else bitching about this, either, all right? Penelope has put a lot of time and energy into this event, so let's make those kids' days, and remember that being healthy is something we shouldn't take for granted."

A bunch of my teammates nod in agreement, Colton glares at me as he pushes a long, black wig on his head, and Vince smirks as I turn around and come face-to-face with Penelope.

"I think I had it handled, Taylor."

People move around us now, the bustle drowning out our voices a little. "I know you did, but I wanted to make sure they heard something from me, too. Cross is lucky I didn't break his nose for his piss-poor attitude."

"Fighting in front of the kids isn't considered appropriate."

I look around the room and then back to her, grinning now. "I don't see any kids yet."

We stand there in a silent stare-off until Hayden comes up to us, ending the moment.

"What do you think?" He twirls around in a sky-blue dress that sparkles when the light hits it with a curly blond wig and tiara on his head. He's still wielding his wand.

"You are the prettiest girl at the ball, Hayden." Penelope giggles while prompting him to keep spinning.

"I know. I gotta say, if football doesn't work out, I wouldn't mind dressing up and doing this professionally. It's kind of fun."

Vince comes up to us now, studying Hayden while shaking his head. "Dear lord."

When I glance over at him, he's in a pink-and-purple ruffled gown and a pink rhinestone tiara, which only makes his bald head glisten even more under the fluorescent lights.

"You're one to talk. You look like Gru from *Despicable Me 2*," I say, fighting my laughter.

"Hey, I've seen that movie, so I'll take that as a compliment." He puffs out his chest. "He's a kick-ass dad, and I like to think I am myself, too. He dressed up so his daughter wouldn't be disappointed. And I'm telling you what, these kids are gonna love this, Penelope." He turns to her now. "I play dress up with my daughters all the time, so this doesn't even faze me. But just know you did good."

"Maybe next time you can bring your girls, Vince," she suggests. "I'd love to meet them."

"They're six and three, so not quite old enough yet. But you bet that when they get older, I'll be dragging them to stuff like this so they understand just how good they have it." He grabs a wand and taps it on my head, the plastic actually hurting for a second. "Now it's time to transform this prince into a princess. Come on, man. Let's find you a dress that makes your butt look good."

Hayden begins to twist in an attempt to see his own butt. "Fuck, does my ass look good in my dress? Should I change?"

Penelope pinches the bridge of her nose. "First, no one can see your ass, Hayden. And second, please try not to use the f-word around the kids."

"Oh, shit. Okay."

"No 'shit,' either."

I let Vince lead me away and over to the rack with all of the dresses. I'm not sure where she found costume gowns that would fit three-hundred-pound men, but I'm not surprised that she did. She's a fucking rockstar.

"So what was that little speech for earlier?" Vince says to me, lowering his voice so people can't overhear.

"What speech?"

"Your little outburst after Cross got lippy and Penelope put him in his place. Seems she had it handled to me."

I take a dark-green gown off the rack and slide the zipper

down so I can pull it over my head. "I didn't say she didn't. I just didn't want anyone else to bitch. She doesn't deserve that." Yanking the dress down my torso, I slip my arms through the straps. "She's put a shit-ton of work into this, so we need to, too."

He eyes me suspiciously. "Are you sure that's the only reason?"

"Why? What are you insinuating, Vince?"

"Call me crazy, but I just sense something between you two." He twirls a necklace around his finger, almost hitting me in the face with it before he stops. "If I didn't know any better, I'd say you have a little thing for Miss Klein."

Fuck. Could I really have been that transparent? "I mean, I've definitely enjoyed getting to know her so far."

"But . . ."

"But what? She's working for the team."

"So?"

I freeze. "So?"

He leans in closer and lowers his voice even more. "I'm not one for sneaking around, but if something's there, I say go for it. Don't ask for permission. Make the decision, and if something happens, just apologize later." Leaning back, he winks at me.

Even though in my mind I had already decided on that, it's nice to know that someone else would do the same thing in my shoes. "Thanks, man."

"No problem. Just be careful. We do have a lot of attention on us right now, and even more is coming. But women like that? They don't come around that often. I should know I snagged one myself and married her the second I could."

With a pat on my shoulder, he walks back to where Penelope is starting to gather the players before we go meet the kids. I reach down and grab a red-haired wig from the basket and fix it securely on my head.

"All right, guys. Just go in there, and be yourselves. Have fun, even though seeing some of these kids and what they're going through may not be very fun. But they're really excited for this, and I know they're going to appreciate it."

My teammates start to file out of the room, and I hang back nonchalantly so I can have a moment alone with her. Once the last guy leaves, I make my move.

She looks at me and instantly tries to hide her smile. "Oh boy, Mr. Taylor. You look like a modern day Merida . . . you know, if she took steroids and threw a football for a living."

I brush an errant curl from my face. "I always liked Merida, though. She was badass and didn't need a man to validate her existence. I think a strong, independent woman is sexy, if you haven't caught on to that by now."

She squints, dropping her eyes up and down my body. "You watch Disney movies?"

"Yeah, I do. My cousin's kids happen to have quite the collection, and whenever I go home to visit, her daughter always asks me to watch a few with her."

Her face softens as she locks eyes with me. "That's really sweet."

"What can I say? I guess I'm just a sweet guy."

"Sweet and dirty," she teases. "You haven't told me a joke today yet. Are you feeling all right?"

"Do you *want* me to tell you a dirty joke, Penelope? Could it be that you're actually starting to enjoy our little interactions?"

She twists so I can't see her face, but I hear her response that's just above a whisper. "Maybe . . ."

"Then we should interact more, don't you think?"

Sighing, she spins around to face me again, looking far more irritated than she did just a few seconds ago. "Why didn't you ever text me back?"

"What?"

"When I texted you about the flowers and the massage you left me in Vegas . . . you never texted me back."

"I never got a text from you." Lifting the bottom of the dress up, I reach down to pull my phone from my pocket, open the screen, and scroll through my messages at the speed of light. "No. Nothing is here." I may have programmed her phone number into my phone as soon as I left our first meeting. It was on her business card, so I figured that was okay. And even though I wanted to reach out a hundred times, I also wanted her to make the first move, so I kept my thoughts to myself.

"Are you sure?"

"If you texted me, Penelope, I would have fucking replied."

"Oh. Well, then, something must have happened."

"Maybe you have my number wrong, because believe me, it's all I can do to wait patiently for you to meet me halfway here."

"Maddox, I . . ."

Hayden pops his head in at that very moment, and the urge to punch him in the nose comes on so strong, I have to stop myself from lunging in his direction. "Yo, QB . . . you coming?"

"Yeah, be right there." He nods and leaves as quickly as he came. Turning back to Penelope, I say, "Can we finish this conversation later?"

"Uh, sure."

"I'm serious. I wanna talk about this, about us."

"Okay." Her lips curve in a small smile that has a surge of hope inflating in my chest.

"Okay. Now if you'll excuse me, I have a party to attend." I swing my wig over my shoulder and traipse out the door toward the room where the kids are waiting, beaming with pride from the laugh I hear as I walk away.

❧

"And what is your dog's name?"

"Baxter." The young girl I'm sitting with shows me a picture of him from her phone. Sarah—as she told me her name is—holds up a photo of a wrinkly bulldog with a snaggletooth that I can't help but smile at.

"What a good-lookin' man."

"He's the best. I can't wait to have him sleeping in my bed with me again."

"I bet. When do you get to go home?"

She coughs and adjusts the oxygen tube under her nose. "Hopefully, Monday."

Sarah has been battling Hodgkin's Lymphoma for two years now, and as of last week, her family and doctors realized there are no further treatments to try. The cancer has taken over her body, so she's going home to live out the rest of her life and be with her loved ones before she passes.

I'd be lying if I said I wasn't fighting back tears right now. But this is exactly why I try to give back my time as much as possible. I never want to take for granted the life I get to live.

"Well, I'm sure he's excited to see you, too."

"My mom will FaceTime with me and put the camera up to his

face so he can see and hear my voice, and he always licks the phone."

"He loves you."

"I love him, too." She coughs again. "Would you mind getting me a drink of water, please?" she asks.

"Of course." I rise from the table where Sarah is sitting in her wheelchair and walk over to the table full of refreshments to fill up a cup of water for her. I glance at the trays of food—cookies, fruit, and finger sandwiches—and decide to make her a little plate as well, even though I'm not sure if she's hungry. But I don't want to return empty-handed.

As I walk back to the table, I catch Penelope staring, so I flash her a wink before taking my seat again and asking Sarah more questions about her dog.

Penelope has been busy mingling with the players and kids, snapping pictures and delivering craft materials around the room so the kids can work on something as we talk to them. Surprisingly, Colton Cross seems to be having a great time talking to a teenage boy who fractured both of his legs in a car accident and is doing physical therapy here to regain his mobility. He's a big football fan, too, so we signed a jersey for him and every other kid who wanted one.

"You know what's missing from this party?" Hayden comes up to me, resting his hand on my shoulder.

"What?"

"Music. I've got this kick-ass dress and no music to dance to."

Sarah giggles beside me.

"Well, how about we fix that?" I turn to Sarah. "I'll be right back, okay?"

"Sure. I'm not going anywhere."

Hayden takes my place as I search the room for Penelope. When I find her, I head in her direction, still rocking my Merida-inspired look.

"Hey, Penelope?"

"What's up?" She drops her camera from her face.

"Is there any way we could play some music for the kids?"

"Was there a request for music?"

"Yeah, from me."

She laughs. "Feeling like you need to dance in your fancy dress?"

"I mean, why waste a good outfit, right?" I spin around. "Actually, I think it would be fun for the kids and liven up the party a bit."

Nodding, she reaches into her pocket for her phone. "What shall we play? I have a Bluetooth speaker I can pair my phone to."

"I know just the song. May I?" Holding my hand out to her, she places her phone in my palm hesitantly and then moves over to her bag to grab her speaker, turning it on. I tap to search for the song I'm looking for and wait for it to play. When it does, her eyes widen. "Really?"

"You can never go wrong with Whitney." I hand her phone back to her just as Hayden jumps up from his seat.

"Oh, hell yeah!" he shouts as the opening beats to "I Wanna Dance with Somebody" ring out from the speaker. "Let's dance, everyone!"

I run over to Sarah and help her from her chair, holding her to me as we sway and sing along to the song. The entire room rushes to their feet, and giggles echo as everyone laughs and dances their hearts out. Grown men who tackle each other for a living are spinning around in wigs and dresses, having the time of their lives. And the kids—they're smiling, laughing, and living.

It's a fucking phenomenal moment I hope I never forget.

Sarah doesn't last long, so when she feels weak, I help her back into her chair and make sure she's comfortable. My eighties playlist keeps blaring from the speaker, "Girls Just Wanna Have Fun" following the ballad before it. But when I stand and look for Penelope, I catch a flash of her hair flying through the doorway as she exits the room.

"Sarah, I'll be back in a minute, okay?"

"Don't worry about me." She waves me off, and I waste no time hunting down the woman I've really wanted to be alone with all day.

"Penelope," I whisper through the hall as she walks away, never turning back to acknowledge my presence. In fact, her pace picks up, and then she turns to her right, disappearing from view as I hear the telltale sound of a door opening and closing.

Following in her footsteps, I open the same door and let out the breath I was holding when I find her inside. Her arms are wrapped around her body, and her head is leaning right out of the window in the room as if she craves the fresh air.

"Hey. Is everything okay?"

"You didn't need to follow me."

"Well, I wanted to make sure that you're all right. Is that a problem?" She doesn't answer me. "What's going on?"

"That's a hard question to answer right now, Maddox."

"Can I help you with anything? Is something wrong?"

She sighs, but I hear the tremble in her voice. "It's just not fair."

"What's not?"

"Those kids like Sarah," she whispers, and then I see her reach up and brush her face. *Is she crying?*

Slowly, I take a few steps toward her, ripping the wig from my head and tossing it on a table before placing my arm gently on her shoulder. "I know. It fucking sucks."

"Some of them will never get to dance at a school dance or at their weddings. They won't ever know what it's like to fall in love or drive a car. They haven't even lived, and yet they're stronger than most of the men in that room." Slowly, she faces me, and I can see the pain in her eyes.

"Yup. Moments like these always remind me that growing old is a privilege, not a right."

She smiles softly now. "I love that."

"I keep those words fresh in my mind on the days when I feel like my life or my job is hard. Not everyone gets to live to be seventy or eighty. Not everyone gets to make their dreams come true like I have. That's why I always try not to take my job for granted, give back when I can, and live life to the fullest—to not let opportunity pass me by."

She bobs her head and then shuts her eyes, dropping her arms from her body. "You sure are something else, Maddox Taylor."

"I hope that was meant as a good thing."

"It is, but it shouldn't be." Reaching up, she digs her hands into her hair and takes a step back from me, shaking her head and glancing away. "God, we shouldn't be alone right now. You shouldn't have followed me in here." She points to the door. "You're supposed to be out there with the kids, showing the fans who you are and being the NFL quarterback that everyone knows you as. You're supposed to be building excitement for this next season so they don't think you're pissed about your new team, not worrying about me and my issues at the moment. You shouldn't be sending me flowers or booking me massages . . ."

Taking another step closer to her, I pull her hands from her hair and grasp her upper arms gently, forcing her to look at me. "I will always be grateful for the life I have and the shots I've taken because they've led me here. But right here, right now? I feel like this is where I'm supposed to be at the moment, regardless of what the public is saying, Penelope. I had to make sure that you are okay."

She blinks up at me before I point off to the side of the room.

"Those people? The fans who are watching behind screens? They don't know who I really am. And they don't have to know everything about me in order for me to do my job—including who I spend my private time with."

Her eyes widen.

"But those shots I've taken? It's because I've known the risk was worth the reward. And *you* are worth it. Us together—our connection and chemistry—is worth it to me. It's why I followed you in here . . . because I care about you. I can't stop thinking about you, and as hard as this will be, I can't deny that I don't care what the consequences may be. All I'm asking for is a chance for us to figure out what this is between us without pressure from the outside."

"I have a past, Maddox." Suddenly, I can see her fight is dwindling, but I'm glad. Because her voice is raw right now, so I know this is the real woman coming through, the one who has me wrapped around her finger. "I've been hurt."

And there it is. Her words strike a chord and give me just a morsel of the reason she's fighting this so hard.

"Fuck, I'm sorry, sweetheart. I've been there, too." I lower my head and rest my forehead against hers, breathing her in. Then I whisper, "But there's very little reward without a little pain, Penelope. Don't you feel this?" I take her hand and place it on my chest, right over my beating heart. "This is how my heart beats every time I'm around you."

"I wish I didn't feel it, too, but I'd be lying if I said that I don't—that I'm not curious." She growls and pulls away as I release her from my hands, lifting part of her shield up again. "But how is this supposed to even work? It's not like we can be seen together out in public, just the two of us. One picture snapped at the right time would create a clusterfuck."

"I can be creative. And hell, that's what phones are for. We can talk all night long like two teenagers sneaking around." I waggle my eyebrows at her. "It'll be fun."

A hint of a smile graces her lips. But then she swallows, her lips fall again, and that little divot between her brow returns as she stares into my eyes. "Are you sure about this?"

"About eighty percent." I shrug as her mouth drops open.

"That's it?" She throws her hands up. "That doesn't make me feel better about this situation—"

"How can we ever be one-hundred-percent sure of anything, Pen?" I cut her off. "Life is too short to question whether certain things will work out the way we want them to. Sometimes you just have to have faith and jump in, make a decision from your gut." I point to my stomach, and when she doesn't say anything, I continue. "I *like* you. I want to know everything about you. I just need you to let me. And I promise, I'll give you all the juicy dirt on me, too."

Rolling her eyes, she says, "Fine. But we have to take this slow. I don't do relationships, Maddox. What you got from me already is the extent of time I usually spend with a man, and I won't apologize for it. How I've lived my life is how I've been surviving, and it's been working just fine—until you came along."

Wrapping my arms around her waist, I pull her in so her palms land on my chest. She gasps. "I can go slow. I can be patient with you, Penelope. Hell, you made me work for your attention that first night, so I have no problem putting in the work again." Nuzzling my nose against her cheek, I feel her relax a bit in my arms. And then I whisper in her ear, "And the next time I get you in my bed again, I won't let you run away." Leaning back, I find her eyes again. "But know this—this isn't just about sex for me. As often as I relive that night and as much as I want a repeat, that's not the only reason I'm pursuing you. I want you to trust me on that."

"No sex?"

"I didn't say that. But maybe we take things a little slow . . ." My dick is strongly objecting to this idea, but I know this arrangement is necessary to help her understand my intentions here.

"I don't know . . . I like things hard and fast."

"Fuck. At some point, that will be absolutely necessary. But right now, the only thing I want to do is taste your lips again."

She inhales sharply but doesn't say anything, so I take that as my cue to make my move.

Gently, I cup the back of her neck and stare down into her eyes before cocking my head to the side, going in at the perfect angle. The space separating our mouths diminishes, and when her soft lips meld against mine and she grips my shoulder and pulls me closer, my entire body comes alive.

It's a soft press at first, and I wait to feel her out, to make sure that this is what she wants. But when she grabs the back of my neck and brings me closer, I know. This is exactly what she wants —and thank fuck.

Like the flip of a switch, Penelope takes over my mouth, moving her soft, pillowy lips over mine. God, her mouth has entranced me since that first night, and tasting her again now is even more addicting than it was the first time—and that's how I know this isn't only lust. Because kissing Penelope again just feels *right*, deep in my bones. Which scares me but gives me hope at the same time.

I'd thought I'd been with the right person before, and then I learned very quickly that you can think you know someone, but they can surprise you when you least expect it and show their true colors.

But right now, this need and desire I feel for her is more than just physical, so I owe it to both of us to see what it means. This could crash and burn and be a monumental mistake, or it could be something real. I just hope we both survive the process of figuring out which it is.

We both groan when our tongues touch, sparking my need for her even more. I bury one of my hands in her hair and control her head as desperation builds in my veins, spilling out into this kiss. The same kiss I've done nothing but dream about since I saw her that day in her office.

We stand there for God knows how long devouring each other in slow, drugging, heated kisses as we grip each other tighter and shut out the outside world. And then I reluctantly break us apart, waiting for her eyes to lift and lock on to mine.

When they do, I see nothing but the same desperation I feel staring back at me.

"Fuck," I breathe out, and her answering giggles as she rests her forehead on my chest tell me she feels the same way I do right now.

"Why do you have to be so good at that?"

"I could say the same to you. That kiss was . . ."

"Yeah." She smooths her hands up my chest and lifts her eyes back to mine. "Although next time, I think it would be even better if you weren't wearing a man-sized princess dress."

My eyes drop down to the gown I completely forgot is still on me. "Jesus."

Laughing again, she reaches up and brushes my wild hair from my face. "It's okay. If anyone can pull off wearing that and still kiss me so hard that my panties are officially ruined, it would be you, Maddox Taylor."

Groaning, I lean in to nuzzle her neck. "Fuck, you can't say things like that, Penelope. I've got to go back to the kids, and I probably shouldn't do that with a hard-on."

"Don't worry, your dress should cover it."

I think about what she just said. "Damn, you're right. I think I should wear more dresses around you, then, since you seem to make my dick go from six to noon every time you're near."

She playfully shoves me. "Shut up, Maddox. Now go. I'm sure the guys are looking for you, and I need to get back out there for a group shot and then clean up."

I pull her into me one more time. "Can I call you later then?"

"You have my number?"

"From your business card. And this way, you'll have mine, my correct number."

"Oh, yeah. That makes sense. Sure." She's fighting her smile, but I can tell she likes the idea. Hell, I do, too. I can't wait to find out what makes this woman tick.

"Then look for my call." I press one more soft kiss to her lips. "Talk to you later, Penelope."

"You, too."

I release her, grab my wig and place it back on my head, twisting it in place, and then head for the door. And as I walk down the hall, there's an extra pep in my step because Penelope just gave me an in—and I'm not going to let her regret it.

Chapter 10

Penelope

As soon as I step through the front door to my townhouse, I sigh. Today went well, despite the emotional response seeing the kids evoked in me. And then there's Maddox and his regard for my feelings.

How can he be so sweet and forthright about his feelings but also kiss me breathless and make me want to mount him in a hospital room? The man has confidence and swagger in spades, and fighting my attraction to him has been a challenge I finally have accepted that I might not want to fight anymore.

I set my purse on the counter and plug my phone into the charger before I head upstairs to change my clothes and order something to eat. Normally, I don't mind cooking for myself, but today was a long one, and I have no desire to dirty my clean kitchen.

The townhome I purchased three years ago has become my own little sanctuary. With white walls and cabinetry, every room feels open and bright, and little pops of purple and gray give it that feminine feel. There are three bedrooms and two baths, more than enough space for a single gal like me, but the price was right, so I couldn't pass it up. It's not like I ever planned on filling those rooms with kids or welcoming a man into my home, but it's nice to have ownership over a piece of property I know serves as an investment as well.

After I toss my hair up in a messy bun to get it off my neck, throw on a cami with no bra and my favorite pair of gray sweat shorts, I head back downstairs, settling on sushi for dinner, and then call in my order to my favorite local place and settle into the couch as I wait for my food to be delivered.

Flipping through Netflix, trying to decide what to watch this evening, I'm startled by my phone ringing. I know Maddox is supposed to call tonight—at least that's what he said—but I didn't think he would call this early.

Unfamiliar tingles swarm in my belly as I stand from the couch and head over to my phone. But when I see who's actually calling me—and it's not Maddox—the excitement I was feeling deflates, replaced by uneasiness.

The contact picture I chose for my mom flashes across the screen. It's from my high school graduation, and both of us are smiling brightly at the camera. Jacob's frame is in the background as he was talking to my dad, but his face was out of the shot. However, I know he was there, and every time this picture shows up on my phone, I'm reminded of that.

But that girl in the picture—me—she's a girl who was so naïve to the pain the real world was about to show her, all smiles and tears of happiness. Too bad I couldn't have prepared her for what was about to happen just a few weeks later.

I haven't spoken to my mom in weeks, but that's normal for us. Our communication has become sporadic since I left home, headed for UCLA, and I haven't returned. It's not for a lack of trying from my parents. It's been my choice not to go back to a place that only holds painful memories for me. I ran away from there and vowed not to go back—ever.

Knowing I have time to actually hold a conversation, I decide it's probably a good idea to let my mother know that her only daughter is still here.

"Hi, Mom."

"She lives!" My mother laughs at herself. "I was beginning to think I might have to come out to California and see for myself that you're still breathing."

"Dramatic, much?"

"Where do you think you got it from, darling?"

My mother's right. My loud, opinionated, take-no-prisoners attitude is a direct inheritance from her, and I'm damn proud of it. They say some men don't like loud women—well, I don't like men who can't handle a woman who isn't afraid to voice her opinion, laugh out loud, or stand up for herself. And lord knows, I'm a little bit of all three.

"I got it from my mama."

"Yeah, you did. So how's it going? It's been awhile since we've spoken. Anything new?"

"Uh, yeah, actually. Work has been crazy. I got assigned to a sports team, so that's been interesting."

She goes silent for a minute. "Which team?" she asks hesitantly because she knows the sensitivity of the subject.

"The Los Angeles Bolts."

"Oh, boy. Are you okay, baby? I thought you told your boss you didn't want anything to do with athletes?"

"I did, but he blew smoke up my ass and told me there's no one else he would want for such a high-profile client, so here I am managing over fifty grown men, making them dress up in princess ballgowns and do charity work while smiling for the cameras."

Pride comes through in her voice. "Well, at least you've shown them what you're capable of right out of the gate."

"That was the plan."

"So what exactly are you trying to accomplish for the team?"

I spend a few minutes explaining my goals for the next few months, leaving out my inappropriate and confusing relationship with Maddox.

"Well, I hate to say it, but it sounds like your boss put the right person on the account."

"You have to say that because you're my mom."

"No, baby, I don't. But I know that you are damn good at your job. Charles is right. And even though I know this must be difficult for you, I'm proud of you for pushing through."

I sigh, settling deeper into the couch. "It's definitely been taxing."

"Bring some memories up for you?"

"You could say that."

"You know, it's been a long time, Penelope. People have moved on here . . . maybe it's time you did, too."

"I have moved on, Mom."

She sighs. "No, baby, you ran away."

Damn. She just called me on my shit. And now you can see exactly where I get it from.

"Look, everyone deals with grief in their own way, but maybe it's time to forgive yourself, even though you did nothing wrong. And perhaps working with this football team will help you heal a little." We both sit there in silence for a minute, waiting the other person out before she finally says, "We miss you, Penelope. Your room is still the same way you left it all those years ago. It's been months since we've seen you, and that's only because I convinced your dad to spend Christmas in California this year. He nearly had a heart attack when we entered your home and you had a Christmas tree the size of a small bush. Life is too short—"

"I get it, Mom. I'm falling short as a daughter." I hate that I've hurt my parents through my absence, but have they stopped to maybe consider that it's because I don't want to be hurt by going back home? By seeing places and people everywhere I turn that remind me of a life I buried and don't want to think about ever again?

"You are not failing us. We just wish there was something we could do to help you. I would hate for you to end up alone because you carry around this guilt that you refuse to let go of."

"Well, I'm pretty used to it by now, so . . ."

"Aw, Penelope. Jacob would want you to move on, sweetie. He would want you to live and love again."

Just the mention of his name brings tears to my eyes. This rush of emotions that has broken free from the dam I built to keep it back is hitting me harder and harder lately—and I know exactly who is responsible for it.

"I did meet someone, actually."

"What?" she practically whispers. "When?"

"It's complicated and barely a thing, but about a month ago," I reply, considering mine and Maddox's first encounter barely a stepping stone for where we are now. Although, the more that I think about it, that night is why I've been so hellbent on keeping him at a distance—because he's the one who broke that dam.

"That's incredible, baby. And how does he treat you?"

Growing up, my mother always prefaced any conversation about a boy I liked with that question: How does he treat you? Not, is he handsome? Not, does he come from a good family? But, how does he treat you? She said the answer to that question was more important than any other one she would ask next. I remember having this same conversation with her when Jacob moved to town all those years ago.

It's good to know some things never change.

I smile, thinking about how Maddox's actions today spoke volumes about the man he is. "He isn't afraid to let me know how he feels about me, which is refreshing. Obviously, there's attraction there, but it's more than that. He's genuine and funny, and he has a big heart. He actually reminds me a lot of—"

"That's not a bad thing, Penelope," she says, cutting me off. "Any woman would be lucky to experience that kind of love twice in her life."

I scoff. "Yeah, well, we're not anywhere close to love. I'm just . . . feeling things out for right now."

"Nothing wrong with that. Hell, my motherly heart is bursting at the seams just knowing that you're opening yourself up again."

"It's proving to be more difficult than I thought, but I'm trying, Mom."

"That's all you can do, honey." Her sigh fills the line. "Gosh, I miss you."

"I miss you, too."

"Maybe I need to make a trip out to California so we can spend some time together, just the two of us. Now that your father has retired, he's driving me a little mad." We share a laugh. "Or you could come here, you know?"

"I'm going to be very busy until the season starts, Mom. And I have no idea what my job might look like after that."

I can feel her sigh of disappointment. "Well, if you change your mind, you know where to find me. But don't be shocked if I show up on your doorstep unannounced soon."

"I'll be ready for your hug."

"I love you, Penelope."

"Love you, too, Mom."

"Keep me updated on this man."

I scoff. "Yeah. Okay."

When I hang up with my mom, my stomach lets out a growl just as the doorbell rings. Once I pay for my sushi, I grab a pair of chopsticks from the bag and dig in, standing at my kitchen island as I look out the window over my sink. The complex my townhouse is in has a courtyard in the middle of the units with a swimming pool, and a few families are out there enjoying the evening, unseasonably warm for this early in May in Los Angeles.

I finish my meal, grab my phone off the charger, and settle back into the couch, scouring Netflix for something to watch when an icon for a movie containing Robert Downey, Jr.'s face pops up on my screen, halting my scrolling.

"Damn, he looks young here." I click on the picture and read the description for *U.S. Marshalls*, a film RDJ did in 1998. His face is free of scruff and he definitely looks young enough here that I could be with him—or his dad, if you know what I mean. But it's RDJ, so you know my curiosity is piqued.

However, I barely get through the opening credits when my phone rings once more, and a number that looks familiar flashes across the screen.

This has to be Maddox and his correct number.

As I stare at the screen, I realize I must have transposed two of the digits when I texted him last week, but now nerves flutter across my skin knowing he's initiating our contact this time.

That kiss today meant something. I don't want it to, but it did. And now this conversation tonight is going to propel us down a path we can't return from.

So now here's the question: Do I sit here and talk to him all night and let my feelings break free already? Or do I initiate what I think we both want out of this arrangement?

I think I know what would make me feel more comfortable—and it's not baring my soul to this man on the phone just yet. But on the other hand, I want to hear what he has to say.

"Hello?" I answer on a shaky breath.

"Hey, Pen."

"Maddox." I bite my lip to keep from smiling, feeling like a giddy teenager from just the sound of his voice. Clearing my throat, I rein it in.

"I hope it's not too early for you. I debated calling sooner, but I wasn't sure how long you might have needed to settle in." He blows out a breath.

"You sound nervous," I tease him.

"Would you think of me differently if I said I am?"

I settle into the cushion some more, pulling my knees to my chest. "No, because I am, too."

"I've been waiting to talk to you since the second I left the hospital, Pen. You have no idea how happy I am that you're finally giving this a shot."

"Well, I answered your call, so I think that proves I'm willing to see where this goes."

He chuckles. "So what are you up to?"

"I ordered some sushi earlier and was just about to start a movie when you called."

"Oh, yeah?" I can hear the smile in his voice. "What movie?"

"*U.S. Marshalls*. Have you ever heard of it?"

He's silent for a moment. "You were watching that because Robert Downey, Jr. is in it, weren't you?"

I can't help but laugh. "Naturally."

"I don't know what I'm going to have to do to get you to see that RDJ isn't the guy for you."

"Oh, yeah? And I take it you are?"

"Obviously. And nothing against that movie, but everyone knows the best movies were from the eighties."

"The eighties?"

"Best decade of all time, babe."

"Would this explain your musical choices from earlier today?" I reach for my glass of water on the coffee table and take a sip.

"Absolutely. And I guess I'd better admit it now—that was my workout playlist we were dancing to."

I nearly spit water out across the couch. "You work out to Whitney Houston?"

Maddox laughs. "Oh, yeah. Ask Hayden. He's heard my playlist."

"Yet another surprise about you that I find absolutely charming."

"Charming, huh?"

I clear my throat as I place my glass back on the table. "I may have used that word to describe you."

"To whom?"

"My mom."

"Wow. You're already talking to your mom about me? I think this is moving a lot faster than you're aware of."

"Easy, Maddox. I didn't name you for obvious reasons. But I did tell her that I was . . . *talking* to someone."

"Well, I'm honored to be the guy you're choosing to talk to, Penelope. Honestly, I'm getting a little addicted to the sound of your voice and the sarcasm that accompanies it."

Shaking my head, I laugh. "Well, you'd better get used to it because I majored in public relations and communication, but I minored in sarcasm."

He laughs. "Good to know. So why PR, Penelope?"

"Well, it just seemed like the natural career choice for me. I was always involved in leadership classes in school, and I helped organize events in high school and college, particularly in my sorority. I have a knack for organization and being in charge, so I took my strengths and made a career out of it. What about you? Why football?"

The question seemed like the logical one to reciprocate with, but the thought of his answer makes me nervous. I've been down this road before with someone who loved the game and had a dream—and I watched that dream shatter in a matter of moments.

"What little boy who plays football doesn't dream of making it to the NFL one day? Plus, you could say I had a bit of a man crush on Troy Aikman, the QB for the Cowboys in the nineties, so I just made up my mind that I wanted to be like him, and I worked my ass off to make it happen."

"That's . . . cute."

"Cute?"

"I mean, I'm just envisioning you as a little boy staring up at a poster of Troy Aikman on your ceiling, giving yourself a pep talk about how you're going to be better than him one day." The image does make me smile. "It's adorable."

"Did you have video cameras in my room back then that I don't know about?" I laugh even harder, but he continues talking. "The truth is, I kind of looked at football like you did your career. I found something I was good at, something that required talent but tenacity as well, and I knew that if I didn't at least try to make it, I would regret it. But you know what the best part was about making it to the NFL, Pen?"

"What?" I whisper now, becoming anxious about his answer because the intent in his voice changed. This is no longer a joke, and his sincerity is shining through.

"Paying off my parents' house the first year."

"Wow."

"After everything they did for me growing up—the sacrifices, the practices, the traveling, and everything in between—that was the moment that made it all worth it."

"Maddox . . . that's . . ."

"That's me, Pen. I'm just a normal guy from a small town in Texas who is lucky enough to play football for a living. My life isn't perfect. I've got scars and regrets just like everyone else, but I also know how blessed I am, and I try not to forget that like I told you earlier today."

"I'm in awe."

"You know what the second-best part about being in the NFL is?"

"What?"

"That it led me to you."

Instantly, I'm speechless. I honestly have no words.

"You don't have to say anything to that. I know it may sound a little strong, but like I also said earlier—I know this thing between us is worth the time and energy. And I promise I'm going to prove that to you."

"Sure."

He chuckles. "I'm gonna change the subject now so you don't hang up on me, but I'm not done getting you to see that I'm being honest about wanting you, Pen."

"Okay."

"Now back to this movie. What is your movie-watching snack? Popcorn? Candy?"

"Nice segue. Honestly, it's chips."

"Chips?"

"I mean, if I'm at a movie theater, then of course I'm going to go for the greasy buttered popcorn and a box of Nestle Buncha Crunch."

"Nice combo. Salty and sweet."

"Exactly. But if I'm at home—and especially if I'm about to start or am on my period—I want Lay's Wavy Hickory BBQ potato chips."

"That's very particular, but I appreciate a woman who knows what she likes."

"I could eat an entire bag in one sitting easily. What about you?"

"Well, if it's the season, I try to keep it healthy. I'll eat some diced-up watermelon, cubed pineapple, or frozen grapes."

"That sounds way too healthy."

"But if I'm allowing myself to indulge, I want chocolate-covered raisins or a Milky Way."

"Oh, now you're speaking my language. Those are two of my favorites as well."

"Nice to know that movie snacks aren't something that will derail our relationship."

"W hat's something you wish you had more time to do?"

I'm now lying on the couch, staring up at the ceiling while my phone rests on my chest with Maddox on speaker. "Why do you ask these questions that seem so simple but really aren't?"

"The best questions are. I want to know *you*, Penelope, not just the surface stuff about you. And I want to see if I can get some ideas on how to make you fall in love with me." There's a teasing lilt to his voice, but the mention of love makes my heart rate pick up.

God, he makes me want to tell him everything, which is part of the problem anyway. Letting him in means risking being hurt again.

I fidget with the bottom of my shirt while dragging out my answer. "Easy, tiger, with the use of the l-word."

He laughs. "Yeah. Sorry. But tell me."

I let out a sigh. "Honestly, I wish I spent more time outside or at least made more of an effort to do so. You would think that living in southern California, I would make more time to visit the ocean or the mountains, but I'm always working or being there for my friends because those girls are like my family. And I haven't hiked since college, but that's something I also truly enjoy."

"So are you saying you don't mind getting a little dirty?"

The suggestive tone of his voice makes my body heat up and warmth spread to my core. "I think you already know the answer to that question, Mr. Taylor."

"God, woman, you're killing me."

I rub my thighs together, trying to ease the ache. "You started it. Now it's your turn, Maddox. Answer the question."

"Aw, well, that's easy. I wish I had more time to spend with my cousin and her kids."

"I swear, if you have a list of answers to questions that are designed to make me swoon, I'm going to be pissed."

"Aw, you're swooning for me, Pen?"

"How are you still single?"

He goes silent for a moment before he finally gives me a morsel of him that isn't so perfect. "You're not the only one who's been hurt, Penelope. It's hard to trust people given my job, and sometimes, even the people you think you know can turn around and surprise you."

"I'm sorry."

"I haven't dated since I was a sophomore in college, and even then, it was nothing serious after I broke things off with my fiancée."

My stomach drops. "You were engaged?" I ask in almost a whisper as my heart beats frantically. This detail about him is making my head spin for more reasons than one.

I can hear him blow out a breath. "Yeah. We were high school sweethearts, and I thought she was the one, but she shocked the hell out of me when I found out she was only with me for my potential career. She wanted to be a football wife, live a life where she didn't have to do anything but just spend my money. The straw that broke the camel's back for me was when I overheard a conversation between her and her best friend, where she explained how she planned to get pregnant right after we were married and then file for divorce when the baby was two. That way, she'd never have to work a day in her life with the alimony and child support I would owe her."

"Holy shit, Maddox."

"Yeah. So I get being cautious. Hell, you scare me, too, Penelope. I don't ever think I've felt this strongly this fast about a woman. But I knew if I didn't pursue you, I'd end up regretting it. I hate living with regret, especially if it's for something I had control over."

I feel like his words have a double meaning, but I don't press him further. "I'm sorry that happened to you, Maddox. Truly."

"Thank you."

My hands shake as I reach for my phone, take him off speaker, and hold it back to my ear. "Where did you come from, Maddox Taylor?" I whisper as my heart pounds and my brain accepts that I'm screwed when it comes to this guy.

"Newberry Springs, Texas, ma'am, home of the best cornbread west of the Mississippi."

"What is something you can't live without? Something that if someone asked you to give up, you'd feel like your life was ending?" he asks, changing the subject but intriguing me even further with how blatant he is about keeping this conversation going.

I glanced at my alarm clock on my nightstand earlier once I moved to my bed, but I didn't want to say anything about how late it's gotten because I don't want to end this conversation yet. We've just been talking about anything and everything as the topics shift—movies, music, my girls, places we want to travel to . . . I can't remember the last time I talked to a man like this.

Yes, you can.

I know the answer to his question immediately, but there's nothing wrong with a dramatic pause from time to time.

"Sunsets," I finally answer.

That has his voice lifting. "Sunsets? Not chocolate or wine or coffee?" he finally asks for clarification.

"Nope. Those are all things that you could find a substitute for. But never seeing a sunset again? I'd go insane. You might as well just lock me in a padded room so I can forget they ever existed."

"Why sunsets?"

Looking off to the side as memories hit me, I reply, "I just love that no two sunsets are the same. You might think they are, but they can't be, because no two days are the same. And the colors are always different, too. Some days you're blessed with oranges and pinks, and the next day you get an array of purples and blues, which happen to be my favorite." I bury my face in my pillow as I realize I just rambled on about sunsets to Maddox Taylor.

"My girl likes sunsets. Good to know."

My girl. God, it should be alarming how much I like the sound of that.

"There is one other thing I don't think I could ever live without, though," I continue, eager to hear his reaction to my answer.

"And what is that?"

"Orgasms."

A deep groan filters through the line. "Fuck, Penelope. Can't say that I disagree with that one. And just so you know, I'd be happy to deliver on those orgasms as soon as you're ready. Just say the word, and I'm there."

I giggle. "I don't need your help with that, Maddox. Seriously, you should see my battery-operated toy collection. There's no need for a man anymore in our modern society. Sorry if that bruises your ego, but it's the truth."

"No bruise to this ego, sweetheart. Toys aren't the enemy—they're like a teammate who helps you win the championship." Then he lowers his voice. "But you and I both know that it's always more fun to get to the finish line with your real-life partner in tow."

Warmth spreads through my belly, and I rub my thighs together again. "You're right about that, Mr. Taylor." I bite my lip as I think back to our last experience together, fighting with myself about inviting him over at this very moment so we can relive it and ease this ache between my legs. But I know that would just confuse things for me. For the first time in my adult life, I want to get to know a man outside of the bedroom.

So instead, I redirect our conversation. "What about you?" I ask. "What's something you can't live without? Let me guess: football?"

"I hope you would know me better by now than to assume

that's my answer. I mean, I love the game, but if my career ended tomorrow, I'd know it was for a reason, and I'd find other ways to leave my mark on this world."

"That's a bold statement."

"It's the truth. Your career could be over at any time when you use your body for a living and get tackled to the ground multiple times a day. I just take each game one at a time and consider myself lucky to get to play the next one."

His outlook is refreshing. "So besides football . . ."

"My family, of course, and definitely eighties music."

"Oh my God, really?" I giggle.

"Yes. I'm not lying, Pen. I honestly feel like I grew up a decade too late. I love those beats. They completely change my mood, and life is too short to choose anything but joy."

A twinge of pain radiates from my chest. It's not that I haven't felt happy in the past twelve years, but I definitely haven't actively searched out joy, either.

"If I had you for the night, under me and next to me when we woke up in the morning, what would you want for breakfast?" His next question catches me off guard, particularly because of the way he deepens his voice, the gravel of it almost scraping across my nipples as they instantly grow hard and I remember what it was like to be under him last time.

"Seems to me you think that eventually will happen," I tease.

"Oh, I know it will, which is why I want to plan ahead."

"Hmm . . . not that I want to feed into this ego of yours, but my favorite breakfast would have to be a waffle with strawberries and whipped cream."

"Really? I figured you for more of an omelet girl."

"Nope. I love a sweet breakfast. I order one almost every time I go to brunch with my girls."

"Aw, yes. The ladies who brunch . . ."

I sit up in bed, excited from his words. "Hey, I like that! We should get matching t-shirts."

"Just like having jerseys."

"Yes. I'll be the QB since I'm usually the one calling the shots, Charlotte can be my tailback, Amelia would be the center, and Noelle can be the wide receiver."

I can hear his laughter through the line. "Seems like you've put a lot of thought into this. And based on what you told me earlier about your girls, I think your position assignments are accurate."

Yeah, I told Maddox all about my besties. I swear, he must think I'm a lesbian with how enamored I am of all of them. But if there were any women I would turn for, it would be them.

"Actually, I hadn't thought about it, not until you just said it."

"Penelope?"

"Yeah?"

"Have you realized we've been talking for almost four hours now?"

I glance at my alarm clock on my nightstand and see it's almost midnight. "Holy shit."

"See, babe? I can't remember the last time I wanted to talk to a woman like this."

"Well, I am pretty entertaining."

He chuckles. "You are. And you're funny, witty, smart, and complex—and every little detail I learn about you just makes me want to know you more."

"You say things like that, and somehow they don't sound cheesy . . ."

"I don't want them to. I'm being brutally honest with you, Penelope. I want time with you, as much time as you'll give me."

"Well, I have brunch plans tomorrow since it's Sunday, but I guess I could squeeze in a phone call tomorrow evening."

"It's a date."

"I don't think I've ever had a date on the phone before."

"Then I'm glad I get to be your first." I let out a yawn even though I'm fighting it, but Maddox hears it. "I should probably let you go."

"Yeah, today was exhausting, but . . . the ending was pretty amazing."

"I agree wholeheartedly. I'll talk to you tomorrow, babe. Sweet dreams . . . and not of Robert Downey, Jr., okay? Dream of me, Penelope."

Giggling, I shake my head as I stare at the ceiling again. "I can't help my subconscious, Maddox. But after tonight, I think the chances of you appearing in my dreams are pretty high."

"I'll just have to put in even more effort, then. My goal is to hear you tell me about a dream that I'm the star of. And hell, if I'm doing certifiably dirty things to you in that dream, I'm not opposed to that at all."

"Go to sleep, Maddox."

"Good night, Penelope."

I struggle to end the call and wait until I hear him do it because the truth is I don't want to hang up. I want to keep talking.

After I brush my teeth, go through my nighttime routine, and lay back down in bed, it doesn't take but a few minutes before I'm fast asleep.

And Maddox *does* appear in my dreams—but Jacob does, too.

"**I**'m pregnant!" Noelle screams as she runs into Frankie's Diner, straight for our table.

It's the day after the Children's Hospital fundraiser, and I'm still giddy after talking to Maddox last night. But Noelle's news definitely lifts my soul even more.

I stand from my chair, hold my hands out for her to run into, and then shout, "Hell, yes!"

Charlotte and Amelia squeal beside us as Noelle pummels into me. "It's really happening! I'm going to be a mom!" Her words break off on a sob as she covers her mouth with her hand. "I'm going to be a mom . . ."

Holding her to me, I close my eyes and breathe her in as her emotions take over. And I'm not gonna lie, I'm tearing up right now from her happiness. "You are. You're going to be the best mom *ever*."

When I release her, she stares up at me and then over to the girls. "Thank you. And you three are going to be aunts!"

We all laugh as Amelia and Charlotte take turns hugging Noelle as well.

Once we all get our congratulations in, we take our seats just as Frankie comes by with bottles of champagne.

"Noelle, is it true? Are you going to have a baby?"

Noelle beams up at him. "It's true, Frankie, so no more champagne for me."

I raise my hand in the air. "I'll drink her share, Frankie, so don't start skimping on us, all right?"

He nods in understanding. "You got it. Let me grab the OJ, and then I'll be right back to take your orders."

We watch him saunter off before Amelia speaks up. "So how are you feeling? When did you find out? When we didn't get a text from you after last brunch, I wasn't sure you had good news to report . . ."

"And I didn't want to be nosy and press for info," Charlotte interjects. "We kind of figured you'd tell us when you were ready, whether it was good or bad."

Noelle takes a deep breath and blows it out. "Well, I knew I said I was going to take one of those early tests at brunch last time, but the more I thought about it, I didn't want to disappoint myself if it wasn't necessary, so I decided to wait. I knew Wednesday was when I was supposed to get my period, and that morning, I woke up to some spotting, which instantly made me cry. But then it stopped. It wasn't like my period coming, either, if you know what I mean." We all nod. Being a woman is just a fascinating experience, isn't it?

"So I waited until Thursday and took one after I woke up. The faintest pink line appeared, and I was shocked, like I couldn't believe it was true. I wanted to be sure, so I called my doctor and went in Friday on my lunch break to confirm."

I wrap my arm around her shoulder and pull her into me. "I am so freaking happy for you, Noelle. Seriously. And you know what? My nipples *did* tingle on Wednesday, so now I know my superpower really works."

Charlotte rolls her eyes as my girls laugh. "Yes, it was Penelope's nipples that knew you were pregnant before you did."

Noelle shakes her head, smiling from ear to ear. "I don't even care. I'm just so relieved and nervous and excited. I'm feeling a lot of things, but most of all accomplished. I did this on my own, you guys. I took my life into my own two hands and made things happen for *me*. I don't think I've ever felt so independent in my life."

"You're a badass, Noelle. Hell, we all are. You should have seen the grown men I had dressed in princess gowns yesterday at the hospital. It was priceless."

Amelia perks up in her seat, a knowing look on her face. "And how did everything go at the event?" she asks, double meaning in her words that only I can decipher.

The corner of my mouth lifts, but I hide it as best I can. "It went . . . really well. It was emotional, for sure, but I'm optimistic that my plan and decisions will all pay off."

With a nod, she says, "I have no doubt they will."

Charlotte chimes in. "I can't wait to see the articles and press for that. I'm sure Damien will be excited, too."

"All of the boys will," Amelia adds. "They've been reminding me about meeting Maddox and the other players at the Puppy Palooza event in a few weeks almost every day. They're like little kids when you tell them you're going to go somewhere, so they bug you about it every hour of every day until it happens." She rolls her eyes playfully. "It's adorable but starting to get annoying. I never should have told them about it in the first place. I've learned that with Oliver, but you'd think I wouldn't have to worry about it with grown men."

"Don't worry. I'll be sure to record their reactions so we can use it for blackmail later if necessary."

The girls laugh. "Sounds like a plan."

"All right. If you don't mind, I need to eat, ladies. This fetus needs some food, and then this mom-to-be needs some rest. I can already feel my body doing weird things, and lord knows it's not going to get any easier." Noelle reaches for the menu to figure out what she wants, and then Frankie returns for our order.

For the next two hours, we listen to our friend share all of her fears and anticipation about being a mother while I think about my own in relation to Maddox.

Last night was eye-opening, but it gave me hope, much like how Noelle is feeling right now.

My life is changing, too, and hopefully soon I'll feel confident enough to share my story with my girls. But right now, I just want to keep this change close to the vest—because, ultimately, I'm afraid it will all end just as quickly as it began.

Chapter 11

Maddox

Snapping my fingers, I dance my way over to my locker after my shower as I hum the melody of "Jump" by Van Halen, a classic.

"You look like you either got laid or you know you're *going* to get laid," Hayden says as I unlock my locker.

"No, just happy to be alive, man." The last thing I need is to answer his question insinuating anything, especially because the woman who has me dancing is Penelope. And as much as I know how amazing sex with her is, getting to know each other more is what has me dancing around like a loon—particularly because I know I get to see her tonight.

"Yeah, I'm happy to be alive, too, but I'm much happier when there's a woman to help stroke my stick."

Casting a glance over my shoulder, I furrow my brow at him. "You call your dick a stick?"

He shrugs. "Sure. Stick, rod, lightsaber . . . the possibilities are endless."

"You have problems, Palomar." Laughing, I drop my towel and pull on a pair of briefs.

"My mother tells me the same thing."

"I sincerely hope you don't talk to your mother about your lightsaber."

"Nah, not since she gave me the talk about the fact that it would light up at the most inopportune times for the rest of my life."

"One of the curses of having a dick." I turn to face him. "By the way, nice job on the field today. It really feels like the offense is starting to gel." We're a few weeks into OTAs, and I have to say, our team is looking promising. It's been nice to meet some of the players I haven't already and finally run some plays. Throwing a football around after a long break must be what a writer feels like when they start typing again: The thrill of magic happening runs through your veins.

Hayden beams and puffs out his chest. "I told you all of my studying would pay off."

"Is that why there haven't been any women stroking your stick? Your head's been buried in the playbook? And hey, I'm not complaining, just so you know. You totally nailed that last play."

"Thanks, QB. But yeah, and I'm starting to get antsy." He slams his locker shut. "I need to go out, man. Let loose a bit. Try to meet a decent girl who might let me into her pants, for her benefit as well, of course. You got plans this weekend? Maybe you can be my wingman."

"Nah, sorry, dude. I got some stuff going on."

"What about next weekend after the Puppy Palooza?"

I'm not gonna lie, I was hoping to see Penelope next weekend after the charity event—and the weekend after that, and the one after that.

"I might have something going on, but it's not set in stone yet, so I don't want to commit and then back out on you, you know?"

"Yeah, I understand."

The thing is, he wouldn't understand because I don't know if the guy has ever been addicted to a woman the way I am to Penelope.

Hell, at this point, I may as well just book out every night until the season starts because all I want is to be in her presence or talk to her on the phone, much like we've been doing almost every night since the event at the Los Angeles Children's Hospital.

The woman is so much more complex than I thought in the best way, but I also know there's something she hasn't told me yet that's a critical piece of who she is. Most nights, I can almost hear her contemplate going there—giving me the information that would make all of the pieces of her puzzle fall into place. But right before she lets the words free, she freezes and changes the subject. And it mostly happens when we talk about where we grew up or what we were like as kids.

But here's the thing—I can't be mad at her completely because there's something else she doesn't know about me, either, something no one does. It's one of the few things I've been able to keep from the public eye, and I want it to stay that way—and giving her that information means taking a risk that she won't use it against me if she ever flips a switch on me like Brittney, my ex-fiancée, did.

One day, I want to tell her. Hell, I want to tell her everything. But the timing isn't right, and the last thing I want is for her to look at me differently, for her to share the same disappointment I have in myself at times, the guilt I try to mask every time I help a drunk girl get home from a bar.

There are so many other obstacles for us to face before we need to have that conversation, so for now, I'm letting things lie where they are—which includes focusing instead on the date I'm taking her on tonight.

I just hope she loves it and no one recognizes me while we're out.

"Well, fuck," Hayden says, running a hand through his hair.

"What about Jake, the rookie? Ask him."

Hayden casts his eyes across the locker room where Jake stands, glaring at his phone. "I don't know. He doesn't exactly scream 'let's be buddies,' you know?"

I nod. "I see what you mean. The kid could give the Road Runner a run for his money, but he definitely has a chip on his shoulder."

"And not Ruffles, but more like those chips that stab you in the roof of your mouth and make you hate them for a while."

Turning to face him again, I shake my head. "The way your mind veers off on tangents is scary."

"I know."

After we finish getting dressed and I say goodbye to a few of the other guys, I head home to take care of a few things before I pick up Penelope later from her house. But my phone rings before I can leave the parking lot, though the name on the screen has me instantly smiling.

"Well, well . . . you haven't forgotten about us normal people after all." Leslie berates me as soon as I pick up the line.

"Sorry. I have this little thing called a job that has been keeping me busy."

"Nice try, but OTAs just started a few weeks ago, and I know they're not nearly as intense as training camp. Besides, it's not like you don't have your phone glued to you like the rest of the world, so give me the real reason why you've been distant, Maddox."

"Still a ballbuster, I see."

"And I don't plan on changing any time soon."

I chuckle as I continue the drive back to my house. "Well, I've been spending time with Penelope, and that's why I haven't been calling you every day. There's another woman in my life that's been getting all of my attention. There. Now are you happy?"

She's silent for a minute but then replies, "So it's safe to say you didn't follow my advice?"

"That's the thing about advice . . . it's mostly suggestion, which means I don't have to listen if I don't want to."

I hear her sigh, and then something shifts in the background. "Have you thought about this, Maddox? Like, *truly* thought about this?"

"Yes, and I know there are risks. But I'm going to adopt the 'do what I want and ask for forgiveness later' model here."

"All I can say is if you're willing to jeopardize the season and your job, she must really be something."

"She is, Leslie. Fuck, I can't get enough of her. I want to see her and talk to her constantly. I was drawn to her the second I saw her, and every time we speak, she just sucks me in even more."

"Don't you think this is all a little sudden? I mean, I want you to be happy, Maddox. I do, and I hope you know that. But this situation is reminding me of how fast you fell for Brittney back in high school and look how that turned out."

"Penelope isn't Brittney. She actually isn't fond of my job at all, Leslie. Straight up told me she doesn't date athletes, football players to be exact—and not just because of our current working situation."

"What? Why?"

I run a hand through my hair. "I haven't exactly found that out yet. But I know she's been hurt, and the last thing I want to do is hurt her again, so I'm hoping to find out when she feels it's the right time to tell me."

"But what about *you* getting hurt? Sorry to break it to you, cousin, but when you broke up with Brittney, you didn't exactly handle it very well. And then add in what happened three months later with Grace, and . . . shit, I'm just worried that you'll spiral down a dark path again."

Clenching my jaw, I try not to snap a tooth in half as anger and regret floods my chest. "I know, but damn, Leslie. Way to hit a sore spot."

I can hear her sniffle through the line. "You know that wasn't your fault, Maddox. I'm sorry. God, I'm so sorry for even bringing it up. I just don't want to see you ever get like that again."

"Jesus. I know, Leslie. I know." We're both silent for a minute, but neither of us hangs up. "I'm just worried. I don't want this change in your life to be jaded because you're trying to avoid dealing with the trade by fixating on some woman."

"She's not just *some* woman, Leslie, and I've made my peace with the trade. She's unlike any woman I've ever met. And you know me, *truly* know me. Even after the fucked-up shit that Brittney did, I never would invest my time in someone unless I knew I wouldn't regret it."

I can almost hear the wheels turning in her head. "Are you sure about this, Maddox? Are you sure you're willing to face all the consequences of this?"

"Yes. But more importantly, I'm sure about *her*."

"Oh, Jesus, the man is done for," she teases, and the uplift in her voice makes my chest release pressure again.

"I think I am," I admit, because even though I'm still trying to convince myself to be cautious, I'm a little infatuated with Penelope. And I don't see that changing any time soon.

"I want you to be happy, Maddox. And even though I'm scared for you, you know I'll be here if shit goes sideways."

"I know, and that's why I feel confident enough to pursue this, to pursue her. I'm taking her out tonight, actually. We've mostly been talking on the phone, but I have a surprise for her that I think she'll love."

"Aren't you worried about being seen together?"

"I think we'll be okay. We're not going out to a restaurant or anything." I take the next few moments to explain my plans for this evening, and my cousin's reaction is everything.

"Hell, if I were her, I don't think I'd be able to resist you after a gesture like that."

"Well, good thing we're related." We share a laugh. "But thanks for the vote of confidence. I hope she loves it."

"She will. And maybe as things progress, we can video chat so I can meet her."

"I'd love that eventually, but I still need to wear her down a bit more. She's reluctant to admit what's between us, so until she does, I don't want to scare her off. And you, my dear cousin, can be kind of scary."

"You'd think I wouldn't like hearing that, but I do."

I turn on my street, closing in on my apartment building. "All right. I'm almost home. I'll call you sooner rather than later, okay? I promise."

"Please. And keep me updated on the Penelope situation. Plus, the kids want to talk to you."

"I miss those two rug rats. Maybe I'll call them on Sunday if you guys will be home?"

"We don't have any plans, so that sounds perfect."

"It's a date. Love you, Les."

"Love you, too, Maddox."

I end the call just as I pull my truck into my parking space. As I stare up at my building, I mull over my cousin's concerns. But it only takes me a few moments to focus back on tonight and proving to Penelope that we belong together.

Let the preparation begin.

I pull up to Penelope's house just after five and remind myself not to jump from the truck and run up to her doorstep like an overeager kid. Instead, I take a few deep breaths, check my reflection in the rearview mirror, and then exit my truck and slowly ascend the steps to her door.

I knock and wait for her to answer, and when she does, I have to fight to keep my jaw from dropping and drool from leaking out of my mouth.

"Hey, there, Mr. Taylor." With a teasing grin on her lips, Penelope opens the door wider, revealing her curvy body slathered in purple spandex that makes her look like a fruity popsicle I want to suck on.

"Penelope." I take a step forward and press a kiss to her cheek, reminding myself it's not gentlemanly to maul her the second I see her. "You sure you want to wear this?"

She furrows her brow at me. "Is there something wrong with my outfit?" Turning slowly in a circle, she peers over her shoulder at me as I watch her move around. And the look of mischief in her eyes tells me she knows exactly how she looks and why she wore this outfit—to drive me nuts.

"The exact opposite." I drag a hand over my mouth. "Fuck, maybe this wasn't a good idea."

Chuckling, she motions for me to come inside. "No backing out now, Maddox. Come in. I'm just gonna use the bathroom really quick, and then we can leave. Of course, if you want to tell me where we're going and why I had to dress like this, I wouldn't object to that."

Sticking my hands in my pockets, I shake my head at her. "Nope. It's a surprise."

She shrugs. "Fine. I'll be right back." Sashaying as she walks down a hallway, I trail her with my eyes until she disappears behind a door, and then I take a moment to survey her place.

Her townhouse is open and bright, decorated in mostly white and soft gray with pops of purple here and there—a color I'm beginning to notice she loves. The space is feminine and clean, but it's the pictures on the mantle of her fireplace that catch my attention, drawing me closer to them.

Four gorgeous women, one of which is Penelope, stare back at me with blinding smiles on their faces. Instantly, I know these girls have to be her best friends she's bragged so much about, and I'm pretty sure I know who is who based on what she's told me.

Wild blonde curls circle the face of Amelia, the marriage and sex therapist that Penelope loves so much. Charlotte, the magazine executive, has to be the curvy brunette who's a bit shorter than the rest with the strong mind and determination. And Noelle, the literary agent, has soft brown hair and green eyes that make her look just like the girl next door you knew growing up who's always believed in love.

And even though I have no problem admitting all of these women are beautiful, Penelope undoubtedly stands out among them for me with her blinding smile, full lips, slightly reddish hair, and that seductive gleam in her eyes—the one that hints at her wild side. But I see her softness and loyal heart in there, too.

"Checking out my girls?" she asks, forcing me to spin around and face her as she walks back out to the living room.

"Admiring how beautiful you all are but staring at you the most, obviously," I reply.

She walks up to me, standing just a few inches from my chest, and stares up into my eyes. "Good answer."

Neither of us speaks for a minute, just soaking in the feeling of being in the same room as one another, all alone.

But it doesn't take long before we crash into each other at the same time, our lips connecting and tongues lashing instantly.

Groaning, I bury my hand in her hair and hold her body to mine, plunging my tongue into her mouth, kissing her like I'm starved.

And I am. I have been. I've been starved for *her*.

We kiss and moan frantically before finally coming up for air, breathing heavily as I rest my forehead on hers.

"Fuck, I needed that."

"Me, too," she replies, breathless.

"We need to go, though, before I push you down on this couch and fuck you all night."

She laughs. "There's nothing wrong with that."

"Yes, there is." I lift my head so I can see her eyes clearly. "I want you, Penelope. There's no doubt about that. But that's not all I want from you. I promised you a date, so you're getting one, even if my dick is hard as rock the entire time."

She reaches between us and rubs her hand up and down my cock, making me even harder and forcing me to close my eyes to concentrate and remind myself of the end game here. "You'd rather torture yourself than give in just a bit?"

"Yes, because I want you to believe me when I say that your happiness matters more than my dick."

She rears back. "I don't know if that's incredibly romantic or a little crude."

"Both," I reply on a laugh before grabbing her hand and pulling her toward the door. "Now let's go, or we're going to miss it."

"Miss what?"

"You'll see when we get there."

Penelope grabs her purse and locks her door, and then we're off toward the Westridge-Canyonback Wilderness Park for our date.

When we pull into the parking lot, Penelope turns to face me in her seat. "What are we doing?"

I reach over the center console and cup the side of her face. "We're going on a hike, sweetheart."

A soft smile builds on her lips. "What?"

"You told me last week that one thing you wish you had more time for was hiking, so that's what we're going to do." I reach behind my seat for my backpack filled with snacks and water and find my baseball cap, securing it on top of my head. "Plus, it shouldn't be too crowded, so our chances of being seen together are fairly slim. My hat and sunglasses should help conceal my identity a bit, anyway, and once we get to the top, we're going to watch the sunset together."

Her lips part as she sucks in a breath. "I . . . I don't even know what to say."

"You don't have to say anything, Penelope. I'm just glad we're here together right now, that you made time for me tonight and all of the other nights so far. And hopefully, we'll make more."

In a flash, she leans over the console and captures my lips with her own, thanking me without using any words. And I am totally okay with that.

Once Penelope gives me my lips back, I lock my truck and we head for the trail that I researched would give us the best view and the most privacy, hopefully. The excitement I feel just being with her only solidifies that my idea had merit.

Our shoes crunch along the gravel and dirt for a few minutes before Penelope finally turns to me and speaks. "You sure you don't want me to carry anything?"

I hike the backpack up a little more on my shoulders. "Nope. You just enjoy the view while I carry all of our stuff like a pack mule."

"Suit yourself."

"So how was your day at work?"

She sighs. "Busy. I had a meeting with Liam and a few other people from the Bolts' staff today, actually."

"Oh, yeah? And how did that go?"

"Pretty well." She pauses, which has me concerned. "You sure?"

"Yes, it's just that they put out an idea I think would be great to promote the team during pre-season, but the final details haven't been hammered out yet, so I don't want to say anything until they are."

I nod. "I get it. It's okay, Penelope. You don't have to tell me everything about work. I know it's weird given that we're dating now."

She casts me a glance out of the corner of her eye. "Is that what we're doing?"

"Sorry to break it to you, babe, but that's *exactly* what we're doing."

I watch her chest rise as she inhales deeply and blows out a big breath. "Okay. I guess it's time I just accept that, huh?"

"Is dating a scary word for you?"

She scoffs. "Uh, yeah, it is, Maddox. I haven't been on a date since I was sixteen."

I stop in my tracks, my mouth gaping. "What?"

When she notices I'm not next to her any longer, she turns around. "What?"

"Why, Pen?"

"I already told you," she says and starts walking away from me again, so I eagerly hurry to catch up. "I don't date. Haven't since then."

"Is that because you got hurt in the past?"

She nods. "Yes."

"Wow."

"Look, it's not like I haven't been asked."

"That's not what I'm saying," I retort. "I'm just surprised is all."

"Even our phone dates were new for me, so hopefully you get why this is a big deal to me now. Add in the fact that you're famous *and* in the public eye *and* play football . . . well, it's just a lot to take in."

I reach for her arm and pull her into my chest, spinning her around so she's facing me as we pause on the trail. "Thank you for letting me be the first."

Her smile is like winning the lottery. "What can I say? You're very persuasive."

"You have no idea how persuasive I can be." I let her go, give her butt a little tap—which makes her shriek—and then we keep moving. "We can talk more about that later. Right now, we have a sunset to catch."

Engaging in small talk the rest of the way up the hill, we arrive at the peak just as the sun begins to disappear behind the mountain range in the distance. I'm tickled pink that the colors are on point tonight as we both stare off into the distance, watching purples and blues light up the sky.

"God, what a view."

I look over at her, admiring the upturn of her nose, her smile, and the way she looks so free right now as she gazes at the sight, the tiny hairs on the side of her face waving in the breeze. "You're telling me."

Her eyes find mine, and then she walks over to me, wrapping her arms around my waist at my side as we watch the sun set below the horizon. "Thank you for this."

"You are most welcome, Penelope. Thank you for giving me your time tonight and providing me a legitimate excuse to get out of going to a club with Hayden."

She laughs. "Oh, I'm sure he was devastated."

"He'll get over it. I'd much rather be here with you."

She squeezes me tighter. "There's no place I'd rather be right now, Maddox. Thank you for this. I'm just . . . a little speechless."

I lean down and press my lips to hers softly, teasing her with my tongue gently before pulling away. Slowly, I set down my backpack, check our surroundings for company—thankfully, we're all alone—and then stand behind Penelope so I can wrap my arms around her and pull her into my chest.

"I have one more thing to give you while we're here," I whisper in her ear before placing a kiss on her neck, licking the spot slightly and then grazing my teeth over her skin.

I feel her melt in my arms, breathing in a tad as she leans her head to the side to grant me better access. "Oh, yeah?" Her hands land on top of mine, squeezing them, but I slowly move mine away from her waist and begin to run them up her ribcage.

"You said there were two things you couldn't live without," I declare. "The first one was sunsets."

"Uh-huh." Her skin breaks out in goosebumps as I tease the sides of her breasts with my index fingers, trailing them down the exposed skin of her stomach, toying with the top of her spandex capris.

"And do you remember what the second one was?" I nibble on her earlobe, splaying one hand across her stomach as the other one reaches up to turn her head so she can look at me.

"Are you serious?"

I lean in and bite her bottom lip gently. "As a heart attack, baby. It's time for an orgasm." Her eyes widen, and then she twists her head around, clearly looking for other people. "Don't worry, we're alone." I turn her head back to me. "I'm going to make you come on my hand right now, Penelope, as you watch the sunset. How's that sound?"

"Definitely orgasmic," she breathes out.

"That's the idea, sweetheart."

Kissing her deeply, I run my hands over her hips before pulling her back to me again. When our mouths part, she stares up at me while I reach forward with one hand, playing with the top of her capris once more.

"Maddox," she breathes.

"God, I love hearing you say my name." I move my hand under the fabric, teasing her with my fingertips on the bare skin above her slit. But when I feel that small triangle of hair I know she has down there, my dick grows even harder than it was earlier.

She wiggles her ass against me as our eyes remain locked, and my grip on her grows tighter. "You make me crazy, woman."

"Believe me, the feeling is mutual in more ways than one," she fires back as I dip my finger into her slit and find her soaked for me.

"Look at the sunset, Penelope. Remember this moment as you experience two of your favorite things simultaneously."

She moans, closes her eyes, and then turns to gaze at the colorful sky as I begin to drag my finger over her clit.

Her body reacts to me instantly—her legs widen, she leans her head back on my shoulders, and I can hear her rapid breathing as I slowly circle her bundle of nerves, building her up with precision. Her moans spur me on, so I dip my fingers lower and slide two in, loving how tightly her body grips me.

"Fuck, Maddox."

"Keep watching the sunset, Penelope."

My hand moves on instinct, working her over, listening to her cues—the way she clenches when I go deeper, the way her hips begin to circle with my movements, and the way her nails dig into the top of my hand that's clutching her hip while she approaches her precipice.

"Maddox . . ."

"You're getting close, aren't you, sweetheart?"

"God, yes. Keep going . . . fuck, I'm gonna come." And then she shatters, shouting out into the open night, letting me know how amazing she feels.

I hold her up as her orgasm rolls through her in waves, and she leans her head back on my chest, breathing through her release. Hell, just listening to and watching her come has me fighting not to make a mess in my own pants.

When I feel her start to relax, she lifts her head, opens her eyes, and stares up at me in awe. "I don't even know what to say."

And truthfully, neither do I—because how can I put into words how connected I felt to her in that moment?

So I just kiss her gently and deeply to make sure I never forget this experience as long as I live. I can't stop myself from wondering when I can get this woman alone again because lord only knows the things I want to do to her. This only scratched the surface.

When we part, our eyes lock again, and she says, "Take me home, Maddox."

"What?"

"I want you to take me home. Fuck the rules. We've already broken them. Let's break some more."

"Are you sure?" I ask because it's the gentlemanly thing to do, but my dick instantly jumped at her words.

"Yes. I want you to fuck me—again."

"Fuck."

She spins and palms me through my shorts. "Do you think you're up to the challenge, Mr. Taylor?"

"Oh, I'm sure. I've been thinking about this moment since I saw you again, Penelope. And boy, do I have some ideas of what we could do."

"You're not the only one. I might have thought of a few moves we could try as well."

"Then what are we waiting for?" I take her hand in mine and begin our trek back down the mountain as my body vibrates with adrenaline for what's about to happen.

I obviously didn't anticipate our night ending like this, but I'm not complaining, either.

Penelope has let me in, she's opening up, and now I get to explore our physical connection even more. And believe me, you won't hear me whining about that one bit.

Chapter 12

Penelope

Sex. I need sex now.

And not just because I'm a woman with needs and that orgasm was just a tease of pleasure that I haven't had since the last time Maddox and I hooked up.

No, I need sex because I need to shut off these feelings that Maddox keeps bringing up in me.

He took me hiking, watched the sunset with me, and then made me come—how the hell am I supposed to resist that? How the hell am I supposed to maintain some dignity and pump the brakes on what we're doing if he keeps acting fucking perfectly?

I can't. And that's why I need to reset, go back to what I know —and what I know is that Maddox can deliver one hell of an orgasm. And perhaps reminding my body what sex feels like will help me squash these other emotions that are building up inside of me, threatening to take over and crush my control.

The drive back to Maddox's place is quiet, riddled with sexual tension. Little does he know that I'm also at war with myself mentally, but hopefully that will shut off the moment I have his dick inside me again.

We arrive at Maddox's apartment, and I stumble a little once I get a glimpse at the inside. How is it this comfortable and decorated already?

"What's that look on your face for?" he asks as I walk across his living room to the sliding glass door to check out the view. It's a modest place for a professional football player, but I also realize he had to move across the country fairly quickly, so he was probably just looking for a place to put his bed for the time being.

"You've decorated. It's just surprising for a man to care about stuff like that." There are a few framed posters on the wall of his jersey and articles featuring his accomplishments, books on some shelves by the television, and a navy throw blanket on the couch. The walls aren't completely bare, and I'm seriously surprised.

He shoves his hands in his pockets as he grins at me. "Well, besides the few hours of practice I've had each day, I haven't had much to do. That is, besides pursuing you."

I twist to face him again. "Then how about you cash in on your prize?"

He cocks a brow. "My prize?"

I rip my sports bra off and then shove down my spandex capris, standing before him in nothing but my thong. "Isn't this what you wanted? Because I sure as hell know it's what I want."

Taking a few steps toward me, he studies my face. "You're not some prize to be won, Penelope. I want nothing more than to bend you over the arm of my couch and spank you for thinking otherwise, though I'd be lying if I said that the thought doesn't turn me on immensely."

Swallowing the lump in my throat, I practically beg. "Just, please, fuck me already, Maddox. I . . . I need it."

A look of understanding crosses his face, and with lightning speed, he reaches out, pulls me into his chest, and caresses my face. "If that's what you need, then I can do that for you. I want to give you anything you need, sweetheart."

Slowly, he lowers his mouth to mine, and the spark that ignites when our lips touch is enough to flip that switch in my brain, the one that allows me to focus on the physical touch instead of the intensity of my emotions.

Maddox reaches down and grabs my ass, lifting me up so my legs can wrap around his waist. Then he stalks further into the apartment. "Shower first."

"That's not necessary," I mumble against his lips.

"No, it is, babe. I'm sweaty in places where I want your mouth, but I won't ask you to go there until I'm clean."

Laughing, I lean back from his face a bit. "Good point."

Maddox sets me down on the tiled bathroom floor and turns the shower on as I shove down my thong so I'm completely naked now. Then he begins stripping in front of me, and the sight has me squeezing my legs together in an attempt to quell the ache that's thrumming throughout my body.

Jesus, I almost forgot how sexy his body is—his hard and defined chest, his pierced nipples, his tattoos—every detail is calling out to me, and suddenly I feel like a dog that can't stop panting.

I want to lick every inch of him.

Once he takes off his shoes and pushes down his shorts, he

yanks me into his chest again, kissing me thoroughly as we step into the shower.

Water cascades over us as I reach down and begin to stroke him, playing with his piercing as he grows rock-hard in my hand.

"Jesus, woman."

"How long do you think this is going to take? I want this cock inside of me."

He bites my neck and licks my collarbone as the water rains down on us. "Patience, baby."

"I'm past that point, Maddox. I'm primed and ready to go. I need—"

He places a finger over my lips, cutting me off. "I know what you need. But you're not getting my cock until I say you can, understood?"

"Oh, really?" I drop to my knees, fist his cock, and then take him as far back in my throat as I can.

"Fucking Christ," he growls as he reaches backward for the wall to steady himself, staring down at me while I suck him off like a woman wanting to get to the center of a Tootsie Pop.

He allows me to show him how serious I am for a few moments before he snaps back to reality. "You want this cock, Penelope?" I nod while he's still in my mouth. "Fine. I'll give you this cock then, baby. But not in here." He reaches down, lifts me up by my arms, and then moves behind him and shuts off the water. And before I can speak, he has me in his embrace again, and we're walking into his bedroom.

He tosses me on his bed, pinning my hands above my head. "Listen closely, Penelope. I know you like to be in control, and the last thing I want is to fight you right now." He drags his nose up the column of my throat. "I want to please you, babe, but you need to let me do that. Trust me to make you feel good instead of rushing through this."

"Then do it. Do it so this pressure inside of me can be released."

He lets go of me, leans over to his nightstand, and extracts a condom from his drawer, ripping the wrapper and sheathing himself as I lie there and wait.

My entire body feels like it's on fire, and the only hose that can put out these flames is the massive one between Maddox's legs.

He hovers over me again, latching onto my nipple and sucking the bud into his mouth with force, eliciting a moan from me.

Fuck, yes. This is what I need. More of this. More of his body. More of everything but these thoughts running rampant through my mind.

I reach between us, line him up to my entrance, and then pull him into me until we both groan out our relief. "Oh God."

"Fuck, Penelope. God, this pussy. I've thought about having you again for far too long."

Pulling his lips to mine, I shut him up with my mouth.

No talking, no feelings, just pleasure—and lots of it, please.

Maddox thrusts and pounds into me, making every nerve ending in my body come alive. We're both still wet from the shower, so our bodies slide across one another with ease. But the pressure that I felt everywhere before is now centrally located at the apex of my thighs, building and mounting as he continues to fuck me.

I focus on the sounds of our skin slapping together and the tingles in my nipples. I reach down and squeeze his ass, appreciating his muscles there because let's face it—it's one of the best physical parts of him.

But then he pushes up and locks eyes with me, and my heart squeezes tightly in my chest. "This is what you wanted, right?"

"Yes. More, Maddox . . ."

He thrusts harder, making me scream. "Tell me. Tell me how much you wanted this, Penelope."

I shake my head, closing my eyes and blocking out his words.

But then he stops moving. "Say it."

My eyes pop open, and I find him smirking down at me.

I don't want to give in, but I surely don't want this to end just yet, either. So I relent. "Yes, I wanted this. I wanted your cock again, Maddox."

The pleased look on his face has me wanting to punch him. "Glad you can finally admit that."

"Oh, you're just so happy with yourself now, aren't you?"

"Yes, I am. Even more so, because now you're giving me other parts of you, too." He presses his lips to mine again, and a sharp sting of emotional reaction flashes through my chest.

Those words have my heart picking up speed again.

Before I can find my footing, Maddox lifts me up from the bed and takes us over to a chair in the corner. He sits back as I straddle his lap, the two of us still connected.

Light from outside cracks through the blinds, bathing us in a glow of white light and shadows, creating a heavenly mood in the room. Staring down at him, I begin rocking back and forth, lifting up and down, using him to chase the release that I so desperately need at this moment.

But his next words have me snapping right back to reality. "That's right, baby. Ride me. Tell me who this pussy belongs to." He lands a rough smack on my ass, but I instantly stop moving.

This man is in for a hard lesson right now.

"Me," I answer firmly.

Maddox blinks up at me. "Come again?"

Reaching forward, I grip his face in my hand, squeezing his cheeks together so his lips purse like a fish. "This pussy belongs to *me*, Maddox. This is *my* body, not yours. As far as I'm concerned, you are on a rent-to-own contract right now, and until you can prove that you deserve to have my body and I agree to give it to you, this pussy"—I squeeze the pussy in question around his cock, which makes him groan—"is mine."

Maddox stares at me, his gaze penetrating mine. "Marry me."

I throw my head back in laughter as I release his face, moving my hips again. "Fuck you, Maddox."

He grips the back of my head, digging his fingers into my hair, tugging slightly, and nibbles on my neck, inhaling sharply as we grind on each other. "You are unlike any woman I've ever met, Penelope. God, what you do to me . . ."

"Damn straight. I'm one of a kind, a special edition." I sit down on him as hard as I can, making us both gasp.

"And I love getting to know all the things that make you so special." My heartbeat grows stronger at his words. "Are you getting close, Penelope?" He reaches down to stroke my clit with his thumb, and suddenly, I'm seconds away from release.

"Yes. Keep doing that."

"I'm gonna come so fucking hard, baby. Come apart with me, Penelope."

I grind faster, his thumb moves quicker, and our bodies slap and bump against each other as we chase our mutual pleasure.

"I'm there . . . oh, fuck, I'm coming!" I scream out as my orgasm slams into me. Maddox grips my hip hard as he rubs my clit through it, and then he moans loudly when he reaches the edge as well. We gyrate and grind as my orgasm runs through my veins, bursting with electricity as sparks fly behind my eyelids.

Digging my nails into his shoulders, I hang on to him until the aftershocks subside and I can feel my toes again. Maddox buries his face in my neck, and we stay like that, clinging to each other, until I leave the vortex I had just spiraled down.

"Fuck, Penelope. I can't feel my legs."

Laughing, I lift off him and walk on unsteady limbs to find my clothes. "That definitely was a good game, Maddox. Good team-work." I find my thong in the bathroom and then walk down the hall to the living room to find my top and capris.

The sound of Maddox's feet slapping on the tile echoes behind me. "What are you doing?"

I spin around as I pull my bra and pants back on and find him wearing nothing but a pair of gray sweatpants. *Really? The guy isn't playing fair.*

"I'm getting dressed."

"Why?"

"Because I need to go home now."

His brow pinches. "You're not going to stay?"

"I mean, we got what we wanted. I'm tired, and it's been a long week. Let's just call this what it is."

"And what is that exactly?"

"Releasing all of the buildup that's been mounting for months. We're both consenting adults. We had sex, but now I need to get back to reality."

"So that's it? Our date from earlier is over?"

"Well, yeah. I mean, it was great. Seriously—gorgeous view and top notch orgasm. But now . . ."

He stares down at the floor with a pinch in his brow, but then he sighs heavily, never lifting his head. "Fine, then. I'll take you home."

Like the flip of a switch, Maddox grows silent and broody. I wait for him to put a shirt on, and then he takes me back out to his truck.

The drive back to my place is uncomfortable, but I'm not sure what to say. I got what I needed, what usually works for me. But this time? I don't feel good afterward. Honestly? I feel like absolute shit.

I can tell that Maddox wants to say something, that words are on the tip of his tongue, but he never speaks. And without knowing what's going on between us at the moment, I'm scared to say anything myself.

When he pulls up to my townhouse, he puts the truck in park and then leans over the center console to plant a kiss on my cheek. "Have a good night, Penelope."

"You, too, Maddox." I exit the truck and turn back to get one last look at him, but he's not looking in my direction. He shifts into reverse and leaves just as quickly as he came—and I'm left standing there wondering how an amazing night turned so terribly wrong so quickly.

I'm pretty sure I have no one to blame but myself.

Chapter 13

Maddox

"You look stressed, QB." Vince comes up beside me as I'm walking out to my car after practice. "Definitely weren't yourself out on the field today."

Yeah, that's one way of putting it. "My head and heart just weren't in it today, man."

The truth is, I'm having trouble focusing on anything right now, especially football. It's Tuesday, and I haven't heard from Penelope since Friday night. Since I dropped her off at her house after our date.

Our date. Yeah, not sure how the perfectly planned evening was so fucking amazing and then soured so quickly, but Penelope made sure I knew *exactly* where we stood by the time I dropped her off at her home.

And fuck if it's not building this irritation inside of me, this mounting anger that she took the first opportunity to push me away again and ran with it.

"This wouldn't have to do with Penelope, would it?"

We stop at my truck as I unlock it and throw my bag inside, turning to lean up against it. I meet his eyes. "And what makes you think that?"

"Oh, just a lucky guess."

I run my hand through my hair and blow out a breath. "Fuck, Vince. The woman is making me insane."

"News flash, Taylor—that's what women do."

"But you're married. It's different."

"It is, but that doesn't mean my wife doesn't do or say shit that sends me into a tailspin sometimes, even after being together for eight years. Did something happen between the two of you?"

"I took her out Friday night. Things were going well, and then we, uh . . ."

"Slept together?" he clarifies.

"Yeah. Again."

Holding a hand up, he makes the sound of screeching brakes. "Hold up. *Again*?"

Chuckling, I lean back against the truck further to get comfortable before going back to almost three months ago when Penelope and I met the first time.

"Holy shit. No wonder the sexual tension between the two of you was wound so tight."

"Well, we released some of it Friday night, but then right after, she bailed."

The corner of his mouth tips up. "I see."

"I know I'm coming on strong, but fuck . . . I'm in uncharted territory here. The woman is . . . not the commitment type."

"Justice was the same way," he replies, and a light bulb flicks on in my head. *He has experience with this? Now's the time to pick his brain.*

"Really? And how did you deal with that?"

He sighs. "It wasn't easy. There were times where we both ran away because we were afraid of facing our feelings. But then one day, I looked her in the eye and told her that I wasn't going anywhere, that I would fight her to the ends of the earth until she understood that we belonged together. That I wasn't going to let her push me away anymore."

"And what did she say?"

"That I was crazy but she felt the same, that she was overwhelmed but didn't want to be without me." He shrugs. "From then on, we made sure we talked about instances where she felt I was smothering her and vice versa. Communication is key."

"You sound like Dr. Phil."

"Nah, just a man who's learned how to avoid unnecessary fighting and build a marriage that I'm truly happy in."

"Well, Penelope and I aren't exactly as far as it sounds like you and Justice were in your feelings at this point, but I think maybe I do need to force her to listen to me a bit. I wouldn't be jeopardizing my career and reputation for just any woman, Vince. I know she's worth it—all of this shit." I tilt my head back. "My ex did a number on me, too, man—used me for my career when I thought I knew who she was. I don't think that's what's happening here with Penelope, but I can't help but question what the fuck is going on."

"Do you think she's hiding something? Or has an ulterior motive?"

"I don't know. There's definitely part of her she keeps close to the vest, but I'm hoping she'll tell me when she's ready."

"Exactly. And that's why I can see this is messing with your head. You *like* her."

"I really fucking do."

"Then tell her how it's going to be, Maddox—in your own way, of course. Let her know that you understand her fears, but running from you isn't going to work."

Vince's words hit home. I think it's exactly what I needed to hear at this moment.

Determination builds within me, and I stand up straighter. Then an idea pops into my head that I can't ignore. "You're right. I'm not going to let her push me away when we haven't even really started."

He claps me on the shoulder. "That's the spirit. Now get your head on straight, do what you need to do, and I'll see you back here tomorrow."

"Thanks, Vince." I rest my hand on his shoulder. "Seriously. I appreciate the advice."

"You're a good man, Taylor. I'd hate to see you not get the woman you want and deserve. Every man needs one at some point."

I don't think I've ever heard something so true.

So with renewed confidence, I hop into my truck, crank the engine, and head straight for Penelope's office.

This can't fucking wait.

"Garret? Where are those invoices I asked for?" Penelope comes walking out of her office in a black pencil skirt and purple blouse, her hair down around her face in soft curls. She's looking down at her phone and hasn't even realized that I'm standing there in front of her and Garret is nowhere to be found.

And he won't be here for a while, because I asked him to pick up some lunch for Penelope and me for our "meeting," an errand that will take at least thirty minutes to complete with afternoon traffic. He was more than happy to oblige.

Usually, I wouldn't use my fame to get what I want, but this is one time I'm willing to bend my rules. Well, maybe the second, that is, as I stare at the woman in front of me that I'm risking a hell of a lot for.

"Garret won't be back for a while, but he asked me to give you these."

Penelope jumps and drops her phone to the floor, clutching her palms to her chest. "Jesus Christ, Maddox. What are you doing here?"

"What? Surprised to see me? Did I catch you off guard?" I take a few steps so I'm right in front of her.

"Uh, yeah!" Then she looks at me, her forehead creased. "Did we have a meeting I wasn't aware of or something?"

"Yeah . . . or something." I walk past her and through her open office door, waiting for her to join me. But she just stands there, assessing me curiously, before finally grabbing her phone from the floor and sauntering past me. I shut the door as soon as she walks in.

"Maddox, what the hell is going on?" She spins to face me, her hands on her hips.

"We need to talk."

"Okay. About?"

"Friday night."

Her face goes white. "I'm really busy."

"Bullshit. Now answer the question. Why did you run from me?"

"I-I didn't."

"Yes, you fucking did, Penelope. But you know what? That's fine. Because I'm not letting you get away again." Suddenly, I watch fear race through her as her eyes dart around the room, searching for a way to escape. "You don't have to be scared of me, Penelope, but we're going to talk about something right now, and we're going to do it so you can't deny me some answers." I lock the door behind me and then make my way over to where she's standing, pulling her lips to mine before she can object.

This woman. *Christ*. She tastes like heaven and hell all wrapped up into one sassy package that I can't fucking get enough of.

Her hands wrap around my neck and pull me closer as I take out my frustration with her on her mouth. Carefully, I walk us over to her desk and lift her up on the edge of it, raising her skirt as I begin to rub that hot spot between her legs.

"Maddox," she hisses. "We can't here."

"Oh, yes, we fucking can. But you can stop me at any time." I stare her down, a clear challenge.

She just glares at me.

"Then this is how it's going to be, Penelope. I'm gonna make you come with my mouth and maybe my cock, and then we're going to fucking talk." I rip her thong in half and toss it to the side, diving my face between her legs.

"Jesus. Maddox!" she whispers, moaning a little too loudly. I reach up and cover her mouth with my hand, and our eyes lock while she watches me lick every crevice of her.

I swirl my tongue around her clit, sucking and nibbling on the bud until she's writhing, and then I stop and move my hand that was covering her mouth.

"What the hell?"

"Why did you run from me the other night, Pen?"

She groans and drops her head back. "You're seriously doing this to me right now?"

"Damn right, woman. Now answer the question."

"This is just mean."

"It's about to get worse if you don't answer me."

"Fine. I don't usually stay after—"

"Sex?"

She nods. "Yeah."

"I'm beginning to see that." I drop my mouth back down to her pussy and lick her again, sticking my tongue as deep as I can inside of her as she writhes against my mouth. My hand smothers her lips again as I bring her seconds from her orgasm and then stop once more.

"You're killing me, Maddox."

"I promise you'll get what you want . . . right after I get what I need."

"And what is that?" she asks, barely breathing at this point.

"For you to tell me the truth about why you won't let me in."

She shakes her head. "I can't."

Fuming now, I stand up, shove my shorts down, rip the condom open that I had in my pocket, cover myself, and then sit back in her desk chair, pulling her down on top of me. We both moan as I slide inside her.

"Bullshit. Now tell me."

"I can't believe I'm being coerced with sex right now."

"You love it. Now talk to me."

She stares down at me, rocking her hips a few times before she relents. "I don't need you in my life, Maddox. The only thing I might miss is this cock, but don't forget that you're here right now because I want you to be, not because I need you to be." She drops her head to my shoulder, still riding me. But I force her to look back at me as our breathing picks up.

"No, I think you *do* need me. In fact, I know you do. I'm just waiting for you to admit it."

We lock eyes as my words attack her mind like a ninja moving quietly in the dark, taking down his enemies one by one without anyone noticing. Because on some level, I know Penelope knows I'm right. She might not need me right now, but with the way things are going between us, I'm hoping that won't be the case for much longer.

"I'm independent and stubborn, so it's hard for me to let someone in."

"I already know those things, so try again."

She rolls her eyes and sighs, so I pull her off of me. "What the—?"

"No more of my cock until you give me something more."

She narrows her eyes at me. "I really hate you right now."

I lick two of my fingers and then press them to her clit, rubbing soft circles around that spot. Moaning, she leans her head back and closes her eyes as I keep building her up. And just watching her as I torture her is making my dick even harder than it was before.

So I stop moving my hands, and she growls. "I'm going to punch you."

"Then answer my question."

Dropping her head down so our eyes meet again, she bites her lip before saying, "I don't want to get hurt again."

"Now we're getting somewhere."

"This entire situation has disaster written all over it."

"I know." I start moving my fingers again as her hips swivel in time with my movements. "But that doesn't change the fact that we're both here regardless, trying to figure out what this is."

"You scare me."

Light bulb. "Ah, I see." Happy with her confession for the time being, I line my cock back up to her and pull her down my length again, groaning as we reconnect.

She breathes heavily in my ear as she starts riding me again. "Are you going to let me come now?" she asks, squeezing her pussy around my cock. And fuck, it's just as good as the two times before.

"Yes, but only because I'm there, too. This conversation isn't over yet."

"Fine. Just make me come . . . please," she begs on a whisper, so I reach between us and rub her clit again to help her get there.

It doesn't take long for us to both come apart at the seams.

Penelope digs her teeth into my shoulder to keep from screaming, and knowing that she's going to leave a mark on me makes my orgasm last a few seconds longer.

When we both relax, I break the silence. "I ordered us lunch. Garret is picking it up."

"You sent my assistant away without me knowing?"

"I needed him gone just in case you planned on screaming . . . which you did."

"Well, if your plan was to make me come, that's a logical side effect." She brushes my hair from my eyes and looks down at me. "You know what, though? I am kind of hungry."

I tilt my head as I study her. "What are you saying?"

"I'm saying I'm hungry, and if you want to still feed me, I wouldn't be opposed to it."

"You'll have lunch with me?"

"As long as we can make this look like a working lunch . . . then, yeah."

That little move of hers is exactly what I need to release this rubber band around my heart right now. "Okay. Let's get cleaned up first."

"Naturally."

Penelope moves her skirt back in place as I dispose of the condom, pull my shorts back up, and watch her gather herself.

I'm starving, so I hope Garret returns sooner rather than later, but nerves are running through me the longer we don't speak.

However, Penelope decides to bite the bullet and address the elephant in the room before I can say anything else. "I'm sorry."

My heart pounds. "For what?"

"For leaving Friday night."

"Thank you."

"That's just how I do things." She looks off to the side.

"No, that's how you *used* to do things."

"Excuse me?"

Her eyes meet mine again, but this time, I intend to be clear. "You're not going to do that to *me*, Penelope."

"Uh . . ."

"I don't care what or who you've done before me, okay? But I will not let you use me. I thought we were . . ." I brush a hand through my hair. "Fuck, I thought things were going well between us."

"They were." I can feel her start to panic. "It's just . . ."

Closing the distance between us, I grab her hand and lead her over to her couch. "Talk to me. What's going through that head of yours?"

"I'm not sure you want the answer to that question."

"If I didn't want to know, I wouldn't have asked."

She's at war with her mind, but I hope there's some sort of breakthrough here. "This is just . . . a lot. I told you that I don't usually do the relationship thing."

"I get that, and I'm sorry if I'm coming on strong, but fuck." I pull her onto my lap again because when we're like this, I feel like she can't hide from me. Then I bury my hands in her hair. "I want to be patient with you, *for* you. It's just hard when every time I feel like we're making progress, you push back."

"It's who I am, Maddox. I hate being told what to do, how to live my life. I've been alone for a very long time . . ."

"Why?"

"Because it's how I chose to survive."

I exhale heavily, accepting that this isn't going to be solved quickly, but at least we're taking steps in the right direction. "That fucking kills me, especially because I know what that's like, too. I've had shit happen that I chose to ignore, buried under alcohol and bad decisions. It almost cost me all of my hard work, Pen. I know it's not easy to face shit, but—"

"I'm sorry. I am. I'm trying . . . but there's all this stress on me right now. And I know we shouldn't be doing this. It's in the back of my head every time we talk or see each other."

"I know, Penelope. I know." Gently, I press my lips to her forehead. "We can take things a bit slower if that's what you really want, but right now, I just want this." I pull her closer to my chest. "I just want you." I simply hug her, wrapping her in my arms.

We sit there in silence, my arms encircling her, making me feel warm, comforted—safe. I don't know if she's ever felt this way, but I want to be the man who gives that to her.

I want to be the man who gives her everything.

My realization slams into me like a freight train, but I can't deny what my intuition knew long before my brain did.

She finally starts to relax, and a weight lifts from my shoulders. "I can't believe you denied me orgasms," she says, breaking the silence.

I can't help but laugh. "It was one of the only things I could think of to get you to talk to me."

"Well, it worked."

We grow quiet again, but I don't want to lose the progress that we've made, so I do what I do best. "What does one saggy boob say to the other saggy boob?"

She leans back and stares down at my smile. And fuck, that look in her eyes is everything I've been looking for—like she wants me, appreciates me, and *likes* me back.

"I don't know, Maddox. What?"

"'If we don't get some support, people will think we're nuts.'"

The laughter I pull from her is like a bright light, alleviating some of the darkness I felt myself being pulled into just a few seconds ago when I wondered if I made the right decision to come here today.

But as I hold her and we laugh together, I know my gut didn't steer me wrong. Now let's hope I can continue to move forward with her without too much more whiplash.

Chapter 14

Penelope

"I t's a good thing we didn't bring Oliver today, or we would definitely be going home with a dog." Amelia comes up beside me as I answer an email on my phone.

Ethan, her brother Nick, Damien, and Jeffrey all went off to get something to drink, leaving her and me alone for a few minutes. Charlotte is running around somewhere as well, and Noelle told us she would be late, so right now, it's just the two of us standing around as the Puppy Palooza event gets underway.

It wouldn't be a true community event if our whole gang wasn't here.

"No shit, huh? And here's the thing—since he's the cutest kid ever, I would be giving him tips on how to convince you to let him take one."

She laughs. "I know you would."

"By the way, how did my little man like his present?"

Amelia smiles. "He loved it, but I have to tell you, I took the gnome out of the T-Rex's mouth before I gave it to him."

"Probably a good call."

I recently saw a Facebook ad for a garden T-Rex that had gnomes crawling all over him, so naturally I had to buy it for my favorite little boy in the world: Oliver, Ethan's son. It looked like the dinosaur was trying to eat some gnomes as a snack, but I figured any little boy would be tickled pink to have a dinosaur in his yard. And after Amelia went to great lengths to feed into his belief in magic with her own gnomes, I wanted to give him something from his Aunt Penelope, too.

"He loves it, though, and he loves you. But like I said, it's a good thing his grandma took him today, or the T-Rex and gnomes would be fighting off a puppy, I have no doubt."

All around us, puppies and full-grown dogs are barking up a storm, stealing the hearts of anyone who walks past at the annual Puppy Palooza, a charity event thrown every year to raise money for the no-kill animal shelter in Los Angeles.

Charlotte's magazine, *Revision*, is a sponsor every year, which is how I found out about the event. But since my new role is to gain positive exposure for the Los Angeles Bolts, this year, some very physically fit and charming football players are going to be washing dogs and helping with adoption paperwork in hopes of worming their way into the hearts of football fans in southern California.

Amelia nudges me with her shoulder, forcing me to look up at her from my phone. "I haven't heard much from you lately on the Maddox front. How's that going?"

I sigh and shove my phone into my back pocket. "Um?" I can't fight my smile. "Things are going well. I mean, if giving you an orgasm in front of a sunset is the sort of thing that's on the top of your bucket list."

Amelia's eyes go wide, and her lips curl up in a smile. "Holy shit, Penelope."

I lower my voice. "It was freaking incredible. He took me on a hike so we could be alone, you know? And then he made me come on his hand while we watched the sun sink down behind the mountains," I muse.

"Based on the look in your eyes, I'm gonna say that's not the only thing he's been doing for you."

Glancing around the park, I pull Amelia to the side so we're around fewer people who can eavesdrop. "Well, after our hike, I demanded he fuck me. I've been so horny since he was the last guy I slept with, so I needed that release. But then, I . . ."

"What?"

I sigh. "I ran off."

"You didn't?" she asks, her brow furrowed.

"Believe me, it wasn't my finest moment. I keep reliving it, too, like an awkward conversation where you go back and repeat every stupid thing you said and did." I shake my head. "It wasn't pretty."

"Well, how did he react?"

"Ha. Oh, the man just hunted me down at my office and denied me an orgasm until I talked to him about it."

She folds her lips in. "Sounds like you've met your match, Penelope."

"Ugh, he's too much. Too handsome. Too funny. Too bossy."

"That's not a bad thing, girl. Believe me, being bossed around is hot."

"I'm glad to know that Ethan is delivering in the bedroom, my friend, but can we focus back on me for a second?"

She nods. "Right. So what's going through your head? Talk it out with me."

"It's complicated. Maddox's awakened a side of me that I've locked up for far too long—the side that wants more from a man than just sex. But dear God is the sex fucking fantastic. So I guess I just thought if I could go back to that, focus on the physical with him again, the emotional stuff would go away. But I was wrong."

"I could have told you that."

"I got what I wanted from him, and I honestly thought that would solve everything. But it didn't. It made things worse. The feelings didn't go away, they just grew stronger."

"So you ran, but he came back for you?"

"He did. And I told him that leaving after sex is what I do, but he told me I wasn't going to do that with him, no matter what I've done in the past. Normally, I wouldn't give a rat's ass if a man—or anyone, for that matter—had a problem with how I chose to live my life."

"But this isn't just anyone—it's Maddox, the man who's been nothing but straightforward with you about his feelings."

"Exactly, so I tried to do the same. And since then, we've been talking on the phone almost every night. He sends me texts every day, and he listens to what I say. I actually *want* to talk to him." I close my eyes. "I'm so freaking screwed. This is why I've *only* had sex with guys before, Amelia. I got really good at turning my emotions off and just focusing on the physical because I never wanted to be vulnerable again."

I drop my voice to a whisper. "It took me over a year after Jacob died to be able to do that, to sleep with someone else. And the first time I did, I bawled afterward. Cried like a baby for three days. It was hell, but it got easier, and I made sure to stay away from any man who reminded me of him." A few dogs bark off in the distance, reminding me that we need to get back to the event. "But this? Opening up again? It's almost harder in some ways."

Reaching up, she places her hand on my shoulders. "First of all, my heart breaks for you, knowing you've been battling this by yourself. And secondly, you're not screwed. You deserve this, Penelope. Maddox is good for you. This entire experience is. It's forcing you to deal with so many things that you've been burying. Does this mean you called the grief counselor I recommended you to?"

I dart my eyes from hers. "Well . . ."

She shakes her head and sighs. "Penelope, I know you have so much going through your brain right now, honey. But that is precisely why you need to process it all."

"But that's what I have you for," I say, smiling back at her again.

She tilts her head at me. "You do, but you need to talk to someone professionally, Pen. Otherwise, your emotions are going to creep up on you when you least expect it. I'm proud of you for opening yourself up to this possibility, but if you don't really deal with your past, it's going to come back to haunt you at the worst time."

Huffing, I turn back to survey the park again. It's beginning to fill up with people, so I'm keeping an eye out for the players on the team to arrive. "I think I'm doing okay right now, though, so maybe I'll be fine."

Honestly? I'm lying through my teeth. I'm a fucking mess.

I mean, jumping into dating Maddox was something I just

didn't think I could fight anymore, and giving in felt like the right thing to do. But now that we're in the thick of it and he's making me believe in possibilities, I feel like I'm being slapped around in a bounce house from wall to wall and I can't stand up to find the exit.

I *like* him. I *really* do. He's sweet, thoughtful, funny, and fucking hot—let's be real about that, okay?

And I know Maddox isn't Jacob, but I feel like every time I move forward with him—whether emotionally or physically—I'm also being pulled toward my past, reminded about the last guy who made me feel this way.

Am I always going to feel like this? I honestly don't know. But the more I think about it, the more I realize I want to move forward. It's just a lot harder than I thought it would be.

My chest is tight, my mind is muddled, but my heart? It's both broken and mending simultaneously. *Is that even possible?*

"You might be okay. But I also know you, and you feel *big*, Penelope—about your friends, about your job, about issues that are important to you. And if Maddox is making you feel, soon those feelings are going to overpower you, too." She smiles softly. "I just want you to be happy and heal. You deserve that. You deserve to let yourself love again without fear of what might happen."

Shaking my head, I grasp her hand and squeeze it. "Thank you. I know you're right. I'm just . . . trying to adjust to everything Maddox is making me face right now while enjoying the high, too. Is that so bad? The feeling of getting to know someone new, that excitement? I haven't felt that since I was sixteen, Amelia."

"I know. And no, that's not bad. Just don't ignore your past because you're living in the present."

"Wouldn't most people—even therapists, for that matter— advise people *not* to live in the past but to focus on the here and now?"

She arches a brow at me. "Yes, but most people don't have a past like yours."

I can't even argue with her. "Touché, my friend. Touché."

Before either of us can say another word, a commotion commands our attention as Maddox, Hayden, Vince, and a bunch of the other players on the team waltz through the gates of the park, heading in my direction.

And just seeing that beautiful man walking toward me has my heart doing somersaults again.

Dressed in white t-shirts with the Los Angeles Bolts logo on them, they stride across the grass in a line like a scene out of an action movie—or maybe Baywatch would be more appropriate. If they were shirtless, that is. *Perhaps I need to see if I can make that happen. Sex sells, right?*

Amelia playfully nudges me again. "Looks like the boys are here."

"That they are."

A few seconds later, Nick, Damien, Ethan, and Jeffrey make their way over to where Amelia and I are standing under a tree for shade.

"Are they here yet?" Jeffrey asks, nearly bouncing in his excitement.

"They're walking over here right now," I say, pointing toward Maddox and the other guys. Maddox's eyes lock on mine just then, and the spread of his lips makes butterflies take flight in my stomach again.

"Oh my God," Jeffrey squeals and then clears his throat. "Holy shit, I think I might pee my pants."

"If you do, I'm disowning you as a friend," Damien mutters from his side.

"I'll just blame it on a puppy later. Puppies piss on everything, right? Even people?"

Nick chimes in. "I think I'm going to start hyperventilating."

Ethan looks over at him, his eyebrows scrunched together. "I really wish you wouldn't. You guys need to get a grip on yourselves. They're just guys, men who throw and catch a football for a living. It's not a big deal."

At that very moment, Maddox and the boys arrive. "Good morning, Penelope," he says, staring right at me and ignoring the gawking of all of the men standing around me. "The gang's all here, and we're ready to get to work."

"Good morning. Thanks again for coming, guys."

Jeffrey clears his throat beside me, pulling my attention to him. With wide eyes, he juts his head in Maddox's direction. Luckily, I've known the man long enough to pick up on his not-so-subtle hints. Plus, I kind of already knew this moment was coming.

I turn back to Maddox. "Before I take you over to the booth to sign in, I would like to introduce you to some friends of mine. Boys, this is Jeffrey."

Maddox reaches out to shake Jeffrey's hand. "Nice to meet you, Jeffrey."

"Holy shit, you have big hands," he says, offering his for a handshake. "Your dick must be huge."

I almost attest to that but catch myself and instead try not to laugh. I hear Amelia giggling behind me.

"Uh, thanks," Maddox replies, darting his eyes to me for a

second then back to Jeffrey, who's standing stock-still like if he moves, he might fall over.

"Next up for the awkward introductions is Nick. This is Amelia's brother."

Nick steps forward. "Holy shit, man. It's an honor to meet you, truly. I've followed your entire career. You're a legend, and I'm so stoked to see what you do with the Bolts this year."

"Thanks, man. That means a lot. I'm optimistic with our offensive line so far, for sure."

"And this is Damien." I gesture to Damien as he steps forward and shakes Maddox's hand.

"Say, Maddox? What are you doing on June 21st?"

"Uh?" He looks over at me for help, but all I do is shrug. "Nothing for sure yet. Why?"

"How would you like to attend my wedding?"

"Oh my God, Damien! You have to stop inviting people to the wedding! Our caterer is going to kill us!" Charlotte stomps up to the group at that very minute to berate her fiancé.

"Aw, come on, babe. It's Maddox Taylor!" He points to where Maddox is standing now, Hayden and Vince behind him just smiling as they watch my friends fangirl over him. "Who else can say that they've had a professional NFL player at their wedding?"

"Lots of people, I'm sure." She turns to Maddox and waves. "Hi, Maddox. It's nice to meet you. And please forgive my fiancé. He was dropped on his head one too many times as a child."

Maddox laughs. "No problem. But I mean, if you're okay with it, I'd really like to attend. It's not every day you get invited to someone's wedding the second you meet them."

Charlotte's mouth drops open. "Really?"

"Um, Charlotte," I interrupt. "I'm not sure that's such a good idea . . ."

Maddox raises an eyebrow at me. "Really, Penelope? I mean, could you imagine the positive press this could bring for the team?" The inflection of his voice tells me he's got ulterior motives for accepting this invitation. "Maddox Taylor and crew attending a wedding for some good friends? I don't see how you can say no to that."

Amelia snickers behind me. "He has a point, Pen."

"Maddox Taylor is going to the wedding!" Jeffrey screams and then covers his mouth. "Sorry. Oh God, I just sounded like a teenage girl right then, didn't I?"

Damien nods and slaps him on the back. "A perfect impersonation. But I'm glad you did it first so I could hold mine in." He shakes Jeffrey by the shoulders and then jumps up and down. "Maddox Taylor and other players from the Bolts are going to be at my wedding, man! I think I might cry!"

Maddox lets out a hearty laugh. "The pleasure is all mine. In fact, let me introduce you to Vince Dayton and Hayden Palomar." He waves the boys closer. "These two are my right-hand men on the field, and I'd love it if they could come, too."

Charlotte sighs and then smiles back at Damien. "I mean, I guess I can't say no at this point. But just you three, all right?" She points at them. "I can't ask my caterer to feed fifty giant men on top of our two-hundred guests. Plus, our venue isn't big enough to fit an entire football team."

Maddox nods. "Fair enough."

My heart is racing knowing that the man I'm dating secretly will be at their wedding now, and I'll have to fight to pretend there's nothing going on with us in front of my friends. This just got *way* more complicated.

Then I realize Ethan has been standing there this entire time saying absolutely nothing. I turn to him as Amelia does the same.

"Ethan? Babe? Are you okay?" Amelia asks.

He nods. "Yup."

I move closer to him. "Oh my God, Ethan? Are you nervous about meeting the team?"

He shakes his head and pretends he's not freaking out inside. "No . . ."

"Aw, you are, aren't you?" I lean in closer and lower my voice. "You can admit it. It's okay. I don't think any less of you." Amelia giggles beside me, enjoying how I'm teasing him right now.

For such a serious guy, one who was just giving the other guys shit for how they were acting, I find watching him freeze at the thought of meeting professional football players extremely entertaining. I know Ethan loves the sport, so this is blowing my mind right now.

"I just . . ." He lowers his voice. "Jesus, this is so fucking cool. I mean, I feel like Oliver right now—what I wouldn't have given to meet guys like this when I was his age. And here they are." He puts his hand out toward them. "Just standing in front of me, acting like normal people."

"Please, don't cry, baby," Amelia says, rushing over to hug him and widening her eyes at me over his shoulder, mouthing *Oh my God*. "It's okay. Let's take a walk, and then maybe you'll be ready to say hi."

He nods as Amelia pulls him away. "Okay. Yeah, that sounds good."

Shaking my head and laughing, I turn back to the group. Nick,

Jeffrey, and Damien are crowding the boys while Charlotte stands to the side, frantically texting on her phone.

I move to stand beside her. "I'm sorry. We knew the boys meeting Maddox was going to be entertaining, but I never imagined Damien was going to invite them to your wedding."

"Yeah, you and me both." She looks up and smiles at Damien. "It's okay, though. He's so fucking happy about it that I'm pretty sure I'm going to be hearing about this now every day until then."

"Only three weeks left," I say, bumping my shoulder with hers.

"I know." She looks over at Maddox, who's staring at us. "And if I didn't know any better, I'd say that Maddox's eagerness to accept the invitation was because of you."

"Oh, no." I scoff. "He just loves his fans. Our working relationship has been much better since I put him in a ballgown, too."

Charlotte arches a brow. "You sure that's all that's going on?"

"Uh-huh," I reply without meeting her eyes, and then I head back over to Hayden, Vince, and the man who is going to be getting a not-so-pleasant phone call from me tonight for putting me in this position.

I hate lying to my friend, but now is not the time to reveal my indiscretions in front of multiple witnesses and thousands of citizens of Los Angeles. So instead, I focus back on work while still keeping my secret relationship close to the vest.

"Come on, boys. Let's get you checked in and to your assigned stations."

Hayden rubs his palms together. "I'm ready, Penelope. Let's play with some puppies."

～

The morning goes swimmingly. The boys made quite an impression on the people of LA who turned up at the event, especially the women. And I'm not going to lie—watching them pose while holding puppies was like an estrogen hit for any pair of ovaries, mine included.

Maybe a calendar of the team full of photos from the event is the next marketing move we make?

Raises hand in the air. *"I'll take four, please. One for me, and three for my best friends."*

I can hear the screaming now.

While the boys gave some puppies baths and helped with adoption paperwork, I made sure to take plenty of photos and run the booth that we set up to raffle off season tickets for the Bolts.

All in all, I'd say the day was a success, and in about thirty minutes, the employees from the shelter will be serving lunch for all of the volunteers. I leave one of my associates in charge of the booth while I walk off to find Maddox and the guys so I can congratulate them on an awesome event.

But then I run into Noelle.

"Sorry I'm so late. I lost track of time while reading, and then my video meeting went over." She reaches into her shirt and pulls out what appears to be a chicken nugget.

"Um, that's okay." I shake my head at her. "I'm sorry, but is that a chicken nugget?"

She rips half of it with her teeth and talks to me while chewing. "Yeah. So?"

"Do you always walk around with chicken nuggets in your bra?"

She sighs. "No, but I am starving right now. I was eating them on the way over but wasn't finished, so I just decided to stick them in there instead of bringing in the bag and my purse." She pauses and then stares down at the other half of the nugget in her hand. "I put them in a napkin, though, if it makes it any better." She pops the rest of the nugget in her mouth. "Now that I think about it, it does seem kind of odd."

I chuckle at my friend who, in a few years, just might find chicken nuggets in her bra that her child put in there. "You know, I think it's innovative." Wrapping my arm around her shoulders, I lead her over to the table where Maddox, Hayden, Vince, Jeffrey, Damien, Nick, and Ethan are all standing, chatting about manly things, I presume. "You might be on to something."

"You're not just saying that?" she asks around another mouthful of food, questioning her own sanity right now, I'm sure.

"No, babe. And you look good. Better than you did last weekend."

Last Sunday at brunch, I thought Noelle was going to toss her cookies at the table. The smells and sights of certain foods were making her nauseous beyond belief. Stuff like that just makes me *so* excited for what I might experience during pregnancy one day.

Whoa. Where did that thought come from?

Avoiding an internal freak-out, I push that thought aside as we arrive next to the boys and Noelle pulls another chicken nugget from her bra.

"Hey, boys. Maddox, Vince, and Hayden—this is Noelle, the last of my best friends who just arrived."

At that moment, I notice each of the guys has what looks like a cookie in his hands, but every face is scrunched up in disgust.

Maddox tosses the cookie to the table, wipes his hand on his shorts, and then moves to shakes Noelle's. "Pleasure to meet you, Noelle."

"Likewise."

My eyes dart around the group again and then behind them to the table where a basket of favors sits for the community to take as a thank-you for visiting the event today. But those definitely aren't meant for people.

Oh. My. God. They didn't.

Jeffrey confirms my suspicions first. "Where did you get a chicken nugget from?" he asks Noelle. "I'd gladly eat that over these cookies."

Noelle finishes chewing and then replies, "I brought them. They're one of the only things I can eat right now and not throw up."

"Fuck, I should have brought food." He tosses the last remnants of his cookie on the table and licks his lips like he just ate poison. "The food they provided for us is disgusting, Penelope."

"Um, Jeffrey . . ."

A few of the other guys chime in.

"It tastes like cardboard."

"No, more like worms."

"I imagine this is what licking an asshole tastes like."

"Maybe your asshole. My asshole is clean."

"Fuck you, this was your idea!"

"I didn't know they were going to be gross. I mean, look," Jeffrey says, grabbing another cookie from the basket and holding it up. "It's wrapped in a clear bag with a yellow bow on top, looking perfectly appetizing. And it's shaped like a bone, which I thought was a cute idea because of the dogs, you know. But then you taste it, and . . ." He visibly shudders.

"Um, guys. You're not going to like what I'm about to tell you." They all spin to face me, and I almost don't have the heart to break the news. *Almost.* But when have I ever not taken advantage of a humorous moment? "Those aren't cookies, and they're not for humans. Those are dog biscuits, boys."

The looks I get back at me are fucking priceless.

"What the fuck, Jeffrey!" Damien shouts, throwing his biscuit on the table and then scraping his tongue with his fingernails.

Ethan and Nick start dry heaving, and then Maddox, Hayden, and Vince share a look before tossing their biscuits, too, and searching for something to drink.

"I need water!" Hayden shouts. "Fuck, Penelope. Do you have gum? A mint? A toothbrush?"

Noelle pulls a pack of gum from her bra, which apparently is serving more of a purpose than a purse right now. "I have gum!"

The boys rush her, and I have to step in front of her to protect her, splaying my hands to the side. "Whoa. Easy does it, boys. One at a time."

Standing guard, I wait for Noelle to dispense a piece to each man as they frantically chew the gum to relieve the taste of the dog biscuits they tried to consume.

God, why am I not having this filmed?

After everyone settles down, I lead them over to the building at the park where lunch is being served. But Maddox hangs back nonchalantly so we can speak. I haven't been alone with him all day, so I can't say that I wasn't eager for a moment with him, too.

"Are you hungry? I heard they're serving burgers, but if you would rather have more dog biscuits, I'm sure they would let you take some of those, too." I try to stifle my laugh, but it's no use. I have to let it out.

"Ha ha. Very funny. I'll have you know, I only took one bite and knew something was off. Jeffrey ate almost the whole thing."

"Oh, Jeffrey."

"That is definitely something I won't forget and will think twice about trying in the future."

"I can imagine."

We take a few more steps side by side before he speaks again. "Say, I know we didn't talk about hanging out tonight, but would you want to? Maybe back at my place? Or yours? I promise, I'll brush my teeth and scrub my tongue before you come over."

Excitement builds in my chest only for it to leave just as quickly. "Oh, I'd love to, but I have to go through the pictures from today, and I actually have a phone meeting with Liam."

I can see his shoulders fall. "Oh, okay."

I glance around us before placing my hand on his shoulder. "Seriously. I would if I could, but Liam was adamant about it."

"I get it." He smiles, so I remove my hand from him. "Maybe tomorrow then?"

"After brunch with the girls, I'm free."

He leans over and whispers in my ear just before we walk through the doors. "I can't wait to get you alone again."

My entire body heats up from his words. I turn to face him, staring up into those hazel eyes that look brighter in the sunlight. "Tomorrow may be the last chance I have for a while. I . . . I have stuff going on the next few weeks for the wedding, which means I need to get ahead at work." Any other time, I have no problem remembering words. But when he's this near, it becomes a difficult feat for me. Why does he have to be so fucking hot? "But I do want to see you. I just don't know if I'll have time after this weekend."

The corner of his lips lift. "We'll figure something out, Penelope, but definitely plan on tomorrow." He drags a hand down his face. "Fuck, I want you so much right now."

"Well, you'd better restrain yourself. The last thing we need is unwanted attention." I'm trying to remind him of our working boundaries, but I'd be lying if I wasn't contemplating how the two of us could be alone right now.

He chuckles and then puts his hand out, gesturing for me to walk in ahead of him. "I guess we can just pick up this conversation tomorrow."

"Sounds like a plan."

"No. It's a date." He winks at me over his shoulder and saunters off, leaving me yearning for him and borderline irritated that the longer this secret rendezvous exists, the harder it's going to be to resist him.

Chapter 15

Maddox

"**P**erfect." I lean down to smell the garlic and onions sautéing in the pan, and I feel like Matthew McConaughey in *How to Lose a Guy in Ten Days* when he's cooking dinner for Kate Hudson. Penelope's house smells phenomenal as the pasta boils next to the sauce I'm working on, and soft eighties music plays in the background, of course.

After last night, a night out with Hayden that left me feeling unfulfilled, I couldn't wait until it was time to arrive at Penelope's place where I demanded I cook dinner for us this evening. I wanted to hang out at her house since the last time I was here was to pick her up for our hike. I thought maybe being in her space would make her feel more comfortable, and besides, she lives closer to the place that I'm taking her later.

I used to love going out with my teammates, bonding over a

few drinks and letting loose after abusing our bodies day in and day out. So when Hayden suggested it as we were leaving the Puppy Palooza, I agreed, especially since I couldn't spend the night with Penelope. But turns out, the only thing I want to do after a long day now is see her.

The woman has made everything in my life shift.

The event yesterday was a good time, accidentally eating dog treats aside. And seeing her with her friends exposed me to an entirely different side of her. The pride she exhibited when she introduced them to me and her teasing with the boys—teasing that showed her playful side I'm already a big fan of—had me holding myself back from just exposing us to them right there.

I'm proud that a woman like her is giving me her time. She's independent and bold, confident in who she is, prides herself in her work, and cares about those close to her.

But I can't let anyone know that she's mine.

I hate that we have to keep hiding. I hate that the longer we keep this a secret, the greater the risk of being found out. And I hate that if I could convince her to come forward and tell the right people about us, we could probably spin this in a positive way. But if I suggest that, I'm afraid she'll run for the hills again.

Every time we see each other, I notice she's relaxing around me more. And tonight, I plan on making sure that we keep pushing our relationship forward by surprising her yet again with something I'm sure she'll love.

When we made plans for me to come over so I could make her dinner and I suggested Italian, her response was "That's one sure-fire way to win me over: with carbs." And that response right there had me falling for her even more.

She's not like the women who try to get my attention. She's

not impressed by what I do and how much money I make. Hell, she's proved time and again that she can control a situation without anyone's assistance, a clear confirmation of what she told me in her office that day: *I'm independent and stubborn.* And *You're here right now because I want you to be, not because I need you to be.*

I just hope she keeps wanting me around the longer this relationship goes on.

I know there are still parts of my past I need to open up about as well, which might make me sound like a hypocrite since I'm frustrated that she won't do the same. I'm just afraid that it might make matters worse if she finds out too soon or will make her feel obligated to reciprocate before she's ready. That's why I'm going to play tonight by ear—feel her out, see if she's getting more comfortable or if she's gearing up to push me away again.

"Are you sure you don't want any help?" Penelope asks, sitting on one of the stools on the other side of her kitchen counter, sipping a glass of red wine. "I know how to cook. I won't mess it up, I promise."

"It's not that I think you will. I just want to do something for you. When's the last time someone did that? When's the last time a man cooked for you, for that matter?" I look over my shoulder, waiting for her response.

"Never," she replies, swirling her wine in her glass.

I almost drop my spoon. "Never?"

"I told you, Maddox." She points to her chest with her free hand. "I don't do relationships. I don't even date."

"Wow. Well, then this is just another first of yours I get to claim."

She arches her brow. "There are other things you could claim as well, you know?"

Letting out a groan, I go back to stirring the onions and garlic and then pour in the can of crushed tomatoes. "Don't worry, I have plans for later."

She chuckles. "Yeah, so do I."

I finish up dinner and then take two plates over to her dining room table that I decorated with candles, placemats, and flowers I brought.

That's right. I'm pulling out all the stops tonight. *Wine and dine, baby.*

"This looks and smells amazing. I feel like I'm living in a rom-com movie right now. Thank you again." I reach across the table to refill her wine glass.

"You're welcome." I take a drink of my water and then dig in. "And this is what you deserve, Penelope. Those movies aren't popular with women for nothing."

"You're not going to have wine?"

"Nope. I'll need to drive in a bit, and I have a hard no-drinking-and-driving policy."

"And just where do you plan on taking me?" she asks before pulling a bite of noodles into her mouth. She lets out a moan as the flavors hit her tongue.

"It's a surprise."

"You and your surprises." She finishes chewing and then wipes her mouth. "This pasta is amazing, Maddox. Where did you learn to cook like this?"

"From my mom. She always made sure we knew how to make at least a few dishes before we left home."

"Do you cook a lot for yourself?"

"Only during the off-season. Normally, I have a personal chef who will come in during the season and prep meals for me. But when I have the time, I do enjoy making a few things on my own. One of my guilty pleasures is watching cooking shows sometimes."

She smiles at me, clearly amused. "I can't get over how there are so many facets to you. I just never would have thought when I met you that you would turn out to be so . . ."

"What?"

"Quirky," she says.

"Quirky?"

"Yeah. You tell dirty jokes to defuse tense situations, you have an infatuation with eighties music, you're a momma's boy, obviously, but when we're alone . . ."

"What?" I ask, my heart rate increasing immediately.

"You grow so serious, so demanding." She leans back in her chair. "It's so fucking hot. It's like you have a Dr. Jekyll and Mr. Hyde personality, and it's not a bad thing."

"I try not to take life too seriously because I think the energy we put out in the world comes back to us tenfold. So if I try to make people laugh, be supportive of my family and teammates, and give back when I can, the hope is that those actions will make their way back when I need them." She smiles. "And as far as in the bedroom? Well, you make me a little crazy, Pen, so that's just the side that comes out around you."

"Well, I think you're doing a damn good job, in all respects."

"Thank you. So what *did* you think of me the night we met then?"

"Honestly? I thought you were a smooth talker who was definitely looking to get laid."

"I wanted you, but I also didn't expect anything."

"I know. I remember you telling me that. It's one of the reasons I felt comfortable going home with you."

"And look how that turned out," I tease.

She laughs and then takes another drink of wine. "I mean, not many other girls could say they've had dinner cooked for them by Maddox Taylor, that's for sure."

"No other girl can say that, Penelope."

Her smile falls, and then I see her swallow. "Really?"

"Yes. You're the only one, Pen." She pauses mid-sip and stares at me, unblinking, so I clear my throat, not wanting to feed into the nervousness that just grew between us. "Are you done?"

"Oh, yeah. Thank you."

I clear our plates and then begin washing dishes.

"I can do that."

"Nope. I've got it."

"But you cooked," she argues.

"And I'm also cleaning. Just give me five minutes, and then we'll leave."

After I'm done washing the dishes, I tell Penelope to grab a sweater, and then we hop in my truck, headed for our next destination. And when I pull up to the beach just as the sun begins to set, she gasps.

"Maddox."

"Come on, or we're going to miss it."

I round the hood of my truck and open her door, helping her down and then grabbing the blanket that I tucked into the back seat and the basket of candy I bought earlier today. Once I lock it, I take Penelope's hand and head for the sand, over to a small cove in the rocks that I know will give us a little privacy. I also brought a ball cap just in case, but I feel like after the sun goes down and it grows dark, I probably won't have to worry about being recognized anymore.

"This is risky, Maddox," she whispers as we kick off our sandals and march through the sand.

"Most things that are worth it are."

When we arrive at the spot I scoped out last week, I lay the blanket down and motion for Penelope to sit right between my legs so her back is to my chest. Reaching for the basket of candy, I hold it out in front of her. "What's your poison tonight?"

She searches through her choices and then snags the box of Buncha Crunch I put in there just for her. "These are mine."

"I thought you might like those." I pull out a Milky Way, chomp into it, and then turn to watch the sun settle in the sky.

"This is incredible, Maddox. I can't believe you did this."

"Well, we already went on a hike. I figured we might as well knock this off your list, too. But there will be no pushing me away later, got it?"

She nods and then rests her head on my shoulder, twisting so her face lines up with my neck, and then she places a soft kiss against my skin. "I won't. I would be a certifiable ass if I did that this time."

"Glad to know you're not afraid to admit when you're wrong."

"Careful there, Maddox, or my elbow just might find your crotch behind me." She jabs me in the ribs to emphasize her point.

I wince. "You would only be hurting yourself then, Penelope, because I'm pretty sure that would put me out of commission for the rest of the night."

She sighs. "Damn, you're right."

"Best words to hear from a woman."

She elbows me again as we laugh and eat more of our candy.

"The sky is beautiful tonight," she says, staring off into the distance as the waves crash onto the sand. A salty breeze wafts around us, and she buries herself in my chest for warmth, which I'm not complaining about.

"It is. Do you think everyone around the world sees the same sunset?" I ask. "I mean, I always wondered if certain places get better views of shit like that."

"I thought the same thing when I moved out here from Ohio because I could have sworn that a sunset on the beach was better than some I saw back home."

"Ohio, huh?"

She tenses up and then replies, "Yup." And that's all she says. "Tell me, were they this golden in Newberry Springs, Texas?"

"Believe it or not, I think they were more orange and pink than golden. I played many a football game as the sun was going down, and I remember how orange the sky always was because the stadium lights stood out against it."

She nods. "Sounds very memorable."

"Some of my best memories of playing the game."

"More than now with a stadium full of screaming fans?"

"I'd say so. I mean, back then, the stands were full of people I knew. Now, I play and know my parents aren't there and neither is my cousin, Leslie, with her kids and husband. My aunts and uncles. They're the people who stood behind me and pushed me into this career that I wanted so badly. They're the people I truly play for. The fans are just an added bonus."

"Have they ever been to a professional game?"

"Oh, yeah. In fact, I got them flights and tickets for a game the week of Thanksgiving so we can spend the holiday together since I won't make it home."

"You're really close to them, aren't you?"

"Definitely. I miss Leslie's kids the most, Gavin and Stella. They're six and three, respectively, and missing them grow up is what kills me the most about this trade. Gavin is starting peewee football, and Stella is in dance. I wish I could be there for those types of things. At least when I was in New Orleans, the traveling wasn't so bad. But now . . ."

"I'm sorry the trade took you away from them. It sounds like you lost a lot with the move."

I pull her closer to my chest. "I didn't *lose* anything, things just changed. And hey, look at what I gained, too." Nuzzling her neck, I whisper, "If I hadn't been traded, we wouldn't be here together right now, Penelope. There was plenty of good that came into my life with this change—the biggest part being you."

She turns to face me. "You just have no problem putting your feelings out there like that, do you?"

I cup the side of her face, stroking her cheek with my thumb. "Why hold back? Why not just live in the moment and let it over-take you?"

Open up to me, Pen. Tell me what you're feeling. Stay in this moment with me.

"Because sometimes one moment can change everything," she replies. And even though I feel there is so much more to her answer, I swallow down my desire to keep pushing her, and instead I kiss her, holding her in my arms, soaking up this moment for the both of us.

❦

"How did your meeting with Liam go last night?" I ask as we head back to Penelope's place.

"Oh, it went okay. I swear he thinks I'm incompetent, but I had no problem putting him in his place."

My blood starts to boil. "What did he say?"

"It's what he doesn't say, like he's sure I'm going to fuck something up. Always asking me questions, making sure I have things in place that we've discussed time and time again. I'm an organized person, and his micromanaging is beginning to piss me off."

"I'll talk to him."

She places her hand on my forearm as I turn into her complex. "Please, don't. You going to bat for me is just going to make things worse and invite questions. This is my job on the line, Maddox. I can handle Liam."

"Fuck. Okay. But it pisses me off that he's acting this way. I saw it the first time he met you. And I'm pretty sure his reservations and irritations with you are of the sexist variety."

"Well, don't worry. I've never let the fact that I have a vagina keep me from doing anything in my life, particularly proving someone wrong."

Laughing, I shift my truck into park and then turn to her. "Don't beat around the bush with how you really feel."

"Was that supposed to be a vagina pun?"

"Maybe."

"Well, this bush is trimmed to perfection and ready for some action. Care to check out my landscaping job?"

I yank her to me by the neck, hovering my lips over hers. "Show me your lady garden, Penelope."

She laughs. "I've actually used that phrase to describe it before. The girls said it was disturbing." She tilts her head. "And now that I've heard it from someone else, I think I'd have to agree."

I press a kiss to her lips, and then we exit my truck. Once we get back inside her house, she leads me to her room, pushes me down on the edge of her bed, and then backs away slowly.

"What are you doing?"

"Well, since you pulled out all the stops earlier to make me feel special, I thought I'd return the favor."

"I'm listening . . ."

"You're not the only one who listens, Maddox." She winks and then heads for her closet. "I'll be right back."

My dick is already straining against my shorts from our little conversation in my truck. But as I sit here, waiting for Penelope to return, I don't know how I will ever learn to control myself around this woman.

After what feels like forever, the door to her walk-in closet slowly opens, and she appears before me, bare-legged and wearing only a football jersey—*my* new jersey for the Los Angeles Bolts.

Jesus fuck.

Running my hand down my face, I gasp and then groan at the sight of her, her torso covered in the purple-and-yellow colors of the team. "Holy shit."

"You like?" She spins around so I can see the back: my last name over the number nine. And I swear I might ask her to marry me this very second. This sight—I never want to forget this.

"Um, yeah. You could say that." I reach down to adjust myself, feeling pre-cum drip out of the tip of my dick.

Giggling, she turns back to face me and then saunters over to where I'm sitting, looking fucking delectable and so goddamn sexy that I'm barely holding it together. She straddles me and brushes my hair from my face. "You're not the only one who listens," she says.

"What do you mean?"

"That day in my office before Liam got there during one of our first meetings. You made a comment about how seeing me in your jersey and nothing but your jersey would be a fantasy of yours."

"Hmm, I did." I run my hands up her bare thighs to her hips, finding her completely naked under this thing.

"At the time, I thought you were delusional for thinking that might ever happen. But obviously, I was a fool for thinking I'd be able to resist you."

"The feeling is mutual, Pen. The moment I saw you again, I just . . ." I trail off, trying to think of a way to get her to understand how drawn to her I was. But I just can't explain it. It was one of those gut feelings that a person just can't ignore.

She lifts my chin and looks down at me. "I need you to fuck me, Maddox. Please."

Burying my hand in her hair, I tilt her head back and lick up the column of her neck, nibbling as I go. "Say that again."

"Fuck me, Maddox."

"How bad do you want my cock, baby?"

"So bad." She rubs herself over my crotch, wetting my shorts as she does.

"I want you aching for my dick, Penelope. I want you screaming, begging, and practically convulsing before I give you my cock tonight. Do you think you can handle it?"

"Yes." She moans before I pull her lips to mine and devour her mouth. She reaches between us and pulls on the hem of my shirt, lifting it up and breaking us apart just long enough to extract the fabric from my body. Then we find each other's mouths again.

I run my hands along the curve of her ass, up her ribcage, and then find her breasts, playing with her nipples with my thumbs. For a moment, I debate taking my jerscy off of her, but then I realize there's one thing I need to see before I do.

"Get on your knees."

She leans back and stares down at me. "I hate that you try to tell me what to do," she says, but her entire body drops to the floor, her legs folding under her as she obeys my command.

"No, you don't. That's why you listened." Gripping her chin lightly, I direct her gaze to mine and continue. "Because deep down, you know this is what you want and need. It's what we both need. You want to relinquish control, and I want to watch you do it. So let me give that to you, and I'll gladly let you return the favor."

"Only because I know that the reward at the end of this is entirely worth it." She smirks and then reaches up to undo the button at my waist as I stand. I grab a condom from my wallet and toss it on the bed before I help her take my shorts off so I'm completely naked before her. I stroke myself a few times, teasing her even more.

"You like watching me stroke my cock, Penelope?' She nods, licking her lips. "What if I just stood here and took care of myself? How would that make you feel?"

"Frustrated."

"Hmm. And what about your pussy? Is your pussy dripping for me right now at the thought of that?"

She dips her fingers between her legs and then lifts them back out, her hand glistening with her arousal.

"Fuck. That's what I want my cock to look like when you're done sucking me off. Do you understand?" I bend at the waist and suck her fingers clean.

"Yes, Maddox."

"Jesus. I'm close to coming already with those two words alone, Penelope."

She simply smiles up at me and says, "Then bring it here, Mr. Taylor." And then she's opening her mouth and sticking out her tongue.

Unable to wait another second, I bring my cock to her lips and allow her to play with the head, flicking my piercing back and forth as she teases me with her tongue. She reaches up to cradle my balls, rolling them as her tongue moves from the base of me all the way up to the tip. And she keeps doing that, bringing me closer to my orgasm than I should want.

But right now, all I want to do is come down her throat.

As if she can read my mind, she takes me as far back as she can, gagging before she releases me and then starting the process all over again—pulling me in, sucking as she lets me back out, swirling her tongue with such finesse that I know I'm not going to last much longer.

"Fuck, I'm gonna come, Penelope."

She nods and keeps working me over—rolling my balls in her hand, stroking my length that she can't take all the way in, and sucking me over and over until stars form behind my eyelids and I'm cursing as the first hot spurt of cum shoots out of me.

"Jesus . . . Christ."

Penelope keeps sucking, pulling me in as I unleash my release in her mouth, and she swallows it all like a fucking champ.

When she's done, she releases me and then leans back on her heels, staring up at me, a proud grin on her face.

"That was fucking incredible," I say, stroking her cheek before helping her stand and assisting her onto the bed.

She crawls on all fours to the center of the bed, giving me a perfect view of her ass until she spins around and curls her finger, beckoning me to her.

"Take off the jersey, baby." As sad as I am to see the purple-and-yellow brand come off of her, I want her completely naked for what I have planned next.

She does as she's told, granting me such a gorgeous view that I take a mental picture to save for later.

"Where are your toys, Pen?"

She arches a brow at me. "My toys? You mean like my Barbies?"

"Don't get sassy, woman, or I'll just make this worse for you."

She giggles and then points to the nightstand next to her bed. Feeling myself grow hard again, I stroke my length as I walk over and open the drawer, finding so many fucking brightly colored sex toys staring back at me. "You weren't kidding about having quite the collection, were you?"

"Nope," she says proudly.

I reach in and take out something I've never seen before, a wand that's no bigger than my hand but has an opening on the end. "What does this do?"

"It sucks on my clit until I'm making a mess on my sheets."

Turning toward her, I catch the gleam in her eyes. "Then this is what we're going to use. Lie back."

She lays down so she's perpendicular to the headboard and spreads her legs open, giving me a view of her perfect pussy—pink, wet, and ready. And as much as I want to drive into her right now, I told her I was going to torture her, and that's exactly what I intend to do.

I move toward the edge of the bed, tossing the toy to the side, and then hover over her, propping myself up so our bodies aren't touching. "You are so fucking perfect, Penelope."

She reaches up and runs her nails through the scruff on my jaw. "Maddox, I . . ."

Leaning down, I latch on to her nipple, teasing her as I circle my tongue around. She arches her back, pushing her chest up to grant me better access. I rub her other breast with my thumb, flicking and rolling her peak until she's writhing before I switch sides.

"So good," she cries, gripping onto the sides of my head as I worship her breasts. And then, as I keep kissing her nipples and nibbling on them, the head of my dick collides with her clit, and she gasps as we connect. "Oh my God."

I abandon her chest to look down between us as I rock back and forth, using my piercing to tease her bundle of nerves and drive her wild. "You like that?"

"God, yes. Fuck, it feels so good."

"You're so fucking wet, Pen." I move my cock down further around her entrance, gathering her arousal, and then bring it back to her clit, rubbing her back and forth again.

"I'm about to be wetter."

"Not yet." I pull away, and she groans in frustration.

"Maddox . . ."

"I told you. I want you begging for my cock by the time I'm done with you." I push myself up and then drop to my knees before her as her head pops up to see where I went. I lean forward, dragging my tongue through her, tasting her, practically drowning in need for her all over again. "God, I could do this all night, baby."

She pushes her hips up into my face. "I'd love to see that."

I rim her entrance with my tongue. "I don't think you could handle that."

"You're right. I'm already dying, Maddox. Please. I need you to fuck me."

"I fucking love it when you beg. Hearing you want me, knowing you're fucking drenched because of me? It's such a fucking turn-on."

"All I want is you," she says. My heart bursts from the declaration. She probably said it in the heat of the moment not realizing that, subconsciously, she's admitting much more.

I'll take it. I'll make it so she'll never want anyone else.

I reach for the toy now and turn it on, listening to the sucking sounds it makes. She lifts her head again and watches as I place it over her clit, instantly making her cry out. "Oh, *fuck*, yes."

"Goddamn." As I hold the toy steady, I slowly slide two fingers inside her and hiss as she squeezes her pussy around me and liquid leaks out of her all over my hand. I take my time working her over, sliding in and out, hooking my fingers to tease that spot inside her that I know will make her burst.

She's squirming on the bed, burying her hands in my hair,

cursing and chanting to God as I get her to the edge of her orgasm —and then I stop.

"Maddox!" she screams. "Please! I was so close."

"I know. And now you're ready for my cock." I reach for the condom, cover myself with lightning speed, and then slide right into Penelope, pistoning my hips and fucking her like I promised, knowing neither of us is going to last very long at this rate.

"God, yes!"

"Fuck, Pen."

"Maddox!"

"Are you gonna come all over my cock, baby?"

She gasps as I fuck her, thrusting so hard and fast inside her that the entire bed is shaking.

"Yes . . . yes . . . yes!" She shatters, screaming so loud I'm sure the neighbors can hear her, but I don't give a fuck. I keep pounding into her, drawing out every last tremor of her release as I reach my own, slamming into her so hard at the end that I'm afraid I've hurt her.

But the sated look on her face tells me she's okay—her eyes are closed, her mouth is open, and her chest is heaving with every breath she draws in. Sweat covers both of our bodies.

I collapse on top of her, burying my face in her hair with my dick still inside her.

She finally speaks. "Holy shit."

"Penelope." I kiss her neck, her jaw, and then her lips. "Jesus, woman. You drive me senseless."

"Well, I definitely don't mind the consequences of that."

I press a kiss to the tip of her nose and then push myself off her. "Stay right here." I walk into her bathroom to dispose of the condom, and then I wet a washcloth and bring it back out to find her still spent on the bed, barely moving. Slowly, I wipe between her legs, cleaning her gently, and then press a kiss to her clit. "There. Gotta take care of my girl."

She bites her lip and then closes her legs.

"Aw, come on. Don't go all shy on me now, Pen. Can you finally admit that this pussy belongs to me now?"

She smirks. "You're definitely getting closer to partial ownership, but at the end of the day, it will always belong to me first."

Chapter 16

Penelope

"Hello, Liam."

"Penelope. What the fuck is going on with Maddox?"

"Uh, excuse me?" My pulse spikes as I wonder what exactly the point of this phone call is because the worst-case scenario is playing through my head right now, and I feel like I'm about to puke.

Did Liam find out about us?

We've been trying to be careful, but last night he *did* take me to the beach. Not a completely private area to be sneaking around, hoping not to get caught together.

My gut told me it wasn't a bright idea, but then we watched the sunset together, and all of that caution went right out the window.

Obviously, my head is not on straight at all when it comes to this man.

"The tabloids!" Liam shouts into the phone, pulling me back to the conversation. "Have you seen the fucking tabloids this morning?"

"No. I usually don't worry about that stuff until I get into the office." My normal clients don't usually have me worrying about tabloids anyway since I tend to work with companies, not people.

"Well, that's a shame. As someone who works in PR and at the suggestion of your boss, I thought we had the best of the best working for the Bolts, which means that you should barely be sleeping because our reputation is on the line." He blows out a breath.

"Is there a point to this call besides you trying to tell me how much I suck at my job?"

A notification dings followed by a link that pops up on my phone. "Read this article, and then tell me that I don't have every right to be pissed. I thought you had him under control, Penelope. I thought you had him hypnotized like every other man on the team. But I guess I have to hover over you now, too."

He hangs up, leaving me fuming as I yank my phone down from my ear and click on the screen. I instantly feel my blood boil, understanding why Liam is so freaking pissed this morning—because he has every right to be, as do I now.

What the actual fuck?

You know those days when you wake up and just know you might murder someone? Like your hormones are all dressed in gladiator armor and are coming together, ready to fuck some shit up?

Well, add in an NFL quarterback who just took the last two months of your hard work and basically ripped it to shreds, and now? I don't think I need another reason to be storming into a locker room full of naked men at the moment, especially after our amazing time together last night.

Huffing in time with the click of my heels on the floor, I rush past men with gaping mouths who are scrambling for towels to cover their junk.

News flash—I've seen many penises, and none of them even compared to Maddox's, so I really don't care about sizing up their junk.

"Maddox!" I shout, trying not to crinkle the gossip magazine in my hands any more but failing as my arms pump in time with my legs, moving me closer to the man who is going to feel the wrath of all my hormones today. I feel like a scene from the movie *300* is playing in the background as I close in on him.

"He's over there!" A voice shouts, and I turn just in time to see Vince pointing me in the direction I'm already headed.

"Thank you!"

"You do know you're in the men's locker room, right, Penelope?"

"Well aware, Vince. But thanks for the clarification. I'm not sure what gave it away—the half-naked men, the smell of sweaty balls, or the fact that all of you are staring at me, not sure if you should be afraid or if you're falling in love."

His laugh rings out as I turn the corner and come face to ass with Maddox.

God, I couldn't forget that ass even if I tried.

Focus, Penelope. Do not let that man's ass derail you from the problem he's created for you.

"Maddox Taylor!"

He twists around so fast he almost falls to the floor. "Penelope? What the hell are you doing in here?"

Oh God, he doesn't have a towel on.

Don't drop your eyes, Pen. Don't do it.

But the piercing . . . it's like a sparkling, shiny toy you just can't help but want to reach out and touch.

Now's not the time to salivate over the man's dick, the dick reminding you that the last time you had sex with him was less than twelve hours ago.

"We need to talk. Now."

His eyes scan the room behind me where I'm sure most of his team are standing, watching our conversation unfold. "Uh, okay. Do you mind if I get dressed first?"

Without dropping my eyes from his, I say, "Do it quickly. I don't have all day. I'll meet you in the media room. You have five minutes." Then I spin on my heels and march right back out of the locker room to the room down the hall, hoping it's unlocked and we can have some privacy.

In less than four minutes, Maddox appears, his hair still wet and his clothes barely situated on his body.

At least he took my timeline seriously.

He shuts the door quietly behind him, cautiously entering the room. After we both end up standing there in silence for a few moments, he breaks it using his signature move. "What do a near-sighted gynecologist and a puppy have in common?"

"Maddox . . . seriously?"

He grins. "Just answer the question."

Rolling my eyes, I say, "I don't know, Maddox. What?"

"A wet nose."

I tuck my lips in to hide my smile, but that little reprieve from my anger doesn't last long. "You have problems."

"Yes, I do, starting with why you're so pissed at me right now. When you stormed into the locker room, I thought I'd pop off with some flirtatious remark about how if you wanted to see me naked so badly, all you had to do was ask. But given the way your nostrils are flaring and the vibe your body language is giving off, I'm gonna say this isn't a friendly visit."

"So the man's not all muscles and does have a brain," I fire back with a low blow that I know isn't necessary. But dammit—right now, I am pissed.

Just pissed, or hurt, too, Pen? Especially after what you guys shared last night.

I slam the paper on the table in front of me, pointing to the picture of Maddox on the front page along with the headline, "Guess Taylor Hasn't Changed His Ways After All." "Care to explain this?"

"What do you want me to explain?" His entire face changes—that soft, teasing smile from before becomes a hard line between his lips, and his arms fold over his broad chest. "Seems to me you already think you know what's going on in this picture."

"When was this taken, Maddox?"

He peers down at the picture again. "Saturday. That's the outfit

I wore when I went out with Hayden and a couple of the other guys from the team after the Puppy Palooza."

"That's what I thought. Why on earth would you think that, after volunteering at a community event, it would be smart to go out drinking with your buddies and get photographed getting into a car with a woman?"

His brow lifts. "I didn't know I needed permission to go out and drink legally."

"That's not the problem here, Maddox, and you know it." I blow out a breath, turn around, and then throw my hands up in the air. "How am I supposed to repair your image and help the team's image if you keep doing shit like this? The same fucking thing happened that night we met at the club. And why are you out at clubs at all when you should be focused on football?"

"First, don't worry about my focus on football. And second, you know I didn't go home with that girl the night we met, Penelope. You know that for a fact." He points at me across the room.

I swallow my words and contemplate his as he reminds me yet again of how fucked up this situation is given our past transgressions.

This is why we shouldn't be dating. My mind is muddled, unable to separate him as a client from the man I'm seeing.

Oh God, I fucked up.

And the worst part is, I *care*. I care about what this looks like, and not just from a professional perspective. Because the day after this, we spent hours together at my place, and he gave me some of the best sex of my life.

"Okay, but that doesn't explain why you were with her in the first place or why this picture looks the way it does." I hold out the paper to him. "You're literally smiling as you put her in the back of this cab. You look like you're about to get lucky and you're happy about it."

"You're just going to have to trust me."

"And you're just going to have to give me more information to work with. I need a reason, Maddox. I need you to fill in the holes in this story."

"You need a professional reason, or is this because you don't believe me?"

I rear back like he just slapped me. But the truth is, I don't know what to believe at this moment, other than that I feel like a fool.

He continues quickly after he sees my reaction. "I was helping her get home, Penelope, but I didn't go home with her. I would never do that to you."

"Why? Why help her get home and risk a picture like this being taken?"

He sighs and then puts his hands out to the side. "I'm a silent ambassador for a hotline that helps provide rides for women and men so they can get home safely when they've had too much to drink," he explains. "There. Now are you happy?"

"You do what?"

"Call it a savior complex, but if I see someone who I can tell has lost their ability to make decisions that won't put them or anyone else in harm's way, I have to step in." Emotion is clogging his voice now, but I know he has more to say, so I simply watch him. "I slip them the card for the service with the number and then get a text when a driver arrives, so I help them out to the car. But you never see pictures of me helping guys, do you? Because those pictures aren't going to sell magazines and generate clicks."

"I'm sorry," I interrupt, shaking my head, stunned by this

information that is taking my brain far too long to process. "You are a *silent* ambassador for this?"

"My cousin runs it. We developed it in college after . . ." But he doesn't elaborate, and now I know there's more to this story. He looks off to the side like he's being transported back in time. "Let's just say it's a cause I feel very strongly about."

My heart is pounding as I try to soak in all of this information. He does this to *help* women? He's not hooking up with them?

That's what he said, Penelope. Now focus. You need more information.

"Why the silent ambassador? Why not use your fame to help promote something like this?"

This man and his heart—now I feel horrible that I thought the worst. But seriously, these pictures don't help tell a different story than the one everyone assumes is true.

He drops his hands and shakes his head. "Because then it would blow up, and not in a good way. You've seen how my life is —everyone wants to know everything about me. You should see my DMs on Instagram and TikTok, Penelope. It's insane. Women offering to have my babies and marry me, stalking me every time I post a picture and someone finds out where I am. Imagine them knowing about my connection to this and then using it as a way to get to me." He clenches his jaw. "It would defeat the entire purpose of what I do—why it means so much to me."

"And what is that reason?"

He huffs and crosses his arms over his chest again. "How about you tell me the real reason you're so pissed off about this first?"

"What—what are you talking about?" I stammer.

"You know exactly what I'm referring to. I know an angry

woman when I see one, but I don't think it's the picture that has you pissed off, sweetheart."

I shake my head. "No. That's not how this is going to work."

"So, what? You're allowed to call me on my shit, but I'm not allowed to call you on yours?"

"It's my job to know your shit, Maddox."

"Well, since we're dating, I think I'm entitled to know yours, too."

Shaking from my racing heart, I stare across the room at him, suddenly feeling like the walls are going to cave in. His face softens, and then he takes a few steps toward me, but I put up my hand to stop him. "It's too risky, Maddox. Someone could walk in here any second."

He nods and then shoves his hands in his pockets. "If you think that little display in the locker room isn't already prompting questions, then you're sadly mistaken. If you think women are gossips, you should listen to a bunch of athletes in the locker room, sweetheart. They're probably still talking about it as we speak."

"Don't worry. I can spin this. The photo is public knowledge, and we'll just say that this meeting was also necessary to tell you about the next PR move the team wants you to do."

"Which is?"

I take a deep breath and then decide there's no better time than now to tell him what Liam wants him and a few of the other players to do. We finalized the details during our call Saturday night, the same night Maddox went out to the club. I should have told him yesterday, but I didn't want to ruin our night. Plus, I was trying to separate our working relationship from our personal one as much as possible.

Although I'm quickly realizing that it's becoming harder and harder to do that.

"The team wants a media crew to follow you back home to your football camp to film your life behind the scenes. They want clips to use for promo, and they're going to do a team spotlight on ESPN during pre-season to generate more buzz."

He takes a step back and runs a hand through his hair as he turns. "This has already been arranged?"

"Pretty much. And I'm the one who's been assigned to you."

That has him spinning around to face me again. "What?"

"Each player participating in this has a representative traveling with them. Since I obviously can't be in multiple places at once, Liam insisted that I follow you since you're the most high-profile player right now." I point down to the picture again. "And not in a good way at the moment."

"So that means we'll be flying there together? Spending a week alone?"

"For work," I clarify.

"For work," he repeats, smirking because he knows damn well that time away with just the two of us will probably involve a lot more play than work.

"I have a few conditions."

"Which are?"

"I get to sign off on any information that's being shown. There are certain things about my life that I don't want people knowing if I can help it. And I don't want my family exposed to more publicity than they already deal with. My job doesn't need to make their lives harder."

I tilt my head at him. "Well, we need *some* content with you and them. That's the point, Maddox. The fans need to know you.

They *want* to know you, the real you. So I need you to give me something and them something that will appease all of the invested parties. Because whether you are a talented player or not isn't the question. The question is: Can you maintain your dignity while still playing according to the rules? And the rules of the NFL are that you will always be held to a higher standard. That means these pictures need to stop."

He nods, hopefully understanding that in order for me to be able to do my job and do it well, he might have to break a few of his rules about letting the public into his private life.

"I'll help you hide your involvement with the hotline if that's what you want. But we need to find a different way for you to help these girls out to their cars."

"Okay. I will try to think of something. I'll also talk to my family so I can give you bits and pieces, but there is a limit as to what I'm willing to share, Penelope. And I have my reasons for that."

"I understand. Just let me know when we get close to crossing that limit, and we can discuss how to move forward. Everyone has things they don't want to share and talk about."

"Like you?"

"What?"

He closes the distance between us again, and I stay firmly planted where I am as I wait to hear what he says next. "There's something you're not telling me, too."

"I-I'm not ready, Maddox. Please . . ." I don't want to get into this right now. This conversation is not appropriate to have where anyone could walk in at any moment. And after we just argued like that? The last thing I want to do is bring up my past and make this entire situation worse.

His brow furrows as he stares down at me, clearly frustrated but still showing me compassion. "Okay, but tell me this: When *are* you going to tell me, Penelope? Because I feel like what you're holding back is big . . . and I just need to know if it's so big that you're not willing to move past it."

It suddenly feels hard to breathe. "It's . . . complicated, Maddox. But I am trying to work past it."

No, you're not. Why haven't you called the grief counselor then, Penelope?

"I hope so. I don't want there to be things between us, sweetheart." He takes another step toward me, reaching out to cup my face. "Like secrets . . . or clothes."

My body is primed just from his touch. "Clothes?"

Leaning forward, he runs his nose along my jaw, making my breath hitch. "Yeah, Pen. Clothes. Did you wear this dress on purpose today, to make me crazy?"

His hands encircle my hips, which are covered by the teal dress I chose this morning, before he pulls me into his chest. And the rational concern I had before about someone walking in on us goes out the window in a flash. "Maybe . . ."

"And was your intention to walk in on me naked?"

"No, it just ended up being an added bonus."

"You weren't looking at any other dicks as you walked through the locker room, were you, Penelope?"

I bite my lip. "Two months ago, I would have been all over that. But now . . ."

"Now what?"

I lean back and stare into his eyes. "Now the only dick I care to see is yours, Maddox. And believe me, you should definitely take that as a compliment."

"I could take that comment one of two ways, but I'm going to choose to focus on the fact that my dick is your favorite one now."

"Good choice. Now, if you'll allow me to get back to doing my job, I would appreciate it."

"Great. But first, you need to stop talking and kiss me."

"Maddox, we can't."

"I'm not taking no for an answer, Penelope. I feel like we just had our first big fight, and now I need to remind you that you're the only woman I want, the only one who makes me irrational and so fucking needy that I can't wait to remind you of why I couldn't let you go when I saw you again."

I roll my eyes playfully even though I'm only a few seconds away from pushing him down on the chair behind me and straddling him like one of those mechanical bull rides.

And just so you know, I never get bucked off of those.

I reach down and cup him through his shorts, suddenly throwing all of my caution to the wind. "Why do we have to wait? You could come over tonight, you know."

"Jesus, woman. If you don't stop, I'm gonna take you over this table right now. Just give me your lips."

I laugh and move my hand away from his junk. "Fine, but make it—" I don't even get to finish my sentence before Maddox's lips are on mine and we're both moaning out loud.

Gripping him tightly, I wrap my arms around his neck and fight to get as close to him as possible, his need for me evident in how hard he grabs me by the ass and pulls me into him.

We're frantic, horny, and desperate for each other. And if I didn't have so many things on my mind between work and Charlotte and Damien's wedding—plus the fact that we're in a public space where people could walk in on us—I'd give in to him right now.

A noise in the hall startles us apart, and we jump away from each other like the other person just burst into flames.

"Shit. You need to go," I whisper to him.

"My dick is hard as a rock. I can't go out there yet," he hisses back.

"Fine. I'll go first." I take a few steps toward the door and then turn back one more time to get a glimpse of him. "Behave yourself, Maddox."

"I should say the same thing to you, Penelope. You're the only person who makes me want to break the rules, sweetheart."

"Yeah, I know what you mean," I reply softly. Because while Maddox might be talking about the rules of our working relationship, I'm referring to the ones that I've used to guard my heart up to this point.

And as of now, I think it's safe to say those rules are being thrown completely out the window.

Chapter 17

Maddox

Three Weeks Later

"You know what the best part about weddings is?" Hayden stands next to me, shoving yet another appetizer in his mouth. "The free food and booze."

"Really? I couldn't tell."

He holds out his hands. One is holding his beer, and the other is balancing a small plate piled high with bacon-wrapped shrimp, mini fried wontons, and bruschetta. "I'm starving, man. Practice has been kicking my ass."

"Yeah, tell me about it." The conditioning we've been doing during OTAs lately has been intense, to say the least. But at least I know my endurance is up—and tonight, I feel like I'm going to need it.

A prickle of awareness shoots up my spine as I see Penelope

off in the distance, posing for pictures with the bridal party in a blush dress that looks absolutely stunning on her. But the moment her eyes lock on to me, my body is instantly aware of our connection.

Leslie is right—this pull I have to her was fast and intense, but I know there's a reason I'm drawn to her. I'm still determined to find out what it is. Even more, I'm hoping once I introduce Penelope to my cousin in a few weeks, she'll see what I see: that the woman is witty and beautiful—and the person I've been looking for all my life.

When Penelope told me a few weeks ago that she would be following me home with a film crew, the first idea that raced through my mind was introducing her to my family. I know she'll fit right in with her sarcasm, smile, and spirit. Underneath that wall she has guarding her heart is a woman who sees the beauty in the small things, who values friendship above all else, and who fights for her independence. She's also fiery and fierce regarding things she feels strongly about; exactly the type of woman I know my parents want me to end up with.

The question is: Does Penelope want to be that woman?

Deep down, I think I already know the answer. But then Leslie's voice comes back, inserting doubt.

Is it Leslie's voice or yours, Maddox?

There's something missing, some vital piece of who she is that she hasn't revealed yet. I'm hoping as we grow closer, she'll open up to me more.

I need that from her so that I can do the same. I'm sure once we visit Texas, I'm going to have to let her know just what I've been keeping close to the vest as well. And even though I've debated telling her already, I know that divulging everything while in my hometown will help my story make much more sense.

People mill around us, conversing while sipping champagne and beer as we all wait for the reception to start. It truly is a beautiful wedding, the type of black-tie event one would see in a magazine or on a Pinterest post.

White flowers are everywhere with pops of pink and yellow in the décor. Tall trees with hanging crystals sit atop each table, and mood lighting climbs up the walls. White linen covers every surface, and waiters in black suits and ties meander around the room, attending to guests.

It's romantic and classy, but I'm irritated that I can't celebrate the event the way I want to—with Penelope on my arm.

"Why didn't we have a champagne bar at our wedding?" Justice, Vince's wife, asks, pulling my attention to the two of them as they come up to Hayden and me.

"Because you wanted a signature cocktail, sweetie," Vince replies, rolling his eyes at me. He can act like his wife is annoying him all he wants, but I know the man is wrapped around the woman's fingers.

"I know, but it's such a great idea. There are so many different flavors and add-ins to choose from." Then she turns to me. "Thanks for getting an invite to the wedding by the way, Maddox. It's been awhile since Vince and I had a night out, just the two of us."

I chuckle. "No problem."

"And I know Vince probably won't tell you himself, but he's really loved getting to know you." She reaches up and places her hand on my shoulder.

"Babe!" he chastises.

"Oh, don't act like you haven't been talking about him since you met him." She looks back at me and winks. "That's how I know he likes you. All I hear is 'Maddox, this' and 'Maddox, that.' Speaking of which, how's it going with Penelope?"

Hayden's ears perk up, and my stomach drops. Vince's eyes go wide as he looks between me and his wife. "Uh, babe? Now's not a good time to—"

Hayden cuts him off. "What's going on with Penelope?"

Justice finally absorbs the looks on all of our faces and then lifts her champagne glass to her lips before saying, "I mean with the team. Vince says she's been doing a great job organizing the events and such."

I feel my shoulders relax, and I watch Vince's do the same. "Yes, she has. The team is lucky to have her. And Liam says that ticket sales have already increased since this time last year, so what we're doing is working."

"Any woman who can wrangle a team of fully grown men is a badass in my book." She drains her glass and then turns to Vince. "I need more champagne."

"I don't think you do," Vince retorts.

Hayden shoves his last shrimp in his mouth. "I'll go with you, Justice. I need more beer and food."

Vince and I watch the two of them walk off before he turns to me, shaking his head. "I'm sorry, bro."

"What the fuck, man? You told her about me and Penelope?" I hiss.

"She's my wife, Maddox. We tell each other everything. Don't worry, though. I think Hayden bought her cover."

I sigh and pinch the bridge of my nose. "I hope so. I don't need anyone else knowing about this right now. She's already on edge about our relationship given the pictures that surfaced of me at the club a few weeks ago." I hold up a finger and thumb with an inch of space between them. "I'm this close to breaking down her walls, man. I don't need anything else to make her run."

After she confronted me about the picture of me helping that woman home, I called Leslie and told her I had to lay low for a while and wouldn't be going out. She understood, and then I filled her in on what happened with Penelope and the fact that she would be coming home with me for almost a week. She didn't seem thrilled with the idea, but she knew that my job was on the line if I didn't follow through with the press they wanted. She told me she just hoped I wasn't thinking with my dick anymore.

I assured her that I'm way past that point.

We talked about how I could protect everything we've worked for without jeopardizing giving help to more women and men, and she suggested that I meet with the owner of the club and tell him about the program. She thought they could advertise it to their customers and have an employee be in charge of helping the patrons to their rides, eliminating me from the process entirely. I agreed it was a good idea, so after an NDA was approved, we signed a contract.

Now I feel more comfortable knowing the hotline can still serve the people it's supposed to help. In fact, I have meetings with more club owners next week to expand the project.

It was freaking genius, and Leslie's idea helped alleviate some of my stress. It doesn't sit right with me that I can't help someone myself given my personal connection to the cause, but maybe this is for the best.

Now, I'm just trying to focus on building the relationship I've established with Penelope, even though we haven't seen much of each other in the past two weeks. Between practices and her assistance with this wedding, I've only seen her alone and in-person twice.

I'm burning for her right now, and I can't wait until we can leave later and spend the next week fucking each other's brains out.

I have one more week of OTAs and then two weeks off until training camp starts, and one of those weeks—five days, anyway—will be spent in Texas at my football camp. I'm both excited and nervous to bring Penelope back home, but I'm optimistic that her seeing where I came from and the things that are important to me will give her the confidence to trust me with whatever she's holding inside.

She never speaks of her family, her background, or her life before she moved to LA. She swears she's working on whatever is going through her mind, but the longer I feel like I have to climb this wall between us, the more my patience is wearing thin.

I want this woman. The past three months have been challenging and have forced me to adapt to a lot of change very quickly, but the biggest challenge has been Penelope and getting her to see that life doesn't have to be lived alone.

I know that from personal experience.

Like flicking a switch, just the mention of her has my eyes searching for her again, but the entire bridal party isn't anywhere to be found. Then the voice of the DJ asking us to take our seats so he can announce the bride and groom cuts into my thoughts just a second later.

"Listen, I'll talk to Justice and tell her to keep her mouth shut about that for the rest of tonight, but I hope you two figure out what's going on between you soon. You deserve happiness, man."

He stares off at his wife, who's walking back toward us now. "Having a woman you can't get enough of is the best. And then when you make little mini versions of the two of you?" He sighs. "There's nothing better."

I watch him walk away, intercepting Justice with a loving embrace before they find their seats, and that's when it hits me: I want that kind of love. I want that kind of relationship.

And I want it with Penelope.

Music filters through the speakers, and the DJ starts to announce the bridal party as they walk into the room. Jeffrey beams as he struts in with Penelope on his arm, and in that moment, I'm fucking jealous—jealous that I can't walk around with her on my arm as well.

He spins her around as she laughs, and then they make their way over to the round table situated by the head table, where the bridal party will all sit together.

Nick and Noelle walk in next followed by Amelia and Ethan, and that same look I saw from Vince earlier with his wife is exactly the look Ethan is giving Amelia right now.

When a man falls, he falls hard, huh?

After Charlotte and Damien make their entrance, dinner is served. I take my seat with Hayden, Vince, and Justice, and we make small talk about the upcoming season with our tablemates before speeches and cake cutting commence.

And as usual, I watch Penelope charm her audience during her speech. She makes jokes, evokes emotion, and leaves everyone feeling the love that Charlotte and Damien have been blessed with.

"Some people find the person they're supposed to be with early in life, and some have to wait until much later. You two proved that timing is everything. I can't wait to watch you build a life together, and I'm honored that I get to be a part of it. To Charlotte and Damien!"

Everyone raises their glasses, and then the DJ turns up the music as the dance floor fills up.

I excuse myself to use the restroom before I run across the reception hall and shove my tongue into Penelope's mouth. The urge to touch and kiss her is so strong, I don't know if I'm going to be able to last all night without claiming her in front of everyone.

A voice behind me pulls me from my thoughts. "Maddox?"

I spin around to find Amelia chasing after me, moving as quickly as she can in her heels. I pause in the hall, waiting for her to catch up, and then look around to make sure we're alone.

"Hey, Amelia."

"You headed to the bathroom?"

"Yeah, that beer ran right through me."

She chuckles. "The champagne is doing the same for me. Do you mind if I talk to you for a minute, though?"

"Uh, sure."

We walk down the hall a bit before she pulls me off to the side and lowers her voice. "Don't tell Penelope that we're having this conversation, okay? She would kill me."

I arch a brow at her. "Okay . . ."

"I know about you two."

Now both of my brows lift. "You know what?"

She shoots me one of those looks that says *Don't play stupid.* "I know you're seeing each other."

"She told you?"

"I sort of pulled it out of her, but yes. Charlotte and Noelle don't know, though, and neither do the guys."

"What about Ethan?" I ask, thinking about how Vince told his wife about Penelope and me.

"Okay, Ethan knows, but I only told him last week."

I scoff. "Nothing is a secret when you're in a couple, is it?"

She chuckles. "Not really. But that's why I want to talk to you." She takes a deep breath. "I love my friend. God, do I love her, but she can be hardheaded—if you haven't figured that out yet."

"You don't say?" I tease.

"But she likes you, Maddox. I can hear it in her voice when she speaks about you. The fact that she's let you in this far, despite all of the obstacles you two face, is amazing."

"I care about her, Amelia." *I'm fucking in love with her.*

"I know you do, and that's why I'm asking you . . . please, don't give up on her. She's going to fight this. If you think she's fought you thus far, you haven't seen anything yet."

"What do you mean?"

"I mean, if you look up the definition of stubborn in the dictionary, you'd find her picture, Maddox. She's not one to be in tune with her feelings, but I'm trying to get her to own them. But ultimately, it's up to her to admit what she wants."

"And you think she wants me?"

She nods, smiling. "I know she does. She just has to realize it for herself. And if she can't, you just might need to coerce her."

I think back to when I denied her orgasms in her office. "I have no problem doing that."

Pleased with my response, she continues. "I had a feeling. You're good for her; you challenge her. And she needs to be broken down a bit before you can help repair all of the damage she's holding inside."

The way Amelia is speaking right now sends my mind spinning. *What the hell happened to this woman?*

I sigh, looking behind her to make sure that we're still alone. "Is there anything I can do to make this easier on her?"

"You're doing everything right so far, Maddox. Just keep telling her how you feel. Sooner or later, she's going to have to accept that she feels the same way."

"Thanks, Amelia."

"No problem. Oh, and if you can, maybe ask her to dance. I'm sure you two could probably get away with that without inviting too many questions."

"I don't know. Every time I'm near her, I just want her more."

"That's not necessarily a bad problem to have." She winks at me and then heads for the bathroom, leaving me alone in the hall.

I take a moment to absorb her words and then use the restroom like I intended to before marching back out to the reception, intent on getting Penelope alone soon so we can unleash two weeks of unresolved sexual tension on each other.

Right now, I think that's what we both need to clear our heads.

When I come back from the bathroom, the first thing I see is Hayden dancing with Penelope. I shouldn't be annoyed. I know Hayden doesn't mean much by it. The kid is a natural flirt, and it's not like they're dancing to a slow song.

But inside, I'm irritated, angry that I can't claim her in front of this entire room full of people, leaving no doubt in anyone's mind who she belongs to. I notice how Damien holds Charlotte as they laugh and dance together, how Ethan broods over Amelia and keeps her close whenever she's near, and the frustration builds. Because I can't do that—not yet, that is.

"Mind if I cut in?" I ask as I get closer to where the two of them are moving at the edge of the wooden dance floor.

Hayden spins around and does the Q-Tip. The only reason I even know what dance he's doing is because I've seen *Hitch* one too many times. "I'm not sure you can keep up with me, Taylor."

"This may come as a shock to you, but I actually wanted to dance with Penelope." The song shifts from "Yeah" by Usher to an acoustic version of "Hearts on Fire" by ILLENIUM and Dabin featuring Lights.

"I'm wounded, QB," he teases but then grabs Penelope's hand and places it in mine. "Have fun, you two. I need to hit the head." He saunters off as I pull her into me, holding her close with a valid reason now.

"Maddox, I don't know if this is a good idea." Her eyes scour the room.

"Well, it's a good thing Charlotte and Damien instituted that no cell phone rule for their wedding, huh? No pictures to suggest anything, so we're just two people sharing a dance."

She relaxes a bit in my arms and then leans her head against mine. Because of our height difference, the top of her head lines up with my mouth. "True."

"You look so beautiful tonight, Penelope," I whisper in her ear and inhale deeply, savoring her floral scent. "Seeing you and not being able to touch you has been pure torture."

"I know what you mean. Nice tie, by the way." Her eyes drop to the maroon tie I chose for this evening.

"Thanks. I hear Ironman's suit is the same color."

She laughs and then puts her head back in the same spot,

resting on mine. "Are you trying to entice me with reminders of Robert Downey, Jr.?"

"Is it working?"

She shakes her head. "No, and it's not necessary. You are enticing all on your own, Mr. Taylor."

The desire in her voice is evident as we continue to sway. "So how long do you need to be here?"

"I mean, now that my speech is done, I guess I could leave at any moment."

"Is that right?"

"I should probably stick around, though, at least for a little bit, so it's not entirely noticeable that I left so soon."

"True."

"Although, I'm sure there *might* be a way to persuade me to leave . . ." She leans back slightly and stares up into my eyes just as the song ends.

"Well, you're leaving with me tonight, so if you need an itinerary of the evening, I'd be more than willing to provide it to you. Though the list of things that need to be done is rather short."

"How short?"

"Only one item on it."

"Well, that doesn't sound promising at all."

Leaning down to her ear, I clarify my intentions. Though let's be honest—I think we both know what's going to happen here, and no clarification is needed. But I want her to know that I'm not playing around. "The list only has one item on it, Penelope, and that's *you*."

"Me?"

"Uh-huh. That's the only thing I plan to do tonight—you, over and over again. And even though it's short, sweet, and to the point, none of the things I intend to do to you tonight fall into any of those categories." Her breath hitches. "No, what I have planned is long, dirty, and full of points I need to make to ensure you know where I stand."

"And where is that?" she practically pants.

"That I want you. You and no one else. I want you under me, on top of me, and all over every surface of my apartment. I want you screaming my name, pulling on my hair, falling to your knees. But more importantly, I want you alone where I don't have to worry about anyone seeing us—until the only two people who exist in the world tonight are you and me."

"Hmm," she hums, taking a step back. "That actually sounds like a pretty detailed list. I think you might need some help with that after all."

Smirking, I pull my jacket tighter and hope to God my pants aren't completely tented right now. "Yeah, I think I do. Meet me behind the hotel. I'll call us a ride so we're not seen leaving together in front of the building."

"Okay. Let me say my goodbyes, and then I'll see you there."

"Don't keep me waiting, Penelope."

"Believe me. I need and want this just as much as you do."

Penelope spins on her heels, making her way over to her friends, and then I'm off to do the same thing.

I spot Hayden by the bar, flirting with the girl serving drinks. "Hey, man. I'm gonna head home."

"Already?" He sets his beer on the counter and pretends to pout. "The night's just getting started. Vince already left and now you."

"Vince left?"

"Yeah, he and Justice wanted to bone before they went home."

He sighs. "Sometimes I think being married has some perks, you know? Like regular sex with someone who wants to do it with you whenever you feel like it."

I bob my head from side to side. "You have a point. But sorry, man. I have things to do tomorrow, and this week kicked my ass."

"I get it. Have a good night, QB. See you on Monday."

"Behave, Palomar."

Before I head out the back, I make sure I thank Damien for the invitation. He practically cries when I hug him. And the funny thing is, if the roles were reversed, I might act the same way.

I remember growing up idolizing all of the football players I watched on television, wishing and hoping one day that I'd be one. And now that I am, I know how meaningful something like attending someone's wedding is, because when we stick to our word and show up when we say we will, we foster faith in humanity. That's how we make the world a better place—by being there for someone else.

I've failed in that respect before, and I refuse to do it again.

When I walk out the back door of the hotel and see Penelope standing there under the glow of the street lamp waiting for me, I know: She's the one I want to be there for now. And I need her to know that I'm serious about that, no matter how hard she's trying to fight it.

My plans to go slow with her flew out the window the second I shut the door to my apartment behind us. Penelope practically tackled me as we stripped each other down as fast as we could. And now we're in my bedroom with nothing but moonlight filling the room.

"Get on your knees."

"Don't tell me what to do," she says as she drops to the floor.

"Funny. Seems you like being told what to do. Every time I command you to do so, your body obeys before your mouth can argue."

"Maybe it's because I know it's going to result in your cock in my mouth."

"Then take what you want, baby."

With her eyes locked on mine, Penelope sticks out her tongue and licks me from base to tip before she starts flicking the ring through the head of my dick, slowly teasing me with her tongue. But the look in her eyes is what truly has me hypnotized.

"That's right, Penelope. Now suck me."

Swirling her tongue around the head, she licks and then draws me in, pulling me to the back of her throat. I hiss as the wet heat of her mouth consumes me, pushing a hand into her hair so I can hold on to her as if it might help me stay standing.

She works me over, licking, sucking, playing with my balls, and driving me fucking insane with her mouth.

Funny how her words do the same thing.

"So good, baby. So fucking good."

"I want you inside me, Maddox," she says after releasing my dick with a pop.

She stands, so I capture her lips, kissing her deeply as I back us up to the wall behind her. Reaching under her thighs, I hoist her up and press her to the wall, pinning her there with my hips.

But then I remember I haven't put on a condom yet. "Fuck." I lean my forehead on her chest, sucking her nipple because it's there.

"What?"

"I need to grab a condom."

"You don't . . . have to . . . if you don't want to."

I lift my head and find her eyes. "What are you saying?"

"I'm saying I'm clean and on the pill, so if you're okay with that . . ."

Jesus Christ. She wants me bare.

"Of course I want that, Penelope. You sure?"

She nods as her face softens, but her eyes are full of emotion. "Yeah, I do. Now fuck me, please."

I line myself up to her entrance and slowly push in.

The first inch is hot and wet. With the second inch, I'm biting my lip to keep my composure. By the time I'm all the way in, her eyes are rolling back in her head and I'm squeezing her hip so tightly I'm gonna leave a mark.

"Holy fuck." I latch on to her nipple again as I thrust in and out of her, hoping it will be a distraction from how fucking incredible she feels. My blood is running hot through my veins as I feel every inch of her hug every inch of me.

I've never had sex without a condom before, even with my ex-fiancée. We were young, and I didn't want to risk getting her pregnant. I'm glad I had the common sense to think about that given how that entire relationship panned out.

But with Penelope? If she told me she were pregnant tomorrow, I would be ecstatic. Hell, that would mean we'd be attached forever. And that's what I want.

"Maddox. Oh, God . . . it's so good."

I pull back and slide out of her slowly just so I can catch my breath. But the look in her eyes as our gazes meet causes something to shift in my chest.

"Penelope . . ." I stare into her eyes, holding back the words I so desperately want to say.

"Maddox." She gasps and presses her lips to mine chastely before pulling away.

We stay there like that, our eyes locked, breathing each other in as I move in and out of her—swiveling my hips, dragging out long strokes, pressing our bodies together so she can't fight our connection.

My heart rate climbs and so does that flash up my spine warning that I'm about to come.

"Keep going, Maddox. Oh, God," she moans, closing her eyes. "Keep going."

"I'm there, baby. Are you?" I reach up and pinch her nipple, tweaking it just slightly.

And that sets her off.

"God, yes!" She clings to me, and we both snap at the same time, the ache that was building finally detonating and radiating out through all of my limbs.

My knees almost buckle, but I hold it together long enough for her screaming to subside and my dick to stop twitching. My legs are practically numb, but I can't move. I don't want to. If I could stay attached to her like this for the rest of my life, I'd die a happy man.

Once we relax, I wrap my arms around her and carry her to the bathroom, holding her in my arms as I wait for the water in the shower to heat up.

All we do is kiss, letting our mouths do the talking and saying the words that I don't think either of us could vocalize right now—

well, at least maybe not her.

Me, on the other hand? I have three words on the tip of my tongue that are just dying to come out.

"What about sunrises?" I scoot closer to Penelope and kiss her shoulder as we lie in bed. We spent the rest of the night exploring sex with nothing between us, and it was fucking incredible, but not quite as incredible as waking up with her next to me.

That's right, ladies and gentleman—she stayed the night, even though it took a little coaxing.

I could tell she was overwhelmed at one point, after the second time we had sex, so I put on a movie to quiet her mind, one starring Robert Downey, Jr., of course. It only took about twenty minutes of me softly rubbing her head as she rested it in my lap before she was sleeping in my arms.

But then about an hour later, I woke up with my dick in her mouth, and then she rode me until we passed out again.

And believe me, I'm not complaining.

"What about them?" she asks, stretching her limbs and then pushing her ass into my crotch.

"Well, I know sunsets are one thing you can't live without. But what about sunrises?" I press my lips to her skin again. "Those are pretty spectacular as well."

"I don't disagree, but there's something about the end of a day that makes the sunset more poignant."

"What do you mean by that?"

She twists to face me now, tucking her hands under her head.

And God, the woman looks radiant in sunlight. Her green eyes sparkle, the red in her hair is highlighted and shines against her tan skin, and her entire body looks relaxed, like she's not ready to greet the world just yet. "Sunsets are like the curtain closing on the day. They're a time for reflection. And I just feel like the colors are more vibrant when you get to look at one and ask yourself if you made a difference that day."

"Is that important to you? Making a difference?"

She cracks a small smile. "Yeah, more as I get older, I think. I mean, I actually feel like since I was assigned to the Bolts that my job gives me more of a purpose now, you know?"

"How so?"

Note to self: Get Penelope talking in the morning. Apparently, she hasn't realized I'm pulling out my Jedi mind trick yet. Probably because she hasn't had her coffee.

"Don't get me wrong; I'm good at my job. I can spin a story, create an image, build a brand, and right a wrong with the click of a few buttons. But now? Doing the charity work with you guys, meeting these men who aren't just muscle heads but genuinely love a game that I grew up watching myself—it just gives me this warm, fuzzy feeling that I haven't felt in a long time."

"Warm and fuzzy, huh?" I pull her close to me, and the press of her silky skin on my thighs has my dick perking up in seconds.

"Uh-huh." She reaches down between us and cups my junk. "Speaking of warm, I have a very warm spot you could put this in." She spreads her legs open and brings my cock to her slit, rubbing it through her wetness. And I'm already fighting to not come in her hand.

Fuck, what this woman does to me.

"Sounds like a good way to start the day. Then I'm going to

make you waffles with strawberries, and then we're going to fuck some more so you have plenty of things to reflect on when the sun sets later. Sound good?"

"Sounds amazing," she murmurs before rubbing the head of my cock all over her clit, teasing us both.

"What goes in hard and dry but comes out soft and wet?" I ask her, catching her lips for a chaste kiss.

"Your dick, Maddox. That's an easy one."

I roll on top of her, thrust inside her with little effort, and then slowly begin rocking, loving the way she gasps as I bottom out.

"No, Penelope, you dirty girl." I lean down to nibble on her earlobe before I whisper, "The answer is gum."

Chapter 18

Penelope

Two Weeks Later

"What's this?" I come out of Maddox's bedroom in nothing but his shirt and find him at the counter, chopping up fruit.

"This is called breakfast, Penelope. Also known as the most important meal of the day."

"Thank you, wiseass. But why are you making this? I told you that I'm meeting the girls for brunch today. Charlotte and Damien are finally back from their honeymoon, and Amelia and Ethan are back from their . . . engagement-moon?" I question, wondering if that's even a thing. But I brush it off. "Whatever you want to call it, I'll be eating with them."

He drops the knife to the cutting board and then saunters toward me, his shorts hanging low on his hips. The sight of those deep cuts of his vee make me want to tackle him to the floor and hump his brains out—which is alarming, given how much sex we've been having over the past two weeks.

He's such an attentive lover, treating me like a queen but also the dirty girl that I am when I want to be. We've explored everything—a little anal play, so many positions that I didn't know my body could be contorted into—and every time, it just keeps getting better and better.

The sex is amazing, but the threat of tomorrow has me needing a break from this rollercoaster that I'm on. Because last night, it finally hit me: I'm falling for him.

And I feel like admitting that out loud is wrong, especially considering the timing of that revelation.

The night after the wedding was . . . game-changing. I felt like a switch was flipped. Letting Maddox into me with nothing between us sent me into a tailspin, one where all I want is to mount the man and cuddle up in his arms.

I don't know what came over me that night, why I even suggested foregoing protection. Maybe it was seeing one of my best friends marry the man she loves and how happy she is. Maybe it was the fact that Maddox and I had barely seen each other prior to that and I wanted to get as close to him as I possibly could.

Or maybe it was a way for me to let him in the only way I knew how—because the other way is pressing down on me as time continues to tick by, the season growing closer and the timeline of my job with the team dwindling rapidly.

We haven't had a conversation about what's going to happen after my contract with the Bolts is up, and part of me doesn't want to. I'm comfortable right now with the way things are, and I think that talking too much about the future is only going to exacerbate the anxiety that I'm feeling.

But the anniversary of tomorrow is adding to that, too.

I still haven't called the grief counselor that Amelia suggested to me. I still haven't told Maddox about Jacob, and I still haven't accepted the fact that the only person in control of all of those things is me.

Maddox pulls me into his chest. "I know you're going to brunch, babe. The fruit is for my oatmeal. I'm going to get a workout in after you leave while my cleaning lady comes by, and then maybe we can have dinner tonight, if you're not sick of me yet."

"Oh. Um, maybe. But I kind of want to see what the girls are up to, and then I need to catch up on some work." Slowly, I peel his arms off of me and walk around him to the coffee pot, where I find a cup of coffee already made for me, just the way I like it.

Seriously, why can't the man *not* do the sweetest things for me all the time? Why do I not want to go to brunch and instead stay here with him? Why do I want to be near him still even though he's practically been buried inside me for the past two weeks?

I can feel his eyes on me, but I keep my back to him as I taste that first sip of my coffee, glad I waited until after my shower to drink this so I can chug it down and then run.

"No big deal," he says, the tone of his voice slightly concerning. "We'll have plenty of time together in Texas. We leave Wednesday night, right?"

I spin around at his suggestion. "Yeah. I have to make sure I get ahead on work before I leave, too. There's a bunch of data I need to sort through, a few articles to approve, and I have a meeting with Liam to go over final details about what he wants filmed."

"I understand." He nods and then goes back to the counter to pick up his coffee. "I am looking forward to celebrating the Fourth of July back at home with you, though. There's nothing like a family barbecue and fireworks to come home to."

"Oh. Yeah, I guess."

"What do you mean, you guess?"

I shrug and stare down at my mug. "That's just not what I do on the Fourth of July."

"What do you usually do?"

"Watch movies in my house by myself. My girls are usually off doing things with their families, so I don't like to intrude."

Actually, you decline their invitations because you usually spend the entire weekend depressed and trying to escape your memories, Penelope.

"What about your family?"

"What about them?"

"You don't ever go home for the Fourth?"

"No."

"Why not?"

Without thinking, I say, "I haven't been home in twelve years, and I have no intention of going now." My stomach drops. Nausea builds in my throat, and now I have to deal with the fact that Maddox is not going to let that comment go.

Fuck.

"Twelve years?" he practically shouts.

"Oh, wow, will you look at the time," I say, placing my coffee cup in the sink and then sliding right past him. "I'd better get going."

"Penelope," he calls after me as I race down the hallway to his room, tossing his shirt aside and frantically searching for my clothes.

"I have to go."

"Penelope . . ."

"Have you seen my clothes?" I scan the floor and then remember I took them off in the bathroom right before we had sex in the shower last night.

But Maddox grabs my wrist and spins me around until I collide with his chest. "Penelope, stop."

Shaking my head, I close my eyes. "I need to go, Maddox."

"No, you need to talk to me."

"No, I don't," I fire back, opening my eyes and shooting laser beams at him with them. He can't make me do anything, and the last thing I want to do right now is get into a battle with him.

The girls will be waiting on me, and I need some space. Actually, I'd really love a time machine so I can go back and take away the words I just let slip from my lips, but you know, this isn't *Back to the Future*.

No, this is a clusterfuck of the past and the present colliding at the worst time.

"Is that how this is going to be?" he asks. That's when I realize I'm very naked and he is still in his shorts.

"Yes."

"Huh."

Before I can say another word, he lifts me up, tosses me on the bed, and then smothers me with his body. His lips land on mine, and then he's ravishing my mouth, diving his tongue deep, running his hands all over my curves, parting my legs and stroking me where it counts.

I'm suddenly overwhelmed by how desperate he feels, because I can feel that desperation inside of me as well.

I don't know that I'll ever get enough of this man.

But then it hits me—I know what he's doing. He's using sex to get me to talk like he did last time. But this time, I'm prepared. I can resist him. I can fight right back. I can—

"What the . . . ?"

The sound of metal hitting metal hits my ears first, followed by the feel of something around my wrist. *What the actual fuck?*

"Did you just . . ."

Maddox releases his hold on my wrist, the one that is now handcuffed to his bed frame, and sits back on his heels, admiring his handiwork. Meanwhile, I'm still in shock over what just happened. I can't even form words as I watch him reach into his nightstand and pull out another pair of handcuffs, gripping my free wrist and repeating the process, but this time with my knowledge.

He just fucking handcuffed me to his bed.

"Have you lost your damn mind?"

"What? I thought you'd like this? You did say it was one of your fantasies awhile back?"

"Yeah, when I'm a willing participant. But right now, this feels more like being held as a prisoner."

He shrugs. "I think it's a mixture of both." And then he rises from the bed and stares down at me, blatantly pleased with himself.

"Why are you doing this?" Tears start to build in my eyes, but I blink them away.

"Because I think you need some time to think about why you're fighting this so much."

"What?" I twist my head as I look up to confirm the cuffs

locking me to the iron bars of his headboard, my anxiety from before morphing into anger. "Unlock these right now, Maddox, or you'd better sleep with one eye open from now on!" I start to kick and thrash, but the pull against my wrists sends a pain up my arm, stopping me fairly quickly.

His chuckles make me even angrier. "What are you going to do about it? In fact, that's a pretty angry threat from someone who doesn't have the use of her hands right now." He leans over me, brushing his lips against mine. Then he kisses his way down my neck and over to my breasts where he circles his tongue around both of my nipples and then slowly descends upon the apex of my thighs. With one drag of his tongue through my slit, I moan and arch against the bed, wondering how I can simultaneously hate and crave the man at the same time.

But then he pulls away.

"Maddox Taylor, I swear to God . . ."

"Sorry to break it to you, Penelope, but even he can't save you right now. I'm officially putting you in a time-out so you can think about why you won't give in to me completely, why you shut down every time I ask you to open up to me. I know we're good at sex. I mean, hell—sex with you is unreal, woman. But you're keeping a part of you under lock and key, and you won't let me in. I know you want to; it's written all over your face. But you're choosing not to. So until you're willing to talk to me, this is where you'll stay." He dangles the keys in front of my face and then sets them on the nightstand right next to the bed, just out of reach, taunting me with my freedom.

"I have a life! I'm supposed to meet the girls for brunch in thirty minutes!" I shout as I watch him walk down the hall, not even bothering to look back in my direction.

"Not sure when I'll be back! Get comfortable!"

And those are the last words I hear before he opens and shuts the door to his apartment, leaving me all alone and imprisoned with no way to free myself and nothing but time to plot his murder.

Walking past the window of Frankie's, I can see Charlotte speaking to my two other friends. I'm sure they're wondering where the hell I am, and boy, do I have a story for them—one that gives me no choice but to come clean about Maddox and me for it to make sense.

Though right now, "Maddox and me" is iffy. I'm still so pissed at that fucker that he might want to stay clear of me for a while.

As soon as I reach the handle on the glass door, I burst into Frankie's, my hair looking like a rat's nest and my eyes wild with rage, I'm sure. Wearing a barely there purple dress and heels—because that's what I had on last night when I arrived at Maddox's—I stomp across the restaurant toward my girls and plop down into my seat, seething.

"Uh, hello? Where have you been?" Noelle asks, clearly not keying in to my mood.

"I'm going to kill him," I grate out.

"Who?" Charlotte asks.

"Maddox Taylor." No sense in beating around the bush. Plus, once they know who has messed with me, they can all help me devise a plan to get back at him.

I need to order three hundred of something. What shall I choose?

All of my girls shoot wide-eyed looks in my direction. Yeah, seems about right.

"I'm sorry?" Charlotte asks, clearing her throat. "Did you just say Maddox Taylor? The football player?"

I take a deep breath through my nose and blow it out of my mouth harshly. "Yup, and lower your voice, please. I don't need the entire diner to know about my morning."

"And why are we planning to murder him?" Charlotte interrogates further. "I mean, I'm all for trying to get away with murder. I've actually always wondered if I could get away with it. I think I could; I'm smart enough." She nods enthusiastically. "I've watched enough murder documentaries and listened to one too many murder podcasts . . . but my hair is always getting everywhere, girls. Even Damien complains about it."

Noelle cuts her off. "Jesus, Charlotte. Let her speak." She turns to me, her brows scrunched together. "Honey, what's going on? Don't get me wrong, I'm glad you're okay and that we don't have to file a missing person's report for you anymore. But why on earth are you pissed off at Maddox Taylor?"

I reach into my purse and pull out a pair of handcuffs, slapping them on the table. The loud clash of metal hitting the surface draws the attention of people around us.

"Did you get arrested?" Noelle asks.

Charlotte rolls her eyes. "Jesus, Noelle. Really? Do you think if she got arrested they would have let her go and take the handcuffs with her?"

Noelle scoffs. "Jeez. Sorry. Pregnancy brain is a real thing, all right?"

Amelia decides this is the appropriate time to chime in. "Penelope, why do you have handcuffs in your purse, and what does this have to do with Maddox?" I'm sure she has as many questions as the girls, even though she knew about my relationship with him when they didn't.

I huff, crossing my arms over my chest. "Because that dick-head fucked me within an inch of my life last night and several times all week then handcuffed me to his bed this morning and left me there as a punishment."

All of their mouths drop open, but I'm still fuming so I can't address their otherwise comical reactions right now.

"He handcuffed you to the bed? And just left you there? How did you get out?" Charlotte questions, clearly invested in the story of how I weaseled my way out of that situation. I mean, doesn't everybody contemplate what they would do in such a position at least once in their life?

I mean, I know I have. I just never thought I would actually ever be in that kind of debacle against my will.

I shake my head, popping my tongue against my cheek, trying to calm myself down as I explain how I got out. Something I will unfortunately be reliving for a long time. "His cleaning lady came in and found me butt-ass naked on his bed. The keys were right on the nightstand, so she was able to unlock me—but not before she saw my snatch."

They all laugh under their breaths. I swear Charlotte even snorts before she covers her mouth with her hand.

"Jesus, Penelope. What are you going to do now? And you and Maddox Taylor? When the hell did this happen?" Noelle probes, leaning over the table.

I reach for my mimosa and drain half of it before replying. "Buckle up for one hell of a story, ladies, especially because this one is just getting started." My eyes dart to Amelia, and with a nod of her head, I know she's telling me what I accepted walking in here—it's time to let everything out.

"First of all, I want to apologize for keeping this from you and Noelle." I flick my eyes back and forth between them.

Charlotte lifts a brow. "What are you talking about? Amelia knew?"

Amelia grimaces beside her. "Yeah, I did. But only because I pulled it out of her."

"Interesting," Charlotte says. "We can revisit that later. Keep talking, please."

Taking a deep breath again, I start. "I met Maddox Taylor back in March at that vodka party Charles assigned me to."

Their mouths drop open, and Charlotte asks, "What?"

"And I slept with him that night."

"Holy shit!" Noelle pipes up. "Why didn't you say anything?"

"Because I never thought I'd see him again. He lived on the other side of the country, you know? But he was alluring and persistent, so I gave in, which is something I wouldn't normally do, especially because—"

"—he's an athlete," Charlotte finishes for me, and I simply nod. "I remember your rule from college: no athletes. But you know, I always thought it was strange."

"Well, I'm about to let you know why that's my rule. We're getting there."

Noelle rubs my shoulder. "Hey, we're not going anywhere, okay? Just relax, breathe, and tell us how you ended up with these as a souvenir." She reaches for the handcuffs and dangles them in front of my face, giggling.

I snatch them back and put them in my purse again. "It's not funny."

"Oh, but it is. Come on, Pen. You have to admit this is a little funny. If it happened to one of us, you'd be on the floor, dying of laughter."

"One day, I'm sure I'll be able to laugh about this. But right now . . ." I drop my eyes to my lap. "There's a lot you don't know, Noelle."

She catches the change in my demeanor quickly. "Okay. I'm sorry. Please continue."

Sighing, I lift my head again and drain the rest of my mimosa, sliding the glass toward Charlotte for a refill. "The last man I was in a relationship with was a football player."

Both of their foreheads crease, and Charlotte fills my glass while Noelle asks, "When was this?"

"In high school, before I ever met you girls."

Their faces smooth at the same time. Noelle breathes, "Your young love."

I nod. "His name was Jacob. We were high school sweethearts, and he had a full scholarship to play football for Ohio State. We were supposed to go to college together. He was determined to get drafted to the NFL, and he was the man I thought I was going to spend the rest of my life with."

They grow quiet, and I look to Amelia for help.

"It's okay, Pen. It's time to let this out."

Charlotte looks over at her and then back at me. "What happened, Penelope?"

"Three weeks after we graduated from high school, he died."

Noelle and Charlotte both gasp. "Oh my God, honey. I'm so sorry."

I look up at the three of them, and they're all blurry. I hadn't even realized it, but tears are streaming down my face at this point.

Noelle hands me a napkin, and I start dabbing my eyes and then blowing my nose.

This is why I didn't want to tell them. I hate looking weak. I hate letting my emotions overwhelm me. But there's no turning back now. And even though I've been fighting this, it feels good to know these girls are here for me.

I can't believe I ever expected anything else but that reaction from them.

Noelle speaks up once I've collected myself. "How did he die? If you don't mind me asking."

"He—he drowned. And it was my fault."

"Oh, Penelope." Charlotte stands from her chair and moves over to hug me. "First of all, I'm sure it wasn't your fault. And second, why on earth didn't you tell us this? You've never said one word in the twelve years that we've known you. And we tell each other *everything* . . ."

"Let me try to explain." I fiddle with my fingers to buy myself some time before I continue. "When I moved out here to go to school, I wanted a fresh start. I didn't want to think of him, be reminded of him. The life I had planned with him was not going to happen anymore, so I just . . . shut it away. You girls were the only thing that kept me from going down a really dark hole and never coming out. You gave me a family out here. You gave me hope that my future would still be bright because I'd always have the three of you."

I smile at them. "I'm sorry I didn't tell you, but I didn't tell anyone. I shoved it down and left it there. You girls saved me from the darkest time of my life, and I didn't ever want to go back to that darkness. And even more than that, I was determined to never fall in love again."

Noelle rubs my shoulder as Amelia tears up across from me, mouthing "I'm so proud of you."

I flash her a half-hearted smile as Charlotte releases me and takes her seat again. "Wow. Okay. That was a lot, but I hope you know that we will always be there, no matter what, Pen. We could have helped you through this, too, but I get why you didn't say anything. I feel like so much about you makes sense now."

I chuckle. "Thanks."

"But I feel like we're still missing pieces of the story with Maddox."

Shuddering, I breathe in again, preparing myself to fill in the gaps. "You are. Well, the night we met, something about him got under my skin. The sex was . . ."

"Mind-blowing?" Noelle asks and then her eyes bug out. "Oh my God! That morning, when you were talking about Garret and his taxidermist, that wasn't about him, was it? It was about you and Maddox!"

"Ding, ding, ding!" I reply sarcastically.

"I knew that didn't make sense," she scoffs. "Who the hell is a taxidermist anymore?"

"I'm sure they still exist, but let's get back to the story, shall we?"

She nods. "Okay, yes. I feel like I'm living in one of my romance novels right now." She claps her hands, making me laugh, which I needed right now.

"So anyway, the reaction I had to him I haven't had since Jacob, and it freaked me out. That's why I didn't say anything, particularly because I didn't think I'd ever have to address it. Then, flash forward to six weeks later, and Charles tells me I'm the new PR rep for the Bolts—and Maddox had just been traded a few weeks before. All of those feelings came rushing back, and apparently I wasn't the only one who felt them."

"He felt it, too?" Charlotte clarifies.

"Oh, the boy was determined to get me to cave again. And no matter what I told him—how I don't do relationships or how this would jeopardize both of our careers—the man would *not* take no for an answer—and ultimately, I was tired of fighting what I felt."

"You like him," Amelia announces with a smile on her face.

"I do. And I don't think 'like' is a strong enough word anymore."

I swear Amelia is holding back a squeal.

"So you've been seeing each other in secret?" Charlotte interjects.

"Yup."

She smacks the table. "God, I knew it! I saw the way he looked at you at the Puppy Palooza and the night of our wedding —the man looked starved for you, like he wanted to mark you in front of everyone."

"You have no idea how commanding the man can be, and it's so fucking hot. And ladies—he's pierced."

Their eyes go wide. "Damn."

"You know when you see a new dick for the first time?"

Noelle furrows her brow at me. "Yeah?"

"And there's like an adjustment period?"

"What do you mean?"

"You have to adjust to the sight of that one. Penises come in all shapes and sizes, right? And no two are alike. So when you meet a new one, you have to prepare yourself for what it might look like. And even sometimes, if it's a repeater dick, the second observation still takes you by surprise."

By now, all of my friends are staring at me. "Oh my God, the dick adjustment period, Penelope? Really?"

"Yup. Well, with Maddox, there was no adjustment period, ladies. Just pure adoration and obsession manifesting itself like someone snapped their fingers." I sigh. "And now I'm addicted. This is one penis I don't think I can leave behind."

"Then don't," Amelia interjects. "Don't leave him behind."

"He's ruined everything, you guys!" I reach up and push my fingers into my hair, yanking a bit in my frustration because the reality of my confession is hitting me square in the chest. "My life is ruined because Maddox Taylor swaggered in with his giant pierced cock and made me start feeling shit again."

"Uh, Penelope, I know you're basically going through an existential crisis right now, but why does it mean your life is ruined? Just because Maddox is making you open up?"

I point a finger at my chest now. "Because for the last twelve years, I've kept my heart locked up tight with multiple keys, and now the cages have burst wide open, and all of these feelings are flying out. I haven't allowed myself to feel something for a man since Jacob—until now."

"That's just . . . sad," Charlotte says softly. "I feel sorry for you. That's no way to live."

"Or Maddox was the only one with the key, so now she's forced to deal with what happened back then." Amelia arches a brow across the table at me, and suddenly my anger is being directed toward her.

It's not her fault for speaking the truth, Pen. Calm down.

Charlotte smiles and then turns back to me. "I have more questions."

"Fine."

"Why the hell did he handcuff you to the bed? I mean, by the way you marched in here about ready to plot his death, I take it that move wasn't a kinky one between the two of you that you agreed to."

I huff out a laugh. "No, it wasn't, unfortunately. It was his way of trying to teach me a lesson, of punishing me because I wouldn't talk about something with him."

"You *were* pushing him away," Amelia clarifies. "And it sounds like he wasn't going to accept it."

"I don't want to. It's just . . ." I run my fingers through my hair. "He doesn't know about Jacob. He doesn't know how scared I am to let him in completely. He doesn't know—"

Amelia cuts me off. "The only way he *will* know is if you tell him, Pen. And he deserves that."

"Why can't I work past this? Why do I feel like my emotions are suffocating me? I'm a grown-ass woman who has no problem taking control of every other aspect of her life, no problem speaking up in any other situation and letting her feelings be known."

Amelia chimes in again. "Because although you've gotten older, you never had to mature emotionally—at least in relation-ships, that is. You've used physical connection as a means to cope, to bury any feelings of intimacy. You've never taken time to get to know a man, date one, or think about his feelings because you shut off your own."

My throat grows tight. "Wow. Don't hold back."

"I'm not going to, Penelope, because you need to hear this. Otherwise, you're going to destroy this relationship before it ever really gets off the ground." Her face softens. "I love you. We all do. But it's time to grow up, to stop running from your feelings and your fear, and to face your past so you can make room for Maddox in your future. The eighteen-year-old girl inside of you is begging for room to grow, to work past her trauma and love again. It's what Jacob would want for you. It's what we *all* want for you."

Charlotte and Noelle nod and reach for my hands. Amelia keeps talking.

"I've said this once before, and I'll say it again—you love *so* hard. Us girls? We are so freaking lucky to have you in our lives. But now it's our turn to love *you*, to push you and support you as you navigate this shift in your life. Maddox is head over heels for you. Anyone who was watching you two at the wedding saw it. So the question is: Are you ready to move on, Penelope?"

Inhaling deeply, my entire body shudders as a few more tears fall. "I want to. I don't want to be afraid anymore." The realization slams into me. "And I don't want to lose him."

"Then I think you know what you have to do."

"I need to tell Maddox everything." My throat goes tight at the thought.

She nods. "You do."

"And I need to speak with someone."

She smiles. "You already know who to call. Healing from grief and trauma isn't linear, Penelope, and everyone handles it differently. It's circular, an up-and-down type of ride, and sadly, it never truly ends. You will always feel what you went through, just at a different level at times. But if you hide from it, you will always remain at the bottom, in the lulls that you feel you can't climb out of. Maddox is lending you a hand, babe. He's offering to help you up, to help you climb the staircase or hold your hand on the rollercoaster so you have something to squeeze. It comes down to if you're going to let him."

Leaning back in my chair, I sigh and stare at the three people who know me better than I know myself before finally muttering, "Fuck."

Their laughter is everything I needed at this moment.

"You've got this. If anyone can tackle a problem head-on, it's you, Pen," Charlotte says.

"Normally, I wouldn't disagree with you. But this is a problem I don't have much experience with."

"None of us do. Hell, look at me and Damien. Look at Amelia and Ethan. We had our miscommunications, our disagreements, our obstacles to overcome. But we worked past them because we didn't want to live with regrets, didn't want to live a life without the person we knew we were meant to be with."

I tilt my head as I look at my girls. "You know, when you girls found Damien and Ethan, I was genuinely happy for you. I abso-lutely believed you deserved love and knew how badly you wanted it. I just never wanted that or thought it would happen to me. But now? Maddox is the only guy I've ever thought about breaking my rules for. He's the only one who fought me right back when I tried to push him away."

"And that's how you know it's time to face everything, Pen," Amelia says. "The past, the present, and the future."

Later that afternoon, after brunch, I shower, change into my comfy clothes, throw my hair up off my neck, and go to the back of my closet to retrieve something I only let myself look at once a year.

By now, I'm sure that Maddox knows I escaped, judging by the missed calls I had on my phone. But I don't want to speak to him—not just because I'm upset with him, but because I have other things on my mind, other battles to fight that are far more pressing at the moment. And perhaps some space from him will help me get my head on straight.

Blowing dust off the dark leather, I stare down at the photo album, and all the memories it brings up slam into me at once.

Feeling my eyes well with tears already, I take the photo album over to my bed and sit down in the middle of my comforter, criss-cross applesauce style. I brace myself for what I'm going to see when I open it and then turn the page, coming face-to-face with the only boy I've ever loved—until now.

Jacob's smile blinds me as the picture from our first date stares back at me—his spiked hair with bleached tips, our braces catching the light from the disposable camera, his blue eyes that were so bright, they gave the sky a run for its money in hue.

His arm is wrapped around my shoulder as he pulls me into his chest, and both our chins are cut off by the bottom edge of the picture since back then we had no idea if our picture was a decent one until we got the film developed.

I turn the page, fighting back tears as I see the next picture, the one from our sophomore Homecoming, the first dance he took me to. I remember him picking me up from my house, shaking my dad's hand as I came down the stairs in my red dress, my hair in ringlets that really would be a crime to wear nowadays.

I just keep flipping through past years of memories—football games and pictures of him in his uniform, hugging me after he won; holidays when we would buy each other bottles of cologne and perfume as gifts or the year he got me a promise ring that I wore until a year after he died; and high school graduation, when we smiled so proudly and optimistically, thinking we had nothing but our future ahead of us.

With each passing picture, the images grow blurrier until I finally collapse and curl up in a ball as sobs rack my body. I cry for every mistake I've made since then. I cry for not having the courage to go back home and face the town I left behind that's full of all these memories. And I cry for the man I hurt over and over again for the past three months because I felt guilty for wanting the same things with him that I wanted with Jacob.

I cry until I can't open my eyes. I cry until I finally pass out.

And when I wake up the next morning on the anniversary of Jacob's passing, I cry some more as I dial the number for the grief counselor, schedule an appointment, and book a flight to the place I vowed I'd never return to.

Then I turn off my phone for the rest of the day, wanting to grieve one last time in peace.

Chapter 19

Maddox

"Taylor!" Liam's voice comes through the line at an alarming volume.

"Jesus, Liam." I sit up in bed, running a hand down my face as I try to wake up. I passed out earlier after being up all night, trying to get a hold of Penelope. I'd seriously fucked up, and I knew it. So I'd barely slept, and with no reply from her by mid-afternoon, my body finally succumbed to the adrenaline rush that peaked and then crashed with my anxiety. "What the fuck? Why are you yelling?"

"Penelope isn't answering her goddamn phone."

I know that, but I can't tell him why, so I deflect. "Okay. How is that my problem?"

"You two leave for Texas in two days, and I can't get a hold of our PR rep. What the fuck is going on?"

"Like I would know?"

"The woman is a flake. I don't understand why the team hired her or even allowed her on this account."

I sit up straighter as fury runs through my veins. "You'd better watch your tone, Liam. I'm sure there's a reason why you can't reach her, and it has nothing to do with her work ethic, all right?"

Who are you trying to convince there, Maddox? Him or you?

As soon as I left Penelope handcuffed to my bed yesterday, I felt like I took things too far. But dammit, she shut down on me again, and I was done. The next time I see her, we're going to talk, I'm going to tell her how I feel, and then we're going to make a decision about going public with our relationship.

That is, if I can get the woman to talk to me. At this rate, I wonder if she'll even follow through with going home with me.

I fucked up. I pushed her too hard. Now, all I want is to apologize and move forward, but I'm scared that pushing her to talk to me too soon might make matters even worse.

I called her so many times yesterday that I lost count, but each time it went to voicemail, so I finally gave up.

She's obviously pissed at me and doesn't want to talk. But after this conversation with Liam right now that's making me want to punch something, I think I might just have to show up at her house and *make* her talk to me—because now I'm getting worried.

Did something happen to her? Did her phone die when she was on a mountain, hiking somewhere to clear her head? Did she walk on the beach at night and get kidnapped?

My mind is running through a hundred different scenarios at the moment, none of which I like at all. But Liam's voice pulls me from my thoughts.

"There'd better be a reason she's not fucking answering my

calls, because if the owner catches wind of this, it's her job on the line. Training camp starts next week. The last thing we need is for her to go rogue right now."

"Listen, calm your fucking tits, man."

"Excuse me?"

"Everything is fine. The team's not in jeopardy. Hell, when that picture of me ran in the tabloids a month ago, she spun the story to make me look like a fucking gentleman." And she did, painting me as the Good Samaritan who was just opening a car door for a lady. In fact, she fostered a counter-campaign, distributing an article to as many media outlets as possible that explained the reason I get photographed at times with women in that situation: me exhibiting my southern charm and chivalry. The news outlets went apeshit over it.

"She's damn good at what she does, and there has to be a reason why she isn't talking to you at the moment, so chill the fuck out." I blow out a breath, trying to calm myself down. "Look, I met a few of her friends at the Puppy Palooza event. Maybe I'll get in contact with them and see if they know where she is or how to get a hold of her. Maybe her phone broke or something, and she's in the process of getting a new one. You never know what's going on in someone else's life, so you shouldn't go assuming the worst, okay?"

He huffs, and I can only hope that some of those words got through to him. "Fine. But if I don't hear from her by tomorrow morning, I'm going to the owners. I won't let this team go down because of her."

"That won't be necessary. Now, relax for a moment, and let me see what I can find out."

"You'd better do something, Maddox, because this isn't just

her ass on the line. It's yours, too." Then the line goes dead, and I have a strong fucking urge to throw my phone against the wall.

"Jesus." Standing from my bed, I head to my closet to change my clothes. I run into the bathroom to check my appearance really quick since I'm sure I look like shit from a lack of sleep. Dark circles under my eyes reveal the stress my heart and mind have been under, but other than that, I just look like a man in love with a woman who *he* pushed away this time.

I need to fix this, once and for all. So I hop in my truck and race across town, hoping Penelope will answer the door when I knock.

"P enelope?" I bang louder, hoping I don't rattle the walls, but I could have sworn I heard movement inside just a second ago. If she's in there and not answering, that means she doesn't want to see me. And I don't know how I'm going to take that.

"Penelope, open up, please. I'm sorry. I'm so fucking sorry about yesterday. But I need to talk to you. There's shit going on with Liam, and—" My phone ringing cuts me off.

I pull it from my pocket and see Leslie's name across the screen. I momentarily debate just calling her back later, but from the looks of it, Penelope's not home, anyway. And maybe my cousin can give me some advice.

Reluctantly, I answer and lean against the door. "Hey, Les."

"Uncle Maddox!" Stella shouts over the call. Even though I'm technically their second cousins, Leslie's kids call me their uncle, and I don't mind it at all. Her voice instantly makes me smile, granting me a moment of reprieve from all the stress.

"Stella Bella! How are you, my princess?"

"I miss you, Uncle Maddox. When you come home?"

"I'll be there in a few days, Stella. And we are gonna play tea party and watch all of the princess movies, okay?"

"Yay!" she shouts, and I can hear Leslie laughing in the background.

"Listen, can I talk to your mommy, please? It's really important."

"Okay, Uncle Maddox. I love you!"

"I love you, too, princess." There's a shuffling noise, and then Leslie's voice comes through. "Hey, Mad. Is everything okay?"

"I fucked up, Les. With Penelope."

"Oh, shit!"

"Mommy, you said a bad word!" Stella shouts in the background.

"Bad words are for grown-ups, sweetie. It's okay," she says and then focuses back on me. "What happened?"

I briefly explain to her how things have been going and how I might have restrained Penelope yesterday because she wouldn't talk to me. By the end of it, I can almost visualize the look on her face, the one that says I'm a complete fucking idiot.

"Well, I'd be pissed at you, too, if I was dating you and you left me like that."

"I know. It wasn't my finest moment. But do you remember slapping me out of my stupidity after Grace died? It worked, so maybe sometimes a little tough love is the answer."

"Yes, but I don't think that's the only reason she's not returning your calls right now, given that you've always been suspicious that she's been hiding something. You of all people should have respected that. You know what it's like to fight demons in your head when you're still living in the past."

"I know. But now I can't find her, Leslie. I can't—I can't fucking lose her."

"Then don't. Give her some space, but when you see her next, vow to cherish her. Make her realize she's the only woman you want in your life. And never make her doubt you, Maddox. That's how you keep a woman. It's not about being perfect and never making mistakes. It's about being a man she knows she can depend on even when you fuck up."

"I don't know where she might be."

She clicks her tongue. "Yeah, you do. Come on, you know her. Use your head, use your resources, figure out who she might run to if she's running from you."

Just like that, a spark ignites in my mind. "Fuck, I've got an idea."

"Yeah, you do. Now go, Maddox. Fight for her. Show her the man you are—because even though I know I was hesitant about this before, I can hear it in your voice. You love her."

"She's the one, Leslie."

"The one who's going to drive you crazy but make every instance worth it."

"**M**addox?" Amelia spins around in her office to find me standing there, nearly out of breath.

"Hey, Amelia. I hope I'm not interrupting anything."

She sets a file folder down on her desk and then looks back up at me. "No, I'm in between my last two clients right now, actually, so your timing is impeccable. How can I help you?"

"Have you talked to Penelope lately?"

The way her face falls tells me she knows something. "Um, yes. At brunch yesterday and then a bit this morning."

"So she's okay?"

Amelia sighs. "Yes and no."

"She won't answer my calls or Liam's. He's pissed, and I'm worried. The last time I saw her, I . . . well, let's just say, I left her in an uncomfortable situation."

Amelia folds her lips in to hide her smile. "Oh, I'm aware. She was an hour late to brunch."

"Fuck. She was pissed, wasn't she?"

"I mean, I know I told you to push her, I just didn't think you had it in you. Nice cuffs, by the way. Those are ones I recommend to clients as well for comfort." She winks, and I shift my weight beneath her knowing gaze. But then I remember that talking about sex is part of her job, so my stomach untwists fairly quickly.

"Well, I think I pushed her too far. She won't talk to me, and she's not home."

"I know."

I take a step toward her. "You know where she is?"

"Yes. She went back to Ohio for a few days."

My heart stops beating for a minute. "She did?"

"Maddox, remember when I spoke to you at the wedding? When I told you she was working through things and you needed to be patient with her?"

"Yeah?"

"Well, this time right now is what I meant. She's working

through it, Maddox. And knowing Penelope, she's doing it on her own timetable. If she doesn't want to talk to you, don't take it personally, just respect it. Give her the space she wants, and I promise, she'll come around. She always does. That woman is one of the best people I know, and your presence has made her have to face a plethora of issues she never dealt with from her young adult life. But the fact that she even boarded a plane this morning to go home for the first time in twelve years says something. It tells me she knows that even though doing that is scary for her, you are worth it."

"Fuck, Amelia." I run a hand through my hair as I begin to pace her office. "You sure I should just let her be?"

She simply nods. "Yes. Give her a few days."

"But we're supposed to leave for Texas tomorrow for the filming."

"I would talk to Charles because I'm sure she already has, and he'll have a plan in place. But don't act like you know anything else, given your working relationship."

"I'm so sick of hiding how I feel about her, Amelia. I want the whole fucking world to know."

Her smile is comforting. "I can tell, and you'll get there. You're just on the bumpy and scary part of the ride right now. Every relationship goes through them, often more than once. Think of this like the big hill you climb on a rollercoaster before you drop down and scream."

"I fucking hate rollercoasters."

That makes her laugh. "Sorry. That was the only analogy I could think of."

I let out the breath I was holding and then turn for the door. "It's okay. Thanks for the advice."

"No problem. And Maddox?"

I spin to face her. "Yeah?"

"I'm rooting for you two."

"Yeah, me, too."

Two days later, I'm boarding a plane with Liam, who looks like one smug motherfucker as I battle my anxiety about taking off. I hate flying and would have felt far more comfortable with Penelope by my side, but I still haven't heard from her. And since she was gone, Liam stepped up to accompany me home for the film footage and my football camp.

When we landed, Leslie picked me up from the airport and drove me home while Liam took an Uber to his hotel. She tried to console me as best she could given the situation, but ultimately this trip—one that I had been looking forward to for the past month—is quickly becoming an emotional nightmare.

I fucking miss her. I wonder if she's okay. I wonder if she's thinking about me, too. Is this space going to do her some good, or will she return and realize that she doesn't want me anymore?

I hate that I honestly can't answer those questions with confidence.

I go to my parents' house that night for dinner. I play with Stella and Gavin and watch movies with them until we all fall asleep. The next morning, I wake up and do the best I can to celebrate the Fourth of July with my family. But as the sun sets in the distance and the sky lights up with purples and blues, I know the only thing that would make the night complete is having Penelope by my side.

So I send her a text, even though Amelia and Leslie told me not to. But I hope it's the right move to get her to see that we belong together.

Because I can't imagine a world where we don't.

Chapter 20

Penelope

"Oh my God, she's actually here, Brad. She's actually here." The moment I come around the corner with my suitcase to look for my mom, I hear her voice. Tears fill her eyes as she rushes toward me, and I intercept her for a hug. We squeeze each other so hard that I swear she makes more tears fall.

When she releases me, I look up and find my dad barely holding it together. "Hey, sweet pea."

"Hey, Dad." I take a moment to greet him, too, knowing that this homecoming of mine is just as emotional for my parents as it is for me.

I made it here. I went home. The plane ride was nerve-wracking, and my chest has been tight since I booked the flight, but right now, I'm so fucking relieved to see my parents that I feel like I climbed a mountain and finally made it to the top.

Once we all wipe our tears and blow our noses on the tissues my mother always has in her purse, we make our way to the car. And then my parents drive me home through Waynesville, Ohio.

The girls offered to come with me when I texted them and told them where I was headed, but I was adamant that I needed to do this on my own. But knowing they all would have dropped everything and put their lives on hold to accompany me is exactly why those women are the best girls I've ever known.

I feel like I'm being transported back in time as I look out the window and notice that while so much hasn't changed, so much has. Trees still line the roads, and small shops and businesses are still flourishing in some parts, but there are more people now, more bustle, more memories hitting me as we drive.

"We're getting an Old Navy next month, Penelope!" my mother exclaims as we cruise past one of the few shopping complexes in town.

"Oh, boy. Waynesville is moving up in the world, isn't it?"

She laughs and then reaches between the seats to search for my hand. "I'm so glad you're home, my girl."

"I know, Mom."

"And I know there must be a reason that you returned after all this time. Especially today, of all days."

I swallow down the lump in my throat. "There is."

"Then we can talk more when we get home."

My dad pulls into the garage, and my heart aches when I see that my childhood home looks the same as it always has. The dark-green shutters got a fresh coat of paint, and the yard is filled with more flowers than it was back then, but otherwise, it's the same white house that was filled with love and a life that I left behind so long ago.

"I'm gonna get dinner ready while you get settled, sweet pea. Still like your steak medium rare?"

"Yeah, Dad. Thanks."

The scent of my mom's favorite candle hits me the second I walk in the door, fruity and vibrant. The walls are now a soft gray compared to the beige they were when I was growing up, and the kitchen cupboards look brand new. But familiar pictures hang on the walls, a larger television sits on the stand I cracked my head open on once, and the lines in the wall where my dad measured my height are still easy to detect as I walk by.

"Did you guys change the kitchen?"

"No, just did a little repurposing of things. Now that your father's retired, he hasn't got much to keep him busy, so he's found projects around the house to work on."

"No, *you've* found projects for *me* to work on, Cecelia."

My mother laughs and then goes to fill two glasses with water for us.

My father was a diesel mechanic for thirty years, and my mother still teaches kindergarten. She's retiring at the end of next year after thirty-five years of teaching, and I know they're eager to start traveling soon.

"It looks great. God, this is so weird." I laugh nervously. "Sorry, I just . . ."

Mom rests her palm on my shoulder. "It's okay, Pen. Let's go to your room to talk."

My mother leads me down the hall and opens the door to my room, where, just as she said before, the space looks exactly how I left it.

A few boyband posters still line the walls (*NSYNC fan for life), the walls are the same shade of lilac I demanded when I turned fourteen because I was and still am obsessed with the color purple, and my twin bed is still made and in the same corner where I slept under the window that I used to sneak Jacob in and out of at night.

My lip trembles, and I know my mom senses it because she rushes over to me and holds me to her chest, encircling me in her arms.

"It's okay, Penelope. It's okay. Shh."

"I'm so sorry, Mom. I'm so sorry it's been so long."

"I know, baby. But you're here now, and that's what matters."

"I had to come back. I-I need to move on."

"Does this have something to do with the man you started seeing a few months ago?" I nod against her shoulder. "Well, then, I guess it's time we talk."

I wipe my nose on the sleeve of my light sweater, and then we both settle onto my bed. "God, where do I start?"

"Anywhere you want, my girl. Take your time."

I draw in a deep breath and then let it out. "The man I'm seeing is Maddox Taylor."

My mother's eyes bug out. "Oh my. He's, uh . . ."

"Really fucking hot, Mom."

She nods in agreement as we both laugh. "That's one way to put it, yes."

"But he plays for the Bolts now, the team that I've been doing PR for over the past three months. We've been seeing each other in secret."

Her eyes widen. "I see."

I stare down at my lap, picking at my cuticles. "I haven't made things easy on him, but he's been very adamant about his feelings for me, and I . . . I'd be lying if I said I didn't feel the same."

"Oh, sweetheart, I'm so happy for you."

"He doesn't know about Jacob, Mom," I say, lifting my eyes to hers.

"Oh."

"I haven't told him, and he knows I'm hiding something. We sort of had a fight the other morning, and when I got home, I stared at pictures of Jacob and me, trying to convince myself that it's okay to love again."

"Penelope," she whispers.

"I feel guilty for falling for someone else. I think that's what I've always feared, that being with another man in that way would mean I didn't love Jacob anymore."

My mom gives me a soft smile and reaches for my hand. "The road to get to where we're supposed to be is never easy. All of the good we ever get to experience is at the cost of struggles and pain, Penelope. We have to work for the blessings in our life. We have to experience failure, make mistakes, and endure heartache along the way. Because if we don't, we will never appreciate the truly beautiful things when we obtain them." She wipes a tear from under my eye. "You experienced loss and pain at a very young age, sweetheart. And since then, you've been fighting to never experience it again. But in doing so, you've also been robbing yourself of love. And I know love when I see it. You are in love with that man, Penelope. Now's the time to let someone else in."

"But—"

"You will always love him, Pen. But he's gone. He's not coming back, and he would have wanted you to move on."

"I'm scared, but I'm tired of being scared. If that even makes sense."

"It does."

"And Maddox is . . ." I sigh, smiling softly. "He's this giant teddy bear of a man, but he's commanding and alpha when he needs to be." She bounces her eyebrows, which makes me blush. "I feel safe with him, protected, and seen. He makes me laugh, and I love just being with him, doing simple things like watching a movie together. He calls me on my crap, and I do the same right back to him. It's so similar to what Jacob and I shared but on an entirely different level, too. I don't want to compare them because I know that's not fair. But I guess in my brain, it feels like I'm having to make a choice between the two of them, and I feel guilty for choosing the man who's alive even though that's the logical choice, you know?" I groan. "Ugh, it's so frustrating."

My mom strokes my cheek with her thumb. "It's easy for us to idolize young love, particularly when it's our first experience with the feeling. I'm not saying you didn't love Jacob, because I know you did. I remember the two of you together, and it was a beautiful thing. But love takes on a new meaning and look as we get older. Love is a choice, not a feeling, Penelope. You can still love Jacob and remember him while also loving Maddox. But Maddox doesn't deserve to wonder why you're being secretive. He doesn't deserve to be compared to Jacob, either. So now's the time for you to decide what choice you're going to make about Maddox and the future you want with him."

"I know. That's why I came home. I need to say goodbye to my past so I can walk confidently into my future."

"Well, for my own selfish reasons, I'm glad you're here. But I'm also so damn proud of you for finally taking this step. The stubborn girl that you are, I knew it would take the right man to pull you out of that box you started to live your life in after Jacob died. And if my gut is any indication, I'd say this man is the man for you."

"I really think he is." Letting out a sigh, I fall back on my bed. "I'm so drained."

My mom stands from the bed and then leans over me, brushing the hair from my eyes. "Then take a nap, sweetie. I'll have Dad wait on dinner a bit. And then I think there's somewhere you need to go today."

"Yeah, I think that sounds like a good plan. I love you, Mom."

"I love you, too, Penelope. And I'm really glad you're home."

Ever since I saw *Now and Then* as a kid, I've been terrified of being in a cemetery at night. And if I don't make this quick, that's exactly the predicament I'm going to find myself in.

The sun is falling in the sky at what feels like rapid speed, but I have to do this today. It's symbolic. And though it's been twelve years, it doesn't take me long to find exactly where I need to go.

I remember the funeral like it was yesterday, standing beside Jacob's casket in disbelief that it was happening, hundreds of calla lilies all around, everyone dressed in black, and tears flowing freely as I stood there in shock, convincing myself that this was all a dream.

But now it's just me, descending upon the spot where the first love of my life was laid to rest, my eyes filling with moisture as I get closer to his headstone.

"Holy shit," I mutter to myself, collapsing on the ground as soon as I arrive. I close my eyes and let my tears fall as I place my hands on my knees, regret freely flowing through me that it took me this long to come back here.

"Jacob, I'm so sorry I've been gone this entire time. I-I haven't handled this the right way, but I'm here now. I'm here."

A soft breeze whips past as I lay the bouquet of calla lilies down on his grave and read his name on the gray stone over and over.

"Jesus. I just—I need a minute, okay?" Shaking my head, I let my guilt consume me and then dissipate until I feel strong enough to speak.

"I met someone. That's why I'm here. He reminds me so much of you. But I want you to know that he'll never replace you. I'll never forget you. I loved you and always will, and I'm so sorry I didn't listen to you that day. But I don't want to be alone anymore. I want to love again. I want to be loved the way you loved me." I reach up and wipe under my eyes. "You will always be such an important part of my life, but my future is waiting for me. I just wanted to say goodbye before I take that final step, and I hope you'll be cheering me on as I do."

I spin around and lay down in the grass, staring up at the sky as it changes color, relieved that I finally got to say those words to him here. My eyes continue to leak, and my heart continues to crack and then mend in my chest as I release the turmoil I've been holding on to for years. It almost feels like someone is lifting a hundred-pound brick off my chest.

Peace washes over me, calm infiltrates my veins, and my body feels lighter when I turn my head to watch the sun drop closer to the horizon.

And that's when my phone dings, making me jump.

I reach in my pocket and swipe across the screen to find a text from Maddox, and my heart skips a beat.

The first thing he sent is a picture of the sunset. And I gasp. Because then I read his message.

Maddox: *Is it the same one you're looking at wherever you are in the world right now?*

And then, a few seconds later, a follow-up text comes through.

Maddox: *I miss you, but I'll be here when you're ready. You and I are meant to be, Penelope. And that's something I will not let you argue with me about.*

It's like he knew I needed to hear this, at this very moment.

And now I know what else I need to do.

"Who are you?" A little girl dressed in a princess dress stares up at me through a screen door. After four hours of traveling, the last thing I expected was to be interrogated by a miniature person. But then it dawns on me—this must be Stella.

"Uh, I'm Penelope. Is your mommy or daddy home?"

"Mommy! There's a lady at the door!" she shouts, running off and leaving me sweltering in the humidity but amused at how short a kid's attention span can be.

Luckily, just a few seconds later, a woman with a short blonde bob approaches me, wiping her hands on a dish towel. "Can I help you?"

"I hope so. Are you Leslie?"

She arches a brow at me. "Who's asking?"

"My name is Penelope Klein, and I—"

"Oh, shit." She turns around, probably to see if the munchkin from before overheard her, and then faces me once more. "You're here?"

"Yes, I am. I'm sorry to show up unannounced like this, but your house was closer to the airport than anyone else's on my list, so . . ."

On the flight down to Texas, I searched through all of the contact information I had for the filming cast and crew—the filming I was supposed to be in charge of—and researched the closest relative of Maddox's so I could get in contact with them. I'd tried calling him, but he wasn't picking up. I'm hoping that's just because his phone died, not because he changed his mind about us. Hopefully, Leslie can allay my doubts in just a few moments.

She opens the screen door, steps outside, and closes the actual door behind her. "I'm surprised to see you. Maddox made it sound like you wouldn't be joining us at all anymore."

"Well, I was able to take care of some personal items quicker than I anticipated, and I wanted to be here for the duration of the trip. I need to speak with him desperately. Do you know where he is? He's not answering my calls."

Crossing her arms over her chest, she stares me down. "He's probably still at the high school where the camp was held, and he usually turns his phone off while he's there. Today was the last day —he always insists on being the last to leave." I sigh out my relief. "But I'm going to tell you right now: If you're here to break his heart even more—"

"I'm not," I interject. "I'm not, Leslie. Gosh, I'm sure Maddox has told you a little bit about our relationship, and I have to say, the man is a saint for putting up with me." She nods but doesn't say anything. "I just needed some time to get my head on straight. Sometimes, as women, we live up there in a constant circle of thoughts, you know? But I'm here. I need to talk to him. And I hope that after we speak, you and I will get the chance to know each other better."

Her face softens.

"I know how much he loves you and your family. He speaks of you all the time. You guys are one of the most important parts of his life, so I would love to get the chance to find out why. But he and I need to iron out a few things first."

She studies me with a narrowed gaze. "You know, I wasn't sure if getting involved with you was a good idea. He's told me all about your relationship and the secrecy of it."

"I assumed."

"But I can tell by the way he's hurting right now that he's serious about you. And if you're just as serious about him, then go put the man out of his misery. Then we can celebrate with a glass of wine."

Relief floods my chest as my lips break out into an effortless smile, one I haven't felt eager to display in days. "I would love that. Although, I'm more of a champagne girl, myself."

She grins. "Maybe you and I will be better friends than I thought."

By now, my smile must be blinding her. "Thank you. I hope to see you again very soon."

With a nod, I take off down her driveway, fire up my rental car again, and find the address of the high school in my GPS. Soon I'm driving as fast as I can legally go, racing the sun going down in the distance.

I'm coming, Maddox. I'm almost where I need to be—in your arms.

Walking across a football field at night still does something to me. The way the lights blind me if I look directly at them. The way the grass smells after a long, hot day. The way the bleachers that are usually full of screaming fans stand eerily empty and cold but echoes of cheers can still be heard if I listen closely.

Those sounds and smells hold some of my most precious memories, but tonight, I hope they can hold one more.

I see him before he hears me. He's throwing a football into a net, practicing his release and stance. His body is so powerful and exquisite that I take just a few more moments to admire it before I break the silence around us.

"Why can't you hear rabbits making love?"

He drops the ball as he spins and finds me standing there about ten feet away from him. "Holy shit. You scared me."

"Just consider it payback for all the times you did the same to me."

He wants to smile. I can see the corners of his mouth lift, but he fights them down. "I guess I deserve that."

"You didn't answer my question."

"What was it?"

"Why can't you hear rabbits making love?"

"I don't know. Why, Penelope?"

"Because they have cotton balls."

His smile spreads wide and bright this time, and suddenly he's moving toward me, pulling me to him by my waist. "Are you here? Are you really fucking here?" he asks as our foreheads connect and my emotions get the better of me.

I don't want to cry anymore, but I can't help it. Seeing him right now, feeling his arms around me again, I am so grateful I went back home and laid my past to rest. So I break down again, but this time, he's holding me up.

Chapter 21

Maddox

I lean back, looking down at her just to make sure that this is real, and the woman I see standing in front of me looks like she's been cutting onions for hours.

"You—you haven't been answering your phone. I tried calling you so many times."

"I know, but I needed space. I needed time." A tear slips from the corner of her eye, making me question what has her this emotional right now.

"Liam tried to call you, too, after we found out you weren't going to Texas with me. He went off on me over the phone because he couldn't get a hold of you, but I had nothing to offer him until I spoke with Amelia."

"Well, forgive me for taking a few personal days, all right? Charles knew. I made sure all my t's were crossed before I took off. But the last thing I wanted was to answer my phone for anyone that day, Maddox." More tears fall as she looks away from me.

"Sweetheart, are you okay?"

She closes her eyes and shakes her head as her hands reach for my shirt. And I don't wait any longer—I just react.

I sweep her up into my arms and carry her over to the bleachers. Sobs run through her as I sit down, holding her in my lap as she cries.

I just wait for her to gather herself. My gut tells me something else is going on here, but I don't want to question her until she's found some composure.

I've never seen her like this. I mean, I can recall instances where fear clouded her eyes, and I know that she can show emotion, even if it's not intentional. But this is beyond a minor inconvenience in her life. No, this cry is the kind that comes from deep pain.

As she continues to shudder, I rub my fingers up and down her back. "Penelope, you're scaring me, baby. Are you hurt?"

She nods and grips me tighter. And my heart lurches.

Fuck. If something happened to her and I wasn't there for her, I will lose my ever-loving mind knowing it was because I pushed her too hard, pushed her away from me. Who knows what she's been through in the past four days, but I hope these tears aren't because of me.

Smoothing my hand across her face, I lift her chin so she's looking up at me. Her skin is red and blotchy again, and her eyes are heavy and swollen. "What happened? Did someone do something to you?"

The next words she speaks have my heart breaking in two. "I did. I'm the one who hurt me, Maddox. That's the worst part." The pain I see in the eyes staring back at me isn't just the type of pain that a person carries in their heart; it's the type that takes over their entire body, buries in their bones, their brain, and their soul. It's every stage of grief running through them on an endless cycle that feels like it's never going to end.

And the only reason I know this is because I've been there—and it's not a pleasant place to be.

"I'm the one who fucked myself up. The reason that doing this with you scares me shitless is because it means I have someone to lose again." She lays her forehead back on my chest and shudders as more tears leak from her eyes.

"Shh, it's okay. I'm not going anywhere."

"You don't know that," she counters.

"Why on earth would I be going anywhere, Pen? Don't you know how out of my mind I've been for the last four days knowing you wouldn't answer my calls?"

"Yeah, about that," she says, looking up at me again. "I have half a mind to knee you in the balls right now for leaving me like that. Your cleaning lady saw my freaking vagina, Maddox."

I press a kiss to her forehead. "I'm sorry, but if it's any consolation, you have the perfect pussy, baby." She rolls her eyes, a hint of a smile on her face, but it's gone as quickly as it appeared. "Dammit, Pen, you pissed me off, but that's no excuse. After I left, I knew I shouldn't have left you like that. So I went back right away. But by the time I got there, you were already gone."

"I'm angry with myself if it makes you feel any better."

"No, it doesn't." She rests her head on my shoulder this time, and I can feel her body start to relax. Rubbing up and down her arm, I wait for her heart rate to slow, and then I continue to prod her. "What's going on, Pen? I feel like this isn't just about what happened between us on Sunday."

"It's not."

"Then what is it? Does it have to do with why you finally went home?"

"You knew where I was?"

"I kind of tracked Amelia down when you went missing. I needed to make sure that you were okay. Don't be mad at her for telling me."

She nods and takes a shaky breath. "I'm not. But I need to talk to you about something."

My pulse races. "Okay . . ."

"It's about why I hadn't been home in twelve years. It's about why I kept pushing you away, why I have avoided relationships my entire adult life," she says, locking her eyes on mine. "Until you."

I swallow against the lump in my throat. "I'm right here. I'm not going anywhere. I want you to talk to me."

This is it. I can feel it. This woman is finally going to confide in me about what she's been hiding, and I'd be lying if I said I wasn't slightly terrified.

The sound of her inhaling has me doing the same, and then I listen as she fiddles with her hands in her lap. "I was in love once. His name was Jacob, and we were high school sweethearts. We planned to get married and spend the rest of our lives together. But twelve years ago on Monday, he died."

"Fuck, Penelope. I'm so sorry. I—"

She puts her hand in front of my face. "I need to get this out, okay? Otherwise, I'm going to stop, and I can't do that. I don't want to keep this from you anymore."

I press my lips to hers gently. "I'm listening."

"As I was saying, this week was the anniversary of his death. He was my first love, my first everything, my best friend. And he played football, just like you." Suddenly, her no-football-players rule makes a hell of a lot more sense. "He had a full scholarship to play for Ohio State, and it looked like he would have a promising career in the NFL if he kept up his momentum. But three weeks after we graduated from high school, we had plans to go to the lake with some friends of ours right before the Fourth of July. Jacob was complaining about a headache, but I kept telling him he would feel better once we got to the water. I gave him some ibuprofen, convincing him he just needed to let it kick in, and he'd be fine."

She pauses, shaking her head. "He said he didn't feel right, but I suggested maybe he was dehydrated, you know? It was hot, sweltering really, and I just wanted to hang out with everyone, soak up our last summer before real life started."

I continue to rub her arm as she finds the strength to continue.

"There was a small hill on the edge of the lake that everyone would jump off into the water, doing flips and showing off in front of our friends. A few of his friends, including me, convinced him to jump off, too, so he did. But he never came back up."

"Jesus."

"He had a brain aneurysm, Maddox, and it ruptured while he was underwater or right before he jumped. The autopsy report basically concluded that the timing was everything, and for him, it was fatal."

"Babe . . ."

"For so long, I've believed that it was my fault, Maddox. I'm the reason he died." She starts crying again. "If I had just listened to him, had us stay home instead of going to the lake, he might have survived. But I was being selfish. I told him to suck it up. And because of me, he didn't even have a chance of surviving . . ." She buries her face in my chest again, and I hold her to me, breathing in her sorrow while simultaneously feeling relieved that I finally understand her so much better now.

"He was the only boy I ever loved, and I played a part in why he's not here anymore. So I ran away from home and haven't been back since. I haven't dated, haven't let any other man in because I couldn't stand the thought of loving someone like I loved him. But even that wasn't enough."

"Penelope, this was not your fault."

She shakes her head.

"No, it wasn't. Listen to me." I tilt her chin up again so I can see her eyes. "You magnificent woman. There was no way for you to know what was going to happen, no way that you could have prevented that. The fact that you've been carrying around this guilt for so long makes my heart break for you. Because, Pen?"

"Yeah?" she asks, wiping her nose.

"I know what that's like, baby. I know exactly how it feels to think you're responsible for someone else's death."

Her mouth falls open. "What? How?"

"I had a cousin, Leslie's sister, actually. And she died in a drunk driving accident, one that she should have never been in if it wasn't for me."

Chapter 22

Penelope

"What?" My stomach plummets, and I actually cover my heart with my hand because I'm afraid it might come out of my chest completely if I don't.

"Fuck, it makes so much sense now," Maddox whispers, resting his forehead on mine. Normally, I love it when he does that, but right now, I can't focus on anything other than what he just told me.

"Maddox. I-I'm so confused."

"You don't need to be, Pen. Because I'm not. Now I understand. I get why I felt connected to you before I ever truly got to know you." He runs his knuckles down my jawline. "I think our souls knew we needed each other, baby. Mine recognized the guilt in yours, but perhaps together, we can completely heal."

Oh my God, his words. My heart lurches from them, wishing I

could reach out and hold *his* heart in my hands. "Your cousin died?"

"And I blamed myself for it, Pen. Just like you did with Jacob." He blows out a breath as he stares across the field. "Leslie and I had finally both turned twenty-one, and Grace wanted to take us out and party. I broke up with Brittney, my fiancé, about three months earlier, so the idea of letting loose and trying to get back out there seemed promising, and I was tired of wallowing. Grace was older than us, but she insisted that we needed to experience the club scene and wanted to show us the ropes. She told us she would be the designated driver, but as soon as we got to the club, she started drinking. Up until that point, I'd always thought she had a bit of a drinking problem, but it wasn't until that night that I got up close and personal with it."

He adjusts me on his lap, and I settle in, completely invested in this story because my heart resonates with it.

"She was relentless, doing shot after shot, and after I had two drinks myself, I knew she wouldn't be able to drive us home, so I stopped drinking for the night. It only took a few hours, but she was wasted, and I knew Leslie and I needed to get her home. I told Leslie to take her to the bathroom and then we would get going, but I ran into a buddy of mine from school on my way out and got caught up in a conversation with him." He looks off to the side of the field. "Leslie came up to me God knows how long later and asked me where Grace was. I told her I thought she was with her, but apparently, while Leslie finished in the bathroom, Grace snuck out and decided to drive herself home. She crashed her car into a telephone pole and died on impact."

"Oh my God, Maddox."

"I instantly blamed myself, Pen. I spiraled out of control. If we hadn't gone to the club, if I had just ended my conversation sooner, if I had just stopped her from taking all of those shots, if I had just done this or that, she wouldn't have died."

"Fuck, you sound like me in my head."

He cups my face. "Exactly. You can go through all the would-haves and should-haves, but it doesn't change anything. Grace made the choice to drive that night, and she died. There's nothing different I could have done. And the same goes for you."

"But . . ." My bottom lip trembles.

"No, let me finish." I nod, so he continues. "After the funeral, I started drinking heavily, which is ironic, really. I started skipping practice. I blew off classes, locked myself away in my apartment, and stopped talking to my family. I shut out Leslie, who was not only my cousin and Grace's sister but also someone who felt the same guilt I did. But then one day, Leslie burst into my apartment and smacked me across the face."

"Wow."

"She told me that I'd be a fool to let all of my hard work go to waste because Grace made a decision to drive that night. And although we both wished we could go back and do everything differently, wishing wasn't going to change anything. The best thing we could do was continue to live, to honor her life by saving other women and men from making the same choice, and to follow our dreams, like mine of playing in the NFL."

I lick my lips as tears fall again.

"I'm not going to say that I snapped right out of my depression and guilt because that would be a lie. I had rough days and had to fight like hell to get my grades back up so I could pass my classes. I started seeing a therapist, and it took me a long time to feel at peace with what happened. But when I got drafted, my life started to fall into place, so I vowed never to take it for granted. It's why I live my life the way I do now. Losing Grace reminded me that life's too fucking short, that helping other people will always make the world a better place, and that fighting for the life we want is the only way to make all of our dreams come true." He presses his lips to mine softly before rearing back.

"This is what kept me going, Penelope." He waves his hand out toward the field. "My family, my career that I wanted more than anything, my home. Without this support system, I would have crumbled after everything happened with Grace and Brittney. I shut out the world for a while, convinced myself that I couldn't let anyone in. But then my entire world went dark. It took Leslie and my parents to pull me out of the spiral I was going down. It took learning about how other people's lives have changed in an instant to remind myself that life is precious. We only get one, baby. And I can say, without a shadow of a doubt, that I want to live mine with you."

"I don't know what to say."

"Then let me continue." He stares down into my eyes. "I am so fucking sorry that you lost someone you loved, and I understand why not letting anyone else in felt like the logical solution to you. But Penelope, I don't think we stood a chance to resist one another when we met. And now that I know we share a similar experience, I'm certain fate brought us together." He inhales and then holds my face in his palm. "I am so fucking in love with you, Penelope Klein. I am so sorry that you loved and lost, but I *found* you, Pen. We found each other, and I want to prove to you that you can have it all, even when life gets shitty, even when we experience heartache and guilt. I want to be your future, Penelope Klein—if you'll let me."

"I want that, too," I admit on a shaky breath as relief floods through me. And then I say the words I've only ever said to one other person. "And I love you. After everything we went through to get to this point, the last thing I want to do is walk away. I went home finally. I had to say goodbye to my past because my future is right here . . . with you. *You are* worth the risk. *You are* worth my job. *You are* worth everything I have been through to get here, and as long as we're together, none of the other shit matters. I love you so much, Maddox Taylor. You saw me when I didn't want to be seen, pursued me when I was fine with being alone. But now, all I see and all I want is you and me together, forever. I don't want to be afraid anymore of letting you in." We both exhale at the same time. "God, I hate to say it, but I feel so much better now that you know. I was afraid you would look at me differently."

"Why on earth would you think that?"

"Because I've held on to this other person and the love I had for him for so long, like I was afraid to let go of him." My eyes shift to the field as the sun sets in the distance. "Part of me still is, but the other part of me knows that it's time."

"You don't have to let go of him, babe. He will always be a part of you—who you were, who you are, and who you will become. But you deserve to keep living, Penelope. You deserve to be loved again. And you deserve to forgive yourself for what happened because it was not your fault."

"It's hard."

"I know it is."

"You remind me so much of him, too."

"Then I'm honored. If he earned your love, then I know he was one hell of a guy."

I look back up at him. "You're the only other man I could have ever seen myself with, Maddox. I don't say that lightly. And I'm sorry for everything that I've put you through."

"You are worth it, Penelope. That's what I've been trying to get you to understand. It's why I couldn't walk away from you."

"Thank you for not giving up on me. It means more to me than you'll ever know."

~

"Are you sure you're up for this?"

I nod even though I know the way I look right now must be atrocious. "I'm sure. My face is puffy and blotchy, though, so I hope they don't mind."

He brushes my hair from my face, holding my hand as we stand on the front porch of his parents' house. When we left the field, he called Leslie and asked her to gather the kids and meet us there to introduce me to his family while I followed him in my rental car. I could see how eager he was—after being alone all week—to show me his home and have me meet the people who helped shape him into the incredible man he is, so I really couldn't say no.

"They're going to love you. It doesn't matter what you look like. And honestly, you look so fucking beautiful right now, like a peace has come over you."

"I do feel more at peace," I reply on a sigh. "But I also feel like my eyelids are halfway closed because they're so swollen."

"We won't stay long. I just want them to meet you." He lifts my hand and kisses the back of it. "They need to meet the woman I love before I introduce her to the world."

"You still sure about that?"

"Positive. I finally get to claim you as mine, Penelope Klein. I'm getting hard just thinking about it."

"Probably not the best way to walk into your parents' house, but if you think you can keep your dick in check . . ." I shrug, and he pulls me into his chest.

"Don't worry. I can wait until later to show you exactly how hard it makes me."

Moaning, I pull his lips to mine. "I'm counting on it."

"Ew! Uncle Maddox is kissing a lady!" a small voice shouts, breaking us apart just as quickly as our lips met.

"Stella Bella!" Maddox releases me, opens the door, and scoops up the little girl I met earlier, her giggles echoing through the house as he runs inside with her.

Leslie holds the door open so I can follow him through. "Good to see you again, Penelope."

"Likewise, Leslie. You got that champagne? I could really use a glass after today."

She smiles and nods at me. "You've got it."

"Is that her?" A tall brunette with the same hazel eyes as Maddox comes around the corner, practically dancing on her toes.

"Hi. I'm Penelope. It's so nice to—" I'm cut off by who I assume is Maddox's mother yanking me into her for a hug.

"Oh my gosh, you are just the most gorgeous thing," she squeals.

"Miranda, let her go. Jesus." A male voice rings out behind us, pulling my attention in his direction.

Once Miranda lets go of me, I come face-to-face with a man who is as big and brawny as Maddox and is covered in tattoos, just like his son.

If the way this man looks is any indication of what Maddox will look like in twenty-to-thirty years, sign me up, please!

"Hi. It's so nice to meet you both. Thank you for welcoming me into your home," I say as my eyes finally glance around to take in the ranch-style house that Maddox called home as a child. It has the same feel as my childhood home—photos all over the walls, smells of freshly made food cooked with love, and little quirks that show how well lived-in the space is.

Out of nowhere, Maddox comes up beside me, kisses the top of my head as he wraps his arm around my waist, and pulls me tightly to his chest. "Mom, Dad. This is Penelope. She's the PR rep the Bolts hired—and my girlfriend."

"I have heard so much about you," Miranda says.

I look up at Maddox, and all he does is shrug. "I told you, I'm a momma's boy."

"All good things, I hope?"

She nods and leads me into the kitchen where Leslie hands me a glass of champagne. I give her a silent "thank you" and then take a seat at the kitchen counter.

"Are you hungry, dear? I made drumsticks earlier, baked beans, coleslaw . . ."

"You wanna eat?" Maddox asks as he pulls two plates from the cupboard. And at that moment, I realize the last time I ate was about six this morning.

"Yes, please."

"So tell us all about you, Penelope," Miranda begins.

"Let the girl relax for a moment," Maddox's dad interjects, cracking open a beer. "The last thing the woman probably needs is a Southern woman's inquisition," he says in a twang that instantly makes me smile.

"No, tell us how you two met," Leslie chimes in, leaning against the counter, ready for all the dirt.

And in that moment, I feel it. The love, the friendship, the community this man has makes him exactly who he is.

So I don't hold back because I think honesty is the best policy, after all. "Well, it all started with a dirty joke . . ."

"**S**trip for me, babe." Maddox releases my lips just long enough for him to rip his shirt over his head and toss it somewhere in the room.

We made it back to his house after dinner with his family and long after the sun had set, and now we're making up for lost time.

He captures my mouth again as I work to unbutton my shorts and shove them and my underwear down my legs. His hands lift my shirt from my head, and he pinches the back of my bra to release it from my body before he lifts me and carries me over to the bed.

Standing back, he shoves his own shorts and underwear down, and then he climbs over me, making my breath catch.

"Are you okay?"

"Yes. I'm more than okay," I say, staring up at him, pushing his hair from his face.

"Fuck, I love you, Penelope."

"I love you, too, Maddox."

"I want everything with you." He kisses my lips. "And I mean that." His mouth climbs down my neck before finding my nipple and sucking it between his lips. "Tonight changed everything, Pen."

"I want that, too. And I just want to feel close to you right now. Make love to me, please."

Lifting his head again, we lock eyes as Maddox slides inside me, pumping his hips in a slow rhythm that has my limbs tingling and my nails scratching his back.

"I'll never get enough of this, of you," he whispers before kissing me softly, and then his hips do a dance that my entire body can't get enough of.

We barely speak as we reconnect physically, reinforcing everything we discussed earlier.

This man is my future. He's my person. He broke down my walls and forced me to see that I do deserve love and that he's the man I've been waiting for to show me that. He welcomed me into his family, he let me cry and share my past with him, and he's holding me together as I push past my fears.

He's everything I need, and I can't believe he's mine.

"I'm gonna come, Pen," he announces as his thrusts pick up speed. And just hearing him say those words has my own orgasm teetering on the brink.

"Me, too. Fuck, Maddox."

"God, I love you," he groans as he reaches between us and rubs my clit, and I pop off like a bottle rocket right alongside him, clinging to him like the lifeline he is—*my lifeline*.

I'm so fucking happy that I cry—but this time, they're tears of joy.

Jacob helped me discover the girl I was, but Maddox helped me find her again. And now is the time for me to just be happy—to accept my past and be hopeful for my future with a man who showed me how to live again and embrace the fear of falling in love.

Chapter 23

Penelope

"What is that?" I lift my head, my hand scrubbing my face as my eyes adjust to the light coming through the windows. A phone ringing in the distance pulls me out of my haze, and I leap out of bed to go fetch it.

We came home from Texas last night, and this morning, Maddox has to report to training camp. I won't be able to talk to him for at least five days since the coaches want the players completely focused on the game and nothing else. It's a small sacrifice to pay before we can come clean about our relationship, but I know it will be worth it in the end.

As of right now, though, I'm pretty sure I've only had three hours of sleep between the flight and Maddox fucking me the second we arrived at my place. Now add in the fact that my phone is ringing off the hook, and the way this day is starting is pissing me off.

"Motherfucker!" I shout as I stub my toe on the corner of my bed in pursuit of my purse, which I finally locate after my phone's done ringing. I pull it from its confines and stare down at it, which makes my stomach drop instantly. "Holy shit!"

"What's going on, Pen?" Maddox leans up in bed, rubbing his eyes.

"I have thirty missed calls." Scrolling down the screen, I see all of the girls have called me, along with Charles and Liam, more than five times each.

"Okay . . ."

"Something must be going on." I open a text from Charlotte and click on the link, and I'm presented with a picture of Maddox and me from the other night—the night when he held me in the bleachers as I confessed my entire past to him—and there's an article accompanying it.

Looks like Maddox Taylor isn't as focused on his new season as a Bolt as the team wants you to believe, because this weekend, he was caught back in his hometown of Newberry Springs, Texas, getting up close and personal with Penelope Klein, the PR rep the Bolts hired to build excitement for the upcoming season. All summer, we've seen stories of Taylor and the Los Angeles Bolts attending charity functions and running drills, preparing for another season of football while giving back to the community. But it seems he had other interests as well, and perhaps Miss Klein and Edelman PR have some explaining to do about preferential treatment of their clients.

"Oh my God! Maddox!"

He leaps from the bed as I cover my mouth. My hands are shaking. "What?"

I hand him my phone as my feet begin to move, and I frantically search for clothes.

"Shit. Shit!" Maddox yanks on his hair. "What the fuck? Who took this?"

"Anyone could have, Maddox. We weren't exactly paying attention to our surroundings at that moment." I find a pair of clean slacks in my closet and start pulling them up my legs. "But now we have a much bigger problem on our hands." I pull a blouse from a hanger, and after clasping a bra on my chest, I shrug it on. "Jesus, Charles is going to be livid with me. Fuck! This is exactly what we were trying to avoid."

Maddox's alarm goes off on his phone a few seconds later. "Fuck. I have to go. And I'm not going to be able to speak to you for days."

Longing rushes through me. "I know. We'll figure this out. There has to be a way for us to spin this."

"If anyone can tackle this, it's you, baby." Maddox pulls my mouth to his and then kisses me like he won't see me for five days. If we had more time, I'd take one more ride on that pierced cock of his to satisfy my need for him. But the truth is, I don't think I'll ever get enough of him.

"I love you." He lifts my hand and presses his lips to my knuckles. "But you'd better not run from me again, baby."

"I'm not going anywhere, Maddox. I'll figure this out. I love you, too. Now go before you're late and get fined."

I watch him leave and then take a deep breath before scrolling through my phone, ready to do damage control.

~

"**I** freaking knew it!" Garret shouts the second I round the corner of the hallway toward my office.

"Knew what?"

"That you were taking a ride on Maddox Taylor's dick to pound town."

"Well, obviously you can see why I couldn't tell you, Garret," I hiss as people mill about the office, shooting curious glances in my direction when they walk past. "But if it makes you feel any better, you were involved in one of my lies to cover this up."

His jaw drops open. "You bitch!"

"What? I thought you'd be happy to be part of the gossip."

He purses his lips, and his head tilts to one side as he thinks about what I just said. "You know what? You're right!"

I laugh. "Glad I could make you happy, but the reality is, this has just turned into a PR nightmare."

Garret waves his hand in the air. "Please, girl. If anyone can spin this, it's you."

"It's a little different when *I'm* the one whose job is on the line, hun." I unlock the door to my office and head for my desk. "Is Charles in yet?"

"Oh, yeah, he is. He actually wanted me to tell you to go to his office as soon as you arrived."

"Jesus, you're just now telling me?"

"Well, yeah. I had to interrogate you a bit before you go get chewed to bits." Garret nibbles on his thumb. "Do you think he's going to fire you? I swear, Pen, if you get fired, I will follow you. We can start our own firm. I can't work under any of the other bitches in this office. I will die."

"Calm down, Garret. Let's not overreact until we need to." Not gonna lie, though, I feel like I might throw up right now.

"Good luck. I'll be here with coffee and cookies when you get back."

I plant a kiss on his cheek before I head for Charles's office. "That's why you're the best assistant ever."

"Don't you forget it."

Trying to calm myself before I walk into the lion's den, I do some square breathing and arrive at his assistant's desk in under a minute. "Julie, I'm here to see Charles."

She smirks up at me. "Oh, I know. Didn't think you had it in you, Penelope. But then again, you always were—"

"I'd be very careful about how you finish that sentence. Woman to woman, you have no idea about the details of my life, so I'd tread carefully," I seethe just as Charles comes out of his office.

"Penelope. Come in, please."

Shooting a glare at Julie as I walk past, I take a seat in one of the chairs across from his desk and wait for him to settle in on the other side.

"Well, nothing like a scandal to start off a Monday morning, right?"

"Charles, I know this looks bad. And I'm sorry. But I'm not sorry for falling in love with him." His brow lifts, but I continue, wasting no time explaining everything. "Maddox and I connected the night of the Zio's Vodka party, so when you made him a client of mine, we already had a history."

"I see."

"And I tried to keep the working relationship strictly professional, but sometimes, you can't control the connection you have with someone. I know I should have come to you sooner, but after the faith you put in me to handle the Bolts account, I didn't want to let you down. We planned on coming clean to you and the Bolts franchise after training camp, but it seems someone else was intent on exposing this story and ruining all of the work I did. I'm sorry, and if you have to fire me, I understand. But like I said, I'm not sorry for falling in love. What we have is real, and I can't regret that."

Charles purses his lips. "Is this why you had that no-athlete rule?"

"No. That had to do with some personal history that isn't relevant right now. And contrary to what I said, I've really enjoyed working with the team. It's been some of my favorite work I've done."

"Penelope, I'm disappointed." His words have me slouching in my chair.

"I know, but—"

He holds up a hand to cut me off. "Let me finish." I nod and zip my lips. "I'm disappointed because for the past three months, you became the PR rep I always knew you could be, and now all of your hard work looks like it was nothing but a personal mission to romance Maddox Taylor. I'm disappointed because now one of my best agents is caught up in a scandal of epic proportions. And I'm disappointed that you didn't feel that you could tell me this before it got out of hand."

"I know, Charles, but if it's any consolation, I barely came to terms with how I feel about Maddox until a week ago. It's part of the reason I took some personal time. I needed to figure out what I wanted."

"And did you?"

"Yes. I want him. And if that means I lose my job, then so be it."

He hums and then sits up taller in his chair. "What I'm about to say may surprise you, but your personal life should always come before your job, Penelope. Other people in this line of work might disagree, but I'm not them. I'm proud of you for choosing love. Now the question is: Are you willing to fight for it?"

I let out a sigh, my whole body relaxing. "Yes, I am."

"Good. Get ready to go to battle. The first person we need to take down is Liam Nelson. Because he's the one who leaked the photo of you two to the press."

"You and Maddox Taylor?" Jeffrey shrieks as he opens the door to Amelia's house.

"Well, hello to you, too, Jeffrey." I step to the side so I can walk past him, but I can feel him hot on my tail.

"You've seen him naked? You were dating him this entire time and didn't say anything to us?"

Damien comes to my rescue at this moment. "Do you honestly think she could trust you, the gossip king, with something like this?" he says, directing his gaze at Jeffrey. But then he twists to me. "You could have trusted me, though, Penelope. I wouldn't have told a soul." He crosses his heart with his finger. "But tell me this: Did you two hook up the night of our wedding? Please tell me it was our nuptials that finally made you two give in to the underlying attraction between you."

Placing a hand on his shoulder, I burst his bubble. "Sorry,

Damien. I was enjoying every part of Maddox Taylor long before your wedding."

He snaps his fingers. "Damn."

"There she is! The world's most hated woman!" Charlotte jokes as she comes out of Amelia's kitchen, holding a glass of champagne.

It's Wednesday night, two days after my relationship was leaked to the press, and the girls called an emergency dinner so we could catch up after my trip home and then to see Maddox. I didn't realize all of the guys would be here, too, but whatever. The more the merrier. I love our little group, even Jeffrey.

"You think so?" I ask for clarification.

"Oh, yeah. You snagged one of the NFL's most eligible, sought-after bachelors." And then I see a light bulb come on in her head as her eyes widen. "Oh my gosh! Penelope, you have to let *Revision* do an interview with you and Maddox about your relationship when you're ready. If you don't, I don't think we can be friends anymore."

I laugh and walk into the kitchen to fetch my own glass of bubbly. "I'm not making any promises. Hell, I barely got to speak to Maddox before he had to leave for training camp, and so much has happened since then. The last thing we're thinking about is doing interviews."

Amelia and Noelle walk through the sliding patio door at that moment, joining us. Ethan and Nick are trailing behind them.

"You're here!" Nick shouts, reaching for me to give me a hug. "I swear, I love you, Pen, but now if you don't bring Maddox around, there will be words."

Ethan slugs him. "Jesus, man."

"What? We officially have an NFL quarterback as part of the

group now. Don't act like you don't want to hang out with the guy as much as the rest of us. Sucks he's at training camp right now. I mean, I get it. But later on, he'd better be here. And if we could get season tickets, that would be great, too." He turns to Ethan, who looks ready to punch him. "What? Don't act like you haven't thought about asking him."

Damien chuckles. "Nah, he'll probably just get stage fright again and forget how to speak."

"Fuck you, Damien," Ethan retorts.

"Boys, you need to go! Girl talk is about to commence, and your drama needs to be taken elsewhere," Charlotte declares, waving her hands to shoo them out of the kitchen.

They all grab another beer and then head outside, where Ethan is preparing burgers on the grill.

"Hi, Auntie Penelope!" Oliver squeals, pausing only to hug my legs as he runs past then darting outside to the pool.

"Um, hi."

"He's been waiting for Ethan to go outside so he could swim. I told him he had to wait," Amelia explains.

"I'll catch up with him later then."

"Okay, tell us. How did Ohio go? And then Texas?" Noelle finally speaks up. "I mean, judging by that picture, things went well, and you two are official now."

The smile on my lips says it all. "Yes, we are, although that's obviously not how we planned to let everyone know." My face falls. "But I went home, and it was hard. My parents were obviously thrilled I was there. And I visited Jacob's grave."

The girls' expressions are nearly identical, their sympathy touching after that revelation.

"But I'm glad I went. And then after another day spending

time with my parents, I knew I couldn't wait until Maddox returned to LA to talk to him. So I booked a flight to Texas to surprise him, where I told him everything."

"We are so proud of you, Pen." Amelia's eyes are clouded with moisture as she looks at me.

"Thank you. And if it weren't for you three, I know I would have never gotten here. I-I can't even begin to tell you how grateful I am to all of you. And again, I'm so sorry I didn't say anything sooner." I feel my own throat close up with emotion.

"We know, Pen. We know." Noelle squeezes my hand. "And you're done running, right?"

"Yes. I'm done. In fact, today was a turning point in this entire thing."

"How so?" Charlotte asks.

I take a sip of champagne and then explain what I learned. "Well, on Monday, when I met with Charles, I found out it was Liam who leaked the photo of us. And apparently, he had more. He'd had us followed numerous times because he suspected something and wanted me to get fired. Apparently, he'd asked to be the Los Angeles Bolts' PR rep within the franchise, but they turned him down. Next thing you know, they hired me."

"Oh my gosh," Amelia whispers.

"So he was waiting for the right time to expose us, but he wasn't very good about covering his tracks. Charles met with the representatives from the team, including the owner, and offered up a suggestion that would spin things in a new direction, one they could use . . ."

"And . . . ?" Noelle raises her eyebrow.

I take a deep breath and try not to smile too hard. "You're looking at the new head of PR for the team, ladies."

"Holy shit!" they all scream in unison.

"Are you serious?" Charlotte asks.

"Yes. And I have Charles to thank. He vouched for me, and I am so excited. Working with the team has been incredible—and now I get to do it full-time!"

"Does Maddox know yet?" Noelle grabs my hand again.

"No. I haven't spoken to him since Monday. The first week of training camp is no-contact, and it's killing me. Especially the lack of contact with his dick."

Noelle rolls her eyes. "God, I miss penis. The further I get into this pregnancy, the more I realize that these hormones are going to be the death of me. I might need to find a friend with benefits just to appease that need, you know?"

Jeffrey walks into our conversation at that very moment. "Uh, I can help with that, Noelle." He bounces his eyebrows.

"Thanks, Jeffrey, but no offense, you're just not my type."

"How do you know? I could be packing heat down here," he says, gesturing to his crotch.

"Are you?" she challenges.

"Guess you'll just have to give me a chance and find out."

Noelle shakes her head. "Never gonna happen."

"Never say never," Charlotte retorts with a wink, making us all laugh.

"Ugh, fine. But just know the offer stands," Jeffrey says before he walks down the hall to the bathroom.

"Men," Noelle mutters.

"Yeah, they can be annoying, but God, we sure do love them, huh?" Amelia says wistfully.

And for the first time, I can agree. "Yes, we do. And I can't wait to see mine and put this whole mess behind us."

Chapter 24

Maddox

"You sure about this?" Hayden whispers in my ear as we wait offstage for the press conference to start.

"I have to, Hayden. I hate the shit that people are saying about her, and both my agent and the Bolts agreed that it needs to be done."

"I mean, I'm on your side. Seriously, Penelope is the type of woman you fight for. At this moment, I'm mad that you pursued her first." He nudges me playfully. "But I always kind of suspected there was something there."

"Yeah, they weren't very subtle about it, were they?" Vince says, slinging his arm around my shoulder.

"It's hard to be when every time I'm around her, I just want everyone to know she's mine."

"Spoken like a man in love," Vince agrees, releasing me from his hold.

"It's been killing me this week not being able to respond. But now I have the green light, so I'm going for it."

It's the Friday of our first week of training camp, which means I could finally have contact with the outside world. But on Monday, after I showed up, I immediately spoke to my coaches and the owners and told them what I wanted to do. They agreed but told me I had to wait until Friday, and let me tell you, this has been the longest five days of my life.

Hayden slaps me on the back. "This is kind of fucking exciting, though, right? I mean, I feel like there's nothing better than a love story to gain people's attention. Now everyone is watching what's going to happen with the Bolts."

"Hopefully once they know the entire story, they'll love it even more."

Coach walks up and stares down at me over his clipboard. "You're sure about this, Taylor?"

"She's everything to me, and it's time that everyone knows the real story."

Hayden slaps my ass this time, making me jump. "Go get 'em, man. The team and I are behind you."

"Good to know." Shaking him off, I take a deep breath and then head out across the room to a cacophony of whispers, questions being shouted, and flashing lights.

"Maddox! Maddox!"

I reach the microphone at the podium and adjust it so I don't have to lean down. "Hello, everyone. If you could quiet down, please, I will address the reason I called this press conference today."

The noise in the room decreases to a simmer, and then it becomes so quiet that I could hear a pin drop.

"I'm sure by now you're aware that I am in a relationship with Penelope Klein, the PR rep the Los Angeles Bolts hired during preseason to help build up the image of our team. What you don't know is that Penelope and I met long before I was ever a Bolt."

Whispers commence.

"Both of us never anticipated my trade, but it happened, and everything that occurred after is something I will never regret. She told me we couldn't be together because of our working relationship, but I wasn't taking no for an answer. Call me stubborn, but when a man knows who he wants, he goes after her."

Murmurs of laughter ensue.

"But here's the thing about love. We can seek it out or try to avoid it, but ultimately, it finds you when it's the right time. I am in love with Penelope Klein. She didn't do anything questionable, except maybe decide to give me a chance."

More reporters laugh.

"But I love her, and I won't apologize for that. I won't apologize for fighting for her because our love story hasn't been easy, but it's been entirely worth it."

"What about the Bolts, Maddox?" A reporter shouts. "What do they have to say about your behavior? Do they think you're too distracted by Miss Klein to focus on your game, on a position that they're paying you a lot of money to play?"

"My love life and my ability to play football are two entirely different things, and they agree with me on that. I am dedicated to this team, optimistic about the season, and want the fans to know that my game will be even better because I have a woman by my side who loves the game and supports it, too. This was one instance in my life where those two things happened to intertwine."

"Excuse me, I have a question," a feminine voice calls out from the back of the room, but I can't see a face.

"Yes?"

"What did one butt cheek say to the other?"

I feel my mouth drop open as I pop up on my toes to search the room, hope blooming in my chest. "What?"

And then she stands in the back row, holding a microphone while answering, "Together, we can stop this shit."

Chaos rings out as cameras flash and Penelope heads for the podium where I'm standing. My heart is thrashing against my rib cage as I watch her walk toward me as if in slow motion. When she reaches me, she looks up at me and says, "Hey."

"Hi."

"You didn't have to do this alone, you know."

"I know, but I couldn't get a hold of you to let you know my plans until this morning, and by then, I thought it would just be best to do this without your input because I'm not afraid to tell everyone how much I love you."

Reporters are still shouting to the side of us, but right now, all I see is her.

"Is that how you think this is going to work, Maddox Taylor? That you're going to just make decisions without consulting me first?"

"I think it will depend on the situation."

"Well, as the new PR spokesperson for the Los Angeles Bolts, I'll have you know that what you just did is exactly what I would advise—telling the truth and letting your feelings be known."

"Wait, what? You're—"

"Charles got me the job. He spoke with the owner, got Liam fired, and then told me they would be a fool not to hire me full-time to work for the franchise. So I guess I'm sort of your new boss."

I wrap my arm around her waist, yanking her toward me. "Is that so?"

"Yeah. I mean, if you can handle it."

"As long as I can still boss you around in bed, I'm okay with it."

"You'd better never stop doing that," she whispers and then brings her arms around my neck. "Are you ready for your first lesson in PR, Maddox?"

"What is it?"

She casts her eyes to the reporters going apeshit as we stand together like this and then flits them back to me. "If they're going to stare, at least give them something to stare at."

And then her lips are on mine, my tongue is in her mouth, and I kiss the shit out of her for the entire world to see.

She's mine—*my girl*. And I'm never letting her go.

Chapter 25

Penelope

About Seven Months Later

Popcorn goes flying past my face. "Jesus, Jeffrey!"

"I'm sorry," he says around a mouthful of food. "But did you see that play? Our defense totally slammed Tom Brady to the ground."

"They've been doing it all night," Nick adds.

"Yes, but if you don't calm down, I'm going to punch you out, and then you won't be able to see the rest of the game."

His face falls, and then Charlotte steps between us. "There's no need to threaten bodily harm, Pen. I know this is stressful, but they've got this. There are only thirty seconds left on the clock, and they're up by three points."

I pinch the bridge of my nose. "You're right. I'm sorry. But if the Patriots get within field goal range, they could tie it up. And then it's going to go to overtime. They've worked so hard for this, Char. They fucking deserve it."

And I want this for Maddox more than anything.

After we went public with our relationship, I left Edelman PR right away with Charles's blessing and started my new job as the full-time PR spokesperson for the Los Angeles Bolts. I dove in headfirst, giving my time to a game that I truly enjoyed. And it also meant that I would be able to spend more time with Maddox and the boys during the season.

Charles was sad to see me go, but we both knew it was a professional move I had to make. And I also made the move for love.

When Charles told me it was Liam who sold the picture of us to the tabloids, I knew I had to get my revenge in a way that only I could perfect. With the help of my girls, we came up with a plan to help ruin his day, his week, his month, and even his year.

That was a *Friends* reference, if you didn't catch it.

I'm still wondering how long it took for Liam to discover the dog shit we put in the fender wells of his car. But I know he got the delivery of three-hundred strap-ons to his house because the look on his wife's face when she intercepted the delivery was priceless.

I may have had a photographer documenting the entire thing. Sue me. He deserved it.

However, I can't stay mad at the man forever. It was his selfish desire to get me fired that ultimately got me a job that I love more than anything. But a random glitter bomb once or twice in his mailbox definitely helped me feel better sooner rather than later.

Being immersed in football again is something the heart of this small-town girl wanted and needed—along with the man she gets to go home to every night.

He's kinda hot, loving, and dedicated as well. I think I'll keep him.

"I can't believe we're at the freaking Super Bowl right now!" Damien shouts next to Jeffrey.

"All of my childhood dreams have come true," Ethan adds as his eyes well.

"You guys are too much!" Amelia shouts through her laughter and then taps my shoulder. "How are you hanging in there?"

"I will feel so much better when this is over."

Noelle didn't come today because she gave birth to her daughter about six weeks ago and didn't want to bring the baby out in the cold. Besides, this stadium is so loud right now I can barely hear myself think, which is probably not a good environment for a newborn.

A whistle draws our attention back to the field as Brady catches the snap, surveying the turf for his open receivers. He fakes a pass, draws his arm back, and then sails the ball down the field in a Hail Mary pass.

The stadium goes silent as we watch the ball soar through the air. It stays suspended above the field for what feels like forever, and then, as it descends, it lands in the arms of one of our players, resulting in an interception.

"Holy shit! They won!" I scream as my entire crew does the same. I pull Amelia and Charlotte into my chest. Damien, Ethan, Jeffrey, and Nick all scream and start crying, and the entire stadium breaks out into noise that is unlike anything I've ever heard.

The Bolts take one final knee to end the game, and then

purple-and-yellow confetti falls from the sky, fireworks pop off, and the Bolts players go apeshit on the field.

"I'm going to Maddox!" I scream to my friends who encourage me to leave, so I take the few stairs down to the gate, flashing my access pass that allows me onto the field to the security guard.

Maddox's eyes are already on me when I spot him, and he lifts me from the ground and holds me tight to his body as soon as I leap into his arms.

I wrap my legs around his waist and then find his lips with my own. "You did it!"

"No, *we* did it, Pen. We fucking did it!"

"I didn't play that game. That was all you, baby. You and the boys! You just fucking won the Super Bowl, Maddox! I'm so proud of you!"

He laughs and kisses me again before gently setting me on the ground. "I wouldn't be here if it weren't for you, sweetheart."

"I'm so grateful I got to be a part of this, baby. This is something you'll never forget."

"I know. But I want to make it that much more memorable." He drops to one knee, and I gasp as I watch him take a ring out of his pants.

"Oh my God! Did you have that in there the entire game?"

He laughs. "No. I had one of the trainers hold on to it for me just in case. But Penelope, I couldn't think of a more perfect time to ask you to marry me."

"Maddox . . ."

Suddenly, the chaos around us goes quiet as I listen to nothing but what he is saying to me at this moment. "Penelope Klein, you are the love of my life. You're the only woman who has ever made me realize that, without a doubt, the most beautiful things in life are meant to be shared with another person, like sunsets and orgasms. Finding true love is always an unusual circumstance, and that's how I know what we have is the real thing, because it was one circumstance that led us together."

Cheers ring out all around us, but all I can hear is him.

"I love your smile, your laugh, and your sass. I love that you can make me feel like the strongest man on the earth because that's what you need, but you're not afraid to be the strong one when I need you to be. I love your drive and passion, the way you are with my family. And I want to spend the rest of my life loving you, if you'll allow me to." He holds out an emerald cut diamond that sparkles in the stadium lights. "Penelope, will you marry me?"

I nod through my tears. "Yes, Maddox. Yes, I'll marry you."

He slides the ring on my finger and then lifts me up, crashing his mouth to mine once more. We stay like that until my friends rush up to us on the field, and that's when I notice the cameras and reporters huddled around us.

"Oh my God!" Charlotte squeals. "This is one of the craziest things I've ever experienced!"

"You're going to be Mrs. Maddox Taylor!" Jeffrey squeals, jumping up and down. Then he coughs to clear his throat, reaches for Maddox's hand to shake, and says in a very deep voice, "Congrats, man."

Maddox laughs. "Thanks, Jeffrey."

"Let me see the ring!" Amelia shouts, pulling my hand to her. "You did good, Maddox. Thank goodness you had some help, huh?"

"You helped him pick out the ring?"

"Naturally. I wanted to make sure that if the girl who swore off love was going to actually get married, she had a rock I knew she'd never be able to turn down."

Reaching for her, I hug her close. "Thank you for helping me get here."

"No, babe. You did that all on your own."

"I think it was partly because I found the right person." I turn back to my fiancé.

"And it was the right time," Maddox says, pulling me into his arms again.

"Yeah, what's the saying? Timing is everything?"

Maddox nods. "Yup. And now's the time when you kiss me again."

THE END

Thank you SO much for reading Penelope and Maddox's story! If you would like a sneak peek into their future, please click here for a bonus epilogue!
And if you enjoyed the book, PLEASE consider leaving a review on Amazon and/or Goodreads!

Noelle's story, *Not as Planned*, will be coming next year, but you can pre-order today here. And keep reading for a sneak peek at her book!

Glimpse into Not as Planned (subject to change after publication)

S carlett lets out a wail just as the flight attendant closes the cabin and everyone prepares for takeoff.

"Come on, baby girl. Let's have a good flight. Please?" My daughter grabs at my shirt, pulling herself forward so her face smashes into my chest, crying out again as she begins to suck on the fabric. "Okay, okay. I take it you're hungry then."

Situating her on my lap as I locate my nursing cover-up from the bag at my feet, Scarlett wiggles and squirms as her cries grow in volume. Panic sets in as I race to put the cover over my head, lift up my shirt underneath, unclasp my nursing bra, and then carefully bring my daughter under the cover without flashing my boob to the rest of the passengers in first class or the flight attendants scurrying around, preparing for takeoff.

The multi-tasking that is required when you're a mom is unparalleled and something that is not talked about enough. I'd like to see a man do what I just did in under thirty seconds.

With eagerness, Scarlett latches onto my nipple, suckling with a contented grunt while digging her nails into my flesh. I peek down into the hole of the cover around my neck. "Easy there, girl." Her eyelashes flutter and then her eyelids slowly close as she takes in her sustenance and the plane prepares to taxi.

Only four more hours of crippling anxiety to suffer through until we land in Chicago.

Normally a flight across the country wouldn't be such a daunting task, but after having my daughter, everything seems far more complicated. I knew what I signed up for being a single mom, but I didn't realize just how lonely and overwhelming it would be at times, how having someone to help would change the mounting stress that takes over during situations that used to be a piece of cake.

My friends help when they can, of course. Charlotte, Amelia, and Penelope love Scarlett as if she's their own. But they're not around all the time, helping with the everyday tasks and giving me a break in those moments where I feel like I'm teetering on the edge of sanity.

And then there's instances like right now, where I'm questioning whether being a mom is all that it's cracked up to be, whether I made the right decision by doing this on my own, that I feel guilty for even thinking those thoughts because this is what I wanted—*what I chose*.

Scarlett releases my breast with a pop and then pushes herself away from me, forcing me to knock elbows with the man beside me as I retrieve her from under the nursing cover and proceed to burp her with my boob still free ranging it underneath. Luckily, she settles in on my shoulder as the plane gains altitude, giving me the false sense of security that this flight might go smoothly after all—especially as my free nipple begins to drip breastmilk all over my thigh.

Ah, the joys of motherhood.

"Shhhhh, it's okay." Pissed off about everything and the confines of our seating arrangement, Scarlett cries as she jumps up and down on my thighs as we close in on the last hour of our flight. At seven months old, she's finally reached the stage where moving around is the only thing that matters, and after being isolated in my lap while declining every baby snack and toy I've offered her, I'm on the brink of a breakdown and she's already headed there.

The man sitting behind me taps me on the shoulder. "Can you quiet her down? She's been fussy this entire flight. Even my earbuds aren't drowning her out."

Rage flashes through my chest, but I rein it in as best as I can. "I'm trying, okay? I'm sorry…"

"Well, try harder!"

As I go to twist around fully to give this man a piece of my mind now as I teeter on brink of snapping, I'm cut off by a familiar voice. "I know you're not speaking to this mother that way."

My head spins around so fast that I nearly fall forward out of my seat, clutching the baby to my chest. And as my eyes drink in the man standing before me, my jaw drops open as my heart hammers uncontrollably when recognition dawns on both of our faces.

Dressed in his pilot's uniform—one that I still have a part of—Grant flashes me a wink before he glares at the man who was just rudely telling me to make my baby stop crying.

"If you had children, you'd know that sometimes there's nothing you can do for a crying baby, and there's sure as hell not much this woman can do stuck in a metal tube in the sky." He leans down and takes Scarlett from my lap, hoisting her up in his arms, cradling her to his chest as if he's done it a thousand times, when he's only done it once. He mouths, "Hi," to me before directing his attention back to the asshole behind me.

I swear the entire flight is just as mesmerized by the sight as I am.

"Well, it's annoying," the disgruntled passenger fires back.

"You're annoying!" Another passenger in first class retorts as more people from the back of the plane join in.

Grant bounces Scarlett up and down and she instantly stops crying, staring at him with wide blue eyes in fascination. "If I were you, I'd keep my mouth shut for the rest of the flight, or you just might see what happens when someone insults a mother that's doing the best she can and other people rally behind her."

The asshole rolls his eyes but cowers down in his seat. "Whatever."

Grant chuckles. "Yeah, that's what I thought." And then he turns his attention back to me. "Fancy seeing you ladies here."

"Thank you," I whisper as I watch him continue to bounce my daughter in a soothing rhythm, her hands reaching out to grab his face as he does. He smiles at her, nuzzling his nose against hers as she squeals in delight. She reaches for his glasses, but he dodges her chubby hands before she grasps them, pretending to eat her fingers instead. She giggles rambunctiously again.

"My pleasure. In fact, I'd say running into you again here was a pleasant surprise."

"I'll say. Um, aren't you supposed to be flying this plane right now?" I dart my eyes between the cockpit and him.

"I came out for a bathroom break. My co-pilot is in there. I assure you, you're in good hands." And then he arches a brow. "Well, not as good as mine, but that's just a matter of opinion."

"Or cockiness."

He grins, his lips curling up under that short mustache and beard that frames his face, a face I hate to admit has flashed through my mind more times than I can count in the last month. And his eyes twinkle behind his glasses, a blueish gray that is only enhanced by the crisp white shirt of his uniform. "No, just a fact."

Scarlett leans her head on his shoulder and stares down at me, perfectly content being in his arms.

Lucky girl.

"I hate to give her back, but duty calls." Grants smoothes his hand up and down her back as he steps closer.

Sitting up taller in my seat, I reach out for her as he hands her off. She fusses a bit but eventually settles into my chest. I think the last three hours of unhappiness have finally drained her. "Well, thank you—again. It seems like you keep saving me."

"Be careful or you're going to give me a savior complex, and who knows what that might do for my ego."

I slowly shake my head at him. "Seriously, Grant. First the coffee shop, now the flight. I don't know how to thank you."

He crouches down in front of my seat, reaching for my hand. "How about this time, you give me your number before we part ways?"

My heart rattles in my chest. "Oh, uh…"

"I mean, how else am I supposed to get my shirt back from you." He winks.

His shirt—the shirt he literally took off his own body to give to me when my breastmilk decided to let down in the middle of the coffee shop that day, soaking my own shirt clear through. The shirt that I still have hanging in my closet that I smell shamelessly each morning as I get dressed. The shirt that resembles the one he's wearing right now, part of his uniform as a commercial pilot, which can only be described as one of those jobs that instantly boosts a man's sex appeal—although I don't feel like Grant needs the extra points.

The man looks like Gabe Kapler, the coach for the San Francisco Giants—*enough said.*

"I guess my number would help with that, wouldn't it?"

His smirk becomes lethal. "Wait for me at the end of the jet way then after we land."

"Okay."

He rises and then winks at me again. "Okay. Enjoy the rest of your flight, Noelle." And then he's gone, disappearing into the cockpit and leaving me stunned by how our paths crossed once more.

Excitement builds in my chest chased by fear. Am I really doing this? Am I really entertaining getting involved with someone at this point in my life, when I have a child to think about?

Don't get ahead of yourself, Noelle. Nothing may come of this. You've been let down by men so many times in the past that this will probably turn out to be the same way. Reading too many romance novels has heightened your expectations of men.

No, it's just made you realize that men could do better, and you deserve that.

And then my mind goes straight to developing the story that's transpired so far, wondering which of my clients I could pitch it to.

Single mom leaks through her nursing pads in a coffee shop so a handsome stranger, who also happens to be a pilot, literally gives her the shirt off his back but has to leave before they can exchange numbers. Then she runs into him again when it turns out he's the pilot of the flight she's on and he defends her and her daughter against a disgruntled passenger but asks for her number before she leaves the airplane.

But what happens next? Does he call? Does she agree to see him again?

I guess I'll leave that part up to the author herself…

Pre-Order her story HERE

Acknowledgments

I am SO happy that this book is finally out in the world! Writing Penelope's story was intense and emotional, and also a little personal, but I hope you feel I did her character justice. I knew she had to be a complex woman behind her shield and getting to know her as I dove into her background resonated with me so much on a personal level.

I had a boyfriend in high school that I dated for three and a half years. He was my first everything and we were very serious about each other. Unlike Jacob in the story, this boy didn't die right after we graduated. Instead we broke up and it was devastating. A life I thought I had planned with him suddenly wasn't my future, and I had a hard time finding myself and understanding how to date. There was a lot of heart ache and learned lessons, and even to this day sometimes I wonder what my life would be like if I had stayed with him.

It's like Penelope's mom said—sometimes we idealize young love. And it doesn't make it any less real, it's just that you do so much growing as a person after high school that the person you're with at that age just doesn't make sense in the long run. And that's okay.

I hope that Penelope's story didn't disappoint, and I just

LOVED writing Maddox! He was SO swoony, hot, and exactly the type of hero I knew Penelope needed.

These women have been so fun to write, and my hope is that through this series every reader can find of hint of themselves in one of them and their stories.

Noelle's story is last, but boy, did I save a doozy for the end. I've been dying to write a single mom, and her hero has a storyline that I'm SO excited to dive into. Their story will be the perfect ending to the series, so mark you calendars for February of 2023.

Penelope and Maddox were a couple I am very proud of and definitely will miss, but their story isn't over. You'll get more of them in the last book in the series. And if you haven't already, make sure to download that extended epilogue to give yourself a little sneak peek into their future.

To my husband: Thank you for cheering me on and celebrating my success with me as I release each book. Thank you for under-standing how much joy this hobby brings me. And thank you for being my real life book husband and giving me my own true love story to brag about.

To Liz: You are my right-hand woman. Thank you for answering every phone call when I get excited about a new idea. Thank you for cheering me on and listening to me vent. I couldn't do this without you. Who would have thought we'd be plotting 18 books and counting when this started?

To Keely: One of the best things that has come out of this author journey is my friendship with you. I cherish our friendship so much! Thank you for always being there to chat and cheer me on. I love ya!

To Kelly: This story would not have turned out completely without your support. Thank you for helping me work through my issues and talk out where I was struggling. I feel so lucky to have readers like you.

To Melissa: I am SO grateful we finally got a chance to work together on this book as my editor! Your attention to detail and thoughtfulness shined throughout the process. Thank you for your dedication to my stories and I look forward to working together again.

To Melanie: As always, your expertise and friendship had made this author journey even more rewarding. I'm so grateful for our connection and honest discussions about this author gig. So thankful to have you in my corner.

And to my beta readers, ARC readers, and every reader (both old and new): Thank you for taking a chance on a self-published author. Thank you for sharing my books with others. Thank you for allowing me to share my creativity with people who love the romance genre as much as I do.

And thank you for supporting a wife and mom who found a hobby that she loves.

About the Author

Harlow James is a wife and mom who fell in love with romance novels, so she decided to write her own.

Her books are the perfect blend of emotional, addictive, and steamy romance. If you love stories with a guaranteed Happily Ever After, then Harlow is your new best friend.

When she's not writing, she can be found working her day job, reading every romance novel she can find time for, laughing with her husband and kids, watching re-runs of FRIENDS, and spending time cooking for her friends and family while drinking White Claws and Margaritas.

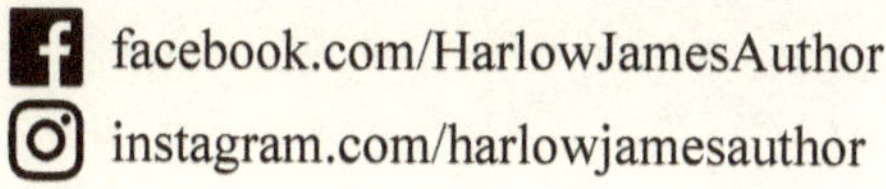

facebook.com/HarlowJamesAuthor
instagram.com/harlowjamesauthor

More Books by Harlow James

One Look, A Baseball Romance Standalone (you can get this for FREE if you sign up for my newsletter)

Guilty as Charged

An intense opposites attract standalone that will melt your kindle. He's an ex-con construction worker. She's a lawyer looking for passion.

McKenzie's Turn to Fall

A holiday romance where a romance author falls for her neighborhood butcher.

The Emerson Falls Series

Tangled (Kane & Olivia)

Enticed (Cooper & Clara)

Captivated (Cash and Piper)

Revived (Luke and Rachel)

Devoted (Brooks and Jess)

The California Billionaires Series

My Unexpected Serenity (Wes and Shayla)

My Unexpected Vow (Hayes and Waverly)

My Unexpected Family (Silas and Chloe)

Lost and Found in Copper Ridge

A holiday romance in which two people book a stay in a cabin for the same amount of time thanks to a serendipitous $5 bill.

<u>The Ladies Who Brunch</u>

<u>Never Say Never (Charlotte and Damien)</u>

<u>No One Else (Amelia and Ethan)</u>

<u>Now's The Time (Penelope and Maddox)</u>

<u>Not As Planned (Noelle and Grant)</u>